Fire
Sea

Bantam Spectra Books
by Margaret Weis and Tracy Hickman

THE DARKSWORD TRILOGY
Forging the Darksword
Doom of the Darksword
Triumph of the Darksword

DARKSWORD ADVENTURES

ROSE OF THE PROPHET
The Will of the Wanderer
The Paladin of the Night
The Prophet of Akhran

THE DEATH GATE CYCLE
Dragon Wing
Elven Star
Fire Sea

and by Margaret Weis

STAR OF THE GUARDIANS
The Lost King
King's Test

THE DEATH GATE CYCLE

VOLUME ◆ 3

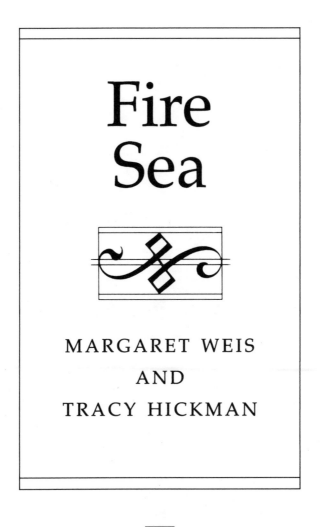

Fire
Sea

MARGARET WEIS
AND
TRACY HICKMAN

SPECTRA ™

BANTAM BOOKS
NEW YORK · TORONTO · LONDON · SYDNEY · AUCKLAND

FIRE SEA

A Bantam Spectra Book / August 1991

SPECTRA *and the portrayal of a boxed "s" are
trademarks of Bantam Books, a division of
Bantam Doubleday Dell Publishing Group, Inc.*

All rights reserved.
Copyright © 1991 by Margaret Weis and Tracy Hickman
Cover art copyright © 1991 by Keith Parkinson.
Book design by Robin Hessel-Hoffmann.
Maps designed by GDS/Jeffrey L. Ward

*No part of this book may be reproduced or transmitted in
any form or by any means, electronic or mechanical,
including photocopying, recording, or by any information
storage and retrieval system, without permission in
writing from the publisher.*
For information address: Bantam Books.

Library of Congress Cataloging-in-Publication Data:
Weis, Margaret.
  Fire sea / Margaret Weis and Tracy Hickman ; music by Janet Pack.
    p.   cm. — (The Death Gate cycle ; v. 3)
  ISBN 0-553-07406-7
    I. Hickman, Tracy.   II. Title.   III. Series: Weis, Margaret.
  Death Gate cycle ; v. 3.
PS3573.E3978F5   1991
813'.54—dc20
                                                                90-23935
                                                                    CIP

Published simultaneously in the United States and Canada

PRINTED IN THE UNITED STATES OF AMERICA

0   9   8   7   6   5   4   3   2   1

And he that was dead

came forth.

♦

—*John 11:44*

The Realms of Abarrach

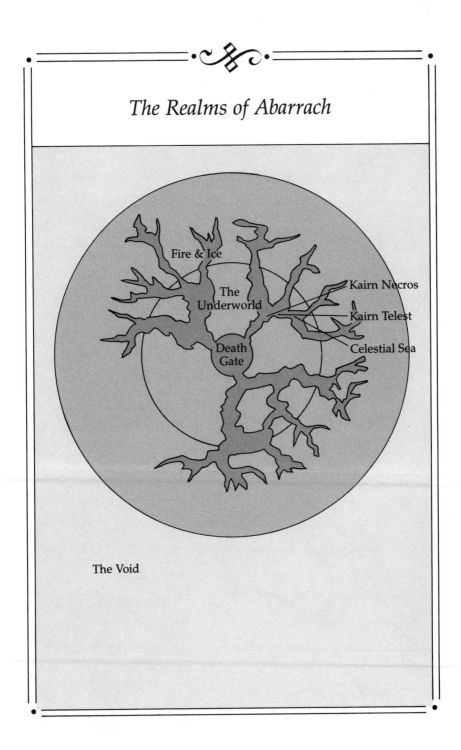

Fire & Ice

The Underworld

Kairn Necros

Kairn Telest

Death Gate

Celestial Sea

The Void

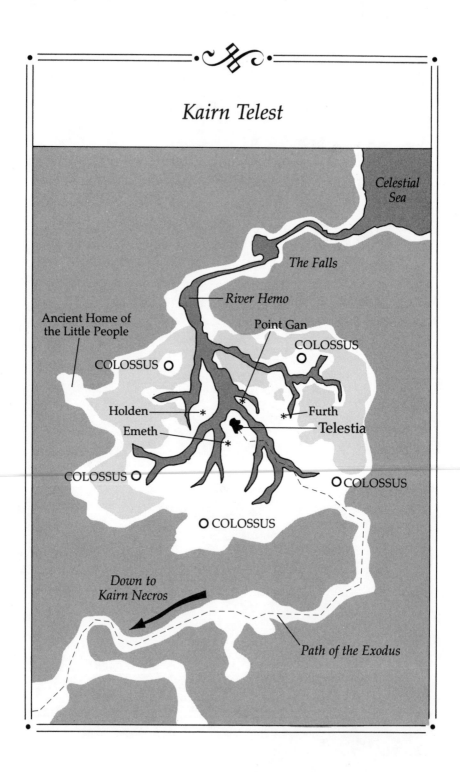

Kairn Telest

Celestial Sea

The Falls

River Hemo

Point Gan

Ancient Home of
the Little People

COLOSSUS

COLOSSUS

Holden

Furth

Emeth

Telestia

COLOSSUS

COLOSSUS

COLOSSUS

Down to
Kairn Necros

Path of the Exodus

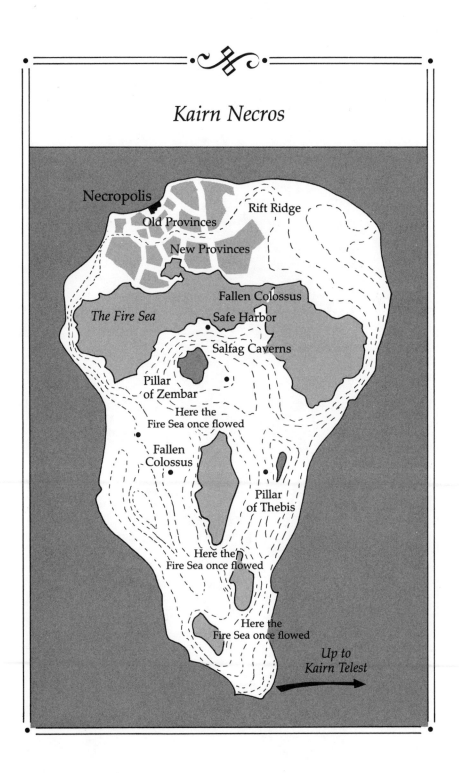

Kairn Necros

Necropolis

Rift Ridge

Old Provinces

New Provinces

Fallen Colossus

The Fire Sea

Safe Harbor

Salfag Caverns

Pillar
of Zembar

Here the
Fire Sea once flowed

Fallen
Colossus

Pillar
of Thebis

Here the
Fire Sea once flowed

Here the
Fire Sea once flowed

*Up to
Kairn Telest*

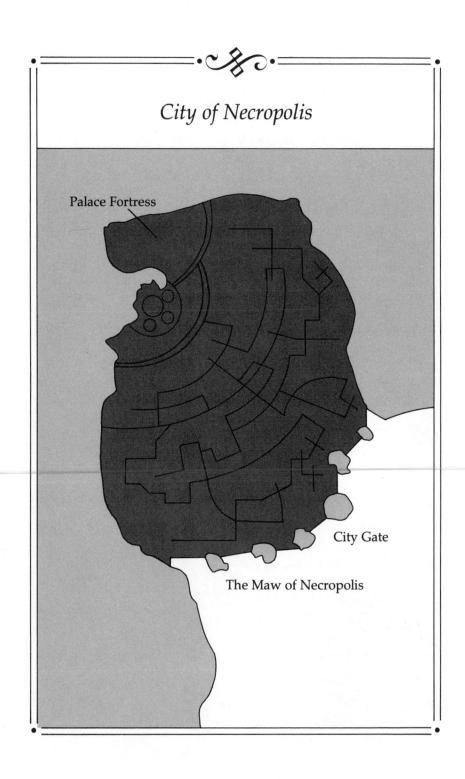

City of Necropolis

Palace Fortress

City Gate

The Maw of Necropolis

Fire
Sea

PROLOGUE

I'VE TRAVELED THROUGH DEATH'S GATE FOUR TIMES, YET I DON'T remember anything about the journey. Each time I've entered the Gate, I've been unconscious. The first trip I made was to the world of Arianus, there and back—a trip that was nearly my last.[1]

On my return trip, I acquired a dragonship, built by the elves of Arianus. It's far stronger and much more suitable than my first ship. I enhanced its magic and brought this ship back with me to the Nexus, where My Lord and I worked diligently to further increase the magic protecting the ship. Runes of power cover almost every inch of its surface.

I flew this ship to my next assignment, the world of Pryan. Once again, I sailed through Death's Gate. Once again, I lost consciousness. I awakened to find myself in a realm where there is no darkness, only endless light.

I performed my task satisfactorily on Pryan, at least as far as My Lord was concerned. He was pleased with my work.

I was not.[2]

On leaving Pryan, I endeavored to remain conscious, to see the Gate and experience it. The magic of my ship protects it and me to the extent that we both arrive at our destination completely safe and undamaged. Why, then, was I blacking out? My Lord hinted that it

---

[1] The Lord of the Nexus underestimated the magical forces that control Death's Gate and failed to provide Haplo with suitable protection for the journey. The Patryn crash-landed and was rescued by the Geg Limbeck (see *Dragon Wing*, vol. 1 of *The Death Gate Cycle*).

[2] Haplo characteristically makes no further mention of what he considers to be his failure on Pryan, but it may relate to the fact that he was very nearly killed by a race of giants whose magic proved far stronger than the Patryn's (see *Elven Star*, vol. 2 of *The Death Gate Cycle*).

must be a weakness in me, a lack of mental discipline. I resolved not to give way. To my chagrin, I remembered nothing.

One moment I was awake, looking forward to entering the small dark hole that seemed far too tiny to contain my ship. The next moment I was safely in the Nexus.

It is important that we learn as much as possible about the journey through Death's Gate. We will be transporting armies of Patryns, who must arrive on these worlds prepared to fight and conquer. My Lord has given the matter considerable study, poring over the texts of the Sartan, our ancient enemy, who built Death's Gate and the worlds to which it leads. He has just now informed me, on the eve of my journey to the world of Abarrach, that he has made a discovery.

◆

I have this moment returned from meeting with My Lord. I confess that I am disappointed. I mean this as no detriment to My Lord—a man I revere above all others in this universe—but his explanation of Death's Gate makes little sense. How can a place exist and yet not exist? How can it have substance and be ephemeral? How does it measure time marching ahead going backward? How can its light be so bright that I am plunged into darkness?

My Lord suggests that the Death's Gate was never meant to be traversed! He can't tell what its function is—or was. Its purpose may have been nothing more than to provide an escape route from a dying universe. I disagree. I have discovered that the Sartan intended there to be some type of communication between worlds. This communication was, for some reason, not established. And the only connection I have found between worlds is Death's Gate.

All the more reason that I must remain conscious on my next journey. My Lord has suggested to me how to discipline myself to achieve my goal. He warns me, however, that the risk is extremely great.

I won't lose my life; my ship's magic protects me from harm. But I could lose my mind.[3]

---

[3] Haplo, *Abarrach, World of Stone*, vol. 4 of *Death Gate Journals.*

CHAPTER • 1

KAIRN TELEST,

ABARRACH

•

"FATHER, WE HAVE NO CHOICE. YESTERDAY, ANOTHER CHILD DIED. The day before, his grandmother. The cold grows more bitter, every day. Yet," his son pauses, "I'm not certain it is the cold, so much, as the darkness, Father. The cold is killing their bodies, but it is the darkness that is killing their spirit. Baltazar is right. We must leave now, while we still have strength enough to make the journey."

Standing outside in the dark hallway, I listen, observe, and wait for the king's reply.[1]

But the old man does not immediately respond. He sits on a throne of gold, decorated with diamonds large as a man's fist, raised up on a dais overlooking a huge hall made of polished marble. He can see very little of the hall. Most of it is lost in shadow. A gas lamp, sputtering and hissing on the floor at his feet, gives off only a dim and feeble light.

Shivering, the old king hunches his shoulders deeper into the fur robes he has piled over and around him. He slides himself nearer the front edge of the throne, nearer the gas lamp, although he knows he will extract no warmth from the flickering flame. I believe it is the comfort of the light he seeks. His son is right. The darkness is killing us.

"Once there was a time," the old king says, "when the lights in

---

[1] From Baltazar, *Remembrances of My Homeland*, a journal chronicling the last days of Kairn Telest kept by the necromancer to the king.

the palace burned all night long. We danced all night long. We'd grow too hot, with the dancing, and we'd run outside the palace walls, run out into the streets beneath the cavern ceiling where it was cool, and we'd throw ourselves into the soft grass and laugh and laugh." He paused. "Your mother loved to dance."

"Yes, Father, I remember." His son's voice is soft and patient.

Edmund knows his father is not rambling. He knows the king has made a decision, the only one he can make. He knows that his father is now saying good-bye.

"The orchestra was over there." The old king lifts a gnarled finger, points to a corner of the hall shrouded in deep darkness. "They'd play all during the sleep-half of the cycle, drinking parfruit wine to keep the fire in their blood. Of course, they all got drunk. By the end of the cycle, half of them weren't playing the same music as the other half. But that didn't matter to us. It only made us laugh more. We laughed a lot, then."

The old man hums to himself, a melody of his youth. I have been standing in the shadows of the hall, all this time, watching the scene through a crack in the nearly closed door. I decide that it is time to make my presence known, if only to Edmund. It is beneath my dignity to snoop. I summon a servant, send it to the king with an irrelevant message. The door creaks open, a draught of chill air wafts through the hall, nearly dousing the flame of the gas lamp. The servant shambles into the hall, its shuffling footfalls leaving behind whispering echoes in the all-but-empty palace.

Edmund raises a warding hand, motions the servant to withdraw. But he glances out the door, acknowledges my presence with a slight nod, and silently bids me wait for him. He does not need to speak or do more than that nod of the head. He and I know each other so well, we can communicate without words.

The servant withdraws, its ambling footsteps taking it back out. It starts to shut the door, but I quietly stop it, send it away. The old king has noticed the servant's entrance and exit, although he pretends that he doesn't. Old age has few prerogatives, few luxuries. Indulging oneself in eccentricities is one of them. Indulging oneself in memory—another.

The old man sighs, looks down at the golden throne on which he sits. His gaze shifts to a throne that stands next to his, a throne done on a smaller scale, meant for a woman's smaller frame, a throne that has long been empty. Perhaps he sees himself, his youthful body strong and tall, leaning over to whisper in her ear, their hands reaching out to each other. Their hands were clasped together always, whenever they were near.

He holds her hand sometimes now, but that hand is chill, colder than the cold pervading our world. The chill hand destroys the past for him. He doesn't go to her much, now. He prefers memory.

"The gold gleamed in the light, then," he tells his son. "The diamonds sparkled sometimes until we couldn't look at them. They were so brilliant they'd make the eyes water. We were rich, rich beyond belief. We reveled in our wealth.

"All in innocence, I think," the old king adds, after some thought. "We were not greedy, not covetous. 'How they'll stare, when they come to us. How they'll stare when they first set eyes on such gold, such jewels!' we'd say to ourselves. The gold and diamonds in this throne alone would have bought a nation back in their world, according to the ancient texts. And our world is filled with such treasures, lying untouched, untapped in the stone.

"I remember the mines. Ah, that was long ago. Long before you were born, My Son. The Little People were still among us, then. They were the last, the toughest, the strongest. The last to survive. My father took me among them when I was very young. I don't remember much about them except their fierce eyes and thick beards that hid their faces and their short, quick fingers. I was frightened of them, but my father said they were really a gentle people, merely rude and impatient with outsiders."

The old king sighs heavily. His hand rubs the cold metal arm of the throne, as if he could bring the light back to it. "I understand now, I think. They were fierce and rude because they were frightened. They saw their doom. My father must have seen it, too. He fought against it, but there was nothing he could do. Our magic wasn't strong enough to save them. It hasn't even been strong enough to save ourselves.

"Look, look at this!" The old king becomes querulous, beats a knotted fist on the gold. "Wealth! Wealth to buy a nation. And my people starving. Worthless, worthless."

He stares at the gold. It looks dull and sullen, almost ugly, reflecting back the feeble fire that burns at the old man's feet. The diamonds no longer sparkle. They, too, look cold and dead. Their fire—their life—is dependent on man's fire, man's life. When that life is gone, the diamonds will be black as the world around them.

"They're not coming, are they, Son?" the old king asks.

"No, Father," his son tells him. Edmund's hand, strong and warm, closes over the old man's gnarled, shivering fingers. "I think, if they were going to come, they would have come by now."

"I want to go outside," the old king says suddenly.

"Are you sure, Father?" Edmund looks at him, concerned.

"Yes, I'm sure!" The old king returns testily. Another luxury of old age—indulging in whims.

Wrapping himself tighter in the fur robes, he rises from the throne, descends the dais. His son stands by to aid his steps, if necessary, but it isn't. The king is old, even by the standards of our race, who are long-lived. But he is in good physical condition, his magic is strong and supports him better than most. He has grown stoop-shouldered, but that is from the weight of the many burdens he's been forced to bear during his long life. His hair is pure white, it whitened when he was in his middle years, whitened during the time of his wife's brief illness that took her from him.

Edmund lifts the gas lamp, carries it with them to light the way. The gas is precious, now; more precious than gold. The king looks at the gas lamps hanging from the ceiling, lamps that are dark and cold. Watching him, I can guess his thoughts. He knows he shouldn't be wasting the gas like this. But it isn't wasting, not really. He is king and someday, someday soon perhaps, his son will be king. He must show him, must tell him, must make him see what it was like before. Because, who knows? The chance might come when his son will return and make it what it once had been.

They leave the throne room, walk out into the dark and drafty corridor. I stand where they may be certain to see me. The light of the gas lamp illuminates me. I see myself reflected in a mirror hanging on a wall across from them. A pale and eager face, emerging from the darkness, its white skin and glittering eyes catching the light, looming suddenly out of the shadows. My body, clad in black robes, is one with the eternal sleep that has settled on this realm. My head appears to be disembodied, hanging suspended in the darkness. The sight is frightening. I startle myself.

The old king sees me, pretends not to. Edmund makes a swift, negating gesture, shakes his own head ever so slightly. I bow and withdraw, returning to the shadows.

"Let Baltazar wait," I hear the old king mutter to himself. "He'll get what he wants eventually. Let him wait now. The necromancer has time. I do not."

They walk the halls of the palace, two sets of footfalls echoing loudly through the empty corridors. But the old man is lost in the past, listening to the sounds of gaiety and music, recalling the shrill giggle of a child playing tag with his father and mother through the halls of the palace.

I, too, remember that time. I was twenty when Prince Edmund was born. The palace teemed with life: aunts and uncles, cousins by birth and by marriage, courtiers—always agreeable and smiling and ready to laugh—council members bustling in and out with business, citizens presenting petitions or requesting judgments. I lived in the palace, serving my apprenticeship to the king's necromancer. A studious youth, I spent far more time in the library than I did on the dance floor. But I must have absorbed more than I thought. Sometimes, in the sleep-half, I imagine I can still hear the music.

"Order," the old king was saying. "It was all orderly, back then. Order was our heritage, order and peace. I don't understand what happened. Why did it change? What brought the chaos, what brought the darkness?"

"We did, Father," replies Edmund steadily. "We must have."

He knows differently, of course. I've taught him better than that. But he will always go out of his way to avoid an argument with his father. Still, after all these years, striving desperately for love.

I follow them, my black slippers make no noise on the cold stone floors. Edmund knows I am with them. He glances back occasionally, as if relying on my strength. I gaze at him with fond pride, the pride I might have felt for my own son. Edmund and I are close, closer than many fathers and sons, closer than he is to his own father, although he won't admit it. His parents were so deeply involved with each other, they had little time for the child their love created. I was the boy's tutor and, over time, became the lonely youth's friend, companion, adviser.

Now he is in his twenties, strong and handsome and virile. He will make a good king, I tell myself, and I repeat the words several times over, as if they were a talisman and would banish the shadow that lies over my heart.

At the end of the hallway stand giant, double doors, marked with symbols whose meanings have been forgotten, symbols that have, with time and progress, been partially obliterated. The old man waits, holding the lamp while his son, muscular shoulders straining, shoves aside the heavy metal bar that keeps the palace doors shut and locked.

The bar is a new addition. The old king frowns at it. Perhaps he is remembering a time, before Edmund was born, when there was no need for a physical barrier. Magic kept the doors shut then. Over the years, however, the magic was needed for other, more important tasks—such as survival.

His son pushes on the doors and they swing open. A blast of cold air blows out the gas lamp. The cold is bitter, fierce, penetrates the fur robes. It reminds the old king that, chill as is the palace, its walls and their magic offer some protection from the blood-freezing, bone-numbing darkness outside.

"Father, are you certain you're up to this?" Edmund asks worriedly.

"Yes," the old man snaps, although my guess is that he wouldn't have gone if he'd been alone. "Don't worry about me. If Baltazar has his way, we'll all be out in this before long."

Yes, he knows I'm near, knows I'm listening. He's jealous of my influence over Edmund. All I can say is, Old man, you had your chance.

"Baltazar has found a route that takes us down through the tunnels, Father. I explained that to you before. The air will grow warmer, the deeper into the world we penetrate."

"Found such a fool notion in a book, I suppose. No use lighting the damn thing," the old king remarks, referring to the lamp. "Don't waste your magic. I don't need a light. Many and many are the times I've stood on this colonnade. I could walk it blindfolded."

I can hear them moving through the darkness. I can almost see the king thrust aside Edmund's proffered arm—the prince is dutiful and loving to a father who little deserves it—and stalk unhesitatingly through the doors. I stand in the hallway and try to ignore the cold biting at my face and hands, numbing my feet.

"I don't hold with books," the king remarks bitterly to his son, whose footfalls I can hear, walking at his side. "Baltazar spends far too much time among the books."

Perhaps anger feels good inside the old man, warm and bright, like the fire of the lamp.

"It was the books told us that *they* were going to return to us and look what came of that! Books." The old king snorts. "I don't trust them. I don't think *we* should trust them! Maybe they were accurate centuries ago, but the world's changed since then. The routes that brought our ancestors to this realm are probably gone, destroyed."

"Baltazar has explored the tunnels, as far as he dared go, and he found them safe, the maps accurate. Remember, Father, that the tunnels are protected by magic, by the powerful, ancient magic that built them, that built this world."

"Ancient magic!" The old king's anger comes fully to the surface, burns in his voice. "The ancient magic has failed. It was the failure of the ancient magic that brought us to this! Ruin where there was once prosperity. Desolation where there was once plenty. Ice where there was once water. Death where there was once life!"

He stands on the portico of the palace and looks before him. His physical eyes see the darkness that has closed over them, sees it broken only by tiny dots of light burning sporadically here and there about the city. Those dots of light represent his people and there are too few of them, far too few. The vast majority of the houses in the realm of Kairn Telest are dark and cold. Like the queen, those who now remain in the houses can do very well without light and warmth; it isn't wasted on them.

His physical eyes see the darkness, just as his physical body feels the pain of the cold, and he rejects it. He looks at his city through the eyes of memory, a gift he tries to share with his son. Now that it is too late.

"In the ancient world, during the time before the Sundering, they say there was an orb of blazing fire they called a sun. I read this in a book," the old king adds drily. "Baltazar isn't the only one who can read. When the world was sundered into four parts, the sun's fire was divided among the four new worlds. The fire was placed in the center of our world. That fire is Abarrach's heart, and like the heart, it has tributaries that carry the life's blood of warmth and energy to the body's limbs."

I hear a rustling sound, a head moving among many layers of clothing. I can imagine the king shifting his gaze from the dying city, huddled in darkness, to stare far beyond the city's walls. He can see nothing, the darkness is complete. But, perhaps, in his mind's eye, he sees a land of light and warmth, a land of green and growing things beneath a high cavern ceiling frescoed with glittering stalactites, a land where children played and laughed.

"Our sun was out there." Another rustling. The old king lifts his hand, points into the eternal darkness.

"The colossus," Edmund says softly.

He is patient with his father. There is much, so much to be done, and he stands with the old man and listens to his memories.

"Someday his son will do the same for him," I whisper hopefully, but the shadow that lies over our future will not lift from my heart.

Foreboding? Premonition? I do not believe in such things, for they imply a higher power, an immortal hand and mind meddling in the affairs of men. But I know, as surely as I know that he will have to leave this land of his birth and his father's birth and of the many fathers before him, that Edmund will be the last king of the Kairn Telest.

I am thankful, then, for the darkness. It hides my tears.

The king is silent, as well; our thoughts running along the same dark course. He knows. Perhaps he loves him now. Now that it is too late.

"I remember the colossus, Father," says his son hastily, mistaking the old man's silence for irritation. "I remember the day you and Baltazar first realized it was failing," he adds, more somberly.

My tears have frozen on my cheeks, saving me the need to wipe them away. And now I, too, walk the paths of memory. I walk them in the light . . . the failing light. . . .

CHAPTER ♦ 2

KAIRN TELEST,

ABARRACH

♦

. . . The council chamber of the king of the realm of Kairn Telest is thronged with people. The king is meeting with the council, made up of prominent citizens whose heads of household served in this capacity when the people first came to Kairn Telest, centuries before. Although matters of an extremely serious nature are under discussion, the meeting is orderly and formal. Each member of the council listens to his fellow members with attention and respect. This includes His Majesty.

The king will issue no royal edicts, set forth no royal commands, make no royal proclamations. All matters are voted on by the council. The king acts as guide and counselor, gives his advice, casts the deciding vote only when the issue is equally divided.

Why have a ruler at all? The people of Kairn Telest have a distinct need for propriety and order. We determined, centuries before, that we needed some type of governmental structure. We considered ourselves, our situation. We knew ourselves to be more a family than a community, and we decided that a monarchy, which provides a parent-figure, combined with a voting council would be the wisest, most appropriate form of government.

We have never had reason to regret the decision of our ancestors. The first queen chosen to rule produced a daughter capable of carrying on her mother's work. That daughter produced a son, and thus has the reign of Kairn Telest been handed down through generation after generation. The people of Kairn Telest are well satisfied and content. In a world that seems to be constantly changing around us—change over which we apparently have no control—our monarchy is a strong and stable influence.

"And so the level of the river is no higher?" the king asks, his gaze going from one concerned face to another.

The council members sit around a central meeting table. The king's chair stands at the head. His chair is more elaborate than the other chairs, but remains on a level equal with theirs.

"If anything, Your Majesty, the river has dropped farther. Or so it was yesterday, when I checked." The head of the Farmer's Guild speaks in frightened, gloom-laden tones. "I didn't go by to see today, because I had to leave early to arrive at the palace on time. But I've little hope that it would have risen in the night."

"And the crops?"

"Unless we get water to the fields in the next five cycles' time, we've lost the bread-grain, for certain. Fortunately, the kairn grass is doing well—it seems to be able to thrive under almost impossible conditions. As for the vegetables, we've set the field hands to hauling water to the gardens, but that's not working. Hauling water is a new task for them. They don't understand it, and you know how difficult they can be when they're given something new."

Heads nod around the table. The king frowns, scratches his bearded chin. The farmer continues, seeming to feel the need to explain, perhaps to offer a defense.

"The hands keep forgetting what they're supposed to be doing and wander off. We find them, back at work on their old jobs, water buckets left to lie on the ground. By my calculations, we've wasted more water this way than we've used on the vegetables."

"And your recommendation?"

"My recommendation." The farmer glances around the table, seeking support. He sighs. "I recommend that we harvest *what* we can, *while* we can. It will be better to save the little we have than to let it all shrivel up and die in the fields. I brought this parfruit to show you. As you see, it's undersize, not yet ripe. It shouldn't be picked for another sixteen cycles, at least. But if we don't gather it now, it'll wither and die on the vine. After the harvest, we can do another planting and perhaps, by that time, the river will have returned to its normal—"

"No," calls a voice, a voice new to the room and to the meeting. I have been kept waiting in the antechamber long enough. It is obvious that the king isn't going to send for me. I must take matters into my own hands. "The river will not return, at least not anytime soon, and then only if some drastic change occurs that I do not foresee. The Hemo is reduced to a muddy trickle and, unless we are indeed fortunate, Your Majesty, I believe it may dry up altogether."

The king turns, scowls in irritation as I enter. He knows that I am far more intelligent than he is and, therefore, he doesn't trust me. But he has come to rely on me. He's been forced to. Those few times he did not, when he went his own way, he came to regret it. That is why I am now necromancer to the king.

"I was planning to send for you when the time was right, Baltazar. But," the king adds, his frown growing deeper, "it seems you can't wait to impart bad news. Please be seated and give the council your report." From the tone of his voice, he would like to blame the bad news on me personally.

I sit down at a chair at the far end of the rectangular meeting table, a table carved of stone. The eyes of those gathered around the table turn slowly, reluctant to look directly at me. I am, I must admit, an unusual sight.

Those who live inside the gigantic caverns of the stone world of Abarrach are naturally pale complected. But my skin is a dead white, a white so pallid it appears to be almost translucent and has a faint bluish cast given by the blood veins that lay close beneath the skin's thin surface.

The unnatural pallor comes from the fact that I spend long hours shut up in the library, reading ancient texts. My jet black hair—extremely rare among my people, whose hair is almost always white, dark brown at the tips—and the black robes of my calling make my complexion appear to be even whiter by contrast.

Few see me on a daily basis, for I keep to the palace, near my beloved library, rarely venturing into town or into the royal court. My appearance at a council meeting is an alarming event. I am a presence to be feared. My coming casts a pall over the hearts of those in attendance, much as if I'd spread my black robes over them.

I begin by standing up. Extending my hands flat on the table, I lean on them slightly so that I seem to loom over those staring back at me in rapt fascination.

"I suggested to His Majesty that I undertake to explore the Hemo, track it back to its source, and see if I could discover what was causing the water to drop so severely. His Majesty agreed that this suggestion was a good one, and I set out."

I notice several council members exchange glances with each other, their brows darkening. This exploration had not been discussed or sanctioned by the council, which means that they are, of course, immediately against it.

The king sees their concern, stirs in his chair, seems about to come to his own defense. I slide into the breach before he can say a word.

"His Majesty proposed that we inform the council and receive their approbation, but I opposed such a move. Not out of any lack of respect for the members of the council," I hasten to assure them, "but out of the need to maintain calm among the populace. His Majesty and I were then of the opinion that the drop in the river level was a freak of nature. Perhaps a seismic disturbance had caused a section of the cavern to collapse and block the river's flow. Perhaps a colony of animals had dammed it up. Why needlessly upset people? Alas"—I am unable to prevent a sigh—"such is not the case."

The council members regard me with growing concern. They have become accustomed to the strangeness of my appearance, and now they begin to discern changes in me. I am aware that I do not look good, even worse than usual. My black eyes are sunken, ringed by purple shadows. The eyelids are heavy and red rimmed. The journey was long and fatiguing. I have not slept in many cycles. My shoulders slump with exhaustion.

The council members forget their irritation at the king acting on his own, without consulting them. They wait, grim faced and unhappy, to hear my report.

"I traveled up the Hemo, following the river's banks. I journeyed beyond civilized lands, through the forests of laze trees that stand on our borders, and came to the end of the wall that forms our kairn. But I did not find the river's source there. A tunnel cuts through the cavern wall and, according to the ancient maps, the Hemo flows into this tunnel. The maps, I discovered, proved accurate. The Hemo has either cut its own path through the cavern wall or the river runs along a path formed for it by those who made our world in the beginning. Or perhaps a combination of both."

The king shakes his head at me, disliking my learned digressions. I see his expression of annoyance and, slightly inclining my head to acknowledge it, return to the subject at hand.

"I followed the tunnel a great distance and discovered a small lake set in a box canyon, at the bottom of what once must have been a magnificent waterfall. There, the Hemo plunges over a sheer rock cliff, falling hundreds of footspans, from a height equal to the height of cavern ceiling above our heads."

The citizens of Kairn Telest appear impressed. I shake my head, warning them not to get their hopes up.

"I could tell, from the vast dimensions of the smooth plane of the wall's rock surface and from the depth of the lake bed below, that the river's flow had once been strong and powerful. Once, I judge, a man standing beneath it might have been crushed by the sheer force of the water falling on him. Now, a child could bathe safely in the trickle that flows down the cliff's side."

My tone is bitter. The king and council members watch me warily, uneasily.

"I traveled on, still seeking the river's source. I climbed up the sides of the canyon wall. And I noticed a strange phenomenon: the higher I climbed, the cooler grew the temperature of the air around me. When I arrived at the top of the falls, near the ceiling of the cavern, I discovered the reason why. I was no longer surrounded by the rock walls of the cavern." My voice grows tense, dark, ominous. "I found myself surrounded by walls of solid ice."

The council members appear startled, they feel the awe and fear I mean to convey. But I can tell from their confused expressions that they do not yet comprehend the danger.

"My friends," I tell them, speaking softly, my eyes moving around the table, gathering them up, and holding them fast, "the ceiling of the cavern, through which the Hemo flows, is rimed with ice. It didn't used to be that way," I add, noting that they still do not understand. My fingers curl slightly. "This is a change, a dire change. But, listen, I will explain further.

"Appalled by my discovery, I continued traveling along the banks of the Hemo. The way was dark and treacherous, the cold was bitter. I marveled at this, for I had not yet passed beyond the range of light and warmth shed by the colossus. Why weren't the colossus working, I wondered?"

"If it was as cold as you claim, how could you go on?" the king demands.

"Fortunately, Your Majesty, my magic is strong and it sustained me," I reply.

He doesn't like to hear that, but he was the one who challenged me. I am reputed to be extremely powerful in magic, more powerful

than most in the realm of Kairn Telest. He thinks that I am showing off.

"I arrived eventually, after much difficulty, at the opening in the
cavern wall through which the Hemo flows," I continue. "According
to the ancient maps, when I looked out of this opening, I should
have seen the Celestial Sea, the freshwater ocean created by the
ancients for our use. What I looked out on, my friends"—I pause,
making certain I have their undivided attention—"was a vast sea of
ice!"

I hiss the final word. The council members shiver, as if I'd
brought the cold back in a cage and set it loose in the Council
Chamber. They stare at me in silence, astounded, appalled, the full
understanding of what I am telling them slowly working its way, like
an arrow tip lodged in an old wound, into their minds.

"How is such a thing possible?" The king is the first to break the
silence. "How can it happen?"

I pass a hand over my brow. I am weary, drained. My magic may
have been strong enough to sustain me, but its use has taken its toll.
"I have spent long hours studying the matter, Your Majesty. I plan to
continue my research to confirm my theory, but I believe I have
determined the answer. If I may make use of this parfruit?"

I lean further over the table, grab a piece of parfruit from the
bowl. I hold up the round, hard-shelled fruit, whose meat is much
prized for the making of parfruit wine, and—with a twist of my
hands—break the fruit in half.

"This," I tell them, pointing to the fruit's large red seed, "represents the center of our world, the magma core. These"—I trace red
veins that extend outward from the seed through the yellowish meat
to the shell—"are the colossus that, by the wisdom and skill and
magic of the ancients, carry the energy obtained from the magma
core throughout the world, bringing warmth and life to what would
otherwise be cold and barren stone. The surface of Abarrach is solid
rock, similar to this hard shell."

I take a bite of the fruit, tearing through the shell with my teeth,
leaving a hollowed out portion that I exhibit.

"This, we will say, represents the Celestial Sea, the ocean of fresh
water above us. The space around here"—I wave my hand around
the parfruit—"is the Void, dark and cold.

"Now, if the colossus do their duty, the cold of the Void is driven
back, the ocean is kept well heated, the water flows freely down

through the tunnel and brings life to our land. But if the colossus fail . . ."

My voice trails off ominously. I shrug and toss the parfruit back onto the table. It rolls and wobbles along, eventually falls over the edge. The council members watch it in a horrible kind of fascination, making no move to touch it. One woman jumps when the fruit hits the floor.

"You're saying that is what's happening? The colossus are failing?"

"I believe so, Your Majesty."

"But, then, shouldn't we see some sign of it? Our colossus still radiate light, heat—"

"May I remind king and council that I commented on the fact that it was the *top* of the cavern only that is rimed in ice. *Not* the cavern wall. I believe our colossus are, if not failing utterly, at least growing weaker. We do not yet notice the change, although I have begun to register a consistent and previously inexplicable drop in the average daily temperature. We may not notice the change for some time. But, if my theory holds true . . ." I hesitate, reluctant to speak.

"Well, go ahead," the king orders me. "Better to see the hole that lies in the path and walk around it than fall into it blindly, as the saying goes."

"I do not think we will be able to avoid this hole," I say quietly. "First, as the ice grows thicker on the Celestial Sea, the Hemo will continue to dwindle and eventually dry up completely."

Exclamations of horrified shock interrupt me. I wait until these die down.

"The temperature in the cavern will drop steadily. The light radiated by the colossus will grow dimmer and soon cease altogether. We will find ourselves in a land of darkness, a land of bitter cold, a land with no water, a land where no food will grow—not even by means of magic. We will find ourselves in the land that is dead, Your Majesty. And if we stay here, we, too, will perish."

I hear a gasp, catch a glimpse of movement near the door. Edmund—he is only fourteen—stands listening. No one else breathes a word. Several of the council members look stricken. Then someone mutters that none of this is proved, it is merely the gloom-and-doom theory of a necromancer who has spent too much time among his books.

"How long?" the king asks harshly.

"Oh, it will not happen tomorrow, Your Majesty. Nor yet many tomorrows from now. But," I continue, my fond gaze going sadly to the door, "the prince, your son, will never rule over the land of Kairn Telest."

The king follows my glance, sees the young man, and frowns. "Edmund, you know better than this! What are you doing here?"

The prince flushes. "Forgive me, Father. I didn't mean to—to interrupt. I came looking for you. Mother is ill. The physician thinks you should come. But when I arrived, I didn't want to disturb the council and so I waited, and then I heard . . . I heard what Baltazar said! Is it true, Father? Will we have to leave—"

"That will do, Edmund. Wait for me. I will be with you presently."

The boy gulps, bows, and fades back, silent and unobtrusive, to stand in the shadows near the doorway. My heart aches for him. I long to comfort him, to explain. I meant to frighten them, not him.

"Forgive me, I must go to my wife."

The king rises to his feet. The council members do likewise; the meeting is obviously at an end.

"I need not tell you to keep this quiet until we have more information," the king continues. "Your own common sense will point out to you the wisdom of such an action. We will meet together again in five cycles' time. However," he adds, his brows knotting together, "I advise that we take the recommendation of the Farmer's Guild and make an early harvest."

The members vote. The recommendation passes. They file out, many casting dark and unhappy glances back at me. They would dearly love to blame this on someone. I meet each gaze with unruffled aplomb, secure in my position. When the last one has left, I glide forward and lay a hand on the arm of the king, who is eager to be gone.

"What is it?" the king demands, obviously irritated at my interruption. He is much concerned about his wife.

"Your Majesty, forgive me for delaying you, but I wanted to mention something to you in private."

The king draws back, away from my touch. "We do nothing in secret on Kairn Telest. Whatever you want to say to me should have been said in the council."

"I would have said it in the council, if I were certain of my facts. I prefer to leave it to the wisdom and discretion of His Majesty to bring up the matter if he thinks it proper that the people should know."

He glares at me. "What is it, Baltazar? Another theory?"

"Yes, Sire. Another theory . . . about the colossus. According to my studies, the magic in the colossus was intended by the ancients to be eternal. The magic in the colossus, Your Majesty, could not possibly fail."

The king regards me in exasperation. "I don't have time for games, Necromancer. You were the one who said the colossus were failing—"

"Yes, Your Majesty. I did. And I believe that they are. But perhaps I chose the wrong word to describe what is happening to our colossus. The word may not be failure, Sire, but destruction. Deliberate destruction."

The king stares at me, then shakes his head. "Come, Edmund," he says, motioning peremptorily to his son. "We will go see your mother."

The young man runs to join his father. The two start to walk away.

"Sire," I call out, the urgency in my voice bringing the king again to a halt. "I believe that somewhere, in realms that exist below Kairn Telest, someone wages a most insidious war on us. And they will defeat us utterly, unless we do something to stop them. Defeat us without so much as letting fly an arrow or tossing a spear. Someone, Sire, is stealing away the warmth and light that give us life!"

"For what purpose, Baltazar? What is the motive for this nefarious scheme?"

I ignore the king's sarcasm. "To use it for themselves, Sire. I thought long and hard on this problem during my journey home to Kairn Telest. What if Abarrach itself is dying? What if the magma heart is shrinking? A kingdom might consider it necessary to steal from its neighbors to protect its own."

"You're mad, Baltazar," says the king. He has his hand on his son's thin shoulder, steering him away from me. But Edmund looks over his shoulder, his eyes large and frightened. I smile at him, reassuringly, and he seems relieved. My smile vanishes, the moment he can no longer see me.

"No, Sire, I am not mad," I say to the shadows. "I wish I were. It would be easier." I rub my eyes, which burn from lack of sleep. "It would be far easier. . . ."

CHAPTER ✦ 3

KAIRN TELEST,

ABARRACH

✦

EDMUND APPEARS ALONE, AT THE DOOR TO THE LIBRARY, WHERE I SIT recording in my journal the conversation that recently took place between father and son, as well as my memories of a time now long past. I lay down the pen and rise respectfully from my desk.

"Your Highness. Please, enter and welcome."

"I'm not interrupting your work?" He stands fidgeting nervously in the doorway. He is unhappy and wants to talk, yet the basis for his unhappiness is his refusal to listen to what he knows I am going to say.

"I have just this moment concluded."

"My father's lying down," Edmund says abruptly. "I am afraid he'll catch a chill, standing outdoors like that. I ordered his servant to prepare a hot posset."

"And what has your father decided?" I ask.

Edmund's troubled face glimmers ghostly in the light of a gas lamp that, for the moment, drives away the darkness of Kairn Telest.

"What can he decide?" he returns in bitter resignation. "There is no decision to be made. We will leave."

We are in my world, in my library. The prince glances around, notes that the books have been given a loving good-bye. The older and more fragile volumes have been packed away in sturdy boxes of woven kairn grass. Other, newer texts, many penned by myself and my apprentices, are neatly labeled, stored away in the deep recesses of dry rock shelves.

Seeing Edmund's glance and reading his thoughts, I smile

shamefacedly. "Foolish of me, isn't it?" My hand caresses the leather-bound cover of the volume that rests before me. It is one of the few that I will take with me: my description of the last days of Kairn Telest. "But I could not bear to leave them in disorder."

"It isn't foolish. Who knows but that someday you will return?" Edmund tries to speak cheerfully. He has become accustomed to speaking cheerfully, accustomed to doing what he can to lift the spirits of his people.

"Who knows? *I* know, My Prince." I shake my head ruefully. "You forget to whom you talk. I am not one of the council members."

"But there *is* a chance," he persists.

It hurts me to shatter his dream. Yet—for the good of all of us—he must be made to face the truth.

"No, Your Highness, there is *not* a chance. The fate that I described to your father ten years earlier is upon us. All my calculations point to one conclusion: our world, Abarrach, is dying."

"Then what is the use of going on?" Edmund demands impatiently. "Why not just stay here? Why endure the hardship and suffering of this trek into unknown regions if we go only to meet death at the end?"

"I do not counsel that you abandon hope and plunge into despair, Edmund. I suggest now, as I have done before, that you turn your hope in another direction."

The prince's face darkens, he is upset and moves slightly away from me. "My father has forbidden you to discuss that subject."

"Your father is a man who lives in the past, not the present," I say bluntly. "Forgive me, Your Highness, but it has always been my practice to speak the truth, no matter how unpleasant. When your mother died, something in your father died, too. He looks backward. It is up to you to look forward!"

"My father is still king," Edmund says sternly.

"Yes," I reply. And I cannot help feeling that this is a fact to be deeply regretted.

Edmund faces me, chin high. "And while he is king we will do as he and the council command. We will travel to the old realm of Kairn Necros, seek out our brethren there, and ask them for help. You were the one who proposed this undertaking, after all."

"I proposed that we travel to Kairn Necros," I correct him. "According to my studies, Kairn Necros is the one place left on this world where we might reasonably expect to find life. It is located on the Fire Sea, and, although the great magma ocean has undoubtedly shrunk, it must still be large enough to provide warmth and energy for the people of its realm. I did *not* counsel that we go to them as beggars!"

Edmund's handsome face flushes, his eyes flash. He is young and proud.

I see the fire in him and do what I can to stoke it.

"Beggars to those who brought about our ruin!" I remind him.

"You don't know that for certain—"

"Bah! All the evidence points one way—to Kairn Necros. Yes, I think we will find the people of that realm alive and well. Why? Because they have stolen our lives from us!"

"Then why did you suggest that we go to them?" Edmund is losing patience. "Do you want war? Is that it?"

"You know what I want, Edmund," I say softly.

The prince sees, too late, that he's been led down the forbidden path. "We leave after we have broken our sleep's fasting," he tells me coldly. "I have certain matters to which I must attend, as do you, Necromancer. Our dead must be prepared for the journey."

He turns to leave. I reach out, catch hold of his fur-cloaked arm.

"Death's Gate!" I tell him. "Think about it, My Prince. That is all I ask. Think about it!"

Disquieted, he pauses, although he does not turn around. I increase the pressure of my hand on the young man's arm, squeezing through the layers of fur and cloth to feel the flesh and bone and muscle, hard and strong beneath. I feel him tremble.

"Remember the words of the prophecy. Death's Gate is our hope, Edmund," I say quietly. "Our only hope."

The prince shakes his head, shakes off my hand, and leaves the library to its flickering flame, its entombed books.

I return to my writing.

♦

The people of Kairn Telest gather in the darkness near the gate of their city wall. The gate has stood open for as long as anyone can remember, for as long as records have been kept, which is from the time of the city's founding. The walls were erected to protect the people from rampaging, predatory animals. These walls were never intended to protect people from one another. Such a concept is unthinkable to us. Travelers, strangers, are always welcome, and so the gates stand open.

But then came the day when it occurred to the people of Kairn Telest that there had been no travelers for a long, long while. It occurred to us that there would be no travelers. There hadn't even been any animals. And so the gates remain open, because to shut them would be a waste of time and a bother. And now the people stand before the open gates, themselves travelers, and wait in silence for their journey to commence.

Their king and prince arrive, accompanied by the army, the soldiers bearing kairn grass torches. Myself—necromancer to the king—and my fellow necromancers and apprentices walk behind. After us trail the palace servants bearing heavy bundles containing clothes and food. One, shambling close behind me, carries a box filled with books.

The king comes to a halt near the open gates. Taking one of the torches from a soldier, His Majesty holds it high. Its light illuminates a small portion of the dark city. He looks out across it. The people turn and look out across it. I turn.

We see wide streets winding among buildings created out of the stone of Abarrach. The gleaming white marble exteriors, decorated with runes whose meanings no one now remembers, reflect back to us the light of our torches. We look upward, to a rise in the cavern floor, to the palace. We can't see it now. It is shrouded in darkness. But we can see a light, a tiny light, burning in one of the windows.

"I left the lamp," the king announces, his voice loud and unusually strong, "to light the way for our return."

The people cheer, because they know he wants them to cheer. But the cheers die away soon, too soon; more than a few cut off by tears.

"The gas fueling that lamp will last about thirty cycles," I remark in a low voice, coming to take my place at the prince's side.

"Be silent!" Edmund rebukes me. "It made my father happy."

"You cannot silence the truth, Your Highness. You can't silence reality," I remind him.

He does not reply.

"We leave Kairn Telest now," the king was continuing, holding the torch high above his head, "but we will be back with newfound wealth. And we will make our realm more glorious and more beautiful than ever."

No one cheers. No one has the heart.

The people of Kairn Telest begin to file out of their city. They travel mostly on foot, carrying their clothes and food wrapped in bundles, though some pull crude carts bearing possessions and those who cannot walk: the infirm, the elderly, small children. Beasts of burden, once used to draw the carts, have long since died off; their flesh consumed for food, their fur used to protect the people from the bitter cold.

Our king is the last to leave. He walks out of the gates without a backward glance, his eyes facing forward confidently to the future, to a new life. His stride is firm, his stance upright. The people, looking at him, grow hopeful. They form an aisle along the road and now there are cheers and now the cheers are heartfelt. The king walks among them, his face alight with dignity.

"Come, Edmund," he commands. The prince leaves me, takes his place at his father's side.

He and his father walk among the people to the head of the line. Holding his torch aloft, the king of Kairn Telest leads his people forth.

◆

A detail of soldiers remains after the others have gone. I wait with them, curious to know their final orders.

It takes them some time and a considerable amount of effort, but at last they succeed in pulling shut the gates, gates marked with runes that no one remembers and that, now, as they march off with the torches, no one can see in the darkness.

CHAPTER ◆ 4

KAIRN TELEST,

ABARRACH

◆

I AM WRITING NOW, UNDER ALMOST IMPOSSIBLE CONDITIONS. I EXPLAIN this to anyone who may perhaps read this volume at a later date and wonder both at the change in style and the change in the handwriting. No, I have not suddenly grown old and feeble, nor am I plagued by illness. The letters straggle across the page because I am forced to write by the dim light of a flickering torch. The only surface I have for a tablet is a slab of flint, foraged for me by one of the soldiers. My magic alone keeps the bloodberry ink from freezing long enough for me to put words to paper.

Plus, I am bone weary. Every muscle in my body aches, my feet are bruised and blistered. But I made a pact with myself and with Edmund to keep this account and I will now record the cycle's events before—

I started to say before I forget them.

Alas, I do not think that I will ever forget.

The first cycle's journeying was not physically difficult for us. The route lies overland, through what were once fields of grain and vegetables, orchards, plains where the herd animals were fed. The paths were easily traversed—physically. Emotionally, the first cycle's journey was devastating.

Once, not so many years ago, the warm, soft light of the colossus beamed upon this land. Now, in the darkness, by the light of torches carried by the soldiers, we saw the fields lying empty, barren, desolate. The brown stubble of the last crop of kairn grass stood in clumps, rattling like bones in the blasts of chill wind that whistled mournfully through cracks in the cavern walls.

The almost joyful, adventurous mood that sent our people marching in hope drained from them and was left behind in the desolate landscape. We trudged in silence over the frozen ground, cold-numbed feet slipping and stumbling on patches of ice and frost. We halted once, for a midday meal, and then pushed on. Children, missing their naps, whimpered fretfully, often falling asleep in their father's arms as they walked.

No one spoke a single word of complaint, but Edmund heard the children's cries. He saw the people's weariness, and knew it was not caused by fatigue but by bitter sorrow. I could see that his heart ached for them, yet we had to keep going. Our food supplies are meager and, with rationing, will last barely the length of time I have estimated will be needed to reach the realm of Kairn Necros.

I considered suggesting to Edmund that he break the unhappy silence. He could talk cheerfully to the people of their future in a new land. But I decided it was best to keep quiet. The silence was almost sacred. Our people were saying good-bye.

Near cycle's end, we came to a colossus. No one said a word but, one by one, the people of Kairn Telest left the path, came to stand beneath the gigantic column of stone. Once, it would have been impossible to have approached the bright and shining source of our life. Now, it stood dead and cold as the land it had forsaken.

The king, accompanied by myself and Edmund and torch-bearing soldiers, moved forward out of the crowd and walked up to the colossus's base. Edmund stared at the huge stone pillar curiously. He had never been close to one before. His expression was awed. He marveled at the girth and mass of the pillar of rock.

I looked at the king. He appeared pained and bewildered and angry, as if the colossus had betrayed him personally.

I, myself, was familiar with the colossus and what it looked like. I had investigated it long ago, seeking to unravel its secrets to save my people. But the mystery of the colossus is forever locked in the past.

Impulsively, Edmund pulled off his fur gloves, reached out his hand to touch the rock, to run his fingers along the sigla-inscribed stone. He paused, however, suddenly fearful of the magic, afraid of being burned or shocked. He looked questioningly at me.

"It won't hurt you," I said, with a shrug. "It lost, long ago, the power to hurt."

"Just as it lost the power to help," Edmund added, but he said the words to himself.

Gingerly, he ran his fingertips over the chill stone. Hesitantly, almost reverently, he traced the pattern of the runes whose meaning and magic are now long forgotten. He lifted his head, looked up and up as far as the torchlight shone on the glistening rock. The sigla extend upward into the darkness and beyond.

"The column rises to the ceiling of the cavern," I commented, thinking it best to speak in the crisp, concise voice of the teacher, as I used to speak to him in the happy days when we were together in the classroom. "Presumably, it extends up through the ceiling to the region of the Celestial Sea. And every bit of it is covered in these runes, that you see here.

"It is frustrating"—I could not help frowning—"but most of these sigla, individually, I know, I understand. The rune's power lies not in the individual sigil, however, but in the combination of sigla. It is that combination that is beyond my ability to comprehend. I copied down the patterns, took them back with me to the library, and spent many hours studying them with the help of the ancient texts.

"But," I continued, speaking so softly that only Edmund could hear my words, "it was like trying to unravel a huge ball made up of myriad tiny threads. A single thread ran smoothly through my fingers. I followed it and it led me to a knot. Patiently I worked, separating one thread from another and then another and then another until my mind ached from the strain. I untangled one knot, only to find, beneath it, another. And by the time I unraveled that one, I had lost hold of the first single thread. And there are millions of knots," I said, looking upward, sighing. "Millions."

The king turned away from the pillar abruptly, his face drawn and darkly lined in the torchlight. He had not spoken a word during the time we'd stood beneath the colossus. It occurred to me, then, that he had not spoken since we left the city gates. He walked off, back to the path. The people lifted their children to their shoulders and started on their way. Most of the soldiers followed after the people, taking the light with them. One only remained near myself and the prince.

Edmund stood before the pillar, pulling on his gloves. I waited for him, sensing that he wanted to talk to me in private.

"These same runes, or others like them, must guard Death's Gate," he said in a low voice, when he was certain no one could overhear. The soldier had backed off, out of courtesy. "Even if we did find it, we could not hope to enter."

My heart beat faster. At last, he was beginning to accept the idea!

"Recall the prophecy, Edmund," was all I said.

I didn't want to appear too eager or press the issue too closely. It is best, with Edmund, to let him turn matters over in his mind, make his own decisions. I learned that when he was a boy in school. Suggest, introduce, recommend. Never insist, never force him. Try to do so, and he becomes hard and cold as this cavern wall that is now, as I write, poking me painfully in the back.

"Prophecy!" he repeated irritably. "Words spoken centuries ago! If they ever do come true, which I must admit I doubt, why should they come to fulfillment in our lifetime?"

"Because, My Prince," I told him, "I do not think that, after our lifetime, there will be any others."

The answer shocked him, as I intended. He stared at me, appalled, said nothing more. Glancing a last time at the colossus, he turned away and hastened to catch up with his father. I knew my words troubled him. I saw his expression, brooding and thoughtful, his shoulders bent.

Edmund, Edmund! How I love you and how it breaks my heart to thrust this terrible burden on you. I look up from my work and watch you walking among the people, making certain they are as comfortable as they can possibly be. I know that you are exhausted, but you will not lie down to sleep until every one of your people is sleeping.

You have not eaten all cycle. I saw you give your ration of food to the old woman who nursed you when you were a babe. You tried to keep the deed hidden, secret. But I saw. I know. And your people are beginning to know, as well, Edmund. By the end of this journey, they will come to understand and appreciate a true king.

But, I digress. I must conclude this quickly. My fingers are cramped with the cold and, despite my best efforts, a thin layer of ice is starting to form across the top of the ink jar.

That colossus of which I wrote marks the border of Kairn Telest. We continued traveling until cycle's end, when we finally arrived at our destination. I searched for and found the entrance to the tunnel that was marked on one of the ancient maps, a tunnel that bores through the kairn wall. I knew it was the right tunnel, because, on entering it, I discovered that its floor sloped gently downward.

"This tunnel," I announced, pointing to the deep darkness inside, "will lead us to regions far below our own kairn. It will lead us deeper into the heart of Abarrach, lead us down to the lands below, to the realm that is lettered on the map as Kairn Necros, to the city of Necropolis."

The people stood in silence, not even the babies cried. We all knew, when we entered that tunnel, that we would leave our homeland behind us.

The king, saying nothing, walked forward and into the tunnel—the first. Edmund and I came behind him; the prince was forced to stoop to avoid hitting his head on the low ceiling. Once the king had made his symbolic gesture, I took the lead, for I am now the guide.

The people began to follow after us. I saw many pause at the entrance to look back, to say farewell, to catch a final glimpse of their homeland. I must admit that I, too, could not refrain from taking a last look. But all we could see was darkness. What light remains, we are taking with us.

We entered the tunnel. The flickering light of the torches reflected off the shining obsidian walls, the shadows of the people slid along the floors. We moved on, delving deeper, spiraling downward.

Behind us, darkness closed over Kairn Telest forever.

CHAPTER ◆ 5

THE TUNNELS OF HOPE,

ABARRACH

◆

WHOEVER READS THIS ACCOUNT (IF ANY ONE OF US IS LEFT ALIVE TO read it, which I am greatly beginning to doubt), he will note a gap in the time period. When I last put down my pen, we had just entered the first of what the map calls the Tunnels of Hope. You will see that I have scratched out that name and written in another.

The Tunnels of Death.

We have spent twenty cycles in these tunnels, far longer than I had anticipated. The map has proved inaccurate, not so far, I must admit, as to the route, which is essentially the same one that our ancestors traveled to reach Kairn Telest.

Then the tunnels were newly formed, with smooth walls, strong ceilings, level floors. I knew that much would have changed during the past centuries; Abarrach is subject to seismic disturbances that send tremors through the ground, but they do little more than rattle the dishes in the cupboards and set the chandeliers in the palace swaying.

I had assumed that our ancestors would have fortified these tunnels with their magic, as they did our palaces, our city walls, our shops, and our houses. If they did so, the runes have either failed or they need to be reforged, reinstated . . . re-runed, for lack of a better term. Or perhaps the ancients did not bother to protect the tunnels, assuming that what destruction took place could be easily cleared by those possessing the knowledge of the sigla.

Of all the possible disasters those early ancestors of ours feared for us, they obviously didn't foresee the worst of all. They never imagined that we would lose the magic.

Time and again we have been forced to make costly delays. We found the tunnel ceiling collapsed in many places, our way blocked by immense boulders that took us several cycles to move. Huge cracks gape in the floor, cracks that only the bravest dared jump, cracks that had to be bridged before the people could cross.

And we are not out of the tunnels yet. Nor, does it seem, that we are near the end. I cannot judge our location precisely. Several major landmarks are gone, carried away by rock slides, or else have altered so over the years that it is impossible to recognize them. I am not even certain, anymore, that we are following the correct route. I have no way of knowing. According to the map, the ancients inscribed runes on the walls that could guide travelers, but—if so—their magic is now beyond our comprehension and use.

We are in desperate straits. Food rations have been cut in half. The flesh has melted from our bones. Children no longer cry from weariness; they cry from hunger. The carts have fallen by the way-side. Beloved possessions became burdens to arms grown weak from starvation and exhaustion. Only the carts needed to bear the elderly and the infirm remain in use and these carts, too, tragically, are beginning to litter the tunnels. The weak among us are starting to die now. My fellow necromancers have taken up their grim tasks.

The burden of the people's suffering has fallen, as I knew it would, on the shoulders of their prince. Edmund watches his father fail before his eyes.

The king was, admittedly, an old man, by the standards of our people. His son was born to him late in life. But, when we left the palace, he was hale, hearty, strong as men half his age. I had a dream in which I saw the king's life as a thread tied back to the golden throne that now stands in the cold darkness of Kairn Telest. As he walked away from the throne, the thread remained tied to it. Slowly, cycle by cycle, the thread is coming unraveled, stretching thinner and thinner the farther he moves from his homeland, until now I fear a harsh or clumsy touch will cause it to snap.

The king takes no interest in anything anymore: what we do, what we say, where we are going. Most of the time, I wonder if he even notices the ground beneath his feet. Edmund walks constantly at his father's side, guiding him like one who has lost the power of sight. No, that is not quite a correct description. The king acts more like a man walking backward, who does not see what lies ahead, only what he is leaving behind.

On the occasions when the prince is called away by his number-less responsibilities, and he must leave his father, Edmund makes certain that two soldiers are on hand to take over his task. The king is tractable, he goes where he is led without question. He moves when he is told to move, he stops when he is told to stop. He eats whatever is put into his hand, never seeming to taste it. I think he would eat a rock, if it were given to him. I also think he would stop eating altogether, if no one brought him food.

For long cycles, at the journey's start, the king said nothing to anyone, not even to his son. Now, he talks almost constantly, but only to himself, never to anyone around him. Anyone that can be counted, that is. He spends a great deal of time talking to his wife—not as she is, among the dead, but as she was, when she was among the living. Our king has forsaken the present, returned to the past.

Matters grew so bad that the council begged the prince to declare himself king. Edmund rebuffed them, in one of the few times I have ever seen him lose his temper. The council members slunk away before his wrath like whipped children. Edmund is right. According to our law, the king is king until his death. But, then, the law never considered the possibility that a king might go insane. Such a thing doesn't happen among our people.

The council members were actually reduced to coming to me (I must say that I relished the moment) and begging me to intervene with Edmund on behalf of the people. I promised to do what I could.

"Edmund, we must talk," I said to him during one of our en-forced stops, waiting while the soldiers cleared away a huge mound of rubble that blocked the path.

His face darkened, turned rebellious. I had often seen such a look when he was a youth and I had forced upon him the study of mathematics, a subject to which he never took. The look he cast me brought back such fond memories that I had to pause and recover myself before I could continue.

"Edmund," I said, deliberately keeping my tone practical, brisk, making this a matter of common sense, "your father is ill. You must take over the leadership of the people—if only for the time being," I said, raising my hand, forestalling his angry refusal, "until His Majesty is once more able to resume his duties.

"You have a responsibility to the people, My Prince," I added. "Never in the history of Kairn Telest have we been in greater danger than we are now. Will you abandon them, out of a false sense of duty and filiality? Would your father want you to abandon them?"

I did not mention, of course, that it was his father who had, himself, abandoned the people. Edmund understood my implication, however. If I had spoken such words aloud, he would angrily deny them. But when they were spoken to him by his own conscience . . .

I saw him glance at his father, who was sitting on a rock, chatting with his past. I saw the trouble and distress on Edmund's face, saw the guilt. I knew then, that my weapon had struck home. Reluctantly, I left him alone, to let the wound rankle.

Why is it always I, who love him, who must repeatedly cause him pain? I wondered sadly, as I walked away.

At the end of that cycle, Edmund called a meeting of the people and informed them that he would be their leader, if they wanted him, but only for the time being. He would retain the title of prince. His father was still king and Edmund confidently expected his father to resume his duties as king when he was well.

The people responded to their prince with enthusiasm, their obvious love and loyalty touched him deeply. Edmund's speech did not ease the people's hunger, but it lifted their hearts and made the hunger easier to bear. I watched him with pride and a newfound hope in my own heart.

They will follow him anywhere, I thought, even through Death's Gate.

But it seems likely that we will find death before we will find Death's Gate. The only positive factor we have encountered on our journey thus far is that the temperature has, at least, moderated; growing somewhat warmer. I begin to think that we have been following the correct route, that we are drawing nearer to our destination—Abarrach's fiery heart.

"It is a hopeful sign," I said to Edmund, at the end of another bleak and cheerless cycle, traversing the tunnels. "A hopeful sign," I repeated confidently.

What fears and misgivings I have, I am keeping to myself. It is needless to pile more burdens on those young shoulders, strong though they may be.

"Look," I continued, pointing at the map, "you will note that when we come to the end of the tunnels, they open up on a great pool of magma, that lies outside. The Lake of Burning Rock, it is named—the first major landmark we would see on entering the Kairn Necros. I cannot be certain, but I believe it is the heat from this lake, seeping up through the tunnel, that we are feeling."

"Which means that we are near the end of our journey," Edmund said, his face—that has grown much too thin—lighting with hope.

"You must eat more, My Prince," I said to him gently. "Eat at least your share. You will not help the people if you fall sick or grow too weak to go on."

He shook his head; I knew he would. But I knew, as well, that he would consider my advice seriously. That sleep-half, I saw him consume what small amount of food was handed to him.

"Yes," I continued, returning to the map, "I believe that we are near the end. I think, in fact, we must be about here." I placed a finger on the parchment. "Two cycles more and we reach the lake, provided that we don't run into any further obstacles."

"And then we are in Kairn Necros. And surely there we will find a realm of plenty. Surely we will find food and water. Look at this huge ocean that they call the Fire Sea." He indicated a large body of magma. "It must bring light and warmth to all this vast region of land. And these cities and towns. Look at this one, Baltazar. Safe Harbor. What a wonderful name. I take that as a hopeful sign. Safe Harbor, where at last our people can find peace and happiness."

He spent a long time, studying the map, imagining aloud what this place or that must look like, how the people would talk, how surprised they will be to see us.

I sat back against the cavern wall and let him talk. It gave me pleasure, to see him hopeful and happy once more. Almost, it made me forget the terrible pangs of hunger gnawing at my vitals, the more terrible fears that gnaw at my waking hours.

Why should I burst his pretty bubble? Why prick it with reality's sharp-edged sword? After all, I know nothing for certain. "Theories," his father, the king, would have termed them in scorn. All I have are theories.

Supposition: The Fire Sea is shrinking. It can no longer provide the vast regions of land around it with warmth and light.

Theory: We will not find realms of plenty. We will find realms as barren, desolate, and deserted as that which we left behind. That is why the people of Kairn Necros stole light and warmth from us.

"They'll be surprised to see us," Edmund says, smiling to himself at the thought.

Yes, I say to myself. Very surprised. Very surprised indeed.

Kairn Necros. Named thus by the ancients who first came to this world, named to honor those who had lost their lives in the Sundering of the old world, named to indicate the end of one life and the beginning—the bright beginning, it was then—of another.

Oh, Edmund, My Prince, My Son. Take that name for your sign. Not Safe Harbor. Safe Harbor is a lie.

Kairn Necros. The Cavern of Death.

CHAPTER ◆ 6

THE LAKE OF

BURNING ROCK, ABARRACH

◆

How can i write an account of this terrible tragedy? how can I make sense of it, record it in some coherent manner? And yet I must. I promised Edmund his father's heroism would be set down for all to remember. Yet my hand shakes so that I can barely hold the pen. Not with cold. The tunnel is warm, now. And to think we welcomed the warmth! My trembling is a reaction to my recent experiences. I must concentrate.

Edmund. I will do this for Edmund.

I lift my eyes from my work and see him sitting across from me, sitting alone, as befits one in mourning. The people have made the ritual gestures of sympathy. They would have given him the customary mourning gift—food, all they have left of value—but their prince (now their king, although he refuses to accept the crown until after the resurrection) forbade it. I composed the body's stiffening limbs and performed the preserving rites. We will carry it with us, of course.

Edmund, in his grief, begged me to give the king the final rites at this time, but I reminded the prince sternly that these rites can be done only after three complete cycles have elapsed. To do so any earlier would be far too dangerous. Our code forbids it for that very reason.

Edmund did not pursue the subject. The fact that he even could consider such an aberration was undoubtedly a result of his dazed confusion and pain. I wish he would sleep. Perhaps he will, now that everyone has left him alone. Although, if he is like me, every time he closes his eyes he will see that awful head rearing up out of the . . .

I look back over what I have written and it occurs to me that I have begun at the end, instead of the beginning. I consider destroying this page and starting again, but my parchment pages are few, too precious to waste. Besides, this is not a tale I am recounting pleasurably over glasses of chilled parfruit wine. And yet, now that I think of it, this might well be an after-dinner type of tale, for tragedy struck us—as so often happens to those in the stories—just when hope shone brightest.

The last two cycles' journeying had been easy, one might almost call them blissful. We came across a stream of fresh water, the first we'd found in the tunnels. Not only were we able to drink our fill and replenish our dwindling water supply, but we discovered fish swimming in the swift current.

Hastily we rigged nets, making them out of anything that came to hand—a woman's shawl, a baby's tattered blanket, a man's worn shirt. Adults stood along the banks, holding the nets that were stretched out from one side to the other. The people were going about their task with a grim earnestness until Edmund, who was leading the fishing party, slipped on a rock and, arms waving wildly, tumbled into the water with a tremendous splash.

We could not tell how deep the stream was, our only source of light being the kairn-grass torches. The people cried out in alarm, several soldiers started to jump to his rescue. Edmund clambered to his feet. The water came only to his shins. Looking foolish, he began to laugh heartily at himself.

Then I heard our people laugh for the first time in many cycles.

Edmund heard them, too. He was dripping wet, yet I am convinced that the drops falling down his cheeks did not come from the stream, but bore the salty flavor of tears. Nor will I ever believe that Edmund, a sure-footed hunter, could have fallen from that bank by accident.

The prince reached out his hand to a friend, a son of one of the council members. The friend, trying to pull Edmund out, slipped on the wet shoreline. Both of them went over backward. The laughter increased, and then everyone was jumping or pretending to fall into the water. What had been a grim task turned into joyous play.

We did manage to catch some fish, eventually. We had a grand feast, that cycle's end, and everyone slept soundly, hunger assuaged and hearts gladdened. We spent an extra cycle's time near the stream; no one wanted to leave a place so blessed by laughter and good feelings. We caught more fish, salted them down, and took them with us to supplement our supplies.

Revived by the food, the water, and the blessed warmth of the tunnel, the people's despair lifted. Their joy was increased when the king himself seemed suddenly to shake off the dark clouds of madness. He looked around, recognized Edmund, spoke to him coherently, and asked to know where we were. The king obviously remembered nothing of our journey.

The prince, blinking back his tears, showed his father the map and pointed out how close we were to the Lake of Burning Rock and, from there, Kairn Necros.

The king ate well, slept soundly, and spoke no more to his dead wife.

The following cycle, everyone was awake early, packed and eager to go on. For the first time, the people began to believe that there might be a better life awaiting them than the life they had come to know in our homeland.

I kept my fears and my doubts to myself. Perhaps it was a mistake, but how could I take away their newfound hope?

A half of a cycle's travel brought us near the end of the tunnel. The floor ceased to slope downward and leveled off. The comfortable warmth had intensified to an uncomfortable heat. A red glow, emanating from the Lake of Burning Rock, lit the cavern with a light so bright we doused the torches. We could hear, echoing through the tunnel, a strange sound.

"What is that noise?" Edmund asked, bringing the people to a halt.

"I believe, Your Highness," I said hesitantly, "that what you are hearing is the sound of gases bubbling up from the depths of the magma."

He looked eager, excited. I'd seen the same expression on his face when he was small and I had offered to take him on an excursion.

"How far are we from the lake?"

"Not far, I should judge, Your Highness."

He started off. I laid a restraining hand on his arm.

"Edmund, take care. Our bodies' magic has activated to protect us from the heat and the poisonous fumes, but our strength is not inexhaustible. We should proceed forward with caution, take our time."

He stopped immediately, looked intently at me. "Why? What is there to fear? Tell me, Baltazar."

He knows me too well. I cannot conceal anything from him.

"My Prince," I said, drawing him to one side, out of earshot of the people and the king. "I cannot put a name to my fear and, therefore, I am loathe to mention it."

I spread the map out on a rock. We bent over it together. The people paid little attention to us. I could see the king watching us with suspicion, however, his brow dark and furrowed.

"Pretend that we are discussing the route, Your Highness. I don't want to unduly worry your father."

Edmund, casting the king a worried glance, did as I requested, wondering in loud tones where we were.

"You see these runes, drawn over this lake on the map?" I said to him in a low voice. "I cannot tell you what they mean, but when I look at them I am filled with dread."

Edmund stared at the sigla. "You have no idea what they say?"

"Their message has been lost in time, My Prince. I cannot decipher it."

"Perhaps they warn only that the way is treacherous."

"That could be it . . ."

"But you don't think so."

"Edmund," I said, feeling my face burn with embarrassment, "I'm not sure what I think. The map itself doesn't indicate a dangerous route. As you can see, a wide path runs around the shores of the lake. A child could travel it with ease."

"The path might be cut or blocked by rock falls. We've certainly seen enough of that during our trip," Edmund stated grimly.

"Yes, but the original mapmaker would have indicated such an occurrence if it had happened during the time he was making the map. If not, he wouldn't have known about it. No, if these runes are meant to warn us of danger, that danger existed when this map was made."

"But that was so long ago! Surely the danger's gone by now. We're like a rune-bone player beset by bad fortune. According to the odds, our luck is bound to change. You worry too much, Baltazar," Edmund added, laughing and clapping me on the shoulder.

"I hope so, My Prince," I replied gravely. "Humor me. Indulge a necromancer's foolish fears. Proceed with caution. Send the soldiers ahead to scout the area—"

I could see the king, glowering at us.

"Well, of course," snapped Edmund, irritated that I should venture to tell him his duty. "I would have done so in any case. I will mention the matter to my father."

Oh, Edmund, if only I had said more. If only you had said less. If only. Our lives are made up of "if onlys."

"Father, Baltazar thinks the path around the lake may be dangerous. You stay behind with the people and let me take the soldiers—"

"Danger!" the old king flared, with a fire that had not burned in either body or mind for a long, long time. Alas, that it should have blazed forth now! "Danger, and you tell me to stay behind! I am king. Or, at least, I was."

The old man's eyes narrowed. "I have noticed that you—with Baltazar's help, no doubt—are attempting to subvert the people's loyalty. I've seen you and the necromancer off in your dark corners, plotting and scheming. It won't work. The people will follow me, as they have always followed me!"

I heard. Everyone heard. The king's accusation echoed through the cavern. It was all I could do to keep from rushing forward and throttling the old man with my bare hands. I cared nothing for what he thought of me. My heart burned from the pain of the wound I saw inflicted on his son.

If only that fool king had known what a loyal and devoted son he had! If only he could have seen Edmund during those long, dreary cycles, walking by his father's side, listening patiently to the old man's mad ramblings. If only he could have seen Edmund, time and again, refuse to accept the crown, although the council knelt at his feet and begged him! If only . . .

But, no more. One must not speak ill of the dead. I can only assume some lingering madness put such ideas in the king's mind.

Edmund had gone deathly white, but he spoke with a quiet dignity that became him well. "You have misunderstood me, Father. It was necessary for me to take on myself certain responsibilities, to make certain decisions during the time of your recent illness. Reluctantly, I did so, as any here"—he gestured to the people, who were staring at their king in shock—"will tell you. No one is more pleased than I am to see you take, once more, your rightful place as ruler of the people of Kairn Telest."

Edmund glanced at me, asking me silently if I wanted to reply to the accusation. I shook my head, kept my mouth closed. How could I, in honesty, deny the wish that had been in my heart, if not on my lips?

His son's words had an effect on the old king. He looked ashamed, as well he might! He started to reach out his hand, started to say something, perhaps apologize, take his son in his arms, beg his forgiveness. But pride—or madness—got the better of him. The king looked over at me, his face hardened. He turned and stalked off, calling loudly for the soldiers.

"Some of you come with me," the king commanded. "The rest of you stay here and guard the people from whatever danger the necromancer theorizes is about to befall us. He is full of theories, our necromancer. His latest is that he fancies himself the father of *my* son!"

Edmund started forward, burning words on his lips. I caught hold of his arm, held him back, shaking my head.

The king set off for the tunnel exit, followed by a small troop of about twenty. The exit was a narrow opening in the rock. The file of soldiers, walking shoulder to shoulder, would have a difficult time squeezing their way through. In the distance, through the opening, the fiery light of the Lake of Burning Rock gleamed a fierce, bright red.

The people looked at each other, looked at Edmund. They seemed uncertain what to do or say. A few of the council members, however, shook their heads and made clucking sounds with their tongues. Edmund cast them a furious glance, and they immediately fell silent. When the king reached the end of the tunnel, he turned to face us.

"You and your necromancer stay with the people, Son," he shouted, and the sneer that curled his lip was audible in his voice. "Your king will return and tell you when it is safe to proceed."

Accompanied by his soldiers, he walked out of the tunnel.

If only . . .

◆

Fire dragons possess remarkable intelligence. One is tempted to say malevolent intelligence, but, in fairness, who are we to judge a creature our ancestors hunted almost to extinction? I have no doubt that, if the dragons could or would speak to us, they would remind us that they have good cause to hate us.

Not that this makes it any easier.

"I should have gone with him!" were the first words Edmund spoke to me, when I gently tried to remove his arms from around his father's broken, bleeding body. "I should have been at his side!"

If, at any moment in my life, I was ever tempted to believe that there might be an immortal plan, a higher power. . . . But no. To all my other faults, I will not add blasphemy!

As his father had commanded him, Edmund stayed behind. He stood tall, dignified, his face impassive. But I, who know him so well, understood that what he longed to do was run after his father. He wanted to explain, to try to make his father understand. If only Edmund had done so, perhaps the old king might have relented and apologized. Perhaps the tragedy would never have occurred.

Edmund is, as I have said, young and proud. He was angry—justifiably so. He had been insulted in front of all the people. He had not been in the wrong. He would not make the first move toward reconciliation. His body trembled with the force of his inheld rage. He stared out the tunnel, said no word. No one said anything. We waited in silence for what seemed to me to be an interminable length of time.

What was wrong? They could have circumnavigated the lake by now, I was thinking to myself, when the scream resounded down the tunnel, echoed horribly off the cavern walls.

All of us recognized the voice of the king. I . . . and his son . . . recognized it as a warning, recognized it as his death cry.

The scream was awful, first choked with terror, then agonized, bubbling with pain. It went on and on, and its dreadful echo reverberated from the rock walls, screamed death to us over and over.

I have never in my life heard anything to equal it. I hope I never hear anything like it again. The scream might have turned the people to stone, as does, purportedly, the look of the legendary basilisk. I know that I stood frozen to the spot, my limbs paralyzed, my mind in little better condition.

The scream jolted Edmund to action.

"Father!" he shouted, and all the love that he had longed for during all the years of his life was in that cry. And, just as in his life, his cry went unanswered.

The prince ran forward, alone.

I heard the clattering of weapons and the confused sounds of battle and, above that, a dreadful roaring. I could now give a name to my fear. I knew now what the runes on the map meant.

The sight of Edmund rushing to meet the same fate as his father impelled me, at last, to act. Swiftly, with what remaining strength I had left, I wove a magical spell, like the nets in which we'd caught the fish, across the tunnel exit. Edmund saw it, tried to ignore it. He crashed full-force into it, fought and struggled against it. Drawing his sword, he attempted to cut his way through.

My magic, its power heightened by my fear for him, was strong. He couldn't get out, nor could the fire dragon—on the other side—break through the net.

At least, I hoped it couldn't. I have studied what the ancients wrote about such creatures, and it is my belief that they underestimated the dragon's intelligence. To be safe, I ordered the people to retreat farther back down the tunnel, telling them to hide in whatever passages they could find. They fled like scared mice, council members and all, and soon no one was left in the front part of the cavern but myself and Edmund.

He struck at me, in his frustration. He pleaded with me, he begged me, he threatened to kill me if I did not remove the magical net. I remained adamant. I could see, now, around the shores of the lake, the terrible carnage taking place.

The dragon's head and neck, part of its upper body, and its dagger-sharp spiked tail reared up out of the molten lava. The head and neck were black, black as the darkness left behind in Kairn Telest. Its eyes glowed a ghastly, blazing red. In its great jaws, it held the body of a struggling soldier and, as Edmund and I watched in horror, it loosed its jaws and dropped the man into the magma.

One by one, the fire dragon took up each of the soldiers, who were attempting, with their pitiful weapons, to battle the creature. One by one, the dragon sent them plunging into the burning lake. It left a single body on the shoreline—the body of the king. When the last soldier was gone, the dragon turned its blazing eyes on Edmund and me and stared at us for long, long moments.

I swear that I heard words, and Edmund told me later that he thought he did, too.

You have paid the price of your passage. You may now cross.

The eyes closed, the black head slithered down beneath the magma and was gone.

Whether I actually heard the fire dragon's voice or not, something inside me told me that all was safe, the dragon would not return. I removed the magical net. Edmund dashed out of the tunnel before I could stop him. I hurried after, keeping my eyes on the boiling, churning lake.

No sign of the dragon. The prince reached his father, gathered the old man's body into his arms.

The king was dead, he had died horribly. A giant hole—inflicted, perhaps, by the sharp spike on a lashing tail—had penetrated his stomach, torn through his bowels. I helped Edmund carry his father's corpse back to the tunnel. The people remained at the far end, refusing to venture anywhere near the lake.

I could not blame them. I wouldn't have gone near it either, if I hadn't heard that voice and known that it could be trusted. The dragon had taken its revenge, if that's what it was, and now was at peace.

I foresee that Edmund will have a difficult time convincing the people that it is safe to walk the path on the shore of the Lake of Burning Rock. But I know in the end that he will succeed, for the people love him and trust him and now, whether he likes it or not, they will name him their king.

We need a king. Once we leave the shores of the lake behind, we will be in Kairn Necros. Edmund maintains we will find there a land of friends. I believe, to my sorrow, we will find there the land of our enemies.

And here is where I have decided to end my account. I have only a few pages of the precious parchment left, and it seems fitting to me to close the journal here, with the death of one king of Kairn Telest and the crowning of a new one. I wish I could see ahead in time, see what the future holds for us, but not all the magical power of the ancients allowed them to look beyond the present moment.

Perhaps that is just as well. To know the future is to be forced to abandon hope. And hope is all that we have left.

Edmund will lead his people forth, but not, if I can persuade him, to Kairn Necros. Who knows? The next journal I keep may be called *The Journey Through Death's Gate*.

—Baltazar, necromancer to the king

CHAPTER ♦ 7

THE NEXUS

♦

Haplo inspected his ship, walked the length and breadth of the sleek, dragon-prowed vessel, studied masts and hull, wings and sails with a critical eye. The ship had survived three passages through Death's Gate, sustaining only minor damage, mostly inflicted by the tytans, the terrifying giants of Pryan.

"What do you think, boy?" Haplo said, reaching down and fondling the ears of a black, nondescript dog, who padded silently along beside him. "Think it's ready to go? Think *we're* ready to go?" He tugged playfully at one of the silky ears. The dog's plumy tail brushed from side to side, the intelligent eyes, that rarely left its master's face, brightened.

"These runes"—Haplo strode forward, laid his hand on a series of burns and carvings inscribed on the ship's hull—"will act to block out all energies, according to My Lord. Nothing, absolutely nothing should be able to penetrate. We'll be shielded and protected as a babe in its mother's womb. Safer," Haplo added, his face darkening, "than any baby born in the Labyrinth."

He ran his fingers over the spidery lines of the runes, reading in his mind their intricate language, searching for any flaw, any defect. His gaze shifted upward to the carved dragon's head. The fierce eyes stared eagerly forward, as if they could already see the end of their goal in sight.

"The magic protects us," Haplo continued his one-sided conversation, the dog not being disposed to talk. "The magic surrounds us.

This time I will not succumb. This time I will witness the journey through Death's Gate!"

The dog yawned, sat down, and scratched at an itch with such violence that he nearly tipped himself over. The Patryn glanced at the animal with some irritation. "A lot you care," he muttered accusingly.

Hearing the note of rebuke in the loved voice, the dog cocked its head and appeared to try to enter into the spirit of the conversation. Unfortunately, the itch proved too great a distraction.

Snorting, Haplo clambered up the ship's side, walked over the top deck, giving it one final inspection.

The ship had been built by the elves of the air world of Arianus. Made to resemble the dragons that the elves could admire but never tame, the ship's prow was the dragon's head, its breast the bridge, its body the hull, its tail the rudder. Wings fashioned of the skin and scales of real dragons guided the vessel through the air currents of that wondrous realm. Slaves (generally human) and elven wizardry combined to keep the great ships afloat.

The ship had been a gift from a grateful elven captain to Haplo. The Patryn modified it to suit his needs, his own ship having been destroyed during his first journey through Death's Gate. The great dragonship no longer required a full crew to man it, or wizards to guide it, or slaves to operate it. Haplo was now captain and crew member. The dog was the ship's only passenger.

The dog, conquering the elusive itch, trotted behind, hoping that the long and boring inspection was nearly at end. The animal adored flying. It spent most of the journey with its face pressed against the porthole, tongue lolling, tail wagging, leaving nose-prints on the glass. The dog was eager to be gone. So was its master. Haplo had discovered two fascinating realms in his journeys through Death's Gate. He had no doubt he would be equally rewarded on this trip.

"Calm down, boy," he said softly, patting the dog's head. "We'll leave in a moment."

The Patryn stood on the top deck, beneath the folds of the dragon's central sail, and looked out on the Nexus, his homeland.

He never left this city without a pang. Disciplined, hard, and unemotional as he considered himself to be, he was forced to blink back the tears whenever he left. The Nexus was beautiful, but he'd seen many lands just as beautiful and never unmanned himself by weeping over them. Perhaps it was the nature of the beauty of the

Nexus—a twilight world whose days were ever either dawn or dusk, whose nights were never dark but always softly brightened by moonlight. Nothing in the Nexus was harsh, nothing in the Nexus existed in extremes except for the people who lived there, people who had emerged from the Labyrinth—a prison world of unspeakable horror. Those who survived the Labyrinth and managed to escape came into the Nexus. Its beauty and peace enfolded them like the embracing arms of a parent comforting a child having a nightmare.

Haplo stood on the deck of his flying ship and gazed out on the green, grassy lawn of his lord's mansion. He remembered the first time he'd risen from the bed where they'd carried him—more dead than alive after his trials in the Labyrinth. He had gone to a window and looked out on this land. He had known, for the first time in his scarred life, peace, tranquility, rest.

Every time he looked out a window onto his homeland, he recalled that moment. Every time he recalled that moment, he blessed and honored his master, the Lord of the Nexus, who had saved him. Every time he blessed his lord, Haplo cursed the Sartan, the demigods who had locked his people into that cruel world. Every time he cursed them, he vowed revenge.

The dog, seeing that they weren't going to leave instantly, flopped down on the deck and lay—nose on paws—patiently waiting. Haplo shook himself out of his reverie, stirred briskly to action, and nearly stepped on the animal. The dog jumped up with a startled yelp.

"There, old boy. Sorry. Keep out from under my feet next time." Haplo turned to descend into the hold, stopped in midstride as he and the world around him rippled.

Ripple. That was the only way to describe it. He had never experienced anything like the strange sensation. The movement started far beneath him, perhaps at the very core of the world, and continued upward in sinuous waves that did not travel horizontally, like a tremor, but vertically, rippling up from the ground through his ship, his feet, his knees, body, head.

Everything around him was distorted by the same effect. For a brief instant, Haplo lost all shape, form, dimension. He was flat, pasted against a flat sky, a flat ground. The ripple passed through and shook them all simultaneously. All except the dog. The dog vanished.

The effect ended as swiftly as it had begun. Haplo fell to his hands and knees. Dizzy, disoriented, he fought off a sickening wave of nausea. He gasped for breath, the ripple effect had compressed the air from his body. When he could breathe, he searched to see if he could discover what had caused the terrifying phenomenon.

The dog returned, standing in front of him, gazing at him reproachfully.

"It wasn't my fault, fellow," Haplo said, darting wary, suspicious glances in all directions.

The Nexus glimmered in its peaceful twilight, leaves on the trees whispered softly. Haplo examined them closely. The stalwart trunks had stood straight and tall and unbent for a hundred generations. But just moments before, he'd seen them ripple like wheat in a windstorm. Nothing moved, he heard no sound—and that in itself was odd. Previous to the ripple, he'd been obliquely aware of animal noises that were now hushed in . . . what? Fear? Awe?

Haplo felt a strange reluctance to move, as if the very act of taking a step would cause the frightening sensation to reoccur. He had to force himself to walk back along the deck, expected every moment to find himself pasted on the landscape once again. He peered over the side of the ship's hull, down onto the lawn.

Nothing.

His gaze scanned the mansion, the windows of his lord's magnificent dwelling. His lord lived alone in the mansion, except for Haplo, and he was only there on occasion. This day, the mansion was empty. The lord was away, fighting his endless battle against the Labyrinth.

Nothing. No one.

"Maybe I imagined it," Haplo muttered.

He wiped chill sweat from his upper lip, noted his hand was trembling. He stared at the runes tattooed on his skin, saw, for the first time, that they were glowing a very faint blue. Hastily, he shoved up his sleeve, saw the blue glow fading from his arms. A glance at his chest, beneath the V-slit collar of his tunic, revealed the same.

"So, I didn't imagine it," he said, comforted. His body had reacted to the phenomenon, reacted instinctively to protect him— protect him from what? A bitter iron taste, as of blood, coated his mouth. He coughed, spit. Turning, he stomped back across the deck. His fear faded with the blue glow, leaving him angry, frustrated.

The ripple had not come from inside the ship. Haplo had watched it pass through the ship, watched it pass through his body, the trunks of the trees, the ground, the mansion, the sky. He hastened below to the bridge. The steering stone, the rune-covered orb he used to guide his vessel, stood on its pedestal. The stone was dark and cold, no light emanating from it.

Haplo glared at the stone in irrational ire, having half-hoped that it might have been responsible. He was irritated to discover it wasn't. His mind cataloged everything else on board: neat coils of rope in the hold; barrels of wine, water, and food; a change of clothes; his journal. The stone was the only magical object.

He'd cleaned away all remnants of the mensch[1]—the elves, humans, dwarf, and insane old wizard who had lately been his passengers on that ill-fated journey to the Elven Star. The tytans had undoubtedly slaughtered them all by now. They couldn't be the cause.

The Patryn stood on the bridge, staring unseeing at the stone, his brain running around like a mouse caught in a maze, darting down this passage and that, sniffing and scrabbling and hoping to find a way out. Memories of the mensch on Pryan wandered to memories of mensch on Arianus and that made him think of the Sartan Haplo'd encountered on Arianus, a Sartan whose mind moved as clumsily as his oversize feet.

None of these memories led him anywhere useful. Nothing like this had happened to him before. He brought to mind all he knew of magic, the sigla that ruled the probabilities, made all things possible. But by all laws of magic known to him, that ripple could not have been. Haplo found himself back where he started.

"I should consult with My Lord," he said to the dog, who was regarding its master with concern. "Ask his advice."

But that would mean postponing his journey through Death's Gate for an indefinite period of time. When the Lord of the Nexus reentered the deadly confines of the Labyrinth, no one could say when—or if—he would return. Upon that return, he would not be pleased to discover that Haplo had been wasting precious time in his absence.

---

[1] A word used by both Sartan and Patryns to refer to the "lesser" races: humans, elves, dwarves.

Haplo pictured the interview with the formidable old man—the only living being the Patryn respected, admired, and feared. He imagined himself attempting to put the strange sensation into words. He imagined his lord's answer.

"A fainting spell. I didn't know you were subject to those, Haplo, My Son. Perhaps you shouldn't go on a journey of such importance."

No, better solve this on his own. He considered searching the rest of his ship, but—again—that would waste time. "And how can I search it when I don't know what I'm looking for?" he demanded, exasperated. "I'm like a kid who sees ghosts in the night, making my mother come in with the candle to prove to me that there's nothing there. Bah! Let's get out of here!"

He strode resolutely over to the steering stone, placed his hands on it. The dog took its accustomed position next to the glass portholes located in the dragon's breast. Apparently its master had come to the end of whatever strange game he'd been playing. Tail wagging, the dog barked excitedly. The ship rose up on the currents of wind and magic and sailed into the purple-streaked sky.

♦

The entry into Death's Gate was an awesome, terrifying experience. A tiny black dot in the twilight sky, the Gate was like a perverse star that shone dark instead of light. The dot did not grow in size, the nearer the ship sailed. Rather, it seemed that the ship itself shrank down to fit inside. Dwindling, diminishing—a frightening sensation and one that Haplo knew was all in his mind, an optical illusion, like seeing pools of water in a burning desert.

This was his third time entering Death's Gate from the Nexus side, and he knew he should be accustomed to the effect. He shouldn't let it frighten him. But now, just as every time before, he stared at that small hole and felt his stomach clench, his breath come short. The closer he flew, the faster the ship sailed. He couldn't stop his forward motion, even if he'd wanted to. Death's Gate was sucking him inside.

The hole began to distort the sky. Streaks of purple and pink, flares of soft red began twisting around it. Either the sky was spinning and he was stationary, or he was spinning and the sky was stationary, he could never tell which. And all the while he was being drawn inside at an ever-increasing rate of speed.

This time, he'd fight the fear. This time—

A shattering crash and an inhuman wail brought Haplo's heart to his mouth. The dog jumped to its feet and was off like an arrow, racing into the ship's interior.

Haplo wrenched his gaze away from the mesmerizing swirl of colors enticing him into the blackness beyond. In the distance, he could hear the dog's bark echoing through the corridors. To judge by the dog's reaction, someone or something was aboard his ship.

Haplo lurched forward. The ship rocked and heaved and bucked. He had difficulty keeping his feet, tottered and staggered into the bulkheads like some old drunk.

The dog's barking grew in loudness and intensity but Haplo noted, oddly, a change in the note. The bark was no longer threatening, it was joyful—the animal greeting someone it knew and recognized.

Perhaps some kid had hidden himself aboard for a prank or a chance for adventure. Haplo couldn't conceive of any Patryn child who would indulge in such mischief. Patryn children, growing up (if they managed to live that long) in the Labyrinth, had very little time for childhood.

After some difficulty, he made his way to the hold, heard a voice, faint and pathetic.

"Nice doggie. Hush, now, nice dog, and go away, and I'll give you this bit of sausage . . ."

Haplo paused in the shadows. The voice sounded familiar. It wasn't a child's, it was a man's and he knew it, although he couldn't quite place it. The Patryn activated the runes on his hands. Bright blue light welled from the sigla, illuminating the darkness of the hold. He stepped inside.

The dog stood spraddle-legged on the deck, barking with all its might at a man cowering in a corner. The man, too, was familiar, a balding head topped by a fringe of hair around the ears, a weary middle-aged face, mild eyes now wide with fear. His body was long and gangly and appeared to have been put together from leftover parts of other bodies. Hands that were too large, feet that were too large, neck too long, head too small. It was his feet that had betrayed the man, entangling him in a coil of rope, undoubtedly the cause of the crash.

"You," Haplo said in disgust. "Sartan."

The man looked up from the barking dog, which he had been

attempting unsuccessfully to bribe with a sausage—part of Haplo's food supply. Seeing the Patryn standing before him, the man gave a faint, self-deprecating smile, and fainted.

"Alfred!" Haplo drew in a seething breath and took a step forward. "How the hell did you—"

The ship slammed headlong into Death's Gate.

CHAPTER ♦ 8

DEATH'S GATE

♦

THE VIOLENCE OF THE IMPACT KNOCKED HAPLO OVER BACKWARD AND sent the dog scrabbling to maintain its balance. The comatose body of Alfred slid gently across the canting deck. Haplo crashed up against the side of the hold, fighting desperately against tremendous unseen forces pressing on him, holding him plastered to the wood. At last the ship righted itself somewhat and he was able to lurch forward. Grabbing hold of the limp shoulder of the man lying at his feet, Haplo shook him viciously.

"Alfred! Damn it, Sartan! Wake up!"

Alfred's eyelids fluttered, the eyes beneath them rolled. He groaned mildly, blinked, and—seeing Haplo's dark and scowling face above him—appeared somewhat alarmed. The Sartan attempted to sit up, the ship listed, and he instinctively grabbed at Haplo's arm to support himself. The Patryn shoved the hand aside roughly.

"What are you doing here? On my ship? Answer me, or by the Labyrinth, I'll—"

Haplo stopped, staring. The ship's bulkheads were closing in around him, the wooden sides drawing nearer and nearer, the deck rushing up to meet the overhead. They were going to be crushed, squeezed flat except, at the same instant, the ship's bulkheads were flying apart, expanding into empty space, the deck was falling out from beneath him, the entire universe was rushing away from him, leaving him alone and small and helpless.

The dog whimpered and crawled toward Haplo, buried its cold

nose in his hand. He clasped the animal thankfully. It was warm and solid and real. The ship was his and stable once more.

"Where are we?" Alfred asked in awe. Apparently, from the terror-stricken expression in the wide, watery eyes, he had just undergone a similar experience.

"Entering Death's Gate," Haplo answered grimly.

Neither spoke for a moment, but looked around, watching, listening with inheld breath.

"Ah." Alfred sighed, nodded. "That would explain it."

"Explain what, Sartan?"

"How I arrived . . . er . . . here," Alfred said, lifting his eyes for an instant to meet Haplo's, immediately lowering them again. "I didn't mean to. You must understand that. I—I was looking for Bane, you see. The little boy you took from Arianus. The child's mother is frantic with worry—"

"Over a kid she gave away eleven years ago. Yeah, I'm in tears. Go on."

Alfred's wan cheeks flushed slightly. "Her circumstances at the time— She had no choice— It was her husband—"

"How did you get on my ship?" Haplo repeated.

"I . . . I managed to locate Death's Gate in Arianus. The Gegs put me in one of the dig-claws—You remember those contraptions?— and lowered me down into the storm, right into Death's Gate itself. I had just entered it when I experienced a sensation as . . . as if I were being pulled apart and then I was jerked violently backward . . . forward . . . I don't know. I blacked out. When I came to myself, I was lying here." Alfred spread his hands helplessly to indicate the hold.

"That must have been the crash I heard." Haplo gazed at Alfred speculatively. "You're not lying. From what I've heard, you miserable Sartan can't lie. But you're not telling me all the truth either."

Alfred's flush deepened, he lowered his eyelids. "Prior to when you left the Nexus," he said in a small voice, "did you experience an odd . . . sensation?"

Haplo refused to commit himself, but Alfred took his silence for acquiescence. "A sort of ripplelike effect? Made you sick? That was me, I'm afraid," he said faintly.

"It figures." The Patryn sat back on his heels, glaring at Alfred. "Now what in the name of the Sundering do I do with you? I—"

Time slowed. The last word Haplo spoke seemed to take a year to emerge from his mouth and another year for his ears to hear it. He reached out a hand to grasp Alfred by the frilly neckerchief around the man's scrawny neck. His hand crept forward a fraction of an inch at a time. Haplo attempted to hasten his motion. He moved slower. Air wasn't coming in fast enough to supply his lungs. He would die of suffocation before he could draw a breath.

But impossibly he was moving fast, far too fast. His hand had grasped Alfred and was worrying the man like the dog worried a rat. He was shouting words that came out gibberish and Alfred was trying desperately to break his grasp and say something back, but the words flew by so swiftly that Haplo couldn't understand them. The dog was lolling on its side, moving in slow motion, and it was up and leaping around the deck like a thing possessed.

Haplo's mind attempted frantically to deal with these dichotomies. Its answer was to give up and shut down. He fought against the darkening mists, focusing his attention on the dog, refusing to see or think about anything else. Eventually, everything either slowed down or speeded up. Normality returned.

It occurred to him that this was the farthest he'd made it into Death's Gate without losing consciousness. He supposed, he thought bitterly, he had Alfred to thank.

"It will keep growing worse," said the Sartan. His face was white, he shook all over.

"How do you know?" Haplo wiped sweat from his forehead, tried to relax, his muscles were bunched and aching from the strain.

"I . . . studied Death's Gate before I entered it. The other times you passed through, you always blacked out, didn't you?"

Haplo didn't answer. He decided to try to make his way to the bridge. Alfred would be safe enough in the hold, for the time being. It was damn certain the Sartan wasn't going anywhere!

Haplo rose to his feet . . . and kept rising. He stood up and up and up until he must crash through the wooden overhead, and he was shrinking, becoming smaller and smaller and smaller until an ant might step on him and never notice.

"Death's Gate. A place that exists and yet does not exist. It has substance and is ephemeral. Time is measured marching ahead going backward. Its light is so bright that I am plunged into darkness."

Haplo wondered how he could talk when he had no voice. He shut his eyes and seemed to be opening them wider. His head, his body were splitting apart, tearing off into two separate and completely opposite directions. His body was rushing together, imploding in on itself. He clasped his hands over his rending skull, reeling, spiraling downward until he lost his balance and tumbled to the deck. He heard, in the distance, someone screaming, but he couldn't hear the scream, because he was deaf. He could see everything clearly because he was completely and totally blind.

Haplo's mind wrestled with itself, attempting to reconcile the unreconcilable. His consciousness dove down further and further inside him, seeking to regain reality, seeking to find some stable point in the universe to which it could cling.

It found . . . Alfred.

Just as Alfred's failing consciousness found Haplo.

◆

Alfred was skidding through a void, plummeting downward, when he came to a sudden halt. The terrible sensations he'd experienced in the Death's Gate ceased. He stood on firm ground and the sky was up above him. Nothing was spinning around him and he wanted to cry from relief when he realized that the body in which he was standing was not his own. It belonged to a child, a boy of about eight or nine. The body was naked, except for a loincloth twisted around the boy's thin limbs. The body was covered with the swirls and whorls of blue and red runes.

Two adults, standing near him, were talking. Alfred knew them, knew them to be his parents, although he'd never seen them before now. He knew, too, that he'd been running, running desperately, running for his life and that he was tired, his body ached and burned, and that he couldn't take another step. He was frightened, horribly frightened, and it seemed to him that he'd been frightened most of his short life; that fear had been his first recognizable emotion.

"It's no use," said the man, his father, gasping for breath. "They're gaining on us."

"We should stop now and fight them," insisted the woman, his mother, "while we have strength left."

Alfred, young as he was, knew that the fight was hopeless. Whatever was chasing them was stronger and faster. He heard terrifying sounds behind him—large bodies crashing through the undergrowth. A wail swelled in his throat, but he fought it back, knowing that to give way to his fear would only make matters worse.

He fumbled at his loincloth, drew out a sharp-pointed dagger, encrusted with dried blood. Obviously, Alfred thought, staring at it, I've killed before.

"The boy?" asked his mother, a question to the man. Whatever was coming was gaining on them rapidly.

The man tensed, fingers closing around a spear in his hand. He seemed to consider. A look passed between the two, a look that Alfred understood and he leapt forward, the word *No!* bubbling frantically to his lips. It was met by a clout on the side of his head that knocked him senseless.

Alfred stepped out of his body and watched his parents drag his limp and unresisting form into a growth of thick bushes, hiding him with brush. Then they ran, luring their enemy as far from their child as they could before they were forced to turn and fight. They weren't acting out of love to save him, but out of instinct, just as a mother bird, pretending to have a broken wing, will lead the fox away from her nest.

When Alfred regained consciousness, he was back in the child's body. Crouching, panic-stricken, in the brush, he watched, in a dazed and dreamlike fashion, the snogs murder his parents.

He wanted to scream, to cry out, but something—instinct again or perhaps only fear freezing his tongue—kept him silent. His parents fought bravely and well, but they were no match for the hulking bodies and sharp fangs and long, razorlike claws of the intelligent snogs. The killing took a long, long time.

And then, mercifully, it was over. His parents' bodies—what was left of them when the snogs had finished their gorging—lay unmoving. His mother's screams had ceased. Then came the frightening moment when Alfred knew that he was next, when he feared that they must see him, that he must be as highly visible as the bright red blood clotting the matted leaves on the ground. But the snogs were weary of their sport. Hunger and lust to kill both satisfied, they moved off, leaving Alfred alone in the brush.

He lay hidden a long time, near the bodies of his parents. The carrion beasts arrived to take their share of the spoils. He was afraid to stay, afraid to leave, and he couldn't help whimpering, if only to hear the sound of his own voice and know that he was alive. And then two men were there, beside him, peering down at him, and he was startled for he hadn't heard them gliding through the brush, moving more silently than the wind.

The men discussed him, as if he weren't there. They eyed the bodies of his parents coldly, spoke of them without sympathy. The men were not cruel, only callous, as if they'd seen murder done all too many times before and the sight could no longer shock them. One of them reached down into the brush, dragged Alfred to his feet. They marched him over to stand beside the bodies of his butchered parents.

"Look at that," the man told Alfred, holding the boy by the scruff of his neck and forcing him to stare at the gruesome sight. "Remember it. And remember this. It wasn't snogs that killed your father and mother. It was those who put us in this prison and left us to die. Who are they, boy? Do you know?" The man's fingers dug painfully into Alfred's flesh.

"The Sartan," Alfred heard himself answer and he knew then that *he* was Sartan and that he'd just killed those who had given him birth.

"Repeat it!" the man ordered him.

"The Sartan!" Alfred cried, and he wept.

"Right. Never forget that, boy. Never forget."

♦

Haplo fell into darkness, cursing, fighting, struggling to retain consciousness. His mind rebelled against him, dragged him under for his own good. He caught a glimpse of a light, as he seemed to be receding farther and farther away, and he exerted every ounce of his being to reach that light. He made it.

The falling sensation ended, all the strange sensations ended and he was filled with a vast sense of peace. He was lying on his back and it seemed to him that he had just awakened from a deep and restful slumber lit by beautiful dreams. He was in no hurry to rouse himself, but lay still, enjoying slipping into and out of sleep, listening to a sweet music in his mind. At length, he knew himself to be fully awake and he opened his eyes.

He lay in a crypt. He was startled, at first, but not frightened, as if he knew where he was but had forgotten and now that he remembered, everything was all right. He felt a sense of excitement and breathless anticipation. Something that he'd been waiting for a long time was about to happen. He wondered how to get out of the crypt, but knew the answer immediately when he asked himself the question. The crypt would open at his command.

Lying back restfully, Haplo glanced down at his body and was amazed to see himself in strange clothes—long white robes. And he saw, with a pang of terror, that the runes tattooed on his hands and arms were gone! And with the runes, his magic. He was helpless, helpless as a mensch!

But the knowledge came to him instantly, almost making him laugh at his own simplicity, that he wasn't powerless. He possessed the magic, but it was inside him, not outside. Experimentally, he lifted his hand and examined it. The hand was slender and delicate. He traced a rune in the air and, at the same time, sang the rune to the air. The door of his crystal crypt opened.

Haplo sat up and swung his legs over the side. He jumped lightly down to the floor; his body tingled all over with the unaccustomed exertion. Turning, he looked back into the crystalline surface of the empty crypt and experienced a profound shock. He was looking at his own reflection, but his face didn't look back. Alfred's did.

He was Alfred!

Haplo staggered, physically jolted by the knowledge. Of course, that explained the absence of runes on his skin. The Sartan magic worked from within to without, whereas Patryn magic worked from without to within.

Confused, Haplo looked from his own empty crypt to one located next to his. He saw in it a woman, young, lovely, her face calm and tranquil in repose. Looking at the woman, Haplo felt a warmth well up inside him and he knew he loved her, knew he had loved her a long, long time. He moved over to her crypt and rested his hands on the chill crystal. He gazed at her fondly, tracing every line of that beloved face.

"Anna," he whispered, and caressed the crystal with his hands.

A chill stole through Haplo, freezing his heart. The woman wasn't breathing. He could see clearly through the glass tomb that wasn't supposed to have been a tomb but only a cocoon, a resting place until it was time for them to emerge and take over their duties.

But she wasn't breathing!

Admittedly, the magical stasis slowed the body's functions. Haplo watched the woman anxiously, willing the fabric across her breast to move, willing the eyelids to flicker. He waited and watched, hands pressed against the glass for hours, waited until his strength gave out, and he crumbled to the floor.

And then, lying on the floor, he lifted his hand and stared at it again. He noticed now what he had not before. The hand was slender and delicate, but it was aged, wrinkled. Blue veins stood out clearly. Dragging himself to his feet, he stared into the crystal of the crypt and he saw his face.

"I am old," he whispered, reaching out to touch the reflection that, when he had gone to sleep, had been bright with youth and alive with eager promise. Now it was aged, skin flabby and sagging, his head bare, the fringe of hair around the ears whitish gray.

"I am old," he repeated, feeling panic surge through him. "I am old! I have aged! And it takes a long, long time for a Sartan to age! But not her! She is not old." He stared back into her crypt. No, she was no older than he remembered her. Which meant she had not aged. Which meant she was . . .

"No!" Haplo cried, clutching at the crystal sides as if he would tear them apart, his fingers sliding down ineffectually. "No! Not dead! Not her dead and me alive! Not me alive and . . . and . . ."

He stepped back, looking around him, looking into the other crypts. Each one of them, except his, held a body. Inside each was a friend, a comrade, a brother, a sister. Those who were to come back to this world with him when it was time, come back to continue the work. There was so much to do! He ran to another crypt.

"Ivor!" he called, pounding on the crystal sides with his fingers. But the man lay unmoving, unresponsive. Frantic, Haplo ran to another and another, calling out each dear name, pleading incoherently with each one to wake, to be!

"Not me! Not me . . . alone!

"Or maybe not," he said, stopping in his mad panic, hope cool and soothing inside him. "Maybe I'm not alone. I haven't been out of the mausoleum yet." He looked toward the archway that stood at the far end of the round chamber. "Yes, there are probably others out there."

But he made no motion toward the door. Hope died, destroyed by logic. There were no others. If there had been, they would have ended the enchantment. He was the only survivor. He was alone. Which meant that somewhere, somehow, something had gone horribly wrong.

"And will I be expected, all by myself, to set it right?"

CHAPTER ◆ 9

FIRE SEA, ABARRACH

◆

HAPLO DID NOT REGAIN CONSCIOUSNESS, HE REGAINED A SENSE OF himself. He had succeeded in his objective, he had remained awake during the journey through Death's Gate. But now he knew why the mind far preferred to make the trip in unknowing darkness. He understood, with a real sense of shaken terror, how near he'd come to slipping into madness. Alfred's reality had been the rope to which he'd clung to save himself. And he wondered, bitterly, if it might not have been better to have let loose his hold.

He lay for a moment on the deck, trying to draw his shattered self back together, attempted to shake off the feelings of grief and dreadful loss and fear that assailed him—all in the name of Alfred. A furry head rested on the Patryn's chest, liquid eyes looked anxiously into his. Haplo stroked the dog's silky ears, scratched its muzzle.

"It's all right, boy. I'm all right," he said, then knew that he would never truly be all right again. He glanced across at the comatose body sprawled on the deck near him.

"Damn you!" he muttered and, sitting up, started to give the body a wakening kick with his foot. He was reminded, forcibly, of the young and beautiful corpse in the crystal tomb. Reaching out a hand, he shook Alfred's shoulder.

"Hey," he said gruffly. "C'mon. C'mon and wake up. I can't leave you down here, Sartan. I want you up on the bridge where I can keep an eye on you. Get moving!"

Alfred sat up instantly, gasping and crying out in horror. He clutched at Haplo's shirt, nearly dragging the Patryn down on top of him. "Help me! Save me! Running! I've been running . . . and they're so close! Please! Please, help me!"

Whatever was going on here, Haplo didn't have time for it. "Hey!" he shouted loudly, straight into the man's face, and slapped him.

Alfred's balding head snapped back, his teeth clicked together. Sucking in a breath, he stared at Haplo and the Patryn saw recognition. He saw something else, completely unexpected: understanding, compassion, sorrow.

Haplo wondered uneasily where Alfred had spent *his* journey through Death's Gate. He had the answer, deep inside, but he wasn't certain he liked it or what it all might mean. He chose to ignore it, at least for the time being.

"Was that? . . . I saw . . ." Alfred began.

"On your feet," Haplo said. Standing up himself, he pulled the clumsy Sartan up with him. "We're not out of danger. If anything, we've just flown into it. I—"

A shattering crash amidships emphasized his words. Haplo staggered, caught himself on an overhead beam. Alfred fell backward, arms flailing wildly, and sat down heavily on the deck.

"Dog, bring him!" Haplo ordered, and hurried forward.

During the Sundering, the Sartan had split the universe, divided it into worlds representative of its four basic elements: air, fire, stone, and water. Haplo had first visited the realm of air, Arianus. He had just returned from the realm of fire, Pryan. His glimpses into each had prepared him, so he had supposed, for what he might find in Abarrach, the world of stone. A subterranean world, he imagined, a world of tunnels and caves, a world of cool and earthy-smelling darkness.

His ship struck something again, listed sideways. Haplo could hear, behind him, a wail and a clattering crash. Alfred, down again. The ship could take such punishment, guarded as it was by its runes, but not indefinitely. Each blow sent tiny tremors through the sigla traced on the hull, forcing them a little farther apart, disrupting their magic ever so slightly. Two had only to completely separate, one from the other, open a crack that would grow wider and wider. That was how Haplo's first trip through Death's Gate had ended.

Making his way forward as rapidly as possible, tossed from side to side by the erratic motion of the heaving ship, Haplo became aware of a lurid glow lighting the darkness around him. The temperature was increasing, growing hotter, much hotter. The runes on his skin began to glow a faint blue, his body's magic reacting instinctively to reduce his temperature to a safe level.

Could his ship be on fire?

Haplo scoffed at the notion. He had passed safely through the suns of Pryan; the runes would most assuredly protect against flame! But there was no denying the fact that the red glow was burning brighter, the temperature growing warmer. Haplo quickened his pace. Emerging onto the bridge with some difficulty, due to the lurching of the vessel, the Patryn stopped and stared, amazement and shock paralyzing him.

His ship was sailing, with incredible speed, down a river of molten lava.

A vast stream of glowing red tinged with flame yellow surged and swirled around the vessel. Darkness arched above him, made darker by contrast to the lurid light of the magma flow below. He was in a gigantic cavern. Vast columns of black rock, around which the lava curled and eddied, soared upward, supporting a ceiling of stone. Numberless stalactites hung down, reaching for him like bony, grasping fingers, their polished surface reflecting the hellish red of the river of fire beneath them.

The ship veered this way and that. Huge stalagmites, with wicked, sword-sharp edges, thrust up from the molten sea like black teeth from a red maw. Haplo understood what had caused the crashes they'd previously experienced. Jolted to action, he moved forward and placed his hands on the steering stone, reacting by instinct more than by conscious thought, his gaze riveted with horrid fascination on the dreadful landscape into which he sailed.

"Blessed Sartan!" murmured a voice behind him. "What frightful place is this?"

Haplo spared Alfred a brief glance.

"Your people made it," he told him. "Dog, watch him."

The dog had obediently herded and harried Alfred to this point by nipping at the man's heels. It plopped itself down on the deck, panting in the heat, fixing its intelligent eyes on the Sartan. Alfred took a step forward. The animal growled, its tail thumped warningly against the deck.

I've nothing against you personally, the dog might have been saying from its expression, *but orders are orders.*

Alfred gulped and froze, leaned weakly against the bulkhead. "Where . . . where are we?" he repeated in a faint voice.

"Abarrach."

"The world of stone. Was this your destination?"

"Of course! What did you expect? That I'm as clumsy as you?"

Alfred was silent, eyes staring out on the awful panorama. "So you are visiting each of the worlds?" he said at length.

Haplo didn't see any reason why he should answer and so he kept quiet and concentrated on his steering. It deserved concentration. The huge boulders sprang up suddenly, without warning. He considered taking to the air, but decided against it. He couldn't determine the height of the cavern's ceiling. The hull could withstand punishment far better than the fragile mast and dragon's head prow.

The heat was intense, even inside the ship, which had the advantage of being protected by runes on the outside. Haplo's skin gleamed a bright blue as the runes cooled him. Alfred, he noticed, was humming beneath his breath, tracing runes in the air with his long-fingered hands and shuffling his feet slightly, his body swaying to the rhythm of the Sartan magic. Flanks heaving, the dog panted loudly, but never took its eyes from Alfred.

"You've been to the second world, I presume," the Sartan continued in a low voice, almost as if he were speaking to himself. "It would be natural for you to travel to them in the order in which they were created, the order they appear on the old charts. Did you . . . did you find any trace of"—Alfred paused, seeming to have trouble speaking—"my people?" he asked finally in a voice so soft that Haplo heard him only because he knew what the question was going to be.

The Patryn didn't immediately answer. What was he going to do with Alfred? This Sartan? This mortal enemy?

Haplo's inclination, and he was astounded by how his hands and fingers itched to perform the action his mind presented to him, was to toss the man into the magma river. But to murder Alfred would be to indulge in his own hatred, a lapse of discipline the Lord of the Nexus would not tolerate. Alfred, a living Sartan—as far as Haplo had discovered, the *only* living Sartan—was an extremely valuable prize.

My Lord will be pleased with this gift, Haplo thought, considering. Far more pleased with this than anything else I could bring him, including my report on this hellish world. I should probably turn around, deliver the Sartan immediately. But . . . but . . .

But that would mean reentering Death's Gate and Haplo, although he hated admitting his weakness to himself, couldn't view that prospect without true alarm. He saw again the rows and rows of tombs, knew again the death of hope and promise, experienced the knowledge of being terribly, horribly, pitifully alone. . . .

He wrenched his mind from the dream or whatever it had been, cursed the eyes that had made him see it. I won't make that journey again, not now, not so soon. Let time blunt it, blur the images. He rationalized: it would be extremely difficult and dangerous to turn the ship around. Better to keep going, complete my mission, explore this world, and then return to the Nexus. Alfred isn't going anywhere without me, that's for damn sure.

One glance at the Sartan's sweat-dewed face, the shivering limbs, and Haplo was reassured. Alfred appeared incapable of making his way to the head without assistance. The Patryn didn't think it likely that his enemy would have either the strength or the ability to wrest the ship away from him and make good an escape.

Haplo met Alfred's eyes, saw—once again—not hatred or fear but understanding, sorrow. It occurred to the Patryn, suddenly, that the Sartan might not want to escape. Haplo considered, discarded the notion. Alfred must know what terrible fate awaited him at the hands of the Lord of the Nexus. And if he didn't, Haplo would obligingly tell him.

"Did you say something, Sartan?" he tossed over his shoulder.

"I asked if you found anything of my people on Pryan," Alfred repeated humbly.

"What I found or didn't find is no concern of yours. It will be up to My Lord to tell you what he thinks you ought to know."

"Are we going back there? To your lord?"

Haplo heard, with a bitter satisfaction, the nervous quaver in the man's voice. So Alfred did know, or at least had a general idea, of the reception he would receive.

"No." Haplo ground the word. "Not yet. I have a job to do and I'm going to do it. I don't think it likely you'll want to wander about this place on your own, but, just in case you're thinking you might give me the slip, the dog will have its eyes on you day and night."

The animal, hearing the reference, brushed the plumy tail on the deck, the mouth widened in a grin, exhibiting razor-sharp teeth.

"Yes," Alfred said in a low voice, "I know about the dog."

Now what's *that* supposed to mean? Haplo wondered irritably, not liking the man's tone, which seemed to border on compassionate when the Patryn would have preferred fear.

"Just a reminder, Sartan. There are things I can do to you, things I would *enjoy* doing to you, that are not at all pleasant and would not ruin your usefulness to My Lord. Do what I tell you and keep out of my way and you won't get hurt. Understand?"

"I am not as weak as you seem to consider me."

Alfred drew himself upright with a semblance of dignity. The dog growled and lifted its head, ears flattened, eyes narrowed. The tail thumped ominously. Alfred shrank backward, stooped shoulders rounding.

Haplo snorted in derision and concentrated on his sailing.

Up ahead, in the distance, the river of magma forked. One large stream branched off to the right, another, smaller, veered to the left. Haplo steered his ship into the right, for no other reason than that it was the larger of the two and appeared easier and safer to travel.

"How could anyone live in such a terrible environ?" Alfred, talking rhetorically to himself, seemed considerably surprised that Haplo responded.

"Mensch certainly couldn't survive, although our kind could. I don't think our trip into this world will be a long one. If there ever *was* life here, it must be dead by now."

"Perhaps Abarrach was never meant to be habitable. Perhaps it was meant to be only an energy source for the other—" Alfred's tongue clicked against the roof of his mouth, he fell abruptly silent.

Haplo grunted, glanced at the man. "Yeah? Go on."

"Nothing." The Sartan's eyes were on his oversize feet. "I was merely speculating."

"You'll have the opportunity to 'speculate' all you want when we return to the Nexus. You'll wish you knew the secrets of the universe and could reveal them, every one, to My Lord before he's finished with you, Sartan."

Alfred kept silent, stared out the glass porthole. Haplo darted glances up and down the black and barren shoreline. Small tributaries of the magma river meandered off among the rock shoals and disappeared into fire-lighted shadow. These might lead somewhere, might lead out. There was nothing above them except rock.

"If we're in the center of the world, in the core, it's possible that there could be life above, on the surface," Alfred remarked, echoing Haplo's thought. He found that extremely irritating.

He considered beaching his ship, proceeding forward on foot, but immediately abandoned the idea. Walking among the slick-sided, sharp, black stalagmites that gleamed with an eerie, lurid brilliance in the magma's reflected glow would be difficult, treacherous. He would stay with the river, at least for the time being . . .

A dull roaring sound came to his ears. A glance at Alfred's face told him the Sartan heard it, too.

"We're moving faster," Alfred said, licking his lips that must be rimed with salt to judge by the sweat trickling down the man's cheeks.

The ship's speed increased, the magma hurtling along as if eager to arrive at some unknown destination. The roaring sound grew louder. Haplo kept his hands on the steering stone, peered ahead anxiously. He saw nothing except vast blackness.

"Rapids! A fall!" Alfred shouted, and the ship plunged over the edge of a gigantic lava cascade.

Haplo clung to the steering stone, the ship fell downward into a vast sea of molten lava. Rocks thrust up out of the swirling fiery mass, black nails grasping for the puny ship that was hurtling down on them.

Shaking himself free of the fascinated horror that gripped him, Haplo elevated his hands on the steering stone and, as his hands lifted, the runes on the stone glowed fiercely, brightly. The ship itself lifted, the magic flowing through the wings, activating them. *Dragon Wing*, as he had named it, wrenched itself free of the magma's clutching grasp and soared out over the molten sea.

Haplo heard behind him a groan and a slithering sound. The dog was on its feet, barking. Alfred lay huddled on the deck, the Sartan's face white as death.

"I think I'm going to be sick," he said faintly.

"Don't do it here!" Haplo barked, noting his own hands shaking, experiencing himself a lurching in his stomach and a bitter taste of bile in his mouth. He concentrated on flying his ship.

Alfred apparently managed to control himself, for the Patryn heard nothing more from him. Haplo sailed his ship upward, hoping to discover that they had flown out of the cavern. As he flew up and up into the darkness, he was disappointed to observe stalactite formations. These were incredibly large—some as much as a mile in diameter. Far, far below gleamed the magma sea, flowing to a horizon that was red on black.

He took the ship back down, near the shoreline. He had caught a glimpse to his right of an object that appeared man-made jutting out into the water. Its lines were too straight and even to have been formed by nature's hand, no matter how magically guided. Moving closer, he saw what looked like a pier, extending from the shore out into the lava ocean.

Haplo brought the ship down. He stared at the formation intently, trying to get a clear view.

"Look!" Alfred cried, sitting up and pointing, startling the dog, who growled. "There, to your left!"

Haplo jerked his head around, thinking they must be about to crash into a stalactite. Nothing loomed ahead of them and it took some moments to determine what Alfred had sighted.

Banks of clouds, created by the extreme heat of the magma sea meeting the cool air of the cavern far above, could be seen in the distance. The clouds drifted and parted, and then myriad tiny lights were visible, blinking out from beneath the clouds like stars.

Except that there could be no stars visible in this underground world.

The mist flew apart in tattered rags, and Haplo could see clearly. Perched on terraced steppes far from the magma sea stood the buildings and towers of an enormous city.

CHAPTER ◆ 10

SAFE HARBOR,

ABARRACH

◆

"Where are you taking the ship?" Alfred asked.

"I'm going to dock at that pier or whatever it is over there," Haplo answered, with a glance and a nod out the window.

"But the city's located on the opposite bank!"

"Precisely."

"Then, why not—"

"It beats the hell out of me, Sartan, how you managed to survive so long. I suppose it's due to that famous fainting routine of yours. What do you plan to do? Waltz up to the walls of a strange city, not knowing who lives there, and ask them nicely to let you in? What do you say when they ask you where you're from? What you're doing here? Why you want inside their city?"

"I would say—that is, I'd tell them—I guess you have a point," Alfred conceded lamely. "But what do we gain by landing over there?" He gestured vaguely. "Whoever lives in this dreadful place"—the Sartan couldn't resist a shudder—"will ask the same questions."

"Maybe." Haplo cast a sharp, scrutinizing gaze at their landing site. "Maybe not. Take a good look at it."

Alfred started to walk to the window. The dog growled, ears pricked, teeth bared. The Sartan froze.

"It's all right. Let him go. Just watch him," Haplo told the dog, who settled back down onto the deck, keeping its intelligent eyes on the Sartan.

Alfred, with a backward glance at the animal, awkwardly crossed the deck; its slight rocking motion sent the Sartan staggering. Haplo shook his head and wondered what the devil he was going to do with Alfred while exploring. Alfred arrived at the window without major mishap and, leaning against the glass, peered through it.

The ship spiraled down out of the air, landed gently on the magma, floated on sluggish, molten waves.

A pier had been shaped out of what had once been a natural groin of obsidian, extending out into the magma sea. Several other man-made structures, built out of the same black rock, faced the pier across a crude street.

"You see any signs of life?" Haplo asked.

"I don't see anyone moving around," Alfred said, staring hard. "Either in the town or on the docks. We're the only ship in sight. The place is deserted."

"Yeah, maybe. You can never tell. This might be their version of night, and everyone's asleep. But at least it's not guarded. If I'm lucky, *I* can be the one asking the questions."

Haplo steered the dragonship into the harbor, his gaze scrutinizing the small town. Probably not so much a town, he decided, as a dockside loading area. The buildings looked, for the most part, like warehouses, although here and there he thought he saw what might be a shop or a tavern.

Who would sail this deadly ocean, deadly to all but those protected by powerful magic—such as Alfred and himself? Haplo was intensely curious about this strange and forbidding world, more curious than he'd been about those worlds whose composition closely resembled his own. But he still didn't know what to do about Alfred.

Apparently the Sartan was following the line of Haplo's thoughts. "What should I do?" Alfred asked meekly.

"I'm thinking about it," Haplo muttered, affecting to be absorbed in the tricky docking maneuver, although that, in reality, was being handled by the magic of the runes of the steering stone.

"I don't want to be left behind. I'm going with you."

"It's not your decision. You'll do what I say, Sartan, and like it. And if I say you'll stay here with the dog to keep an eye on you, you'll stay here. Or you won't like it."

Alfred shook his balding head slowly, with quiet dignity. "You can't threaten me, Haplo. Sartan magic is different from Patryn magic, but it has the same roots and is just as powerful. I haven't used my magic as much as you've been forced by circumstances to use yours. But I am older than you. And you must concede that magic of any type is strengthened by age and by wisdom."

"I must, must I?" Haplo sneered, although his mind went almost immediately to his lord, a man whose years were numberless, and to the vast power he had amassed.

The Patryn eyed his opposite, eyed the representative of a race who had been the only force in the universe who could have halted the Patryn's vaulting ambition, their rightful quest for complete and absolute control over the weak-minded Sartan and the squabbling, chaos-driven mensch.

Alfred didn't look very formidable. His soft face indicated to the Patryn a soft and weak nature. His stoop-shouldered stance implied a cringing, sheepish attitude. Haplo already knew the Sartan was a coward. Worse, Alfred was clad in clothes suited only to a royal drawing room—a shabby frock coat, tight breeches tied at the knee with scraggly black velvet ribbons, lace-trimmed neckerchief, a coat with floppy sleeves, buckle-adorned shoes. But Haplo had seen this man, this weak specimen of a Sartan, charm a marauding dragon with nothing more than a few movements from that clumsy body.

Haplo had no doubt in his mind who would win a contest between the two of them, and he guessed that Alfred didn't either. But a contest would take time and the fighting magicks generated by these two beings—the closest beings to gods the mensch would ever know—would proclaim their presence to everyone within eyesight and earshot.

Besides, on reflection, Haplo didn't particularly want to leave the Sartan on his ship. The dog would prevent Alfred from breathing, if Haplo ordered it. But the Patryn hadn't liked the Sartan's reference to the animal. *I know about the dog*, he'd said. *What* did he know? What was there to know? The dog was a dog. Nothing more, except that the animal had once saved Haplo's life.

The Patryn docked the ship at the silent, empty pier. He kept close watch, more than half-expecting some type of welcome—an official demanding to know their business, an idle straggler, watching their arrival out of curiosity.

No one appeared. Haplo knew little of wharves or shipyards but he took this as a bad sign. Either everyone was fast asleep and completely uninterested in what was happening at their docks or the town was, as Alfred had said, deserted. And towns that were deserted were generally deserted for a reason and that reason was generally not good.

Once the ship was moored, Haplo deactivated the steering stone, placed it once more on its pedestal, its glowing runes extinguished. He began to prepare to disembark. Rummaging in his supplies, he found a roll of plain linen cloth and wound it carefully around his hands and wrists, covering and concealing the runes tattooed on the skin.

The same runes were tattooed over most of his body. He kept himself covered with heavy clothing—a long-sleeved shirt, a leather vest, leather trousers tucked into tall leather boots, a scarf tied close around his neck. No sigla adorned the grim, square-jawed, clean-shaven face, no runes appeared on the palms of the hands or the fingers or the soles of his feet. The rune-magic might interfere with the mental processes and those of the senses: touch, sight, smell, hearing.

"I'm curious," said Alfred, watching the proceedings with interest. "Why do you bother to disguise yourself? It's been centuries since . . . since . . ." he faltered, not certain where to go from here.

"Since you threw us in that torture chamber you called a prison?" Haplo finished, glancing at Alfred coolly.

The Sartan's head bowed. "I didn't realize . . . I didn't understand. Now, I do. I'm sorry."

"Understand? How could you possibly understand unless you've been there?" Haplo paused, wondering again, uncomfortably, where Alfred had spent his journey through Death's Gate. "You'll be sorry, all right, Sartan. We'll see how long you last in the Labyrinth. And to answer your question, I disguise myself because there could be people out there—like yourself, for example—who remember the Patryns. My Lord does not want anyone to remember—not yet, at least."

"There are those such as myself, who would remember and try to stop you. That's what you mean, isn't it?" Alfred sighed. "I cannot stop you. I am one. You, from what I gather, are many. You didn't find any trace of my people alive on Pryan, did you?"

Haplo looked at the man sharply, suspecting some sort of trick, though he couldn't imagine what. He had a sudden vision of those rows of tombs, of the young, dead corpses. He guessed at the

desperate search that had taken Alfred to every part of Arianus—
from the high realms of the self-accursed wizards to the lowly
realms of the slavelike Gegs. He experienced the terrible grief of
coming to realize, finally, that he alone had survived, his race and all
its dreams and plans were dead.

What had gone wrong? How could godlike beings have
dwindled, vanished? And if such a disaster could happen to the
Sartan, could it also happen to us?

Angry, Haplo shrugged off the thought. The Patryns had survived a land determined to slaughter them—proof that they had
been right all along. They were the strongest, the most intelligent,
the fittest to rule.

"I found no trace of the Sartan on Pryan," Haplo said, "except a
city that they'd built."

"A city?" Alfred looked hopeful.

"Abandoned. Long ago. A message they left behind said something about some type of force driving them out."

Alfred appeared bewildered. "But that's impossible. What type
of force could it have been? There is no force, except perhaps your
own, that could destroy or even intimidate us."

Haplo wound the bandages around his right hand, glanced at
the Sartan from beneath lowered brows. He seemed to be sincere,
but Haplo had journeyed with Alfred in Arianus. The Sartan wasn't
as simpleminded as he appeared. Alfred had discovered Haplo to be
a Patryn long before Haplo had discovered Alfred to be a Sartan.

If he did know anything about such a force, he wasn't talking.
The Lord of the Nexus would have it out of him, however.

Haplo tucked the ends of the bandages neatly beneath the shirt
cuffs and whistled to the dog, who leapt eagerly to its feet.

"Are you ready, Sartan?"

Alfred blinked in surprise. "Yes, I'm ready. And, since we're
speaking the human language, it might be better if you called me by
my name instead of 'Sartan.' "

"Hell, I don't even call the dog by name and that animal means a
lot more to me than you do."

"There might be those who remember the Sartan, as well as the
Patryns."

Haplo gnawed his lower lip, conceded that the man had a point.
"Very well, 'Alfred.' " He managed to make it sound insulting. "Although that's not your real name, is it?"

"No. It's one I adopted. Unlike yours, my true name would sound very strange to the mensch."

"What is your real name? Your Sartan name? If you're wondering, I can speak your language—although I don't like to."

Alfred drew himself straighter. "If you speak our language, you know then that to speak our names is to speak the runes and draw on the power of the runes. Therefore, our true names are known only to ourselves and to those who love us. A Sartan's name can be spoken only by another Sartan.

"Just as your name"—Alfred raised a delicate finger, pointed suddenly at Haplo's breast—"is marked on your skin and may be read only by those whom you love and trust. You see, I also speak your language. Although I don't like to."

"Love!" Haplo snorted. "We don't love anyone. Love is the greatest danger there is in the Labyrinth, since whatever you love is certain to die. As for trust, we had to learn it. Your prison taught us that much. We had to trust each other, because that was the only way we could survive. And speaking of survival, you might want to make certain I stay healthy, unless you think you can pilot this ship back through Death's Gate yourself."

"And what happens if my survival depends on you?"

"Oh, I'll see that you survive, all right. Not that you'll thank me for it later."

Alfred looked at the steering stone, the sigla etched on it. He would recognize each sigla, but they were arranged in far different patterns from those he knew. Elven and human languages use the same letters of the alphabet, yet the languages are vastly dissimilar. And although he might be able to speak the Patryn language, Haplo was certain the Sartan couldn't work the Patryn magic.

"No, I'm afraid I couldn't manage steering this ship," Alfred said.

Haplo laughed briefly, derisively, started for the door, then stopped. Turning, he held up a warning hand.

"Don't try that fainting trick with me. I warn you! I can't be responsible for what happens if you pass out."

Alfred shook his head. "I can't control the fainting spells, I'm afraid. Oh, in the beginning I could. I used it to disguise my magic, like those bandages you wear. What else could I do? I could no more reveal I was a demigod than you could! Everyone would have wanted to use me. Greedy men demanding I give them wealth.

Elves demanding I kill the humans. Humans demanding I rid them of the elves . . ."

"And so you fainted."

"I was beset by robbers." Alfred lifted his hands, looked down at them. "I could have obliterated them with a word. I could have turned them to solid stone. I could have melted their feet to the pavement. I could have charmed them utterly . . . and left my mark indelibly on the world. I was frightened—not of them, but of what I had the power to do to them. My mental turmoil and anguish was too great for my mind to bear. When I came to myself, I knew how I had solved the dilemma. I had simply fainted dead away. They took what they wanted and left me alone. And now I can't control the spells. They simply . . . happen."

"You can control it. You just don't want to. It's become an easy way out." The Patryn pointed over the ship's hull to the blazing lava sea, burning bright around them. "But if you faint and fall into a puddle in *this* world, that fainting spell's liable to be your last!

"Let's go, dog. You, too, 'Alfred.' "

CHAPTER • 11

SAFE HARBOR,

ABARRACH

•

Haplo left the ship moored at the dock, its magic keeping it afloat in the air above the magma flow. He was not concerned over anything happening to the vessel, runes of protection guarded it better than he could have guarded it in person, would permit no one to enter in his absence. Not that this appeared likely. No one approached the ship, no dock authority demanded to know their business, no hucksters swarmed over to push their wares, no sailors lounged about, idly eyeing the cut of their jib.

The dog leapt from the deck to the pier below. Haplo followed, landing almost as silently and lightly as the animal. Alfred remained on deck, dithering nervously, pacing back and forth.

Haplo, exasperated, was on the point of leaving the man when suddenly, with desperate courage, Alfred launched himself into the air, arms and legs flailing, and landed in a confused heap on the rock pier. It took him several moments to sort himself out, looking for all the world as if he were endeavoring to decide which limb went where and making mistakes as he went along. Haplo watched, half-amused, wholly irritated, inclined to assist the clumsy Sartan simply to expedite their progress. Alfred at last pulled himself together, discovered no bones were broken, and fell into step beside Haplo and the dog.

They wandered slowly down the pier, Haplo taking his time investigating. He stopped once to stare closely at several bales stacked on the docks. The dog sniffed around them. Alfred gazed at them curiously.

"What are they, do you think?"

"Raw material of some sort," Haplo answered, touching it gingerly. "Fibrous, soft. Might be used for making cloth. I—" He paused, leaned closer to the bale, almost as if he were sniffing it, like his dog. He straightened, pointed. "What do you make of that?"

Alfred appeared rather startled at being thus addressed, but he leaned down, squinting his mild eyes and peering distractedly. "What? I can't—"

"Look closely. Those marks on the sides of the bales."

Alfred thrust his nose nearly into the product, gave a start, paled slightly, and drew back.

"Well?" Haplo demanded.

"I . . . can't be sure."

"The hell you can't."

"The markings are smudged, difficult to read."

Haplo shook his head, and walked on, whistling to the dog, who thought it had found a rat and was pawing frantically at the bottom of a bale.

The town of obsidian was silent, the silence was ominous and oppressive. No heads peered out of the windows, no children ran through the streets. Yet it had obviously once been filled with life, as impossible as that might seem, so near the magma sea whose heat and fumes must kill any ordinary mortal.

Ordinary mortals. Not demigods.

Haplo continued his scrutiny of the various goods and bundles piled up on the pier. Occasionally, he paused and shot a closer glance at one and when he did this, he often pointed it out silently to Alfred, who would look at it, look at Haplo, and shrug his stooped shoulders in perplexity.

The two moved into the town proper. No one hailed them, greeted them, threatened them. Haplo was certain, now, that no one would. The pricking of certain runes on his skin would have alerted him to the presence of anything living; his magic was doing nothing more than keeping his body cool and filtering out harmful properties in the air. Alfred appeared nervous—but then Alfred would have appeared nervous walking into a children's nursery.

Two questions were on Haplo's mind: Who had been here and why weren't they here any longer?

The town itself was a collection of buildings carved of the black rock, fronting a single street. One building, standing almost directly opposite the pier, boasted thick-paned, crude glass windows. Haplo looked inside. Several globes of soft, warm light ranged around the walls, illuminating a large common room filled with tables and chairs. Perhaps an inn.

The inn's door was woven out of a heavy, coarse, grasslike substance, similar to hemp. The fiber had then been coated with a thick, glossy resin that made it smooth and impervious to weather. The door stood partially ajar, not in welcome, but as if the owner had left in such haste he'd neglected to shut it.

Haplo was about to step inside and investigate when a mark on the door caught his attention. He stared at it, the doubt in his mind hardening into finality. He said nothing, his finger jabbed at the door, at the mark on the door.

"Yes," said Alfred quietly, "a rune structure."

"A Sartan rune structure," Haplo corrected, his voice grating harshly.

"A corrupted Sartan rune, or perhaps altered would be a better choice of words. I couldn't speak it, nor use it." Head bobbing, shoulders hunched, Alfred looked singularly like a turtle, emerging from its shell. "And I can't explain it."

"It's the same as those marks we saw on the bales."

"I don't know how you can tell." Alfred wouldn't commit himself. "Those were almost worn off."

Haplo's mind went back to Pryan, to the Sartan city he'd discovered. He'd seen runes there as well, but not on the inns. The inns of Pryan hung out signs of welcome in human, elven, dwarven. He recalled, too, that the dwarf—what had been that fellow's name?— had known something of the rune magic, but only in a crude and childlike fashion. Any three-year-old Sartan could have bettered the Pryan dwarf in a rune-scrying contest.

This rune structure may have been corrupted, but it was sophisticated, runes of protection for the inn, runes of blessing for those who entered. At last, Haplo had found what he had been seeking, what he had been dreading to find—the enemy. And, if he was to judge by appearance, he was standing in an entire civilization of them.

Great. Just great.

Haplo entered the inn, booted feet padding softly across the carpeted floor.

Alfred crept along behind, looked about in amazement. "Whoever was here certainly left in a hurry!"

Haplo was in a bad mood, not inclined for conversation. He continued his investigation in silence. He examined the lamps, was surprised to see that they had no wicks. A jet of air flowed from a small pipe in the wall. The flame burned off the air. Haplo blew out the flame, sniffed, and wrinkled his nose. Breathe that too long without benefit of magic and you'd quietly cease to breathe.

Haplo heard a noise, glanced around. Alfred had automatically and without thinking carefully righted an overturned chair. The dog sniffed a hunk of meat left lying on the floor.

And all around the Patryn, everywhere he turned his glance, were Sartan runes.

"Your people haven't been gone long," he observed, noting the bitterness in his voice, hoping it covered the crawling, twisting knot of fear, of anger, of despair.

"Don't call them that!" Alfred protested. Was he trying hard not to build his hopes too high? Or did he sound as frightened as Haplo? "There's no other evidence—"

"Like hell! Could humans, no matter how advanced in magic, live long in this poisonous atmosphere? Could elves? Dwarves? No! The only people who could survive are your people."

"Or yours!" Alfred pointed out.

"Yeah, well, we all know *that's* not possible!"

"We don't know anything. Mensch might live here. Over time, they might have adapted . . ."

Haplo turned away, sorry he'd brought it up. "It's no use speculating. We'll probably find out soon enough. These people, whoever they are, haven't been gone long."

"How can you tell?"

In answer, the Patryn held up a loaf of bread he'd just broken. "Stale on the outside," Haplo said, poking at it. "Soft in the center. If it'd been left out long, it would be stale all the way through. And no one bothered to put runes of preservation on it, so they expected to eat it, not store it."

"I see." Alfred was admiring. "I never would have noticed."

"You learn to notice, in the Labyrinth. Those who don't, don't survive."

The Sartan, uncomfortable, changed the subject. "Why do you think they left?"

"My guess is war," Haplo answered, lifting a filled wineglass. He sniffed at the contents. The stuff smelled awful.

"War!" Alfred's shocked tone brought the Patryn immediately to attention.

"Yes, come to think of it, that *is* odd, isn't it? You people pride yourselves on peaceful solutions to problems, don't you? But"—he shrugged—"it sure looks that way to me."

"I don't understand—"

Haplo waved an impatient hand. "The door standing ajar, chairs overturned, food left uneaten, not a ship in the harbor."

"I'm afraid I still don't understand."

"A person who leaves his property expecting to come back generally shuts his door and locks it, to keep that property safe until his return. A person who flees his property in fear for his life just leaves. Then, too, these people fled in the middle of a meal, leaving ordinarily portable goods behind them—plates, cutlery, pitchers, bottles—full bottles at that. I'll wager that if you went upstairs, you'd find most of their clothes still in their rooms. They were warned of danger, and they got the hell out of here."

Alfred's eyes widened in sudden horror, realization dawning on him with a sickly light. "But . . . if what you say is true . . . then whatever is coming down on them—"

"—is coming down on us," Haplo finished. He felt more cheerful. Alfred was right. It couldn't be Sartan.

From what he knew of their history, the Sartan had never made war on anyone, not even their most feared enemies. They had shut the Patryns into prison, into a deadly prison, but—according to the records—that prison had been originally designed to rehabilitate, not kill, the prisoner.

"And if they left in such a hurry, it must be quite close by now." Alfred peered nervously out the window. "Shouldn't we be going?"

"Yeah, I guess so. Not much more to be learned around here."

Clumsy footed as he was, the Sartan could move fast enough when he wanted to. Alfred reached the door ahead of any of them, including the dog. Bursting out into the street, he was halfway down the pier, running awkwardly for the ship, when he must have realized he was alone. Turning, he called to Haplo, who was heading in the opposite direction, toward the edge of town.

Alfred's shout echoed loudly among the silent buildings. Haplo ignored him, kept walking. The Sartan cringed, swallowed another shout. He launched into a trot, stumbled over his feet, and fell flat on his face. The dog waited for him, on orders from Haplo, and eventually Alfred caught up.

"If what you say is true," he gasped, breathing heavily from his exertion, "the enemy's bound to be out there!"

"They are," said Haplo coolly. "Look."

Alfred glanced ahead, saw a pool of fresh blood, a broken spear, a dropped shield. He ran a shaking hand nervously over his bald head. "Then . . . then where are you going?"

"To meet them."

CHAPTER ♦ 12

SALFAG CAVERNS,

ABARRACH

♦

THE NARROW STREET HAPLO AND HIS RELUCTANT COMPANION FOL-lowed dwindled down and eventually came to an end among gigan-tic stalagmites thrusting upward around the base of a slick-sided obsidian cliff. The magma sea churned sluggishly at its feet, the rock gleamed brilliantly in the lurid light. The top of the cliff reared upward until it vanished in the steamy darkness. No army was advancing on them from this direction.

Haplo turned, gazed out over a large flat plain behind the small seaside town. He could not see much, most of the land was lost in the shadows of this realm that knew no sun except that within its own heart. But occasionally a stream of lava branched off from the main flow and wandered out onto the vast rock plains. By its reflected light, he saw deserts of oozing, bubbling mud; volcanic mountains of jagged, twisted rock; and—oddly—cylindrical columns of im-mense girth and width vaulting upward into darkness.

"Man-made," Haplo thought and realized, too late, that he'd spoken the thought aloud.

"Yes," Alfred replied, looking upward, craning his neck until he nearly fell over backward. Recalling what Haplo'd said about tum-bling into a puddle, the man looked down, regained his balance hastily. "They must reach straight up to the ceiling of this vast cavern but . . . for what reason? The cave obviously doesn't need the sup-port."

Never in Haplo's wildest imaginings had he envisioned himself standing on a hell-blasted world, calmly discussing geological formations with a Sartan. He didn't like talking to Alfred, he didn't like listening to the high-pitched, querulous voice. But he hoped, through conversation, to lull Alfred into a sense of security. Lead him into discussions that might cause him to slip up, reveal whatever he was concealing about the Sartan and their plans.

"Have you seen pictures or read accounts of this world?" Haplo asked. His tone was casual, he didn't look at Alfred when he spoke, as if the Sartan's reply mattered little to him.

Alfred cast a sharp glance at him, however, and licked his lips with his tongue. He was really a terrible liar.

"No."

"Well, I have. My Lord discovered drawings of all the worlds, left behind by your people when they abandoned us to our fate in the Labyrinth."

Alfred started to say something, checked himself, and kept silent.

"This world of stone your people created looks like a cheese that has been populated by mice," Haplo continued. "It's filled with caverns like this one in which we're standing. These caverns are enormous. One single cave could easily hold the entire elven nation of Tribus. Tunnels and caves run all through the stone world, crisscrossing each other, delving down, spiraling up. Up—to what? What's on the surface?" Haplo gazed at the cylindrical towers, soaring into the shadows above. "What *is* on the surface, Sartan?"

"I thought you were going to call me by my name," Alfred said mildly.

"I will, when it's important," Haplo grunted. "It leaves a bad taste in my mouth.

"To answer your question, I have no idea what is on the surface. You know far more about this world than I do." Alfred's eyes glistened as he considered the possibilities. "I would speculate, however, that—"

"Hush!" Haplo held up a warning hand.

Remembering their danger, Alfred turned deathly white and froze where he stood, body trembling. Haplo clambered over the broken rocks with stealthy ease, being careful to dislodge no small chunk that could fall, rattling, and reveal their presence. The dog, padding softly as its master, went ahead, ears pricked, hackles raised.

Haplo discovered that the street didn't end, as he had thought, against the sheer rock wall. He found a path running along the stalagmites at the cliff's base. A hasty and crude attempt had been made to obliterate the path's existence, or perhaps just slow whatever was coming along it. Piles of rock had been stacked in front of it to hide it. Molten pools of lava made a slip extremely treacherous. Haplo eased himself over the rock piles, following after the dog, who seemed to have an extraordinary talent in picking out safe places for its master to cross. Alfred remained behind, quaking, shivering all over. Haplo could have sworn he heard the man's teeth chatter.

Rounding the last jumble of rock, the Patryn reached the mouth of a cave. Its high, arched entrance was invisible from land, but could be seen clearly from the seaside. A magma tributary flowed into the cave. On one side of the lava flow—Haplo's side—the path continued, leading into the cavern's lava-lighted interior.

Haplo paused near the entrance, listening. The sounds he'd first heard were clearer now—voices, echoing through the cavern. A large number of people, to judge by the sometimes clamorous noise, although occasionally everyone fell silent and one alone continued speaking. The echoes distorted the words, he couldn't understand what language was spoken, and it had a cadence that was unfamiliar to him. Certainly it was not like any of the elven, human, and dwarven dialects he'd heard on Arianus and Pryan.

The Patryn eyed the cave speculatively. The path leading inside was wide, littered with boulders and broken rock. The lava flow lighted the way, but there were pockets and pits of dark shadow along the side of the tunnel where a man—particularly a man accustomed to moving with the silence of the night—might easily hide. Haplo could probably slip up on whatever and whoever were inside that tunnel, get a close look at them, and from that observation make his plans accordingly.

"But what the devil do I do with Alfred?"

Haplo glanced back, saw the tall, gangly Sartan perched on his rock like a stork on a battlement. The Patryn thought of the clumsy feet, clattering among the stones, and he shook his head. No, taking Alfred was impossible. But leaving him? Something was bound to happen to the fool. If nothing else, he'd fall into a pit. And Haplo's lord would not be pleased at losing such a valuable prize.

Damn it all, the Sartan was skilled in magic! And he didn't need to hide it; at least, not yet.

Haplo made his way back quietly, carefully to where Alfred

shivered on his perch. Cupping his hand, putting it to the Sartan's ear, the Patryn whispered, "Don't say a word. Just listen!"

Alfred nodded, to show he understood. His face could have been used as a mask in a play called *Terror.*

"There's a cavern beneath the cliff. Those voices we can hear are coming from inside. They're probably a lot farther off than they sound, the cave's distorting them."

Alfred appeared highly relieved and also ready to turn and head back for the boat. Haplo caught hold of the worn and shabby sleeve of the blue velvet coat. "We're going into the cave."

The Sartan's eyes opened wide, showing red rims around the pale blue iris. He gulped and would have shaken his head if his neck had not gone stiff.

"Those Sartan markings we saw. Don't you want to know the truth? If we left now, we might not ever find out."

Alfred's head drooped, his shoulders slumped. Haplo knew he had his victim netted, he had only to drag him along. At last the Patryn understood the driving force in Alfred's life. Whatever the cost, the Sartan had to know if he was truly alone in this universe or if there were others of his race left alive and, if so, what had happened to them.

Alfred closed his eyes, drew a deep, shivering breath, then nodded. "Yes," his lips mouthed, "I'll come with you."

"It's going to be dangerous. Not a sound. Not one sound or you could get us both killed. Understand?"

The Sartan appeared agonized, looked helplessly down at his own too-large feet, at the hands that dangled at the wrist as if completely beyond their owner's control.

"Use your magic!" Haplo told him irritably.

Alfred drew back, frightened. Haplo said nothing. He merely pointed in the direction of the cave, pointed to the rock-strewn and treacherous path, pointed to the glowing pools of molten rock on either side.

Alfred began to sing, his nasal voice bouncing off the roof of his mouth. He sang softly; Haplo, standing near him, could barely hear it. But the Patryn, sensitive to the slightest noise that might betray them, had to bite his tongue to keep from telling the man to shut up. Sartan rune magic involves sight and sound and movement. If Haplo wanted Alfred to use his magic, Haplo would have to put up with this teeth-jarring chant. He waited and watched.

The Sartan was dancing now, hands weaving the runes his voice conjured, his ungainly feet moving in graceful patterns drawn by his voice. And then Alfred was no longer standing on the rock. He rose slowly into the air, hovered about a foot above the ground. Spreading his hands in a deprecating manner, he smiled down on Haplo.

"This is the easiest," he said.

Haplo supposed so, but he found it disconcerting, and he had to quiet the dog, who seemed to like Alfred well enough on the ground but who took offense at an Alfred floating in midair.

The Sartan had certainly done what was required of him. Alfred, drifting among the rocks, made less sound than the currents of hot wind that swirled around them. Then what's wrong? Haplo wondered irritably. Am I jealous? Because I can't do it myself. Not that I'd want to do it myself!

Patryns draw their magical energy from the possibilities of the seen, the felt, the physical; they take it from the ground, the plants and trees, the rocks, and all objects around them. To let go of reality was to fall into a void of chaos. Sartan magic was of the air, of the unseen, of the possibilities woven in faith and belief. Haplo had the strange sensation that he was being followed by a ghost.

He turned his back on the bobbing Sartan, called the dog to heel, and set his mind to what he was doing, finding the way back along the path. He hoped Alfred struck his head on a rock.

The path inside the cavern proved all that Haplo had foreseen. It was wide, far easier to travel than even he'd supposed. A large wagon could have rolled through it without much difficulty.

Haplo kept to the sides of the cavern wall, making himself one with shadows. The dog, absolutely fascinated by a flying Alfred, lagged behind, staring upward in profound disbelief at the remarkable sight. The Sartan, hands clasped nervously before him, sailed sedately along after them.

They could hear the voices inside the cavern clearly now. It seemed that rounding the next corner in the twisting cave must bring the people speaking into view. But, as Haplo had said, sound bounced among the rocks and off the cavern ceiling. The Patryn and his companion traversed a considerable distance before the clarity of the words spoken warned Haplo that he was finally drawing near.

The magma stream decreased in width, the darkness grew thicker around them. Alfred was now little more than an indistinguishable blur in the fading light. The dog, whenever it stepped into deep shadow, vanished completely. The stream had once been broad and wide; Haplo could see its bed cut cleanly into the rock. But it was drying up, cooling, and he noted the resultant drop in temperature in the darkening cave. The stream ended altogether. Light failed, leaving them in impenetrable darkness.

Haplo came to a halt and was immediately struck from behind by a heavy object. Cursing beneath his breath, he fended off the floating Alfred who, not seeing the Patryn stop, had barreled right into him. Haplo was considering conjuring light—a simple skill, learned in childhood—but the blue glow of the runes would announce his presence on this world. He might as well shout it. Alfred would be no help either, for the same reason.

"Stay here," he whispered to Alfred, who nodded, only too happy to obey. "Dog, watch him."

The dog settled down, head cocked, studying Alfred inquisitively, as if trying to figure out how the man performed such a marvelous feat.

Haplo felt his way along the rock wall. The lava flow behind provided him with lambent light enough to know he wasn't about to plunge into a chasm. He ventured around another bend in the path and saw, at the end, bright light, yellow light, fire light. Light produced by living beings, not light made by lava. And around the light, across the light, and beneath the light, moved the silhouetted shapes of hundreds of people.

The back of the cavern was vast, opening out into a large room capable of holding an army comfortably. And had he found an army? Was this the army that had sent the shore people scurrying away in panic? Haplo watched and listened. He heard them talking, understood what they said. The darkness grew deep around him, he struggled with overwhelming despair and defeat.

He had found an army—an army of Sartan!

What was to be done? Escape! Return through Death's Gate, carry word of this disaster to his lord. But his lord would ask questions, questions Haplo could not now answer.

And Alfred? It had been a mistake to bring him. Haplo cursed himself bitterly. He should have left the Sartan behind on the ship, left him in ignorance. Then he could have taken the Sartan back to the Labyrinth, keeping him in complete ignorance of the fact that his people were alive and well on Abarrach, the world of stone. Now, with just one shout, Alfred could end Haplo's mission, end his lord's hopes and dreams, end Haplo.

"Blessed Sartan," whispered a soft voice behind him, nearly causing Haplo to jump out of his rune-covered skin.

He turned swiftly, to find Alfred hovering in the air overhead, staring down at the fire-lighted bodies moving in the cavern. Haplo tensed, waiting, casting a furious glance at the dog, who had failed its trust.

At least I'll have the satisfaction of killing one Sartan before I die.

Alfred stared into the cavern, his face a pale glimmer in the reflected firelight, his eyes sad and troubled.

"Go ahead, Sartan!" Haplo demanded in a savage whisper. "Why don't you get it over with? Call to them! They're your brothers!"

"Not mine!" Alfred said in hollow tones. "Not mine!"

"What do you mean? That's Sartan they're speaking."

"No, Haplo. The Sartan language is the language of life. Theirs"—Alfred lifted a hand, ghostly in its grace, and pointed—"is the language of death."

CHAPTER ♦ 13

SALFAG CAVERNS,

ABARRACH

♦

"WHAT DO YOU MEAN, LANGUAGE OF DEATH? COME DOWN HERE!" Haplo reached up, caught hold of Alfred, and pulled him nearer. "Now talk!" he ordered in a soft undertone.

"I understand it little more than you do," the Sartan said, looking helpless. "And I'm not sure what I mean. It's just that . . . well, listen for yourself. Can't you tell the difference?"

Haplo did as he was advised, pushing aside the turbulent emotions warring in him to pay close attention. Now that he concentrated, he had to admit Alfred had a point. The Sartan language sounded discordant to Patryn ears. Accustomed to hard, swift, harsh, and uncompromising words that expressed what one had to say in the quickest, simplest, shortest way possible, the Patryns considered the Sartan language elaborate, airy-fairy, cluttered with flights of fancy and unnecessary verbiage and an inexplicable need to explain that which required no explanation.

But to hear these cave-people talk was tantamount to hearing the Sartan language turned inside out. Their words did not fly, they crawled. Their language evoked no images of rainbows and sunshine in Haplo's mind. He saw a pale and sickly light, a light given off by something rotting and corrupt. He heard a sorrow deeper than the dark depths of this world. Haplo prided himself on never feeling "soft" emotion, but this sorrow touched him to the core of his being.

Slowly, he released Alfred from his rough grip. "Do you understand what's going on?"

"No, I don't. Not clearly. But I think I could become accustomed to the language in time."

"Yeah, me, too. Just like I could become accustomed to being hanged. What're you going to do?" Haplo eyed Alfred narrowly.

"Me?" Alfred was astounded. "Do? What do you mean?"

"Are you going to turn me over to them? Tell them I'm the ancient enemy? You probably won't even have to tell them. They'll remember."

Alfred did not answer immediately. His lips parted several times as if he intended to speak, but shut when he changed his mind. Haplo had the impression that the man was not trying to decide what to do, but how to explain his decision.

"This may sound strange to you, Haplo. I have no desire to betray you. Oh, I've heard your threats against me and, believe me, I don't take them lightly. I know what will happen to me in the Nexus. But now we are strangers in a strange world—a world that appears to grow exceedingly more strange the deeper we probe it."

Alfred appeared confused, almost shy. "I can't explain myself, but I feel a . . . a kinship to you, Haplo. Perhaps because of what happened to us going through Death's Gate. I've been where you were. And I think, if I'm right, that you've been where I was. I'm not explaining this very well, am I?"

"Kinship! The hell with all that. Keep in mind one thing—I'm your way out of here. Your *only* way out of here."

"True," said Alfred gravely. "You are right. It appears, then, that while we are on this world we must depend on each other for survival. Would you like me to pledge it?"

Haplo shook his head, fearing he might be called on to pledge something in return. "I'll trust you to save your own skin and because that includes saving mine, I guess that'll be good enough."

Alfred glanced about nervously. "Now that that's settled, shouldn't we be going back to the ship?"

"Are these people Sartan?"

"Ye—es . . ."

"Don't you want to find out more about them? What they're doing on this world?"

"I suppose so . . ." Alfred hesitated.

Haplo ignored his reluctance. "We'll move closer, see if we can figure out what's going on."

The two men and the dog crept ahead, keeping to the shadows

of the tunnel wall, edging their way toward the light until Haplo deemed they were close enough to see without being seen, hear without being heard. He raised a warding hand and Alfred bobbed up close beside him, hovering silently in the air. The dog flopped down on the rock floor, keeping one eye on its master and the other on Alfred.

The cavern was filled with people, all of them Sartan. Sartan appear to be human at first glance, with the exception that their hair rarely varies in color. Even among children, the hair is almost always white, shading toward brown at the bottom. Patryn hair coloration is exactly the opposite. Haplo's hair was brown on top, shading to white at the bottom. Alfred had almost no hair (perhaps the balding was another unconscious attempt at disguise) and was thus not easily recognizable.

Sartan also tended to be taller in height than those of the lesser races. Their magical power and the knowledge of that power gave them extraordinarily beautiful and radiant countenances (Alfred being the exception).

These people were Sartan, beyond doubt. Haplo's eyes darted swiftly over the crowd. He saw only Sartan, none of the lesser races, no elves, no humans, no dwarves.

.   But there was something odd about these Sartan, something wrong. The Patryn had met one living Sartan—Alfred. Haplo had seen visions of the Sartan on Pryan. He'd looked on them with scorn, but he was forced to admit that they were a beautiful, radiant people. These Sartan seemed aged, faded; their radiance dimmed. Some of them were, in fact, hideous to look on. Haplo was repelled by the sight of them and saw his own revulsion reflected strongly in Alfred's eyes.

"They're holding a ceremony of some sort," Alfred whispered.

Haplo was about to tell him to shut up when it occurred to the Patryn that he might learn something to his advantage. He swallowed his words and counseled patience, a hard lesson he'd learned in the Labyrinth.

"A funeral," said Alfred in a pitying tone. "They're holding a funeral for the dead."

"If so, they've waited long enough to entomb them," Haplo muttered.

Twenty corpses of varying ages, from that of a small child to the body of a very old man, lay on the rock floor of the cavern. The crowd

stood at a respectful distance, giving Haplo and Alfred—
unobserved watchers—an excellent view. The corpses were composed, hands folded across the chest, eyes closed in eternal sleep.
But some had obviously been dead a long time. The air was foul with
the odor of decay, although—probably by their magic—the Sartan
had succeeded in keeping the flesh from rotting away.

The skin of the dead was white and waxy, the cheeks and eyes
sunken, the lips blue. On some, the nails had grown abnormally
long, the hair was wild and uncombed. Haplo thought there was
something familiar about the sight of the dead, but he didn't know
what. He was about to mention his notion to Alfred, when the
Sartan signaled him to be quiet and watch.

A man stepped forward, stood before the dead. Prior to the
man's appearance, the crowd had been whispering and murmuring
among themselves. Now, they all fell silent, all eyes turned to him.
Haplo could almost feel their love and respect reach out to the
unknown man.

Haplo was not surprised to hear Alfred whisper, "A Sartan
prince." The Patryn knew a leader when he saw one.

The prince raised his hands to draw their attention, an unnecessary gesture, because it seemed everyone in the cave had their eyes
fixed on him.

"My people"—and it seemed that the man was speaking as
much to the dead as to the living—"we have traveled far from our
homeland, our beloved homeland. . . ."

His voice choked, and he had to pause a moment to regain his
composure. It seemed his people loved him the more for his weakness. Several put hands to their eyes, wiped away tears.

He drew a deep breath, continued. "But that is behind us now.
What is done is done. It is up to us to continue on, to build new lives
on the wreckage of the old.

"Ahead of us"—the prince flung out an arm, pointed, if he had
known it, directly at Haplo and a startled Alfred—"lies the city of
our brethren . . ."

The silence broke, angry mutterings interrupted. The prince
raised his hand in a gentle but peremptory and commanding gesture and the voices ceased, although they left behind the heat of their
emotions, like the heat welling up from the magma sea.

"I say 'our brethren' and I mean 'our brethren.' They are of our
race, perhaps the only ones of our race left on this world or any-

where for that matter. What they did to us—if they did anything to us—they did unknowing. I swear it!"

"Robbed us of all we possessed!" cried one elderly woman, shaking a gnarled fist. The weight of years gave her the right to speak. "We've all heard the rumors you've tried to keep silent. They robbed us of our water, of our heat. Doomed us to die up there of thirst, if the cold didn't kill us first and starvation second. And you say they didn't know! I say they knew and they didn't care!" Snapping her mouth shut, the old woman wagged her head wisely.

The prince smiled at the old woman, a smile that was patient and fond. She obviously recalled pleasant memories. "Nevertheless I say they didn't know, Marta, and I am confident that I speak truly. How could they?" The prince raised his gaze directly to the rock ceiling above his head, but his look seemed to penetrate the stalactites and carry him far above the shadows of the cavern. "We who lived up there have long been parted from our brethren who live here beneath. If their lives have been as difficult as ours, it is no wonder that they have forgotten our very existence. We were fortunate to have wise ones among us, who remembered our past and from whence we came."

Reaching out, the prince laid a hand on the arm of a man who had come to stand beside him. At the sight of this man, Alfred sucked in a deep and horrified breath that echoed among the rocks.

The prince and most of the people standing around him were wrapped in all types and manner of clothing, primarily animal furs, as though the region they'd left had been an exceedingly cold one. The man to whom the prince referred was clad differently. He wore a black skullcap and long black robes that, although the worse for wear, were clean and well kept. The robes were trimmed in silver runes. Haplo recognized these sigla as Sartan, but could make nothing else of them. Obviously, Alfred could but when Haplo cast him an interrogatory glance, the Sartan shook his head and bit his lip.

Haplo returned his attention to the prince.

"We have brought our dead with us these long and hard miles. Many have died along the way." The prince walked over, knelt beside one corpse, who lay in the front of the rest and wore, on its wispy-haired head, a golden crown. "My own father lies among them. And I swear to you"—the prince raised his hand in solemn vow—"I swear to you before our dead that I believe the people in Kairn Necros to be innocent of the harm they did us. I believe that when they hear of it they will weep for us and will take us in and shelter us, as we would do the same for them! I believe this so strongly that I, myself, will go to them alone, unarmed, and throw myself on their mercy!"

The men raised spears, clashing them against shields. The people cried out in shock. Haplo was in shock himself—the peace-loving Sartan were actually wielding weapons. Several pointed at the dead, and Haplo saw that four corpses were those of young men, whose bodies lay on their shields.

The prince was forced to shout to be heard over the clamor. His handsome face grew stern, he sent a flashing-eyed glance around them, and his people hushed, chagrined, at the sight of his anger. "Yes, they attacked us. What did you expect? You came on them too suddenly, armed to the teeth, making demands! If you had re-mained patient—"

"It isn't easy, remaining patient, seeing your children starving!" mumbled one man, his eyes on a thin little boy, clinging to his father's leg. He reached out a hand, fondled the small head. "We asked them only for food and water."

"Asked them at spear point," the prince said, but his face soft-ened in compassion, took the sting from his words. "Raef, don't you think I understand? I held the body of my father in my arms. I—" He lowered his head, put his hands to his eyes.

The man in the black robes said something to him and the prince, nodding, looked up again. "The battle, too, is past and done. We cannot undo it. I take the blame. I should have kept the people together, but I thought it best to send you on while I stayed behind to prepare my father's corpse. I will carry our apologies to our breth-ren. I am certain they will be understanding."

To judge by the low growl among the crowd, the prince's cer-tainty was not shared by his people. The old woman burst into tears. Hastening forward, she clasped her feeble hands on the prince's arm, begged him, as he loved them, not to go.

"What would you have me do, Marta?" the prince asked, gently patting the gnarled hand.

She looked up at him, suddenly fierce. "I would have you fight, like a man! Take back from them what they stole from us!"

The low growl increased in volume, spear clashed against shield. The prince climbed on a boulder, so that he could see and be seen by all the crowd gathered in the cave. His back was to Haplo and Alfred, but Haplo could tell by the rigid stance and the squared shoulders that the man had been pushed almost past endurance.

"My father, your king, is dead. Do you accept me for your ruler?" The edge in his voice sliced through the noise like the whistle of a sword's sharp blade. "Or is there one of you that means to challenge me? If so, step forward! We will have the contest here and now!"

The prince tossed aside his fur cloak, revealing a body young and strong and well muscled. By his movements, he was lithe and obviously skilled in the use of the sword he wore on his hip. For all his anger, he was cool and kept his wits about him. Haplo would have thought twice about confronting this man. No one among the crowd took the prince up on his offer. They appeared ashamed, and all of them lifted their voices in a shout of support that might have been heard in the far-distant city. Again, spear clashed against shield, but it was in homage, not in defiance.

The man in black robes came forward, speaking aloud for the first time. "No one challenges you, Edmund. You are our prince"— another shout—"and we will follow you as we followed your father. It is natural, however, that we fear for your safety. If we lose you, who will we turn to?"

The prince clasped the man's hand, looked around at his people and, when he spoke, his emotion could be heard plainly in his voice. "Now it is I who am ashamed. I lost my temper. I am nothing special, except that I have the honor to be my father's son. Any one of you could lead our people. All of you are worthy."

Many of his people wept. Tears flowed freely down Alfred's face. Haplo, who had never supposed he could feel pity or compassion for anyone outside his own people, looked at these people, noted their shabby clothing, their wan faces, their pitiful children, and he was forced to remind himself sternly that these were Sartan, these were the enemy.

"We should proceed with the ceremony," said the man in black robes, and the prince agreed. He stepped down from his boulder and took his own place among his people.

The man in black robes walked among the corpses. Lifting both hands, he began to make strange designs in the air and, at the same time, he started to chant words in a loud, singsong voice. Moving among the dead, passing up and down the silent rows, he drew a sigil above each one. The eerie singing grew louder, more insistent.

Haplo felt the hair rise on his head, his nerves tingled unpleasantly, his skin crawled, though he had no idea what was being said. This was no ordinary funeral.

"What's he doing? What's going on?"

Alfred's face had gone livid, eyes wide and staring in horror. "He's not entombing the dead! He's raising them!"

CHAPTER • 14

SALFAG CAVERNS,

ABARRACH

♦

"Necromancy!" Haplo whispered in disbelief, conflicting emotions, wild thoughts overwhelming him with confusion. "My Lord was right! The Sartan do possess the secret of bringing back the dead!"

"Yes!" Alfred gasped, wringing his hands. "We did, we do! But it should not be used! Never be used!"

The man in black had begun to dance, weaving gracefully among the corpses, twining in and out between them, hands floating above them, continuing to make the same, singular signs that Haplo recognized now were powerful runes. And then Haplo knew suddenly what had struck him as familiar about the corpses. Looking into the crowd, he noted that many among the living, particularly those huddled near the back of the cavern, were not living at all. They had the same look as the cadavers, the same white flesh, same sunken cheeks and shadowed eyes. Far more of these people were dead than alive!

The necromancer was nearing the end of the ceremony, seemingly. White insubstantial forms rose from the corpses. Possessed of shape and substance, the forms lingered near the bodies from which they sprang. At a commanding gesture from the necromancer, the misty forms drew back, yet each kept near its corpse, like shadows in a sunless world.

These shadows retained the form of the being each had left. Some stood straight and tall over the bodies of straight, tall men. Others stooped over the bodies of the aged. One little one stood near the corpse of the child. Each appeared reluctant to be separated from the bodies, some made a feeble attempt to return, but the necromancer, with a stern and shouted command, drove them away.

"You phantasms have nothing to do with these bodies now. Abandon them! They are no longer dead! Life returns! Get away from them or I will cast you and the body into oblivion!"

From his tone, the wizard would have liked to banish these ethereal shapes altogether, but perhaps that was impossible. Meekly, sorrowfully, the phantasms did as they were commanded, each moving away from its corpse, each standing as near as it dared without risking the ire of the necromancer.

"What have my people done? What have they done?" Alfred moaned.

The dog, leaping up suddenly, gave a sharp, warning bark. Alfred lost his magic, tumbled to the ground. Haplo ripped the bandages from his hands, turned to face the threat. His only hope was to fight and try to escape. The sigla on his skin glowed blue and red, the magic throbbed in his body, but, at the sight of what he faced, he was helpless.

How did one fight something already dead?

Haplo stared, confounded, unable to think through the magic, unable to sort out the possibilities that governed it to find any that might help him. His split-second delay proved costly. A hand reached out, closed over his arm, grasping him with a chill grip that came near freezing his heart. It seemed to him that the runes on his skin actually shriveled up beneath that deadly touch. He cried out in bitter pain, slumped to his knees. The dog, cringing, fell on its belly and howled.

"Alfred!" Haplo cried, through teeth clenched against the agony. "Do something!"

But Alfred took one look at their captors and fainted.

◆

Dead warriors led Haplo and carried the comatose Alfred into the cavern. The dog trotted quietly behind, although it took great care to avoid the touch of the dead, who seemed not to know what to do with the animal. The cadavers laid Alfred down on the floor in front of the necromancer. They brought Haplo, sullen and defiant, to stand before the prince.

Had Edmund's life been measured in gates, as was Haplo's, the prince must have been near the Patryn's age, around twenty-eight.

And it seemed to Haplo, as he looked into the serious, intelligent, shadowed eyes of the prince, that here was a man who had suffered much in those twenty-eight years, perhaps as much as Haplo himself.

"We caught them spying," one of the dead warriors said. The cadaver's voice was almost as chilling as the lifeless touch. Haplo strove to remain motionless, although the pain of the dead fingers biting into his flesh was excruciating.

"Is this one armed?" Edmund asked.

The cadavers—three of them—shook their grisly heads.

"And that one?" The prince glanced at Alfred with a half-smile. "Not that it would matter if he were."

The dead indicated he wasn't. The cadavers had eyes, but the eyes never looked at anything, never shifted or moved, never brightened or dimmed, never closed. Their phantasms, drifting restlessly behind the cadavers, had eyes that retained the wisdom and knowledge of the living. But the phantasms, it seemed, had no voice. They could not speak.

"Restore him to consciousness and treat him gently. Release the other one," the prince ordered the cadavers, who removed their fingers from Haplo's arm. "Return to your watch."

The dead shambled off, the tattered remnants of their clothing fluttering behind them.

The prince gazed curiously at Haplo, particularly Haplo's rune-covered hands. The Patryn waited stolidly to be denounced, to be judged the ancient enemy and turned into a cadaver himself. Edmund reached out to touch.

"Don't worry," the prince said, speaking slowly and loudly as one does to a person who doesn't speak the language. "I won't hurt you."

A flash of searing blue light streaked from the runes, crackled around the prince's fingers. He cried out in shock, more than pain. The jolt was a mild one.

"Damn right," Haplo said, in his own language, testing. "Try that again, and you'll be dead."

The prince drew back, staring. The necromancer, who had been chafing Alfred's temples in a vain attempt to rouse the man, ceased his work and looked up in astonishment.

"What language is that?" The prince spoke in his own, in the corrupt Sartan that Haplo understood, was beginning to understand more clearly all the time, but could not speak. "It's strange. I know what you said, although I swear I've never heard such speech before. And you understand me, although you do not speak my words. And that was rune-magic you used. I recognize the construct. Where do you come from? Necropolis? Did they send you? *Were* you spying on us?"

Haplo cast a mistrustful glance at the necromancer. The wizard appeared powerful and shrewd and might prove his greatest danger. But there was no recognition in the necromancer's piercing, black eyes, and Haplo began to relax. These people had been through so much in the present, perhaps they had lost all knowledge of their past.

The Patryn considered his answer. He had learned enough, from overhearing the conversation earlier, to know that it wouldn't help his cause if he told them he was from what he guessed must be the city they'd seen. This time, the truth seemed far safer than a lie. Besides, he knew that Alfred, once called on to explain himself, would never manage otherwise.

"No, I'm not from the city. I'm a stranger to this part of the world. I sailed here in a ship down the magma sea. You can see my ship." Haplo nodded toward the shoreside town. "I'm—we're"—he included Alfred grudgingly—"not spies."

"Then what were you doing when the dead caught you? They said you had been watching us for a long time. They had been watching you for a long time."

Haplo lifted his chin, gazed steadily at the prince. "We've traveled a vast distance. We entered the town, discovered signs that there'd been a battle, the people all fled. We heard your voices, echoing down the tunnel. In my place, would you have rushed in and proclaimed yourself to me? Or would you have waited, watched, listened, learned what you could?"

The prince smiled slightly, but the eyes remained serious. "In your place, I might have returned to my ship and sailed away from something that did not appear to be any of my concern. And how is that you came by such a companion? One so different from yourself."

Alfred was slowly coming around. The dog stood over him, licking his cheeks. Haplo raised his voice, hoping to jolt Alfred to attention, knowing he would be called to corroborate the Patryn's story.

"My companion's name is Alfred. And you're right. He is different. We come from different worl—er . . . cities. He joined up with me because he had no one else. He is the last survivor of his race."

A sympathetic murmur arose from the crowd. Alfred sat up weakly, cast a swift, frightened glance around him. The dead guards were out of sight. He breathed somewhat easier and, with the help of the necromancer, struggled awkwardly to stand up. Brushing off his clothes, he made a bobbing bow to the prince.

"Is this true?" Edmund said, pity and compassion softening his tone. "Are you the last of your people?"

"I thought I was," said Alfred, speaking Sartan, "until I found you."

"But you are not one of us," Edmund said, growing more and more perplexed. "I understand your speech, as I understand his"—he waved a hand at Haplo—"but it, too, is different. Tell me more."

Alfred appeared highly confused. "I—I don't know what to say."

"Tell us how you came to be here in this cave," suggested the necromancer.

Alfred cast the Patryn a wild look. His hands fluttered vaguely. "I—we sailed . . . in a ship. It's docked over there. Somewhere." He gestured vaguely, having lost all sense of direction. "We heard voices and came looking to see who was down here."

"Yet you thought we might be a hostile army," the prince said. "Why didn't you run away?"

Alfred smiled wanly, gently. "Because we didn't find a hostile army. We found you and your people, honoring your dead."

A nice way to put it, Haplo thought. The prince was impressed with the answer.

"You are one of us. Your words are my words, even though they are different. Far different. In your words"—the prince hesitated, trying to articulate his thoughts—"I see radiant light and a vast expanse of endless blue. I hear rushing wind and I breathe fresh, pure air that needs no magic to filter out its poison. In your words I hear . . . life. And that makes my words sound dark and cold, like this rock on which we stand."

Edmund turned to Haplo. "And you, too, are one of us, but you're not. In your words I hear anger, hatred. I see a darkness that is not cold and lifeless but is alive and moving, like a living entity. I feel trapped, caged, a yearning for escape."

Haplo was impressed, although he endeavored not to show it.

He would have to be careful around this perceptive young man. "I am not like Alfred," the Patryn said, choosing his words carefully, "in that my people still survive. But they are being held prisoner in a place far more terrible than you can ever imagine. The hatred and anger are for those who imprisoned us. I am one of the fortunate who managed to survive and escape. I am looking now for new lands where my people can find homes—"

"You won't find them here," said the necromancer coldly, abruptly.

"No," Edmund agreed. "No, you won't find homes here. This world is dying. Already our dead outnumber the living. If nothing changes, I foresee a time, and it is coming on us very soon, when the dead alone will rule Abarrach."

CHAPTER 15

SALFAG CAVERNS,

ABARRACH

✦

"Now we must proceed with the resurrection. After that, we would be honored if you would be our guests and join our repast. It is meager," Edmund added with a rueful smile, "but we are happy to share what we have."

"Only if you will allow us to add our food to yours," Alfred said, bobbing another awkward bow.

The prince looked at Alfred, at his empty hands. He looked at Haplo and his empty, rune-covered hands. Edmund appeared somewhat puzzled, but was too polite to question. Haplo glanced at Alfred to see if he was astonished over this peculiar statement of the prince's. How could a Sartan food supply be limited when they, like the Patryns, had almost limitless powers of magic to increase it? Haplo caught Alfred glancing with raised eyebrows at him. The Patryn quickly averted his gaze, refusing to give the Sartan the satisfaction of knowing that they were sharing similar thoughts.

At a sign from Edmund, dead warriors escorted the two strangers off to a corner of the cavern by themselves, away from the people, who continued to stare at them curiously, and away from the corpses, still lying on the rock floor.

The necromancer took his place among the dead, whose phantasms began to writhe and stir, as if touched by a hot wind. The corpses continued to lie still and unmoving. The necromancer began his chanting once more, raised his hands and brought them together with a sharp clap. The bodies twitched and jerked, a jolt of magical energy striking each one of them. The small corpse of the child sat up almost immediately and rose to its feet. The eyes of the small phantasm behind it appeared to search for someone in the crowd. A woman, weeping, came forward. The child's cadaver ran to her, white, cold hands outstretched in love and longing. The woman reached out to her child. A man, face drawn in grief, halted her, took the sobbing woman in his arms and drew her away. The little girl's corpse stood in front of them, staring at them. Slowly, the arms of the cadaver dropped to its sides; the wispy, ethereal arms of the phantasm remained outstretched.

"My people . . . what have they done?" Alfred repeated in a tear-choked voice. "What have they done?"

One by one, the cadavers regained the semblance of life. Each time, the eyes of the phantasm sought out loved ones among the living, but the living turned away. One by one, each of the dead took its place in the back of the cavern, joining the crowd of other dead, who stood behind the living. The young warriors joined ranks with their dead fellows. The aged, among the last to be persuaded to return, rose up like weary sleepers who have at last lain down to rest and are loath to awaken. The child lingered near her parents for some time, then finally, withdrew to mingle with other small cadavers. Haplo saw that there were many children among the dead, few among the living. He recalled Edmund's words, *This world is dying*, and he understood.

But Haplo understood something else. These people possessed the key to eternal life! What greater gift could Haplo bring to his lord, to his people? No longer would the Patryns be at the mercy of the Labyrinth. If the Labyrinth killed them, they would simply rise up and fight on, their numbers growing, until finally it was conquered. And then, no army in the universe could stop them, no living army could hope to defeat an army of the dead!

I have only to learn the secret of the rune-magic. And here, Haplo thought, his gaze going to Alfred, is one who can teach me. But I must be patient, bide my time. The Sartan doesn't know yet much more than I do. But he will learn. He can't help himself. And when he does, I'll have him!

The last cadaver to rise to its feet was the elderly man wearing the golden crown. And it seemed likely, at first, that the old man was going to defy them all. Its phantasm was stronger than the others, and it stood over the body defiantly, braving the necromancer's pleas and even—after an apologetic look at the grief-stricken prince—

threats. At last, the necromancer, scowling, shook his head and threw up his hands in a gesture of defeat. Edmund himself stepped forward, spoke to the body lying on the ground at his feet.

"I know how weary you are of life, Father, and how you long for and have earned rest. But think of the alternative. You will sink into dust. Your mind will continue working, yet you will know the hopeless, bitter frustration of being powerless to affect the world around you. You will live like this through the centuries, trapped in nothingness! Resurrection is far better, Father! You will be with us, the people who need you. You can advise us . . ."

The old man's phantasm writhed, rippled in a wind that only it could feel. It appeared frustrated with the fact that it couldn't communicate what it obviously, desperately desired to reveal.

"Father, please!" Edmund pleaded. "Return to us! We need you!"

The phantasm wavered, then dwindled, nearly disappearing. The cadaver stirred. The same magical jolt passed through it that had passed through the others, and it rose, feebly, to its feet.

"Father, my king," said the prince, bowing low.

The phantasm, barely a shadow, twisted in the air like mist rising from a pond. The cadaver lifted its wasted, waxen hand in acceptance of the homage, but then the head with the golden crown and its fixed, expressionless eyes, swiveled this way and that, as if wondering what to do next. The prince's own head bowed, his shoulders slumped. The necromancer drew near.

"I am sorry, Your Highness."

"It isn't your fault, Baltazar. You told me what to expect."

The corpse of the king remained standing before its people, its regal pose a terrible mockery of what the man had once been.

"I had hoped he might be different," said Edmund, speaking in a low voice, as if the dead man might overhear him. "In life, he was so strong, so resolute—"

"The dead can be nothing more than they are, My Lord. For them, their life ends when the mind ceases to function. We can return life to the body, but there our power stops. We cannot give them the ability to learn, to react to the living world around them. Your father will continue to be king, but only to those to whom he was king before their deaths."

The necromancer gestured. The dead king had turned the sightless eyes to the back of the cavern, to the dead who stood there. The corpses bowed in homage and the dead king, its phantasm whispering in grief, abandoned the living who did not know him anymore, and went to join the dead.

Edmund started to go after him. Baltazar plucked him by the sleeve.

"Your Majesty . . ." The necromancer indicated with a glance that they needed to talk in private. The two drew apart from the rest of the people, who made way for them in respect.

Haplo, with a casual gesture, sent the dog after them. The dog pushed near Edmund's leg. Unconsciously, the man's hand reached down to pet the soft fur. Haplo heard, through the animal's ears, every word that was said.

". . . you should take the crown!" the necromancer was urging in low tones.

"No!" The prince's response was sharp. His eyes were on the cadaver of his father, walking with proud and ghastly mien among the legions of the dead. "He wouldn't understand. He is king."

"But, My Liege, we need a living king—"

"Do we?" Edmund's smile was bitter. "Why? The dead out-number us. If the living are content to follow me as their prince, then I am content to remain their prince. Enough, Baltazar. Don't push me."

The youthful voice hardened, the eyes flashed. The necromancer bowed silently, glided off to other duties involving the cadavers. Edmund stood by himself a long while, his thoughts turned inward. The dog whined, nuzzled the hand absently petting him. The prince glanced down, smiled wanly.

"Thank you for your comfort, Friend," he said to the dog. "And you are right, I am being a neglectful host."

Recalled to his guests, Edmund came over to seat himself down on the rock floor beside Haplo and Alfred.

"We had animals like this among us once." Edmund fondled the dog, who wagged its tail and licked his hand. "I remember, as a boy—" He paused, sighed, then shook his head. "But you're not interested in that. Please, be seated. Forgive the informality," he added. "If we were in my palace in my land, I would entertain you with royal ceremony. But, then, if we were in my palace, we'd be freezing to death, so I suppose you prefer it where you are. I know I do. At least, I think I do."

"What terrible occurrence destroyed your kingdom?" Alfred asked.

The prince looked at him with narrowed eyes. "The same occurrence that destroyed yours, undoubtedly. At least, so I must guess, to judge by what I've seen on my travels."

Edmund was regarding them with renewed suspicion. Alfred stammered, appeared highly confused. Haplo sat forward, attempted to salvage the situation by changing the subject. "Did I hear something about food?"

Edmund gestured. "Marta, bring our guests supper!"

The old woman approached respectfully, carrying in her hands several dried fish. She set the fish down before them and, bowing, rose to leave.

But Haplo, watching her, saw her eyes dart jealously to the fish, then to himself and to Alfred.

"Go, old woman," the prince said sharply. His cheeks were flushed. It seemed he had noted the look, as well.

"Wait," Haplo called. Reaching out, he handed some of the fish back. "Take this for yourself. As we said, Your Highness," he added, when he saw Edmund start to protest, "we can provide our own."

"Yes." Alfred joined in eagerly, glad to have something to do. He lifted the fish in his hands. The old woman, clasping the food close to her bosom, hastened away.

"I am deeply shamed," Edmund began, but his words died on his lips.

Alfred was singing the runes to himself, his voice raised in the high-pitched nasal whine that seemed to pierce right through Haplo's head. The Sartan held one fish in his hand, then he held two, then three appeared. Ceasing the chant, Alfred handed the food to the prince, who stared at it, wide-eyed. The Sartan offered another fish, deferentially, to Haplo.

His runes glowed blue and red and where there had been one fish there were now twelve, then twenty-four. Haplo arranged the fish on the flat rock, remembered to give one to the dog, who—with an uneasy glance at the dead—dragged its dinner off to a dark recess to enjoy it in private.

"Such magic is wonderful, truly wonderful," the prince said in awed tones.

"But . . . you can do this," Alfred said, nibbling at the salty-tasting flesh. Hearing a sound, he looked up.

A child, a living child, was staring enviously at the dog. Alfred motioned the boy near and handed the fish to him. The boy caught hold of it, and hurried off. He presented the dried fish to an adult male, who stared at it in astonishment. The child pointed back at them. Haplo had the distinct feeling he was about to go into the seafood trade.

"It is said that in the old days we could perform such feats," Edmund remarked, his awed gaze fixed on the meat. "But now our magic is concentrated on our survival in this world. . . ." He glanced back at the cadavers, standing patiently in the shadows. "And on theirs."

Alfred shuddered, seemed about to say something.

Haplo gave him a swift poke in the ribs, and the Sartan fell meekly silent and began to conjure up more fish.

"You'll find food and supplies in that town," Haplo said, nodding back toward it. "Surely you saw that much while you were there."

"We are not thieves!" Edmund raised his chin proudly. "We will not take what is not ours. If our brethren in the city offer it freely, that will be different. We will work, we will pay them back."

"Some of our people think it is our 'brethren' who should be paying us back, My Liege." The new voice came from Baltazar. He stared with stern eyes at the magic being performed.

Quietly and without fuss, Haplo was replicating fish with his magic and handing it to those who crept near. Alfred was doing the same. A large crowd surrounded them. The necromancer said nothing until everyone had been fed and departed. Crossing his legs beneath the black robes, he seated himself and picked up a bit of the food.

He studied it carefully, as if he expected it to disappear in his hands the moment he touched it. "So you have not yet lost the art."

"Perhaps," said the prince, eyeing Alfred, "your land is different from ours. Perhaps there is hope for the world, after all. I tend to judge everything by what I see. Tell me that I have judged wrongly!"

Alfred couldn't lie, he couldn't tell the truth. He stared at them, opening and closing his mouth.

"It's a big universe," Haplo said easily. "Tell us about your part of it. What he said—your necromancer—about your brethren paying you back. What does that mean?"

"Be wary, Your Majesty," warned Baltazar. "Would you confide

in strangers? We have only their own words to trust that they are not
spies from Necropolis!"

"We have eaten their food, Baltazar." The prince smiled faintly.
"The least we can do in return is answer their questions. Besides,
what does it matter if they are spies? Let them take our story back to
Necropolis. We have nothing to hide.

"The realm of my people is . . . or was . . . up there." Edmund
glanced upward beyond the shadows of the cavern ceiling. "Far, far
up there . . ."

"On the surface of this world?" Haplo asked.

"No, no. That would be impossible. The surface of Abarrach is
either cold and barren rock or vast plains of ice shrouded by darkness. Baltazar has traveled to that realm. He can describe it better
than I."

"Abarrach means world of stone in our language as well as in
yours." Baltazar nodded at Haplo and Alfred. "And it is just that, at
least as far as the ancients—who had the time and talent to devote
themselves to study—were able to determine. Our world consists of
rock through which penetrate countless caverns and tunnels. Our
'sun' is the molten heart burning in Abarrach's core.

"The surface is as His Highness described it. It supports no life
nor any possibility of life. But, beneath the surface, where we had
our homes . . . ah, there the living was very pleasant. Very pleasant."
Baltazar sighed over his memories.

"The colossus—" he began.

"The what?" Alfred interrupted.

"Colossus. Don't you have them in your world?"

"He's not certain," said Haplo. "Tell us what you mean."

"Gigantic round columns of stone—"

"That support the cavern? We saw those outside."

"The Colossus do not support the cavern. Such support isn't
necessary. They were created by magical means by the ancients.
Their purpose was to transfer the heat energy from this part of the
world up to us. It worked. We had bountiful supplies of food, water.
Which makes what happened all the more inexplicable."

"And that was—"

"A drop in our birthrate. Every year the number of children being born to us decreased. In some ways, however, the phenomenon proved fortunate. Our most powerful wizards turned

their attention to the secrets of creating life. Instead, we discovered—"

"—the means of extending life past death!" Alfred exclaimed, voice quivering in shock and disapproval.

Fortunately, perhaps because of the language differences, Baltazar mistook shock for awe. He smiled, nodded complacently. "The addition of the dead to the population proved most beneficial. Keeping them alive *does* leech much of our magical power, but—in past days—we had little need for magic. The dead provided all physical labor. When we noticed that the magma river near our city was beginning to cool, we thought little of it. We continued to receive energy from below, heat traveled up through the colossus. The Little People mined the rock. They built our dwellings for us, and maintained the colossus—"

"Wait!" Haplo stopped Baltazar. "Little People? What Little People?"

The necromancer frowned, thinking back. "I don't know much about them. They are gone now."

"I recall hearing stories about the Little People from my father," Edmund said. "And I met them once. They loved more than anything to dig and delve in the rock. They coveted the minerals they found there, calling them such names as 'gold' and 'silver,' and brought forth jewels of rare and wondrous beauty—"

"Dwarves?" Alfred ventured at a guess.

"That word sounds strangely in my ears. Dwarves." Baltazar looked to the prince, who nodded thoughtfully in agreement. "We had another name for them, but that is near the mark. Dwarves."

"Two other races are believed to populate this world," Alfred continued, either ignoring or simply not seeing Haplo's attempts to stop the Sartan from saying too much. "Elves were one, humans another."

Neither Baltazar nor Edmund appeared to recognize the names.

"Mensch," suggested Haplo, using the term by which both Sartan and Patryns referred to the lesser races.

"Ah, mensch!" Baltazar brightened in recognition. He shrugged. "Reports exist in the writings of our grandfathers. Not that they ever saw any, but they heard of them from their fathers and their fathers before them. These mensch must have been extremely weak. Their races died out almost immediately after they came to Abarrach."

"You mean . . . no more remain on this world! But, they were left in your care." Alfred began in severe tones. "Surely you—"

This had gone far enough. Haplo whistled. The dog left off eating. Following its master's gesture, it trotted over and, plopping itself down beside Alfred, gleefully began to lick the man's face.

"Surely you—stop that! Nice doggie. Go . . . go away, nice doggie." Alfred attempted to shove the dog aside. The dog, thinking this was now a game, entered into the spirit of the contest. "Down! Sit! Nice doggie. No, please. Do go away! I—"

"You're right, necromancer," Haplo struck in coolly. "These mensch are weak. I know something of them and they couldn't have survived in a world such as this, a fact that some should have recognized before they brought them here. It sounds like you'd found the good life. What happened?"

Baltazar frowned, his tone dark. "Disaster. The blow didn't fall at once. It came on us gradually, and that made it worse, I think. Little things began to go wrong. Our water supply mysteriously began to dwindle away. The air grew colder, fouler; poisonous gases were seeping into our atmosphere. We used up more and more of our magic in efforts to protect ourselves from the poison, to reproduce water, to grow food. The Little People—those dwarves as you called them—succumbed. We could do nothing to help them, without endangering ourselves."

"But, your magic—" Alfred protested, having finally persuaded the dog to sit quietly at his side.

"Aren't you listening? Our magic was needed for ourselves! We were the strongest, the fittest, the best suited to survive. We did what we could for the . . . these dwarves, but in the end they died as the other mensch died before them. And then it became more important than ever for us to resurrect and maintain our dead."

Haplo shook his head in profound admiration. "A labor force that never needs rest, never eats the food or drinks the water, doesn't mind the cold, hardship. The perfect slave, the perfect soldier."

"Yes," agreed Baltazar, "without our dead, we living could not have managed."

"But don't you understand what you've done?" Alfred cried in earnest, agonized tones. "Don't you realize—"

"Dog!" Haplo ordered.

The animal jumped back to its feet, tongue lolling, tail wagging.

Alfred raised his hands in front of his face and, with a fearful glance at Haplo, fell silent.

"Certainly we realize," said the necromancer crisply. "We regained an art that was, according to the old records, lost to our people."

"Not lost. Not lost," Alfred said sorrowfully, but he said it beneath his breath. Haplo heard it through the ears of the dog.

"Of course, you must not think us idle in attempting to discover what was going wrong," Edmund added. "We investigated and came at last, and most reluctantly, to the conclusion that the colossus, which had once provided us life, were now responsible for depriving us of it. Warmth and fresh air had once flowed through the columns. Now our heat was being tapped and drawn off—"

"By the people in that city?" Haplo waved his hand in the direction of the buildings over which he'd flown. "That's what you suspect, isn't it?"

He barely listened to the answer. The subject didn't much interest him. He would have preferred to pursue the subject of necromancy, but didn't dare make his intense interest known, either to these men or to Alfred. Patience, he counseled.

"It was an accident. The people of Necropolis could have no way of knowing that they were harming us," Edmund was arguing warmly, his gaze going to the necromancer. Baltazar scowled, and Haplo recognized this as an old disagreement between them.

The necromancer—perhaps because there were strangers present—forebore offering an opinion contrary to that of his ruler. Haplo was about to attempt to turn the conversation back to the dead when a clatter and commotion in the cavern drew everyone's attention. Several cadavers—soldiers by the remnants and fragments of their uniforms—came running from the direction of the cavern's entrance.

The prince rose immediately to his feet, followed by the necromancer. Baltazar caught hold of the prince's arm, pointed. The corpse of the dead king came shuffling forward, also intent on interviewing the guards.

"I told Your Highness this would be a problem," Baltazar said in low tones.

Anger flushed the prince's pale skin. Edmund started to say something, bit off whatever hasty words he might have spoken.

"You were right and I was wrong," he said instead, after a frowning pause. "Are you pleased to hear me confess as much?"

"Your Highness misunderstands me," the necromancer said gently. "I didn't mean—"

"I know you didn't, My Friend." Edmund sighed wearily. Exhaustion drained the color from his thin cheeks. "Forgive me. Please excuse us," he had just the presence of mind to say to his guests, and walked hurriedly over to where the corpse of the king was conferring with the corpses of his subjects.

Haplo made a motion with his hand and the dog, unnoticed, trotted along behind the prince. The living in the cavern had fallen silent. Exchanging grim glances, they began hastily packing away what items they had brought out to aid them in their meager meal. But, when they could turn their attention from their work, their eyes fixed on their prince.

"It isn't honorable for you to spy on them like that, Haplo," Alfred said in a low voice. He glanced unhappily at the dog, standing at the prince's side.

Haplo didn't consider the comment worthy of response.

Alfred fidgeted nervously, toying with his bit of uneaten fish. "What are they saying?" he asked at last.

"Why should you care? It isn't honorable to spy on them," Haplo retorted. "Still, you might be interested to know that these dead, who are apparently scouts, report that an army has landed in the town."

"An army! What about the ship?"

"The runes will keep anyone from coming near it, let alone harming it. What should concern you more is that the army is marching this way."

"An army of the living?" Alfred asked in a low voice, seeming to dread the answer.

"No," Haplo said, watching Alfred closely. "An army of the dead."

Alfred groaned, covered his face with his hand.

Haplo leaned forward. "Listen, Sartan," he said urgently, softly. "I need some answers about this necromancy and I need them quick."

"What makes you think I know anything about it?" Alfred asked uneasily, keeping his eyes averted.

"Because of that handwringing and moaning and whining

you've been doing ever since you saw what was going on. What do you know about the dead?"

"I'm not certain I should tell you," Alfred said, lowering his bald head between hunched shoulders, the turtle ducking into its shell.

Haplo reached out, caught hold of the Sartan's wrist, and gave it a painful twist. "Because we're about to be caught in the middle of a war, Sartan! You're obviously incapable of defending yourself, which leaves your safety and mine up to me. Are you going to talk?"

Alfred grimaced in pain. "I'll . . . tell you what I know."

Haplo grunted in satisfaction, let loose of the man.

Alfred rubbed his bruised flesh. "The cadavers are alive, but only in the sense that they can move around and obey orders. They remember what they did in life, know nothing beyond."

"The king then . . ." Haplo paused, not quite understanding.

"Still thinks of himself as king," Alfred said, his gaze going to the cadaver, to the white head and hoary locks crowned with gold. "He's still trying to rule, because he thinks he is still the ruler. But, of course, he doesn't have any conception of the current situation. He doesn't know where he is, probably thinks he's back in his own homeland."

"But the dead soldiers know—"

"They know how to fight, because they remember what they were trained to do in life. And all a living commander has to do is point out an enemy."

"What are those spirit things that follow the cadavers around like their shadows? What do they have to do with the dead?"

"In a way, they *are* their shadows, the essence of what they were when they were alive. No one knows much about the phantasms, as they are called. Unlike the corpse, the phantasm seems to be aware of what is happening in the world, but it is powerless to act."

Alfred sighed, his gaze going from the dead king to Edmund. "Poor young man. Apparently he believed his father would somehow be different. Did you see the way the old man's phantasm fought against returning to this corrupt form of life? It was as if it knew—Oh, what have they done? What have they done?"

"Well, what *have* they done, Sartan?" Haplo demanded impatiently. "It seems to me that necromancy could have its advantages."

Alfred turned, regarded the Patryn with serious, grave intensity. "Yes, so we thought once, long ago. But we made a terrible discovery. The balance must be maintained. For every person brought back untimely to this life, another person—somewhere—untimely dies." He cast a despairing glance around the people huddled in the cavern. "It is possible, extremely possible, that these people have unwittingly been the doom of our entire race."

CHAPTER 16

SALFAG CAVERNS,

ABARRACH

♦

"Theoretical nonsense!" Haplo snorted in disgust. "You can't prove such a thing."

"Perhaps it already has been proven," Alfred replied.

Haplo rose to his feet, not intending to stay around and listen to any more of the Sartan's whimperings. So the dead had a few memory problems, a short attention span. Haplo considered that if he were in their position, he might not want to dwell on the present either. If he were in their position . . . would he want to be resurrected?

The thought brought him to a standstill. He pictured himself lying on the rock floor, the necromancer standing over him, his body rising . . .

Haplo shoved the question out of his mind, continued walking. He had more important matters to consider.

Maybe not, whispered a voice inside him. If you die on this world—and you very nearly died on two other worlds—then they'll do this to you!

The staring eyes that looked straight ahead into their past. The waxy, white flesh, the blue nails and lips, the lank, uncombed hair. Revulsion twisted his stomach. For an instant, he considered fleeing, running away.

Appalled, he got a grip on himself. What the hell's the matter with me? Running out! Running away! From what? A bunch of corpses!

"The Sartan's doings," he muttered angrily. "That sniveling coward's working on my imagination. If I were dead, I don't suppose it'd matter to me one way or the other." But his gaze shifted from the cadaver to the phantasms, those pathetic, shadowy forms always hovering near their bodies, within reach, yet unable to touch.

"Father, leave this to me," Edmund was talking to the cadaver with praiseworthy patience. "Stay with the people. I will go with the soldiers and see what this is all about."

"We're under attack from the people in the city? What city? I don't remember any city." The dead king sounded querulous, the hollow voice frustrated, confused.

"There isn't time to explain, Father!" The prince's patience was slipping. "Please, don't concern yourself. I will deal with it. The people. You stay with the people."

"Yes, the people." The cadaver caught hold of that, seemed to hang on tightly. "My people. They look to me for leadership. Yet what can I do? Our land is dying! We must leave it, search for somewhere new. My Son, do you hear me? We must leave our land!"

But Edmund was no longer paying attention. He left with the dead soldiers, hastening back through the cavern toward the entrance. The necromancer stayed behind to listen to the cadaver's rambling. The dog, having no instructions to the contrary, trotted along at the prince's heels.

Haplo hurried after the prince but, when he caught up with him, he saw tears glisten on Edmund's cheeks, saw the raw grief in the man's face. The Patryn fell back a pace, stopped to play with the dog, give the prince time to compose himself. Edmund halted, brushed the back of his hand hastily over his eyes, glanced around.

"What do you want?" he demanded, voice harsh.

"Came to get my dog," Haplo said. "He ran off after you before I could catch him. What's the problem?"

"There isn't time . . ." Edmund hurried on ahead again.

The dead soldiers moved swiftly, if clumsily. Walking was difficult for them. They had trouble guiding their steps or making changes in direction if they encountered an obstacle. Consequently, they blundered headlong into the cavern walls, careened off boulders, stumbled over rocks. But although they couldn't seem to comprehend obstacles, no obstacle stopped them. They trundled through red-hot magma pools without hesitation. The glowing lava burned off whatever clothes or armor they might have had left, turned the dead flesh into charred lumps. Nevertheless, the lumps kept on moving.

Haplo felt the revulsion rise in him again. He'd seen sights in the Labyrinth that would have driven most men insane, yet he was forced to harden what he had considered a will of iron in order to keep following along behind the gruesome army.

Edmund shot him a glance, as if the prince would like very much to tell this interloper to go away. Haplo kept his expression purposefully friendly, concerned.

"What did you say was going on?"

"An army from Necropolis has landed on the shores of the town," Edmund answered shortly. Something seemed to occur to him, for he continued, in a more conciliatory tone. "I'm sorry. You have a ship docked there, I believe you said."

Haplo started to reply that the runes on his ship would protect it, thought better of it. "Yeah, I'm worried about it. I'd like to see for myself."

"I'd ask the dead to check it for you, but they're unreliable in their reports. For all I know, they could be describing an enemy they fought ten years ago."

"Why do you use them as scouts, then?"

"Because we cannot spare the living."

So, what Alfred told me was true, Haplo thought. At least that much. And that brought another problem to mind. The Sartan . . . by himself. . . .

"Go back," Haplo ordered the dog. "Stay with Alfred."

The animal obediently did as it was told.

♦

Alfred was exceedingly miserable and almost welcomed the animal's return, although he knew very well it had been sent back by Haplo to spy on him. The dog flopped down beside him, gave the man's hand a swift lick with its tongue and nudged its head beneath his palm to encourage Alfred to scratch behind its ears.

The return of the necromancer was far less welcome. Baltazar was a hale and hearty man. His straight stance, commanding air, long black flowing robes emphasized his height, making him appear taller than he was. He had the ivory-hued skin of these people who had never known sunshine. His hair, unlike that of most Sartan, was so black as to be almost blue. His beard, squared-off about three inches beneath his jaw, glistened like the obsidian rock of his home-land. The black eyes were exceedingly intelligent, shrewd, and in-tent, stabbing whatever it was they looked at and holding it up to the light for further examination.

Baltazar turned those relentless eyes on Alfred, who felt their sharp blade enter and drain him dry.

"I am glad for this opportunity to talk with you alone," said Baltazar.

Alfred wasn't, not in the least, but he had lived much of his life in court and a polite rejoinder came automatically to his lips. "Is . . . is there going to be trouble?" he added, squirming beneath the gaze of the black eyes.

The necromancer smiled and informed Alfred—politely—that, if there was trouble, it was no concern of his.

This was a point Alfred might have argued, because he was among these people, but the Sartan wasn't very good at arguing and so he meekly kept quiet. The dog yawned and lay blinking at them sleepily.

Baltazar was silent. The living in the cave were silent, watching and waiting. The dead were silent, standing around at the back of the cavern, not waiting, because they had nothing for which to wait. They simply stood and would apparently keep standing until one of the living told them otherwise. The king's cadaver didn't seem to know what to do with itself. None of the living spoke to it, and it eventually drifted forlornly to the back of the cave to join its dead subjects in doing nothing.

"You don't approve of necromancy, do you?" Baltazar asked suddenly.

Alfred felt as if the magma flow had diverted course and gone up his legs and body directly to his face. "N—no, I don't."

"Then why didn't you come back for us? Why did you leave us stranded?"

"I—I don't know what you mean."

"Yes, you do." The fury in the necromancer's voice was all the more appalling because the anger was contained, the words spoken softly, for Alfred's ears alone.

Not quite alone. The dog was listening, too.

"Yes, you do. You are Sartan. You are one of us. And you did *not* come from this world."

Alfred was completely nonplussed, he had no idea what to say. He couldn't lie. Yet how he could tell the truth when, as far as he knew, he didn't know it?

Baltazar smiled, but it was a frightening smile, tight-lipped, and filled with a strange and sudden exultation. "I see the world from which you come, I see it in your words. A fat world, a world of light and pure air. And so the ancient legends are true! Our long search must be nearing an end!"

"Search for what?" Alfred asked desperately, hoping to change the subject. He did.

"The way back to those other worlds! The way out of this one!" Baltazar leaned near, his voice pitched low, tense and eager. "Death's Gate!"

Alfred couldn't breathe, he felt as if he were strangling.

"If—if you will excuse me," he stammered, trying to stand, trying to escape. "I . . . I'm not feeling well—"

Baltazar laid a restraining hand on Alfred's arm. "I can arrange for you to feel worse." He cast a glance at one of the cadavers.

Alfred gulped, gasped, and seemed to shrivel. The dog raised its head, growled, asking if the Sartan needed help.

Baltazar appeared startled at Alfred's reaction, the necromancer looked somewhat ashamed.

"I apologize. I shouldn't have threatened you. I am not an evil man. But," he added in a low, passionate voice, "I *am* a desperate one."

Alfred, trembling, sank back down onto the cavern floor. Reaching out an unsteady hand, he gave the dog a hesitant, reassuring pat. The animal lowered its head, resumed its quiet watch.

"That other man, the one with you, the one with the runes tattooed on his skin. What is he? He is not Sartan, not like you, not like me. But he is more like us than the others—the Little People." Baltazar picked up a small, sharp-edged stone, held it to the softly glowing light that filled the cavern. "This stone has two faces, each different, but both part of the same rock. You and I are one side, it seems. He is another. Yet all the same."

Baltazar's black eyes pinned the struggling Alfred to the wall. "Tell me! Tell me about him! Tell me the truth about yourself! Did you come through Death's Gate? Where is it?"

"I can't tell you about Haplo," Alfred answered faintly. "Another man's story is his to tell or to keep hidden, as he chooses." The

Sartan was beginning to panic, decided that he could find refuge in the truth, even if it was only partial truth. "As to how I came here, it . . . was an accident! I didn't mean to."

The necromancer's black eyes bored into him, turned their sharp blade this way and that, probing and piercing. Finally, grunting, he withdrew his gaze. Brooding, Baltazar sat staring at the location on the rock floor where the dead had lately rested.

"You are not lying," he said finally. "You cannot lie, you are not capable of deceit. But you're not telling the truth, either. How can such a dichotomy exist within you?"

"Because I don't know the truth. I don't fully understand it and, therefore, in speaking of the small portion I see only very imperfectly, I might do irreparable harm. It is better if I keep what I know to myself."

Baltazar's black eyes blazed with anger, reflected the yellow firelight. Alfred faced him, steadfast and calm, blanching only slightly. It was the necromancer who broke off the attack, his frustrated rage dwindling to a heavy sorrow.

"It is said that such virtue was once ours. It is said that the very notion of one of our own kind shedding the blood of another was so impossible to conceive that no words existed in our language to speak of it. Well, we have those words now: murder, war, deceit, treachery, trickery, death. Yes, death."

Baltazar rose to his feet. His voice cracked, its hot rage cooled and hardened, like molten rock that has flowed into a pool of chill water. "You will tell me what you know about Death's Gate. And if you won't tell me with your living voice, then you'll tell me with the voice of the dead!" Half-turning, he pointed at the cadavers. "They never forget where they have been, what they have done. They forget only the reasons why they did them! And thus they are quite willing to do them again . . . and again . . . and again."

The necromancer glided away, striding down the tunnel after his prince. Alfred, stricken dumb, gazed after him, too horrified to be able to say a word.

CHAPTER 17

SALFAG CAVERNS,

ABARRACH

♦

"I KNEW I SHOULD NEVER HAVE LEFT THAT WEAKLING ON HIS OWN!" Haplo fumed to himself when Alfred's stammering and confused denials came to his ears through those of the dog. The Patryn almost turned around, returned to try to salvage the situation. He realized, however, that by the time he made his way back through the cavern, the worst of the damage would already be done and so he kept going, following the prince and his army of cadavers to the cavern's end.

By the conclusion of the conversation between Baltazar and Alfred, Haplo'd been glad he'd kept out of it. Now he knew exactly what the necromancer planned. And if Baltazar wanted to take a little trip back through Death's Gate, Haplo would be more than pleased to arrange it. Of course, Alfred would never permit it, but—at this point—Alfred had become expendable. A Sartan necromancer was worth far more than a sniveling Sartan moralist.

There were problems. Baltazar was a Sartan and, as such, inherently good. He could threaten murder, but that was because he was desperate, intensely loyal to his people, to his prince. It was unlikely that he would leave his people, abandon his prince, go off on his own. Haplo's lord would most certainly take a dim view of an army of Sartan marching through Death's Gate and into the Nexus! Still, the Patryn reflected, these snarls in the skein could be worked out.

"The enemy." The prince, slightly ahead of Haplo, came to a halt.

They had reached the end of the cavern. Standing concealed in the shadows, they could see the approaching force—a ragged, tattered army of corpses, shuffling and shambling in what they remembered as military formation. Several of the enemy in the forward ranks had already encountered the prince's troops and skirmishes were occurring on the field.

It was the strangest battle Haplo had ever seen. The dead fought using skills they remembered having used in life, giving and taking sword blows, parrying and thrusting, each obviously intent on killing their opponent. But whether they were fighting this particular enemy or one they had fought years past was open to debate.

One dead soldier parried a thrust his opponent never delivered. Another took a sword through the chest without bothering to defend itself. Blows were dealt in a deliberate, if aimless manner, and were sometimes blocked, and sometimes not. Sword blades wielded by dead hands sank deep into dead flesh that never felt it. The cadavers wrenched the blade free and kept at it, striking each other again and again, doing significant damage but never making much headway.

The battle between the dead might have gone on indefinitely had the strength of both sides been equal. The army from Necropolis was, however, in a far more advanced state of corruption and decay than the prince's army. These dead appeared less well cared for than the prince's dead, if such a thing could be said.

The flesh of the cadavers had, in many instances, fallen from the bones. Each had suffered numerous injuries, most—it appeared—after their deaths. Many of the dead soldiers were missing various parts of their bodies—a bone gone here and there, perhaps a part of an arm or a piece of a leg. Their armor was badly rusted, the leather straps that held it together had almost all rotted away, leaving breastplates dangling by a thread, leg protectors falling down around the cadaver's ankles, often tripping them up.

The corpses made mindless attempts to march over or through obstacles and were constantly impeded by their own falling accoutrements. Thus the army of dead appeared to spend more time tumbling over itself than it did advancing. Those that were fighting were being battered into shapeless heaps of bones and armor over which their phantasms wavered and twisted with pleading, outstretched wisps of arms. It might have been a comic sight, if it hadn't been horrific.

Haplo started to laugh, felt—by the clenching of his stomach—that, if he did so, he might retch.

"Old dead," said the prince, watching them.

"What?" Haplo asked. "What do you mean?"

"Necropolis is using their old dead, the dead of generations past." Edmund motioned to the dead captain of his army. "Send one of your men to fetch Baltazar. You can always tell the old dead." The prince, speaking offhandedly, turned back to Haplo. "The necromancers weren't so skilled in their art. They lacked the knowledge of how to keep the flesh from decaying, of how to maintain the cadavers."

"Do your dead always fight your wars?"

"For the most part they do, now that we have built up substantial armies. Once, the living fought wars." Edmund shook his head. "A tragic waste. But that was many years ago, long before I was born. Necropolis sent the old dead. I wonder," he continued, frowning, "what this means."

"What could it mean?"

"It could be a feint, an attempt to draw us out, force us to reveal our true strength. That's what Baltazar would say," the prince added, smiling. "But it could also be a sign from the people of Necropolis that they don't mean us serious harm. As you can see, our new dead could defeat this lot with ease. I believe Necropolis wants to negotiate."

Edmund gazed ahead, eyes squinting against the bright red glow of the magma sea. "There must be living among them. Yes, I see them. Marching at the rear."

Two black-robed and cowled necromancers walked some distance behind their shabby army, well out of range of spear throw. Haplo was startled to note the presence of living wizards, but realized, on observation, that the necromancers were required not only to lead the army and maintain the magic that held the crumbling bodies together, but also to act as macabre shepherds.

More than once, a corpse came to a standstill, ceased to fight, or sometimes one would fall down and not get back up. The necromancers hastened into their flock, prodding and commanding, urging them forward. When a cadaver fell down, it might, on standing, face the wrong direction and head off on some erratic course directed by its faulty memory. The necromancer, like a conscientious sheepdog, raced after it, turned the dead soldier around, forced it to once more join the fray.

Edmund's dead, which Haplo supposed could be called the "new dead," did not appear subject to these failings. The small skirmishing force fought well, reducing enemy numbers by literally battering the old dead into the ground. The larger portion of the army remained grouped behind their prince in the cavern opening, a skilled army awaiting command. Edmund's only precaution was to continually remind the dead captain of its orders. At each reminder, the captain would nod its head alertly, as if receiving such instructions for the first time. Haplo wondered if the prince's messenger would remember the message by the time it reached Baltazar.

Edmund stirred restlessly. Suddenly, giving way to impulse, he leapt up on a boulder, showing himself to the advancing army. "Hold!" he cried, raising his hand up, palm outward, in a gesture of parley.

"Halt!" cried the enemy necromancers, and both armies, after a moment of confusion, lurched to a stumbling standstill. The necromancers remained stationed behind their troops, able to see and hear, but still protected by their dead.

"Why do you march on my people?" Edmund demanded.

"Why did your people attack the citizens of Safe Harbor?" It was a female who spoke, her voice ringing clear and strong through the sulfurous air.

"Our people did not attack," the prince countered. "We came to the town seeking to buy supplies and were set on—"

"You came armed!" the woman interrupted coldly.

"Of course, we came armed! We have passed through perilous lands. We have been attacked by a fire dragon since we left our homeland. Your people attacked us without provocation! Naturally, we defended ourselves, but we meant them no harm and, as proof, you can see that we left the town with all its wealth safe and untouched, although my people are starving."

The two necromancers conferred together in low voices. The prince remained standing—a proud and lordly figure—on the black rock.

"What you say is true. We saw that much for ourselves," said the other necromancer, a male. He walked forward, moving around the army's right flank, leaving the female at the rear. The wizard lowered his cowl, showing his face. He was young, younger than the prince, with a smooth-shaven jaw, large green eyes, and the long chestnut-colored hair of the Sartan, the white tips curling on his shoulders. His mien was serious and grave and fearless as he advanced on his enemy. "Will you talk with us more?"

"I will, and welcome," said Edmund, starting to jump down from his rock.

The young necromancer held up a warding hand. "No, please. We would not take unfair advantage of you. Have you a minister of the dead who can accompany you?"

"My necromancer is coming now, as we speak," said Edmund, bowing at this show of courtesy. Haplo, glancing back into the cavern, saw the black-robed figure of Baltazar hastening in their direction. Either the cadaver had remembered its message or the necromancer had decided he should be on hand and had already started this way. And there, stumbling along behind him, as clumsy as a cadaver himself, was Alfred, accompanied by the faithful dog.

While waiting for Baltazar to catch up with them, Edmund marshaled his army, permitting enough of his troop strength to be seen to make an impression on the enemy, yet not enough to give away their true numbers. The enemy necromancer waited patiently at the head of his own army. If he was at all impressed with Edmund's show of force, the youthful face didn't reveal it.

The female necromancer kept her face covered, her cowl pulled low over her head. Attracted by the sound of the rich, smooth voice, Haplo was extremely curious to see her features. But she stood unmoving as the rocks around her. Occasionally, he heard her voice, chanting the runes that kept the dead functional.

Baltazar, breathing heavily from the exertion, joined the prince and the two moved out of the tunnel to the neutral territory in front of each army. The young necromancer advanced in his turn, meeting them halfway. Haplo sent the dog trotting after the prince. The Patryn leaned back against a wall, settled himself comfortably.

Alfred, huffing and puffing, tumbled into him. "Did you hear what Baltazar said to me? He knows about Death's Gate!"

"Shhh!" ordered Haplo irritably. "Keep your voice down or everyone in this blasted place will know about Death's Gate! Yes, I heard him. And, if he wants to go, I'll take him."

Alfred stared, aghast. "You can't mean that!"

Haplo kept his eyes fixed on the negotiators, disdained to answer.

"I understand!" Alfred said, voice trembling. "You want . . . this knowledge!" The Sartan pointed a finger at the rows of cadavers lined up in front of them.

"Damn right."

"You will bring doom on us all! You will destroy everything we created!"

"No!" Haplo said, shifting suddenly, jabbing his words into Alfred's breast with his finger. "*You* Sartan destroyed everything! We Patryns will return it to what it was! Now shut up, and let me listen."

"I'll stop you!" Alfred stated, bravely defiant. "I won't let you do this. I—" Loose gravel gave way beneath his foot. He slid, slipped. His hands scrabbled frantically in the air, but there was nothing to hold onto and he landed on the hard rock floor with a thud.

Haplo glanced down at the balding middle-aged man who lay in a pathetic heap at his feet. "Yeah, you do that," the Patryn said, grinning. "You stop me." Lounging against the wall, he turned his attention to the parley.

"What is it you want of us?" the young necromancer was asking, once the formalities of introduction had been effected.

The prince recited his story, telling it well, with dignity and pride. He made no accusations against the people of Kairn Necros but took care to attribute the wrongs his own people had suffered to mischance or ignorance of the true situation.

The Sartan language, even in its corrupt form, is adept at conjuring up images in the mind. By his expression, it was obvious that the young necromancer saw far beneath the surface of Edmund's words. The young man attempted to keep his face impassive, but a flutter of doubt and self-conscious guilt brought a crease to the smooth forehead and a slight tremor to the lips. He glanced swiftly at the female standing motionless at the rear of the army, inviting her help.

The woman, understanding, glided forward and arrived in time to hear the end of the prince's tale.

Removing the cowl from her head with a graceful motion of two fair hands, the woman turned a soft-eyed gaze on Edmund. "Truly, you have suffered much. I am sorry for you and for your people."

The prince bowed. "Your compassion does you honor, mistress—"

"Madam," she corrected him, glancing, with a smile, at the necromancer standing beside her. "My public name[1] is Jera. This man is my husband, Jonathan of the ducal House of Rift Ridge."

---

[1] Sartan have two names, private and public. As Alfred told Haplo previously in the story, a Sartan's private name can give those who know it power over them. A Sartan's private name, therefore, would be revealed only to those he or she loved and trusted.

"My Lord Jonathan, you are blessed in your wife," said Edmund with courtesy. "And you, Your Grace, in your husband."

"Thank you, Your Highness. Your story is indeed a sorrowful one," Jera continued. "And I fear that my people are, in many ways, responsible for your misfortune—"

"I spoke no word of blame," said Edmund.

"No, Your Highness." The woman smiled. "But it is all too easy to see accusation in the images your words conjure. I do not believe, however"—a frown creased the marble-smooth forehead—"that the dynast will take kindly to his subjects coming to him as beggars—"

Edmund drew himself up tall and straight. Baltazar, who had previously said no word, glowered dourly, black brows drawn tight, black eyes reflecting the lurid red of the magma sea.

"Dynast!" Baltazar repeated incredulously. "What dynast? And to whom do you refer as subjects? We are an independent monarchy—"

"Peace, Baltazar." Edmund laid his hand on the wizard's arm. "Your Grace, we do not come to beg of our *brethren*." He emphasized the word. "Among our dead we number farmers, skilled artisans, warriors. We ask only to be given the chance to work, to earn our bread and shelter in your city."

The woman stared at him. "Truly, you didn't know you were under the jurisdiction of Our Most Holy Dynastic Majesty?"

"Your Grace"—Edmund appeared embarrassed at being forced to contradict—"I am the ruler of my people, their only ruler—"

"But, then, of course!" Jera clasped her hands together, her expression bright and eager. "That explains everything. It's all a dreadful misunderstanding! You must come immediately to the capital, Your Highness, and make your obeisance to His Majesty. My husband and I will be honored to escort you and give you introduction."

"Obeisance!" Baltazar's black beard stood out against his livid complexion. "It is rather for this self-proclaimed dynast—"

"I thank you for your gracious invitation, Duchess Jera." Edmund's hand clasped his minister's arm with slightly more pressure than must have been exactly comfortable. "The honor in accompanying you is mine. I cannot leave my people, however, with a hostile army camped before them."

"We will withdraw our army," offered the duke, "if you pledge your word that your army will not sail across the sea."

"Since my army has no ships, such a feat is impossible, Your Grace."

"Begging Your Highness's pardon, a ship is docked at Safe Harbor. We have never seen its like before and we assumed that it—"

"Ah, now I understand!" Edmund nodded, glanced back at Haplo and Alfred. "You saw the ship and thought we intended to sail our army across the sea. As you mentioned, Your Grace, there is much misunderstanding among us. The ship belongs to two strangers, who landed at Safe Harbor just this cycle. We were pleased to entertain them with what hospitality we could, although," the prince added, flushing, pride vying with shame, "they gave us more than we could offer them."

Alfred clambered to his feet. Haplo stood straight. The duchess turned to them. Her face, although not beautiful by any purity or regularity of feature, was made attractive by an expression of singular intelligence and an obviously strong and resolute will. The eyes, a green-flecked brown, were exceedingly fine, reflecting the quickness of the mind that moved behind them. Her gaze flicked over the two strangers and Jera immediately picked out Haplo as the ship's owner.

"We passed your vessel, sir, and found it extremely interesting—"

"What type of runes are those?" her husband interjected with boyish eagerness. "I've never seen—"

"My dear," his wife interposed gently, "this is hardly the time or place for discussions of rune-lore. Prince Edmund will want to inform his people of the honor that awaits him in being presented to His Dynastic Majesty. We will meet you in Safe Harbor, Your Highness, at your convenience." Jera's green eyes focused on Haplo and, behind him, Alfred. "It would be our honor, as well, to introduce these strangers to our fair city."

Haplo regarded the woman thoughtfully. This prince hadn't known him for the ancient enemy, but the Patryn had come to realize, by this conversation, that Edmund's people were nothing more than a small satellite circling a larger and brighter sun. A sun that might be much better informed.

I could leave now and no one would ever blame me, not even My

Lord. But he and I both would always know that I turned tail and ran.

The Patryn bowed. "It is we who would be honored, Your Grace."

Smiling at him, Jera glanced back at the prince. "We will send word ahead of your coming, Your Highness, in order that all may be in readiness to receive you."

"You are most kind, Your Grace," Edmund replied.

Everyone made final polite bows, then the group separated. The duke and duchess returned to their dead army, herded them together (several had wandered away during the talks), prodded them into formation, and headed them back toward Safe Harbor.

Baltazar and the prince reentered the cavern. "A dynast," the necromancer was saying in grim tones. "The people of the sovereign nation of Kairn Telest are nothing but his subjects! Tell me now, Edmund, that the inhabitants of Necropolis brought disaster to us in ignorance!"

The prince was obviously troubled. His eyes went to the far distant city, barely visible beneath the mass of clouds hanging low over it. "What can I do, Baltazar? What can I do for our people if I don't go?"

"I'll tell you, Your Highness! These two"—the necromancer gestured at Haplo and Alfred—"know the location of Death's Gate. These two came through it!"

The prince gazed at them with wondering, astonished eyes. "Death's Gate? Did you? Is it possible that—"

Haplo shook his head. "It wouldn't work, Your Highness. It's a long, long way from here. You'd need ships, a lot of ships, to transport your people."

"Ships!" Edmund smiled sadly. "We have no food, and you talk of ships. Tell me," he added, after a pause. "Do the city people know about . . . Death's Gate?"

"How should I know, Your Highness?" Haplo answered, shrugging.

"*If* he's telling the truth," hissed Baltazar. "And we *can* get ships! They have ships!" He nodded his head toward Necropolis.

"And how will we pay for them, Baltazar?"

"Pay, Your Highness! Haven't we paid already? Haven't we paid with our lives?" the necromancer demanded, fist clenched. "I say it's time we take what we want! Don't go crawling to them, Edmund! Lead us to them! Lead us to war!"

"No! They"—the prince gestured to the departing duke and duchess—"were sympathetic to us. We have no reason to believe the dynast will be less eager to listen and to understand. I will try peaceful means first."

" 'We,' Your Highness. I'm going with you, of course—"

"No." Edmund took the necromancer by the hand. "You stay with the people. If anything happens to me, you will be their leader."

"At last your heart speaks, Your Highness." Baltazar was bitter, sorrowful.

"I truly believe all will be well. But I would be a poor ruler if I did not provide for contingencies." Edmund continued to press the man's hand. "I may rely on you, My Friend? More than friend, mentor . . . my other father?"

"You may rely on me, Your Highness." The last part of the necromancer's sentence was little more than a choked whisper.

Edmund walked back to confer with his people. Baltazar remained behind a moment in the shadows to compose himself.

When the prince was gone, the necromancer raised his head. Ravages of a terrible, heart-wrenching grief had aged the pallid face. The stabbing black-eyed gaze struck Alfred, passed through the trembling body of the Sartan, and bored into Haplo.

I am not an evil man. But I am a desperate one. Haplo heard the necromancer's words echo in the fire-lighted darkness.

"Yes, My Prince," Baltazar promised fervently, softly. "You may rely fully on me. Our people will be safe!"

CHAPTER • 18

NECROPOLIS,

ABARRACH

•

"A MESSAGE, YOUR MAJESTY, FROM JONATHAN, THE DUKE OF RIFT Ridge."

"Duke of Rift Ridge? Isn't he dead?"

"The younger, Your Majesty. You recall, Sire, that you sent him and his wife to deal with those invaders on the far shore—"

"Ah, yes. Quite." The dynast frowned. "This is in regard to the invaders?"

"Yes, Your Majesty."

"Clear the court," the dynast commanded.

The Lord High Chancellor, knowing that this matter would be dealt with circumspectly, had deliberately spoken in low tones, intended for His Majesty's ears alone. The order to clear the court came as no surprise, nor did it present difficulty. The Lord High Chancellor had only to meet the eyes of the ever-watchful chamberlain to have the matter accomplished.

A staff banged on the floor. "His Majesty's audience is ended," announced the chamberlain.

Those with petitions to present rolled their scrolls up with a snap, tucked them back into scroll cases, made their bows, and backed out of the throne room. Those who were merely court hangers-on, who spent as much time near His Dynastic Majesty as possible, hoping for notice from the royal eye, yawned, stretched, and proposed to each other games of rune-bone to ease them through another boring day. The royal cadavers, extremely well preserved and well maintained, escorted the assembly out of the throne room into the vast corridors of the royal palace, shut the doors, and took up positions before them, indicating that His Majesty was in private conference.

When the throne room no longer buzzed with conversation and affected laughter, the dynast commanded, with a wave of his hand, that the Lord High Chancellor was to commence. The Lord High Chancellor did so. Opening a scroll, he began to read.

"His Grace's most reverent respect—"

"Skip all that."

"Yes, Your Majesty."

It took some moments for the Lord High Chancellor to make his way through compliments showered on the dynast's person, compliments showered on his illustrious ancestors, compliments showered on the dynast's just rule, and so forth and so on. The chancellor finally found the heart of the message and delivered it.

" 'The invaders come from the outer circle, Your Majesty, a land known as Kairn Telest, the Green Caverns, due to the . . . er . . . former amount of vegetation grown in that region. Of late, it seems, this region has experienced bad fortune. The magma river has cooled, the people's water source has dried up.' The Green Caverns, it seems, Your Majesty," the Lord High Chancellor added, looking up from his perusal of the message, "could now be called the Bone-Bare[1] Caverns."

His Majesty said nothing, merely grunted in acknowledgment of the Lord High Chancellor's wit. The Lord High Chancellor resumed his reading. " 'Due to this disaster, the people of Kairn Telest have been forced to flee their land. They have encountered innumerable perils on the journey, including—' "

"Yes, yes," said the dynast impatiently. He fixed his Lord High Chancellor with a shrewd look. "Does the duke mention why these people of the Green Caverns felt it necessary to come *here*?"

The Lord High Chancellor hastily scanned the message to the end, read it over again to make certain he'd made no mistake—the dynast had a low tolerance for mistakes—then shook his head. "No, Your Majesty. It might almost seem, from the tone, that these people stumbled on Necropolis by accident."

---

[1] A reference to a move in the game of rune-bone in which an opponent is stripped clean of all his runes. The game of rune-bone is vaguely similar in nature to a game known anciently (pre-Sundering) as *mah-jongg*.

"Hah!" The dynast's lips parted in a thin, cunning smile. He shook his head. "They know, Pons. They know! Well, go on. Give us the gist of it. What are their demands?"

"They make no demands, Your Majesty. Their leader, a Prince"— the Lord High Chancellor referred again to the paper to refresh his memory—"Edmund of some unknown house requests the opportunity to pay his respects to Your Dynastic Majesty. The duke adds in a concluding note that the people of Kairn Telest appear to be in a most wretched state. It has occurred to the duke that it is probable we are in some way responsible for the aforesaid disasters and he hopes Your Majesty will meet with the prince at your earliest opportunity."

"Is this young duke of Rift Ridge dangerous, Pons? Or is the man merely stupid?"

The Lord High Chancellor paused to consider the question. "I don't consider him dangerous, Your Majesty. Nor is he stupid. He is young, idealistic, ingenuous. A touch naive as concerns politics. He is, after all, the younger son and was not raised to have the responsibilities of the dukedom thrust on him so suddenly. Words come from the heart, not his head. I am certain he has no idea what he is saying."

"His wife, though, is another matter."

The Lord High Chancellor appeared grave. "I am afraid so, Your Majesty. Duchess Jera is extremely intelligent."

"And her father, deuce take him, continues to be a confounded nuisance."

"But that is all he is these cycles, Sire. Banishing him to the Old Provinces was a stroke of genius. The earl must do everything in his power merely to survive. He is too weak to cause trouble."

"A stroke of genius for which we have you to thank, Pons. Oh, yes, we remember. You needn't keep reminding us of it. And that old man may be struggling to survive but he has enough breath left in him to continue to speak out against us."

"But who is listening? Your subjects are loyal. They love Your Majesty . . ."

"Stop it, Pons. We get enough of that muck shoveled over our feet from everyone else around here. We expect some sense from you."

The Lord High Chancellor bowed, grateful for the dynast's good opinion; knowing, however, that the flower of royalty would cease to grow unless it was nurtured by the aforementioned muck.

The dynast had withdrawn his attention from his minister. Rising from the throne made of gold and diamonds and the other precious minerals that were so abundant in this world, His Majesty took a turn or two around the large gold-and-silver-inlaid dais. Pacing was a habit of the dynast's; he claimed that movement aided his thought processes. Often the dynast completely discomfited those presenting suits to him by leaping up from the throne and circling it several times before returning to it to pronounce judgment.

At least it kept the courtiers on their toes, Pons reflected with some amusement. Whenever His Majesty rose to his feet, everyone in the court was expected to cease conversation and perform the ritual, reverent obeisance. Courtiers were forever called on to cease their conversation, fold their hands in their sleeves, and bow with heads practically to the floor whenever His Majesty took it into his head to walk out a problem.

Pacing was just one of the dynast's many little eccentricities, the most notable of these being a love of tournament combat and an addiction to the game of rune-bone. Any of the new dead who had been at all proficient in either game during their lives were brought to the palace, where they performed no other service except to offer His Majesty sparring partners during the waking half of the cycle or play at rune-bone with His Majesty far into the sleeping half. Such peculiarities led many to misjudge the dynast, considering him nothing but a shallow-minded gamester. Pons, having seen those many fall, was not among them. His respect for and his fear of His Dynastic Majesty were both deep and well founded.

Pons waited, therefore, in respectful silence for His Majesty to deign to notice him. The matter was obviously serious. The dynast devoted five complete revolutions around the dais to it, his head bowed, hands clasped behind his back.

In his mid-fifties, Kleitus XIV was a well-formed, muscular man of striking appearance whose beauty, when young, had been highly praised in poetry and song. He had aged well and would, as the saying went, make a handsome corpse. A powerful necromancer himself, he had many long years left to stave off that fate.

At last His Majesty ceased his heavy tread. His black fur robes, treated with purple dye to imbue them with the royal hue, rustled softly as he once again settled himself into his throne.

"Death's Gate," he muttered, tapping a ring on the arm of the throne. Gold against gold, it gave out a musical, metallic note. "That's the reason."

"Perhaps Your Majesty worries needlessly. As the duke writes, they could have come here by chance—"

"Chance! Next you will be talking of 'luck,' Pons. You sound like an inept rune-bone player. Strategy, tactics—that's what wins the game. No, you mark our words. They have come here in search of Death's Gate, like so many others before them."

"Let them go, then, Majesty. We have dealt with such madmen before. Good riddance to bad rubbish—"

Kleitus frowned, shook his head. "Not this time. Not these people. We dare not."

The Lord High Chancellor hesitated to ask the next question, not truly certain he wanted to know the answer. But he knew what was expected of him, the echo chamber for his ruler's thoughts. "Why not, Sire?"

"Because these people are not insane. Because . . . Death's Gate has opened, Pons. It has opened and we have seen beyond!"

The Lord High Chancellor had never heard his dynast speak like this, had never heard that crisp and confident voice lowered, awed, even . . . fearful. Pons shivered, as if he felt the first flush of a virulent fever.

Kleitus was staring far off, staring through the thick granite walls of the palace, gazing at a place the Lord High Chancellor could neither see nor even imagine.

"It happened early in the waking hour, Pons. You know that we are a light sleeper. We woke suddenly, startled by a sound that, when we were truly awake, we couldn't place. It was like a door opening . . . or shutting. We sat up and drew aside the bed curtains, thinking there might be some emergency. But we were alone. No one had entered the room.

"The impression that we had heard a door was so powerful, that we lighted the lamp beside the bed and started to call for the guard. We remember. We had one hand on the bed curtain and we were just drawing the other back from lighting the lamp when everything around us . . . rippled."

"Rippled, Your Majesty?" Pons frowned.

"We know, we know. It sounds incredible." Kleitus glanced at his chancellor, smiled ruefully. "We know of no other way to describe it. Everything around us lost shape and substance, dimension. It was as if ourselves and the bed and the curtains and the lamp and the table were suddenly nothing but oil spread over still water. The ripple bent us, bent the floor, the bed, the table. And in an instant, it was gone."

"A dream, Your Majesty. You were not yet awake . . ."

"So we might have supposed. But in that instant, Pons, this is what we saw."

The dynast was a powerful wizard among the Sartan. When he spoke, his words brought sudden images to the mind of his minister. The images flashed past so swiftly that Pons was confused, dazzled. He saw none clearly, but had a dizzying impression of objects whirling about him, similar to an experience in childhood when his mother had been wont to take him by the hands and twirl him around and around in a playful dance.

Pons saw a gigantic machine, whose metal parts were fashioned after the parts of a human body and which was working with frantic intensity at nothing. He saw a human woman with black skin and an elven prince waging war against the prince's own kind. He saw a race of dwarves, led by one in spectacles, rising up against tyranny. He saw a sun-drenched green world and a beautiful shining city, empty, devoid of life. He saw huge creatures, horrible, eyeless, rampaging through a countryside, murdering all who came in their path and he heard them cry, "Where are the citadels?" He saw a race of people, grim, frightening in their hatred and anger, a race with runes traced on their skin. He saw dragons . . .

♦

"There, Pons. You understand?" Kleitus sighed again, half in awe, half in frustration.

"No, Your Majesty!" the chancellor gasped, stammered. "I do not understand! What—where—how long—"

"We know nothing more about these visions than you do. They came to us too fast and when we tried to lay hold of one, it slipped away, like the laze through our fingers. But what we are seeing, Pons, are other worlds! Worlds beyond Death's Gate, as the ancient texts write. We are certain of it! The people must not come to know this, Pons. Not until we are ready."

"No, of course not, Sire."

The dynast's face was grave, his expression hard, resolute. "This realm is dying. We have leeched off other realms to maintain it—"

We have decimated other realms to maintain it, Pons corrected, but only in his own thoughts.

"We've kept the truth from the people for their own good, of course. Otherwise there would be panic, chaos, anarchy. And now comes this prince and his people—"

"—and the truth," said Pons.

"Yes," agreed the dynast. "And the truth."

"Your Majesty, if I may speak freely—"

"Since when, Pons, do you do anything else?"

"Yes, Sire." The Lord High Chancellor smiled faintly. "What if we were to allow these wretched people admittance, establish them—say—in the Old Provinces. The land is almost completely worthless to us now that the Fire Sea has retreated."

"And have these people spread their tales of a dying world? Those who think the earl a doddering old fool would suddenly begin to take him seriously."

"The earl could be handled—" The Lord High Chancellor emitted a delicate cough.

"Yes, but there are more like him. Add to their numbers a prince of Kairn Telest, talking of his cold and barren realm, and his search for a way out, and you will destroy us all. Anarchy, riots! Is that what you want, Pons?"

"By the ash, no!" The Lord High Chancellor shuddered.

"Then quit prattling nonsense. We will portray these invaders as a threat and declare war against them. Wars always unite the people. We need time, Pons! Time! Time to find Death's Gate ourselves, as the prophecy foretold."

"Majesty!" Pons gasped. "You! The prophecy. You?—"

"Of course, Chancellor," Kleitus snapped, appearing slightly put out. "Was there ever any doubt in your mind?"

"No, certainly not, Your Majesty." Pons bowed, thankful for the chance to conceal his face until he could rearrange his features, banish astonishment and replace it with abiding faith. "I am overwhelmed by the suddenness of . . . of everything, too much happening at once." This, at least, was true enough.

"When the time is right, we will lead the people forth from this world of darkness to one of light. We have fulfilled the first part of the prophecy—"

Yes, and so has every necromancer in Abarrach, thought Pons.

"It remains now for us to fulfill the rest," Kleitus continued.

"And can you, Your Majesty?" asked his chancellor, obediently taking his cue from the dynast's slightly raised eyebrow.

"Yes," answered Kleitus.

This astonished even Pons. "Sire! You know the location of Death's Gate?"

"Yes, Pons. At long last, my studies have provided me with the answer. Now you understand why this prince and his ragtag followers, arriving at precisely this moment, are such a nuisance."

A threat, Pons translated. For if you could discover the secret of Death's Gate from the ancient writings, then so could others. The "ripple" you experienced did not enlighten you so much as terrify you. Someone may have beat you to it. *That* is the real reason this prince and his people must be destroyed.

"I stand humbled before your genius, Majesty." The chancellor bowed low.

Pons was, for the most part, sincere. If he had doubts, it was only because he had never quite taken the prophecy seriously. He hadn't even truly believed in it. Obviously, Kleitus did. Not only believed in it, but had gone about fulfilling it! Had he actually discovered Death's Gate? Pons might have been dubious, except for the sight of those fantastic images. The visions had sent a thrill through the chancellor's mind and body as nothing else had done these past forty years. Recalling what he'd seen, he felt, for a moment, quite wild with excitement and was forced to discipline himself severely, wrench himself back from bright and hopeful worlds to the dark and dreary business at hand.

"Your Majesty, how are we to start this war? It is obvious the Kairn Telest do not want to fight—"

"They will fight, Pons," said the dynast, "when they find out that we have executed their prince."

CHAPTER ♦ 19

FIRE SEA,

ABARRACH

♦

Prince edmund told his people where he was going and why. They listened in unhappy silence, afraid of losing their prince, yet knowing that there was no other way.

"Baltazar will be your leader in my absence," Edmund announced simply, at the end. "Follow him, obey him as you would me."

He left amid silence. Not one found words to call out a blessing to him. Although in their hearts they feared for him, they feared a terrible, bitter death even more and so they let him go in silence, choked by their own guilt.

Baltazar accompanied the prince back to the end of the cavern, arguing all the way that Edmund should at least take bodyguards— the most stalwart of the new dead—into Necropolis. The prince refused.

"We come to our brethren in peace. Bodyguards imply mistrust."

"Call it a guard of honor then," Baltazar urged. "It is not right that Your Highness goes unattended. You will look like . . . like . . ."

"Like what I am," Edmund said in grim tones. "A pauper. A prince of the starving, the destitute. If the price we must pay to find help for our people is bending our pride to this dynast then I will kneel gladly at his feet."

"A prince of Kairn Telest, kneeling!" The necromancer's black brows formed a tight-knit knot above shadowed eyes.

Edmund halted, rounded on the man. "We could have remained

standing upright in Kairn Telest, Baltazar. We'd be frozen stiff in that posture, of course—"

"Your Highness is correct. I beg your pardon." Baltazar sighed heavily. "Still, I don't trust them. Admit it to yourself, Edmund, if you refuse to admit it to me or anyone else. These people destroyed our world deliberately. We come on them as a reproach."

"So much the better, Baltazar. Guilt softens the heart—"

"Or hardens it. Be wary, Edmund. Be cautious."

"I will, my dear friend. I will. And, at least, I don't travel quite alone." The prince's gaze glanced off Haplo, lounging idly against the cave wall, and Alfred, endeavoring to pull his foot out of a crack in the floor. The dog sat at the prince's feet and wagged its tail.

"No." Baltazar agreed dryly. "And I like that least of all, somehow. I don't trust these two any more than I trust this so-called dynast. There, there. I'll say nothing more except farewell, Your Highness! Farewell!"

The necromancer clasped the prince close. Edmund returned the embrace fondly and both men separated, the one heading out the cavern, the other remaining behind, watching the red of the Fire Sea bathe the prince in its lurid light. Haplo whistled, and the dog dashed up to trot along at its master's side.

♦

They reached Safe Harbor without incident, if one didn't count stopping to haul the nervous Alfred out of whatever predicament he managed to blunder into along the way. Haplo came close to impatiently ordering the Sartan to utilize his magic, float as he had done when they entered the cavern, let magic lift those clumsy feet up over rocks and crevices.

But Haplo kept quiet. He guessed that both he and Alfred were far stronger in magic than any of these people. He didn't want them to know how strong. Conjuring up fish had them awestruck, and that was a spell a child could perform. Never reveal a weakness to an enemy, never reveal a strength. Now all he had to worry about was Alfred. Haplo decided, after reflection, that Alfred wouldn't be tempted to give away his true powers. The man had spent years trying to conceal his magic. He wasn't about to use it now.

Arriving in Safe Harbor, they met the young duke and duchess standing on the obsidian pier. Both necromancers were admiring— or perhaps inspecting—Haplo's ship.

"Do you know, sir?" The young lord, catching sight of them,

turned from his examination of the ship and hastened toward Haplo. "I've thought of where I've seen runes like this before! The game—rune-bone!" He waited for Haplo's response, obviously expected Haplo to know what he was talking about.

Haplo didn't.

"My dear," said the observant Jera, "the man has no idea what you mean. Why don't we—"

"Oh, really?" Jonathan appeared quite astonished. "I thought everyone—It's played with bones, you know. Runes like those on your ship are inscribed on the bones. Why, say, come to think of it, the same runes are on your hands and arms, too! Why, you might be a walking game wall!" The duke laughed.

"What a dreadful thing to say, Jonathan! You're embarrassing the poor man," remonstrated his wife, although she gazed at Haplo with an intensity the Patryn found disconcerting.

Haplo scratched at the backs of his hands, saw the woman's green eyes focus on the runes tattooed on the skin. He coolly thrust his hands into the pockets of his leather trousers, forced himself to smile pleasantly.

"I'm not embarrassed. I'm interested. I never heard of a game such as you describe. I'd like to see it, learn how it's played."

"Nothing easier! I've a set of rune-bones at home. Perhaps, when we land, we could go back to our house—"

"My dearest," said Jera, amused, "when we land we are going to the palace! With His Highness." She gave her husband a nudge, recalling him to the fact that he had, in his enthusiasm, impolitely ignored the prince.

"I beg Your Highness's pardon." Jonathan flushed red. "It's just that I really never saw anything quite like this ship. . . ."

"No, please don't apologize." Edmund, too, was staring at the ship and at Haplo with new-kindled interest. "It is remarkable. Quite remarkable."

"The dynast will be fascinated!" Jonathan stated. "He adores the game, never misses an evening's play. Wait until he sees you and hears about your ship. He won't let you go," he assured Haplo earnestly.

Haplo didn't find that idea at all encouraging. Alfred cast him an alarmed glance. But the Patryn had an unexpected ally in the duchess.

"Jonathan, I don't believe we should mention the ship to the dynast. After all, Prince Edmund's business is far more serious. And I"—the green eyes turned on Haplo—"would like to have my father's counsel on this matter before we discuss it with anyone else."

The young duke and duchess exchanged glances. Jonathan's face sobered immediately. "A wise suggestion, my dear. My wife has the brains in the family."

"No, no, Jonathan," Jera protested, faintly blushing. "After all, you were the one who noticed the connection between the runes on the ship and the game."

"Common sense, then," Jonathan suggested, smiling at her and patting her hand. "We make a good team. I'm subject to whim, to impulse. I tend to act before I think. Jera keeps me in line. But she, on the other hand, would never do anything exciting or out of the ordinary if I wasn't around to make her life interesting." Leaning down, he kissed her soundly on her cheek.

"Jonathan! Please!" Her face was mantled with blushes. "What will His Highness think of us!"

"His Highness thinks he has rarely seen two people more deeply in love," said Edmund, smiling.

"We have not been married very long, Your Highness," Jera added, still blushing, but with a fond glance at her husband. Her hand twined around his.

Haplo was thankful that the conversation had turned from him. He knelt down beside the dog, made a show of examining the animal.

"Sar—Alfred," he called. "Come here, will you? I think the dog's picked up a rock in his paw. You hold him, will you, while I take a look?"

Alfred looked panicked. "Me, hold . . . hold the—"

"Shut up and do as I say!" Haplo shot him a vicious glance. "He won't hurt you. Not unless I tell him to."

Bending down, the Patryn lifted the animal's left front paw and pretended to examine it. Alfred did as he was told, his hands gingerly and ineffectively grasping the dog's middle.

"What do you make of all this?" Haplo demanded in a low voice.

"I'm not certain. I can't see well," Alfred answered, peering at the paw. "If you could turn it to the light—"

"I don't mean the dog!" Haplo almost shouted in exasperation, fought down his frustration, lowered his voice. "I mean the runes. Did you ever hear anything of this game they're talking about?"

"No, never." Alfred shook his head. "Your people were not a subject to be treated lightly among us. To think of making a game—" He looked at the runes on Haplo's hand, shining blue and red as they worked their magic against the heat of the magma sea. Alfred shivered. "No, it would be impossible!"

"Like me trying to use your runes?" Haplo asked. The dog, pleased with the attention, sat patiently, submitting its paw to being poked and prodded.

"Yes, much the same. It would be difficult for you to touch them, just as you can't easily speak them. Maybe it's coincidence," Alfred offered hopefully. "Meaningless scrawls that have the appearance of runes."

Haplo grunted. "I don't believe in coincidence, Sartan. There, you're all right, boy! What did you mean, whining like that over nothing?"

Playfully, he rolled the dog over, scratched it on the belly. The dog wriggled on its back, indulging in a long luxurious scratch along its spine. Flipping over, it jumped up, shook itself, refreshed. Haplo rose to his feet, ignoring Alfred, who, in attempting to stand, lost his balance and sat down heavily. The duke hastened to assist him.

"Will you sail your ship across the Fire Sea or travel with us?" the duchess asked Haplo.

The Patryn had been pondering this question himself. If they were truly using Patryn runes in that city, there was the possibility, however remote, that someone might be able to break through his carefully planned defenses. The ship would be more difficult for him to reach, docked in this harbor on the opposite shore, but there would be fewer to see it and gape at it and perhaps attempt to meddle with it.

"I'll sail with you, Your Grace," Haplo replied. "And leave my ship here."

"That is wise," the lady said, nodding her head, and it seemed her thoughts had run the same course as the Patryn's. He saw her glance stray to the cloud-covered city, perched on a cliff at the rear of the enormous cavern, and he saw her frown. All was not well there, apparently, but then Haplo had seen few places where living beings existed that were not subject to strife and turmoil. Those had, however, been run by humans, elves, dwarves. This city was run by Sartan, noted for their ability to dwell together in peace and in harmony. Interesting. Very interesting.

The small group walked down the length of the empty, deserted dock toward the duke's ship. It was an iron monster designed—as were most ships in the realms Haplo had traveled—in the shape of a dragon. Far larger than Haplo's elven ship, the black iron dragonship was fearsome in appearance, its huge, ugly, black head rearing up out of the magma sea. Red lights gleamed from its eyes, red fire burned in its gaping mouth, smoke issued in puffs from the iron nostrils.

The army of the dead straggled ahead of them, dropping bits of bone, armor, a hank of hair as they marched. One cadaver, almost completely reduced to a skeleton, suddenly keeled over, its legs crumbling beneath it. The dead soldier lay on the dock in a confused heap of bones and armor, its helm perched at an insane angle on its skull.

The duke and duchess paused, whispering together in hasty conference, considering the feasibility of attempting to raise the thing again. They decided to leave it. Time was pressing. The army continued on, clanking and rattling down the obsidian pier toward the ship. Haplo, glancing back at the skeleton, thought he could see its phantasm hovering over it, wailing like a mother over a dead child.

What was the unheard voice crying? To be brought back to this mockery of life again? Haplo again felt revulsion twist inside him. He turned away, shoving the thought from his mind. Hearing a snuffling sound, he glanced contemptuously at Alfred, saw tears sliding down the man's cheeks.

Haplo sneered, but his own gaze lingered on the wretched army. A Sartan army. He felt unaccountably, uncomfortably disturbed, as if the neatly arranged world he had long envisioned had suddenly turned upside down and inside out.

♦

"What type of magic powers has this ship?" Haplo asked, having walked the length and breadth of the top deck and seen no sign of magic emanations, no Sartan wizards chanting runes, no Sartan runes traced on hull or rudder. Yet the iron dragon sped swiftly across the magma sea, belching clouds of billowing smoke from its nostrils.

"Not magic. Water," answered Jonathan. "Steam, actually." He seemed slightly embarrassed by the fact, defensive at Haplo's look of surprise. "The ships used to be powered by magic, back in the early days."

"Before the magic was needed to raise and maintain the dead," Alfred said, casting a look of pitying horror at the cadavers ranged in ragged lines on the deck.

"Yes, quite true," Jonathan answered, more subdued than Haplo recalled having seen him since their first meeting. "And, to be perfectly honest, to maintain ourselves. You both are learning what magical strength it takes merely to survive down here. The tremendous heat, the noxious fumes take their toll. When we arrive at the city itself, you will be subjected, constantly, to a terrible type of rain that nourishes nothing but eats away at everything—stone, flesh—"

"And yet this land is habitable, compared to the rest of the world, Your Grace," said Edmund, his gaze on the storm-ridden clouds shrouding the city. "Do you think we fled the moment life grew difficult for us? We fled only when it grew impossible! There comes a point when not even the most powerful rune-magic will sustain life in a realm where there is no warmth, where the water itself turns hard as rock, and perpetual darkness falls over the land."

"And every cycle that passes," Jera said softly, "the magma sea on which we sail shrinks a little more, the temperature in the city drops a fraction of a degree. And we are near its core! So my father has determined."

"Is that true?" the prince asked, troubled.

"My dear, you shouldn't be saying such things," Jonathan whispered nervously.

"My husband's right. According to the edicts, it's treason to even think such thoughts. But, yes, Your Highness, I do speak the truth! Myself and others like me and my father will continue to speak the truth, although some don't want to hear it!" Jera lifted her chin proudly. "My father studies scientific subjects, physical laws and properties, matters that are looked down on as being beneath our people's notice. He could have become a necromancer, but he refused, saying that it was time the people of this world focused their attention on the living, not the dead."

Edmund appeared to find this statement somewhat radical. "I agree with that view to a certain extent, but without our dead, how could we living survive? We would be forced to use our magic to perform menial tasks, instead of conserving it for our maintenance."

"If we allowed the dead to die and if we built and used machines, such as the ones powering this ship, and if we worked and studied

and learned more about the resources of our world, it is my father's
belief that we would not only survive but prosper. Perhaps we might
even learn ways to bring life back to regions such as your own, Your
Highness."

"My dear, is this wise, talking like this in front of strangers?"
Jonathan murmured, his cheeks pale.

"Far better to talk like this in front of strangers than those who
call themselves our friends!" Jera answered bitterly. "The time is long
past, says my father, when we should cease to wait for those from
other worlds to come and 'rescue' us. It is time we rescued ourselves."

Her gaze flicked, as if by accident, to the two strangers. Haplo
kept his eyes firmly fixed on the woman, his expression impassive.
He dared not risk a glance at the Sartan, but he knew without
looking that Alfred would look as guilty as if the words *Yes, I Come
From Another World* were written across his forehead.

"And, yet, you, Your Grace, became a necromancer," Edmund
observed, breaking the uncomfortable silence.

"Yes, I did," Jera said, sadly. "It was necessary. We are caught in a
circle that is like a snake, who can maintain its life only by feeding
off its own tail. A necromancer is essential to the running of any
household. Most especially to ours, since we have been banished to
the Old Provinces."

"What are those?" Edmund asked, glad to change the subject,
steer it away from talk he obviously considered dangerous, perhaps
blasphemous.

"You will see. We must pass through them on our way to the
city."

"Perhaps you, Your Highness, and you, gentlemen, would be
interested in observing how the ship operates?" Jonathan offered,
anxious to end this conversation. "You'll find it really quite amusing
and entertaining."

Haplo agreed readily, any type of knowledge about this world
was essential to him. Edmund agreed, perhaps secretly thinking
that ships like these would carry his people to Death's Gate. Alfred
went along simply, Haplo thought uncharitably, so that the inept
Sartan might have the opportunity of falling headfirst down a flight
of iron steps into the ship's hot, dark belly.

The ship was operated by a crew of cadavers, better kept than the army, who had performed their tasks in life and so continued to perform them in death. Haplo explored the mysteries of something called a "boiler" and marveled politely at another essential piece of equipment known as a "paddle wheel," its iron heated red-hot, that churned through the magma, pushing the dragonship along from behind.

The mechanics reminded the Patryn forcibly of the great Kicksey-winsey, the wondrous machine built by the Sartan and now run by the Gegs of Arianus; the wondrous machine whose purpose no one had understood until the child, Bane, figured it out.

The time is long past when we should cease to wait for those from other worlds to come and "rescue" us.

Haplo, ascending back on deck, thankful to leave the terrible heat and oppressive darkness below, recalled Jera's words. The Patryn couldn't help grinning. What sweet irony. The one who had come to "rescue" these Sartan was their ancient enemy. How his lord would laugh!

The iron ship sailed into a harbor, far larger and much busier than the one they had just left. Ships plied the magma sea both above and below where they docked. The thriving New Provinces, Jonathan pointed out, were located near the shores of the Fire Sea, close enough to benefit from the heat, yet far enough not to suffer from it.

Once off the ship, the duke and duchess turned the captaincy of their army over to another necromancer, who shook his head at the sight of the cadavers and marched them off to effect what repairs he could.

Thankful to be rid of their charges, Jera and her husband gave their guests a brief tour of the dockyard. Haplo had the impression that, for all Jera's gloomy talk, Necropolis—to judge by the goods piled up on the docks or being loaded onto ships by teams of cadavers—was a thriving and wealthy community.

They left the pier, heading for the main highway into the city. But, before they reached it, Jera brought the party to a halt, pointed back at the shoreline of the fiery ocean.

"Look, there," she said, her hand extended. "See those three rocks, standing one on top of the other. I placed them in that position before we left. And when I placed them there, the magma sea reached to their base."

The ocean was not at the base any longer. Haplo could have set his hand down in the breadth of empty shoreline left between rock and sea.

"Already, in this short span of time," said Jera, "the magma has receded that far. What will happen to this world, to us, when it has cooled completely?"

CHAPTER 20

NEW PROVINCE HIGHWAY,

ABARRACH

◆

AN OPEN-AIR CARRIAGE AWAITED THE DUKE, DUCHESS, AND THEIR guests. The vehicle was constructed of the same grasslike substance, woven together and covered with a high-gloss finish painted in glowing colors, Haplo had noted in the village.

"A much different material from that used to build your ship," said Jera, climbing into the carriage and seating herself beside Haplo.

The Patryn kept silent, but Alfred tumbled into the trap with his usual grace. "Wood, you mean? Yes, wood is quite common in . . . er . . . well . . ." He realized his error, stammered, but it was too late.

Haplo saw, in the Sartan's enthusiastic words, visions of the trees of Arianus, lifting their green and leafy bows to the sun-drenched blue skies of that distant world.

The Patryn's first impulse was to grab Alfred by his frayed coat collar and shake him. By their expressions, Jera and Jonathan had seen the same visions and were staring at Alfred in undisguised wonder. Bad enough these Sartan knew or guessed they came from a world different from their own. Did Alfred have to show them how much different?

Alfred was climbing into the carriage, still talking, trying to cover his mistake by babbling, and succeeding in doing further damage. Haplo insinuated his booted foot between Alfred's ankles, sent him sprawling headlong across Jera's lap.

The dog, excited by the confusion, decided to add its own and began barking frantically at the beast drawing the carriage—a large fur-bearing creature as long as it was wide with two small beady black eyes and three horns on its massive head. For all its girth, the beast could move swiftly, it whipped out a clawed paw at the pesky dog. The dog leapt nimbly to one side, danced a few paces out of reach, darted forward to nip at the back legs.

"Whoa, pauka! Stop! Get back there!"

The carriage driver—a well-kept cadaver—slashed at the dog with a whip, at the same time struggling to maintain a grip on the reins. The pauka attempted to swing round its head to get a good view (and mouthful) of its antagonist. Those in the carriage were jounced and jostled, the carriage itself seemed likely to tip over, and all thoughts of another world fled in their concern over remaining in this one.

Haplo jumped out. Collaring the dog, he dragged the animal away from the fray. Jonathan and Edmund ran to the head of the pauka, as Haplo learned it was called from certain maledictory phrases being hurled at it by the dead coachman.

"Mind the snout horn!" Jonathan called anxiously to the prince.

"I've dealt with these before," Edmund said coolly, and grabbing a handful of fur, he pulled himself up deftly onto the pauka's broad back. Sitting astride the plunging, frantic beast, the prince caught hold of the curved part of the sharp horn located just behind the snout. Giving it a swift, strong tug, he jerked the pauka's head back.

The pauka's beady eyes opened wide. It gave its head a shake that nearly threw the prince. Edmund clung firmly to the horn, jerked it back a second time. Leaning down, he said a few soothing words and patted the beast on the neck. The pauka paused to consider the matter, cast a baleful glance back at the grinning dog. The prince said something else. The pauka appeared to agree and, with an air of offended dignity, settled stolidly back into the harness.

Jonathan sighed in relief and hastened to the carriage to see if any of the passengers had come to harm. The prince slid off the pauka's back, patted it on the neck. The cadaver retrieved its dropped reins. Alfred was extracted from Jera's lap, from which he emerged extremely red in the face and profuse in his apologies. A small crowd of dockside necromancers, who had gathered around to watch, drifted back to their work, which involved keeping the laboring cadavers at theirs. Everyone climbed aboard the carriage. It rolled off, on iron wheels, the dog trotting along behind, tongue lolling and eyes bright over the remembrance of the fun.

Not a word more was said about wood, but Haplo noted that, during the ride, Jera would glance at him, her lips curving in a smile.

"What lush and fertile land you have!" said Edmund, gazing about him with undisguised envy.

"These are the New Provinces, Your Highness," said Jonathan.

"Land left behind with the falling of the Fire Sea," added the duchess. "Oh, it is prosperous now. But its very prosperity spells our doom."

"We grow mostly kairn grass here," the duke continued with almost desperate cheerfulness. He was aware of the prince's discomfort and cast a pleading glance at his wife, begging her to refrain from bringing up unpleasant subjects.

Jera, with another glance through lowered lids at Haplo, clasped her husband's hand in her own in silent apology. From then on she went out of her way to be charming. Haplo, leaning back in the carriage, watched the change of expression on the mobile face, the flash of wit in the eyes, and thought that only once before in his life had he ever met a woman to equal this one. Intelligent, subtle, quick to think and to act, yet not one to act or speak rashly, she would have made a man a good partner in the Labyrinth. It was extremely unfortunate that she was bonded to another.

What was he thinking? A Sartan woman! Once again, in his mind, he saw the motionless figures resting peacefully in the crystal tombs of the mausoleum. Alfred did this to me. It's all the Sartan's fault. Somehow, he's playing tricks on my mind. The Patryn cast the Sartan a sharp glance. If I catch him at it, he'll die. I don't need him anymore.

But Alfred was hunched miserably in the corner of the carriage, unable to so much as look at the duchess without a wave of blushes sweeping over his bald head. The man appeared incapable of dressing himself without help, yet Haplo didn't trust him. Looking up, feeling eyes on him, he caught Jera, looking back as if she were reading every thought in his mind. Haplo affected to be intensely interested in the conversation going on around him.

"You grow primarily kairn grass here?" Edmund was asking.

Haplo stared at the tall, golden stands of grass undulating in the hot vectors blowing from the magma sea. Cadavers, new dead by the looks of them, worked in the fields, busily cutting the grass with curved sickles, stacking it in bundles that other cadavers pitched onto trundling carts.

"The plant is extremely versatile," Jera said. "It's flame resistant, thrives on heat, drawing its nutrients from the soil. We use its fibers in almost everything, from this carriage to the clothes we wear to a kind of tea we brew."

She was, Haplo realized, speaking to people from another world, a people who wouldn't know kairn grass from paukas. Yet all the while she was talking directly to the prince, who—probably having grown up eating, sleeping, and breathing kairn grass—appeared slightly amazed at being thus edified, but was too polite to say anything.

"Those trees you see growing over there are lanti. They can be found in the wild. We cultivate them. Their blue flowers are known as lanti lace and are highly prized for decoration. Beautiful, aren't they, Your Highness?"

"It has been some time since I have seen the lanti," Edmund said, his expression grim. "If any do still grow in the wild, we did not run across them."

Three thick, stalwart trunks thrust up through the surrounding stands of golden kairn grass. The trunks twined together to form one gigantic braided trunk that soared high up into the air, the tops lost in the mists. The tree's limbs, thin and fragile, gleaming silver-white, were so intertwined that it appeared impossible to separate one from another. Some of these bore flowers of a soft pale blue color.

As the carriage neared the grove of these trees, Haplo noted that the air smelled sweeter, seemed easier to breathe. He saw, by the dimming of the runes on his skin, that his body was using less magic to maintain itself.

"Yes," answered Jera, seeming again to understand his unspoken thoughts. "The flowers of the lanti have the unique ability to draw the poisons from the atmosphere and give back pure air in return. That is why the trees are never cut. To kill a lanti is an offense punishable by oblivion. One may pick the blue flowers, however. They are highly valued, particularly by lovers." She turned a sweet smile on her husband, who squeezed her hand.

"If you took this road," said Jonathan, pointing to a smaller highway that branched off from the major one on which they traveled, "and you continued on it almost to Rift Ridge, you would reach my family's estate. I really should be getting back," he added, looking at the road they were leaving behind with a longing gaze. "The kairn grass is ready to harvest and, although I left Father's cadaver in charge, sometimes it forgets and then nothing is done."

"Your father, too, is dead?" Edmund asked.

"And my elder brother, as well. That is why I'm lord of the manor, although oblivion take me if I ever wanted it or thought I'd come to it. I'm not very responsible, I'm afraid," Jonathan admitted, referring to his own shortcomings with a cheerful candor that was quite engaging. "Fortunately, I have someone at my side who is."

"You underestimate yourself," Jera said crisply. "It comes of being the youngest. He was spoiled as a child, Your Highness. Never made to do anything. Now all that's changed."

"No, you don't spoil me at all," the duke teased.

"What happened to your father and brother? How did they die?" Edmund asked, thinking undoubtedly of his own recent sorrow.

"Of the same mysterious malady that strikes so many of our people," Jonathan answered, almost helplessly. "One moment both were hale and filled with life. The next—" He shrugged.

Haplo looked sharply at Alfred. *Because for every person brought back untimely to life, another—somewhere—untimely dies.*

"What have they done? What have they done?" Alfred's lips moved in a silent litany.

Haplo, thinking about all he'd seen and heard, was beginning to wonder the same.

♦

The carriage left the New Provinces, left behind the tall stands of kairn grass and the lovely, lacy lanti trees. Little by little, the landscape changed.

The air grew cooler, the first drops of rain began to fall, a rain that, when it struck Haplo's skin, caused the protective runes to glow. A shrouding mist closed in. By Jonathan's order, the carriage rolled to a stop, the cadaver driver jumped from his post and hastened around to unfurl a screen of protective fabric over their heads that offered some protection from the rain. Lightning flickered among the trailing clouds, thunder rumbled.

"This area," said Jera, "is known as the Old Provinces. This is where my family lives."

The land was blasted, devoid of life except for a few scraggly rows of sickly looking kairn grass, struggling up through piles of volcanic ash, and some flowerlike plants that gave off a pale and ghostly light. But although the land appeared barren, harvesters moved among the mud pits and slag heaps.

"Why? What are they doing?" Alfred leaned out of the carriage.

"The old dead," answered Jera. "They are working the fields."

"But . . ." whispered Alfred in a horror too profound to be spoken aloud, "there *are* no fields!"

Cadavers in the most deplorable condition, far worse than the army of the old dead, toiled in the drizzling laze. Skeletal arms lifted rusted sickles or, in some cases, no sickles at all but merely went through the motions. Other cadavers, flesh rotting from their bodies, trailed after the harvesters, gathered up nothing, put it carefully nowhere. Barely distinguishable from the mist around them, the phantasms trailed disconsolately after the cadavers. Or perhaps the mist around them was made up of nothing but phantasms belonging to those whose bones had sunk into the ground and would never rise again.

Haplo looked at the mist and saw hands in it and arms and eyes. It clutched at him, it wanted something from him and seemed to be trying to speak to him. Its chill pervaded body and mind.

"Nothing grows here now, although once the land was as lush as the New Provinces. The few stands of kairn grass you see grow along the underground colossus that carry the magma into the city to provide heat. The old dead, who worked this land once themselves when they were alive, are all that remain. We tried moving them to new lands, but they kept drifting back to places they had known, and finally we left them in peace."

"In peace!" Alfred echoed bitterly.

Jera appeared slightly surprised at his attitude. "Why, yes. Don't you do this with your own dead when they grow too old to be of use?"

Here it comes, thought Haplo, who knew he should stop what Alfred was going to say. But he didn't. He kept still, kept quiet.

"We have no necromancers among us," Alfred said, his voice soft and fervent with conviction. "Our dead when they die are allowed to rest after their labors in life."

The three in the carriage said nothing, were stunned into silence. They regarded Alfred with much the same expression of horror as he regarded them.

"You mean," said Jera, recovering from her shock, "you consign your dead, all your dead, to oblivion?"

"To oblivion! I don't understand. What does that mean?" Alfred glanced from one to the other helplessly.

"The body rots, falls to dust. The mind is trapped within, powerless to free itself."

"Mind! What mind? These have no minds!" Alfred waved a hand at the old dead, toiling among the ash and mud.

"Of course, they have minds! They work, they perform useful functions."

"So does that dragonship on which we sailed, but it has no mind. And you're using your dead the same way. But you have done worse than that! Much worse!" cried Alfred.

The prince's expression darkened from one of tolerant curiosity to one of anger. Only his innate courtesy kept him quiet, because what he would say would obviously cause unpleasantness. Jera's brows came together sharply, her chin jutted forward, her back straightened. She would have spoken but her husband held her hand fast, squeezed it tightly. Alfred didn't notice, rushed headlong into an icy, disapproving silence.

"The use of such black arts has been known to our people but expressly forbidden. Surely the ancient texts spoke of such matters. Have those been lost?"

"Perhaps destroyed," suggested Haplo coolly, speaking for the first time.

"And what do you think, sir?" Jera demanded of the Patryn, ignoring the pressure of her husband's hand. "How do your people treat their dead?"

"My people, Your Grace, have all they can do to keep the living alive, without worrying about the dead. And it seems to me that this, for the moment, should be *our* primary concern. Were you aware that there is a troop of soldiers headed this way?"

The prince sat bolt upright, tried to see out the screened carriage. He stared into nothing but mist and rain and hurriedly ducked his head back inside.

"How can you tell?" he demanded, more suspicious of them now than he had been when he first encountered them in the cavern.

"I have extraordinary hearing," Haplo replied dryly. "Listen, you can hear the jingle of their harness."

The jingle of harness, the stamping of what sounded like hooves on rock came to them faintly above the noise of their own carriage.

Jonathan and his wife exchanged startled glances, Jera appeared troubled.

"I take it, then, that troop movement along this highway isn't exactly normal?" Haplo asked, leaning back in the carriage and folding his arms across his chest.

"Probably a royal escort for His Highness," Jonathan said, brightening.

"Yes, that's it. Surely," Jera agreed, with rather too much relief in her voice to be entirely convincing.

Edmund smiled, ever courteous, despite whatever private misgivings he might have had.

The wind rose, the mists thinned. The troops were close and clearly visible. The soldiers were dead, new dead, in superb condition. At sight of the carriage, they came to a halt, formed a line across the highway, blocking the way. The carriage stopped on a hastily given command by Jonathan to his dead driver. The pauka snorted and shook its head restlessly, not liking the beasts the soldiers rode.

Lizardlike creatures, the soldiers' mounts were ugly and misshapen. Two eyes on either side of the head revolved, each independent of the other, giving the impression that they could see in all directions at once. Short and squat, built close to the ground, they had powerful hind legs and a thick, barbed tail. The dead rode on their backs.

"The troops of the dynast," Jera said, speaking in an undertone. "His soldiers alone are permitted to ride mud dragons. And the man in the gray robes leading them is the Lord High Chancellor, the dynast's right hand."

"And the black-robed person riding beside him?"

"The army's necromancer."

The chancellor, mounted astride a mud dragon and looking extremely uncomfortable, said a few words to the captain, who guided its beast forward.

The pauka sniffed and snorted, shook its head at the mud dragon smell, which was foul and rank as if it had climbed out of a pit of poisonous ooze.

"All of you, please step out of the carriage," requested the captain.

Jera glanced at her guests. "I think, perhaps, we better," she said apologetically.

They trooped out of the carriage, the prince graciously assisting the duchess. Alfred stumbled down the two stairs, nearly pitched headfirst into a pit. Haplo stood quietly toward the back of the group. An oblique gesture of his hand brought the dog padding to his side.

The cadaver's expressionless eyes peered at the group, its mouth forming the words the Lord High Chancellor had bidden it say.

"I ride in the name of the Dynast of Abarrach, ruler of Kairn Necros, regent of Old and New Provinces, king of Rift Ridge, king of Salfag, king of Thebis, and liege lord of Kairn Telest."

Edmund flushed darkly at hearing his own kingdom thus claimed, but he held his tongue. The cadaver continued.

"I am looking for one who calls himself king of Kairn Telest."

"I am prince of that land," Edmund said, speaking up proudly. "The king, my father, is dead and but newly raised. That is why I am here and he is not," he added for the benefit of the waiting necromancer, who nodded the black hood in understanding.

The cadaver captain, however, was somewhat at a loss. This new information came outside the scope of its orders. The chancellor indicated in a few words that the prince would serve in place of the king, and the captain, reassured, carried on.

"I am bidden by His Majesty to place the king—"

"Prince," inserted the chancellor patiently.

"—of Kairn Telest under arrest."

"On what charge?" Edmund demanded. Striding forward, he ignored the cadaver, glared at the chancellor.

"Of entering the realms of Thebis and Salfag, realms foreign to him, without first seeking the permission of the dynast to cross their borders—"

"Those so-called realms are uninhabited! And neither myself nor my father ever knew that this 'dynast' even existed!"

The cadaver was continuing its speech, perhaps it hadn't heard the interruption. "And of attacking without provocation the town of Safe Harbor, driving off the peaceful inhabitants, and looting—"

"That is a lie!" Edmund shouted, his fury overtaking his reason.

"Indeed it is!" Jonathan cried impetuously. "My wife and I have just returned from the town. We can testify to the truth of the matter."

"His Most Just Majesty will be only too pleased to hear your side of this dispute. He will let you both know when to come to the palace." It was the chancellor who spoke.

"We're coming to the palace with His Highness," Jonathan stated.

"Quite unnecessary. His Majesty received your report, Your Grace. We require the use of your carriage to the city walls, but, when we arrive in Necropolis, you and the duchess have His Majesty's leave to return to your home."

"But—" Jonathan sputtered. It was his wife's turn to restrain him from speaking his mind.

"My dear, the harvest," she reminded him.

He said nothing, subsided into an unhappy silence.

"And now, before we proceed," continued the chancellor, "His Highness the Prince will understand and forgive me if I ask that he surrender his weapon. And those of his companion, too, I—"

The chancellor's gray hood, hiding his face, turned for the first time toward Haplo. The voice ceased speaking, the hood paused in its rotation, the fabric quivered as if the head it covered were subject to some strong emotion.

The runes on Haplo's skin itched and prickled. What now? he wondered, tensing, sensing danger. The dog, who had been content to flop down in the road during the lull in the proceedings, jumped to its feet, a low growl rumbling in its chest. One of the eyes of the mud dragon swiveled in the direction of the small animal. A red tongue flicked out of the lizard's mouth.

"I have no weapons," said Haplo, raising his hands.

"Nor I," added Alfred in a small and miserable voice, although no one had asked him.

The chancellor shook himself, like a man waking from a doze he never meant to take. With an effort, the gray hood wrenched itself from staring at Haplo back to the prince, who had remained motionless.

"Your sword, Your Highness. No one comes armed into the presence of the dynast."

Edmund stood defiant, irresolute. Duke and duchess kept their gazes lowered, unwilling to influence him in any way, yet obviously hoping he would not cause trouble. Haplo wasn't certain what he hoped the prince would do. The Patryn had been warned by his lord not to become involved in any local dispute, but his lord had certainly not counted on his minion falling into the hands of a Sartan dynast!

Edmund suddenly and swiftly reached down, unbuckled his

sword belt, and held it out to the cadaver. The captain accepted it
gravely, with a salute of a white and wasted hand. Cold with outraged pride and righteous anger, the prince climbed back into the
carriage and seated himself stiffly, staring out over the blasted landscape with studied calm.

Jera and her husband, prey to shame, could not look at Edmund,
who must think now that they had lured him into a trap. Faces
averted, they silently entered the carriage and silently took their
seats. Alfred glanced uncertainly at Haplo, for all the world as if he
were asking for orders! How that man had survived on his own this
long was beyond the Patryn's comprehension. Haplo jerked his head
toward the carriage, and Alfred tumbled in, stumbling over everyone's feet, falling rather than sitting in his seat.

They were all waiting for Haplo. Reaching down, patting the
dog, he turned the animal's head toward Alfred.

"Watch him," he instructed in a soft undertone that no one heard
except the animal. "Whatever happens to me, watch him."

Haplo climbed into the carriage. The cadaver captain rode forward, caught hold of the pauka's reins, and started the grumbling
animal moving, driving the carriage forward toward the city of
Necropolis, the City of the Dead.

CHAPTER 21

NECROPOLIS,

ABARRACH

◆

THE CITY OF NECROPOLIS WAS BUILT AGAINST THE HIGH WALLS OF THE kairn[1] that gave the empire its name. The kairn, one of the largest and oldest on Abarrach, had always been habitated, but had not, until now, been a great population center. Those who traveled to this world in the early years of its history had moved to the more temperate regions nearer the planet's surface, those cities that were located, as was popularly quoted, "between fire and ice."

Abarrach's world had been most carefully designed by the Sartan when their magic first attempted to save their world by sundering it. "All the more astonishing that what had seemed so right had gone so tragically wrong," said Alfred to himself during the dismal, gloom-ridden journey to the city.

Of course, thought Alfred, this world, like the other three worlds, was never meant to remain self-sufficient. They were to have communicated, cooperated. For some reason, unknown, the cooperation failed, left each world cut off, isolated.

But the populations of mensch on Arianus had managed to adapt to their harsh surroundings and survive, even flourish—or they would if their own squabbles and bickering did not kill them off. It was the Sartan, Alfred's race, who had disappeared on Arianus. It

---

[1] *Kairn* is a Sartan word meaning "cavern," a variation on the dwarven word *cairn*, which means "pile of stones." It is interesting to note that the Sartan had no word of their own for cavern prior to their removal to Abarrach and were forced, apparently, to borrow a word from the dwarves.

would have been better—far, far better, he reflected sadly—if his race had disappeared off this one, as well.

"The city of Necropolis," announced the Lord High Chancellor, dismounting awkwardly from his mud dragon. "I am afraid that from here on we must walk. No beasts are allowed inside the city walls. That includes dogs." He stared hard at Haplo's pet.

"I'm not leaving the dog," Haplo said shortly.

"The animal could stay with the carriage," Jera offered, her manner timid. "Would he remain here by himself, if you told him to? We could take him back to our dwelling."

"The dog would, but it won't." Haplo climbed out of the carriage, whistled the dog to him. "Where I go, the dog goes. Or neither of us goes."

"The creature is extremely well trained." Jera, dismounting from the carriage with her husband, turned to the chancellor. "I will vouch for its good behavior while inside the city."

"The law is clear: No beasts inside the city walls," the Lord High Chancellor stated, his face flint-hard and sharp, "except those destined for the marketplace and they must be butchered within the specified time after entering. And if you will not submit to our laws peaceably, sir, then you will submit by force."

"Ah, now," said Haplo, smoothing the rune-covered skin on the back of his hands, "that should be very interesting."

More trouble, Alfred foresaw unhappily. Having his suspicions concerning the dog and its relationship to Haplo, the Sartan had no idea how this would be resolved. Haplo would sooner part with his life than the animal and it seemed, from the look on his face, that he would enjoy the opportunity to fight.

No wonder. Face-to-face, at last, with an enemy who had locked his people into a hellish world for a thousand years. An enemy who had deteriorated in magical skills . . . and in so much else! But could the Patryn deal with the dead? He had been captured easily enough back in the cavern. Alfred had seen pain twist the man's face, and the Sartan knew Haplo well enough to guess that there were few who had ever seen him so incapacitated. But perhaps now he was prepared, perhaps the magic in his body was acclimated.

"I don't have time for such nonsense," said the Lord High Chancellor coldly. "We are late for our audience with His Majesty as it is. Captain, deal with it."

The dog, having grown bored during the conversation, had been unable to resist taking another sniff and mischievous nip at the pauka. Haplo's gaze was fixed on the chancellor. The captain of the guard leaned down, grabbed the dog up in strong arms and, before Haplo could prevent it, the cadaver hurled the animal into a pit of bubbling hot mud.

The dog gave a wild, pain-filled scream. Its front paws scrabbled frantically, liquid eyes fixed in desperate pleading on its master.

Haplo leapt toward it, but the mud was thick and viscous and scalding hot. Before the Patryn could save it, the animal was sucked down beneath the surface and vanished without a trace.

Jera gasped and hid her face in her husband's breast. Jonathan, shocked and appalled, glowered at the chancellor. The prince cried out in bitter, angry protest.

Haplo went berserk.

Runes on his body flared into brilliant life, glowing bright blue and crimson red. The vivid light could be seen through his clothing, welling out beneath the fabric of his shirt, showing clearly the runes drawn on his arms. The leather vest he wore hid those on his back and chest, the leather trousers concealed those on his legs, but so powerful were the runes that a glowing halo was beginning to form around him. Silent, grim, Haplo launched himself directly at the cadaver, who—seeing the threat—went for its sword.

Haplo's lunge carried him to his prey before the captain had its sword halfway clear of the scabbard. But the moment the Patryn's choking hands touched the cadaver's chill flesh, white lightning flared and danced crazily around the two of them. Haplo cried out in agony, staggered backward, limbs twitching and writhing convulsively as the charge passed through his body. He slammed up against the side of the carriage. Groaning, he slid down to lie, seemingly unconscious, in the soft ash that covered the road.

An acrid odor of sulfur filled the air. The cadaver continued, unperturbed, the motion of drawing its sword, then looked to the chancellor for orders.

The Lord High Chancellor was staring, wide-eyed, at Haplo, at the glow of the runes that was just beginning to fade from the skin. The minister licked his dry lips.

"Kill him," was the command.

"What?" Alfred quavered, staring in disbelief. "Kill him? Why?"

"Because," Jera said softly, laying a restraining hand on Alfred's arm, "it is far easier to obtain information from a cadaver than a stubborn, living man. Hush, there is nothing you can do!"

"There is something I can do," Edmund said coldly. "You cannot kill a helpless man! I won't allow it!" He took a step forward, obviously intent on impeding the cadaver in its grisly task.

The captain never paused, but raised its hand in a commanding gesture. Two of its troops ran to obey. Dead soldiers grasped the prince from behind, pinioning his arms skilfully to his sides. Edmund, outraged, struggled to free himself.

"Just a moment, Captain," said the chancellor. "Your Highness, is this man with the strange markings on his skin a citizen of Kairn Telest?"

"You know very well he isn't," answered Edmund. "He is a stranger. I met him just today, over on the opposite shore. But he has done no harm and has seen a faithful companion meet a barbarous death. You have punished him for his effrontery. Let it go at that!"

"Your Highness," said the Lord High Chancellor, "you are a fool. Captain, carry out your orders."

"How can my people . . . *my people* commit these terrible crimes?" Alfred babbled wildly, talking to himself, wringing his hands as if he would wring the answers from his own flesh. "If I stood in the midst of the Patryns, then, yes, I could understand. They were the race that was heartless, ambitious, cruel. . . . We . . . we were the balance. The wave correcting itself. White magic to their black. Good for evil. But I see in Haplo . . . I have seen good in Haplo. . . . And now I see evil in my fellow Sartan. . . . What shall I do? What *shall* I do?"

His immediate answer was: faint.

"No!" Alfred gasped, fighting against his inherent weakness. Blackness crept over him. "Action! Must . . . act. Grab the sword. That's it. Grab the sword."

The Sartan flung himself at the captain of the guard.

That was the plan. Unfortunately, the Sartan ended up flinging only *part* of himself at the captain of the guard. Alfred's upper half went for the sword. His lower half refused to move. He fell flat, landed in a headlong sprawl on top of Haplo.

Alfred, looking at him, saw the Patryn's eyelids flicker.

"Now you've done it!" Haplo shot irritably out of the corner of his mouth. "I had everything under control! Get off me!"

Either the cadaver didn't notice that now it had two victims instead of one, or perhaps it assumed that it was to save time by dispatching both at once.

"I—I can't!" Alfred was paralyzed with fear, unable to move. Looking up in frantic terror, he saw the razor-sharp, if slightly rusted blade, descending.

The Sartan gasped the first runes that came to his lips.

The captain of the dead had been a brave and honorable soldier, well respected and loved by his men. He had died in the Battle of the Pillar of Zembar,[2] of a sword thrust in the gut. The horrible wound could still be seen, a gaping, although now bloodless, hole in the cadaver's stomach.

Alfred's rune-chant appeared to inflict the same killing blow over again.

For a brief instant, a semblance of life flickered in the dead eyes. The cadaver's well-preserved face wrenched with pain, the sword fell from a hand that reached instinctively at its torn vitals. A silent scream came from blue lips.

The cadaver doubled over, clutching its gut. Those watching in stunned shock saw its hands curl around the invisible blade of some unseen attacker. Then, seemingly, the sword was wrenched free. The cadaver gave a last, silent groan and slid to the ground. It did not get back to its feet, it did not continue the attack. The captain lay on the ash-covered ground, dead.

No one moved or spoke; all standing near might have been struck by the same invisible sword. The Lord High Chancellor was the first impelled to action.

"Bring the captain back!" he commanded the court necromancer.

Hastening forward, her black robes fluttering around her, her cowl fallen, unheeded, from her head, the necromancer approached the captain's corpse.

She sang the runes.

---

[2] Fought during the rebellion of the people of Thebis, who refused to pay one-third of their crops in taxes to the dynast. The rebellion failed and almost certainly led to the downfall of a once-great city-state. Fair-minded historians point out that although this tax burden does seem excessive, the people of Thebis thought nothing of charging the dynast and the people of Necropolis a fee of fifty bales of kairn grass per use of the Pillar of Thebis, which supplied much-needed water to the city of Necropolis.

Nothing happened. The captain lay motionless.

The necromancer sucked in a deep breath, eyes widened in astonishment, and then narrowed in anger. She began to chant the runes again, but the magic died on her lips.

The cadaver's phantasm rose up before the necromancer and stood between the wizardess and its corpse.

"Be gone," ordered the necromancer, attempting to brush it aside, as she might brush away smoke from a fire.

The phantasm remained where it was, began to change in appearance. No longer was it a pitiful wisp of fog, but the semblance of a man—strong and proud—who faced the wizardess with dignity. And all realized, who stood watching in amazed awe, that they were seeing the corpse as he had been in life.

The captain faced the necromancer and the watchers saw, or thought they saw, the phantasm shake its head in firm denial. It turned its back on its corpse and walked away, and it seemed a great and sorrowful wail resounded from the mist around them, a wail that was fraught with envy.

Or was it the wind, howling among the rocks?

The necromancer stood gazing at the phantasm in openmouthed stupefaction. When it disappeared, she suddenly became aware of her audience and snapped her mouth shut.

"Good riddance." Bending over the corpse, she spoke the runes again, adding, for good measure, "Get up, damn you!"

The corpse didn't move.

The necromancer's face flushed an ugly red. She kicked at the cadaver. "Get up! Fight! Carry out your orders!"

"Stop it!" Alfred cried in anger, regaining his feet with difficulty. "Stop it! Let the man rest!"

"What have you done?" The necromancer rounded on Alfred. "What have you done to it? What have you done?"

Alfred, taken aback, stumbled over Haplo's ankles. The Patryn groaned and stirred.

"I—I don't know!" Alfred protested, bumping into the side of the carriage.

The necromancer advanced on him. "What have you done?" she demanded, her voice rising to a shrill scream.

"The prophecy!" Jera exclaimed, clutching at her husband. "The prophecy!"

The necromancer overheard, paused in her harangue. She stared at Alfred narrowly, then looked swiftly to the chancellor for orders. He appeared dazed.

"Why doesn't it get up?" he asked in a shaken voice, staring at the corpse.

The necromancer bit her lip, shook her head. She went over to discuss the matter with him in low, urgent undertones.

Jera took advantage of the chancellor's distraction to hasten to Haplo's side. She was solicitous of the Patryn, attentive to him, but the green eyes fixed in silent questioning on the stammering Alfred.

"I—I don't know!" he answered, as confused as anyone there. "Truly, I don't know. It all happened so fast. And . . . I was terrified! That sword—" He shuddered, shivering from cold and reaction. "I'm not very brave, you see. Most of the time I . . . I faint. Ask him." He pointed a shaking finger at Edmund. "When his men captured us, I passed out cold! I wanted to faint this time, but I wouldn't let myself. When I saw the sword . . . I spoke the first words that came to me! I can't recall, for the life of me, what I said!"

"For the life of you!" The necromancer turned, glared at Alfred from the depths of her black hood. "No, but you'll recall them swiftly enough after death. The dead, you see, never lie, never keep anything concealed!"

"I'm telling you the truth," said Alfred meekly, "and I doubt if even my corpse would have very much to add."

Haplo groaned again, almost, it seemed, as if he were responding to Alfred's statement.

"How is he?" Jonathan asked his wife.

Jera's hand reached out to trace the runes on Haplo's skin. "I think he'll be all right. The sigla appear to have absorbed most of the shock. His heartbeat is strong and—"

Haplo's hand closed suddenly and firmly over hers. "Don't ever touch me again!" he whispered, voice hoarse.

Jera flushed, bit her lip. "I'm sorry. I didn't mean—" She flinched, tried to move her arm. "You're hurting me . . ."

Haplo flung her from him, regained his feet by his own power, though he was forced to lean for support against the carriage. Jonathan hastened to his wife's side.

"How dare you treat her like that?" the duke demanded savagely, swinging around on Haplo. "She was only trying to help—"

"Don't, my dear," Jera interrupted. "I deserve his reproach. I had no right. Forgive me, sir."

Haplo grunted, muttered something in ungracious acceptance. He was obviously still not feeling well, but he understood that danger had not lessened.

If anything, thought Alfred, it has increased.

The chancellor was giving new instructions to his troops. Soldiers massed themselves around the prince and his companions, herding them close together.

"What in the name of the Labyrinth did you do?" Haplo hissed, edging nearer the wretched Alfred.

"He fulfilled the prophecy!" said Jera in a low voice.

"Prophecy?" Haplo looked from one to the other. "What prophecy?"

But Jera only shook her head. Rubbing her bruised flesh, she turned away. Her husband put his arm around her protectively.

"What prophecy?" Haplo demanded, turning his accusing stare to Alfred. "What the hell did you do to that corpse?"

"I killed him," said Alfred, adding by way of explanation. "He was going to kill you—"

"So you saved my life by killing a dead man. That figures. Only you—" Haplo stopped talking, stared at the corpse, then looked back at the Sartan. "You say you 'killed' him."

"Yes. He's dead. *Quite* dead."

The Patryn's gaze switched from Alfred to the infuriated necromancer to the sharp-eyed duchess to the watchful, suspicious prince.

"I really didn't mean to," Alfred pleaded unhappily. "I . . . I was frightened."

"Guards! Keep them apart!" The chancellor gestured, and two cadavers hastened to separate Alfred and Haplo. "No talking among yourselves! Any of you! Your Graces." He turned to the duke and duchess. "I'm afraid that this . . . incident changes matters. His Majesty will want to interview all of you. Guards, bring them!"

The chancellor and the necromancer strode on, heading toward the gate in the city walls. The cadavers closed ranks around their captives, separated them one from the other, and ordered them forward.

Alfred saw the Patryn cast one glance at the mud hole into which his faithful dog had disappeared. Haplo's mouth tightened, stern eyes blinked rapidly. Then the guards took him away, blocking him from Alfred's sight.

A moment of confusion followed. Edmund struck aside the chill hands of the cadavers, stated that he would enter the city as a prince, not a captive. He moved forward proudly on his own, his guards trailing behind.

Jera took advantage of the situation to whisper hurried, urgent instructions to her carriage driver. The cadaver nodded and turned the pauka's head toward home, guiding the animal down a road that ran for some distance beneath the city wall. Duke and duchess exchanged glances, they were of one mind on something, but what that could be the unhappy Alfred had no idea.

Nor, at the moment, did he care. He had not been lying. He had no idea what he had done and he wished, with all his heart, he hadn't done it. Lost in dark thoughts, he didn't notice that the duke and duchess fell into step with him, one on either side, the dead guards tramping along behind.

CHAPTER • 22

NECROPOLIS,

ABARRACH

◆

THE INHABITANTS OF NECROPOLIS HAD TAKEN ADVANTAGE OF A PECU-
liar natural rock formation in building their city walls. A long row of
stalagmites, poking up from the cavern floor, extended from one side
of the back end of the cavern around in a half circle, closing it off at
the other end. Stalactites flowed into the stalagmites, forming a wall
that gave the visitor the startling impression he was entering a
gigantic, bared-toothed mouth.

The stalactic form was ancient, dating back to the world's origins,
and was undoubtedly one reason that this point had become one of
Abarrach's earliest outposts of civilization. Old Sartan runes could
occasionally be seen on the massive wall, their magic having once
conveniently filled up gaps left by the natural architecture.

But Sartan magic had dwindled, the continual fall of drizzling
laze had worn most of the sigla away, and no one now remembered
the secret of restoring them. The dead kept the wall in repair, filling
the gaps between the "teeth" with molten lava, pumping magma
into the cavities. The dead also guarded the walls of Necropolis.

The city gates stood open during the dynast's waking time.
Gigantic doors woven of strong kairn grass reinforced by the few
crude runes these Sartan remembered were shut only when the royal
eyes closed in sleep. Time in this sunless world was regulated by the
ruler of Necropolis, which meant that it tended to change depending
on the whim of His or Her Majesty.

Time was, therefore, denoted by such appellations as "the dynast's breakfast hour" or "the dynast's audience hour" or "the dy-

nast's napping hour." An early-rising ruler forced his subjects to rise early to conduct their business under his watchful eye. A late-rising ruler, as was their current dynast, altered the routine of the entire city. Such changes were no great hardship on the living inhabitants, who were generally at leisure to alter their lives to suit their ruler. The dead, who did all the work, never slept.

The Lord High Chancellor and his prisoners entered the city gates during the close of the dynast's audience hour, one of the busiest times of day for the city's inhabitants. Audience hour marked a last moment's flurry of activity before the city shut down for the dynast's luncheon hour and the dynast's napping hour.

Consequently, the narrow streets of Necropolis were crowded with people, both living and dead. The streets were, in reality, tunnels, created either naturally or artificially, designed to give the inhabitants some protection from the constantly falling rain. These tunnels were narrow and twisting and tended to be dark, shadowy places, imperfectly lighted by hissing gas lamps.

Masses of people—both living and dead—crowded into the tunnels. It seemed barely possible for Alfred, the duke and duchess and the guards to add their bodies to the throng. Alfred understood that the law prohibiting beasts in the city streets had not been passed arbitrarily but out of necessity. A mud dragon would have seriously impeded traffic, the huge furry form of pauka would have brought movement in the streets to a complete standstill. Studying the crowds heaving and shoving and pushing around him, Alfred saw that the dead vastly outnumbered the living. His heart seemed to shrivel inside him.

The guards closed ranks around their prisoners, the several groups were almost instantly separated by the crowd. Haplo and the prince vanished from sight. The duke and duchess pressed close to Alfred, one on either side, their hands closing over his arms.

He felt an unusual tenseness, a rigidity in their bodies, and looked at each in doubt and sudden, sickening apprehension.

"Yes," said Jera, her voice pitched low, barely audible above the noise level created by the multitudes jamming the streets, "we're going to try to help you escape. Just do what we tell you, when we tell you."

"But . . . the prince . . . my fri—" Alfred paused. He had been about to term Haplo his "friend" and wondered uneasily if the word was quite proper or even accurate.

Jonathan appeared troubled, glanced at his wife, who shook her head firmly.

The duke sighed. "I'm sorry. But you see that helping them is impossible. We will make certain you get away safely, then perhaps together we can do something to assist your friends."

What he said made sense. How could the duke know that, without Haplo, Alfred was a prisoner no matter where he went on this world? He emitted a small sigh, that no one could possibly have heard. "I suppose it wouldn't matter if I told you that I didn't *want* to escape?"

"You're frightened," said Jera, patting his arm. "That's understandable. But trust us. We'll take care of you. It won't be that difficult," she added, casting a scornful glance at their dead guards, shouldering their way through the crowd.

"No, I didn't think it would," Alfred said, but he said it to himself.

"Our concern is for your safety," added Jonathan.

"Is it?" Alfred asked wistfully.

"Why, of course!" the duke exclaimed, and Alfred had the feeling that the young man actually believed what he said.

The Sartan couldn't help but wonder, with a gentle melancholy, how ready these two would be to risk their lives to save a clumsy-footed bumbling fool instead of a man who'd fulfilled "the prophecy," whatever that might be. He considered asking, decided he really didn't want to know.

"What will happen to the prince, to . . . to Haplo?"

"You heard Pons," said the duchess shortly.

"Who?"

"The chancellor."

"But he's talking about murder!" Alfred was aghast. He could believe it of mensch, believe it of the Patryns . . . but his people!

"It's been done before this," said the duke grimly. "And will be done again after."

"You must think of yourself," Jera added softly. "There'll be time to think of helping your friends escape when you're safe."

"Or at least we might be able to rescue their cadavers," offered Jonathan, and Alfred, looking into the young man's eyes, saw that the duke was completely in earnest.

Everything within Alfred went numb. He was walking in a dream, but if it was a dream, it must be someone else's, because he couldn't wake up. The warm hands of the duke and duchess steered him among the sea of dead, combating the chill flow from the blue-white flesh of the cadavers pressing around them. The odor of decay was strong in his nostrils and emanated not only from the dead but from everything in this world.

The buildings themselves, made of obsidian and granite and cooled lava, were subject to the constant, drizzling, acid-filled laze. Dwellings and shops, like the cadavers, were crumbling, falling apart. Alfred saw, here and there, old runes or what was left of them; sigla whose magic would have brought heat and light to this gloomy, forbidding city. But most were obliterated, either washed away or covered over by makeshift repair work.

Duke and duchess slowed their pace. Alfred glanced at them nervously.

"Up ahead is a cross-tunnel," Jera said, drawing near him. Her face was firm, resolute, her tone urgent, impelling. "We'll encounter the normal traffic tie-ups, confusion. Once we reach that point, be ready to do what we say."

"I think I should warn you—I'm not very good at running, fleeing pursuit, that sort of thing," said Alfred.

Jera smiled, a rather tight smile and lopsided, but her green eyes were warm. "We know," she said, patting his arm again. "Don't worry. It should all be much easier than that."

"*Should* be," breathed her husband, gulping with excitement.

"Calmly, Jonathan," ordered his wife. "Ready?"

"Ready, my dear," said the young man.

They arrived at a junction, where four tunnels converged. People flowed in from four different directions. Alfred caught a quick glimpse of four necromancers, clad in plain black robes, standing in the center of the intersection, directing the streams of traffic.

Jera turned suddenly and began to push and shove irritably at the cadaver guard, who marched directly behind her.

"I tell you," she shouted loudly, "you've made a mistake!"

"Yes, be off with you!" Jonathan raised his voice, stopping to remonstrate with his guard. "You've got the wrong people! Can you understand that? The wrong people! Your prisoners"—he raised his hand and pointed—"went off in that direction!"

The cadaver guards came to a standstill, remaining tightly bunched around Alfred and the duke and duchess as they'd been ordered. People stumbled to a halt around them, the living pausing to see what was going on, the dead attempting single-mindedly to continue on whatever errands they'd been assigned.

A bottleneck occurred. Those in the back of the crowd, who couldn't see, began to push and shove those ahead of them, demanding in strident tones to know what was holding up traffic. The situation was deteriorating, and the necromancers moved with alacrity to find out what was wrong and attempt to clear up the snarl.

A cross-tunnel monitor clad in plain black robes made his way through the mass. Noting the red trim on the black robes of the duke and duchess, the necromancer recognized minor royalty and bowed low. He did, however, glance slightly askance at the cadavers, who wore the royal insignia.

"How can I assist Your Graces?" asked the monitor. "What is the problem?"

"I'm really not sure," said Jonathan, the picture of innocent confusion. "You see, my wife and our friend and I were walking along minding our own business when these . . . these"—he waved a hand at the guards as if there existed no words to describe them—"suddenly surrounded us and began to march us off toward the palace!"

"They've been ordered to guard a prisoner, but they've apparently mislaid him and latched on to us," said Jera, glancing about helplessly.

Traffic was growing more and more snarled. Two of the monitors attempted to direct the flow around the group. A fourth, appearing harassed, tried to herd them over to the side of the road but the walls of the tunnels prevented them from moving very far. Alfred, standing head and shoulders above most of the rest of the crowd, could see that the backup was spreading through all four streets. At this rate, the entire city might be brought to a halt.

Someone was treading heavily on his foot, someone else had his elbow in his ribs. Jera was plastered up against him, her hair tickled his chin. The monitor himself was caught in the tide and had to battle his way out or he would have been carried along in the surging mob.

"We came in the front gate at the same time as the Lord High Chancellor and three political prisoners!" Jonathan shouted to be heard in the echoing tunnels. "Did you see them? A prince of some barbarian tribe and a man who looked like a walking rune-bone game?"

"Yes, we saw them. *And* the Lord High Chancellor."

"Well, there was a third man, and this lot was guarding him and then suddenly they were guarding us and he's escaped somewhere."

"Perhaps," said the increasingly flustered monitor, "Your Graces could simply go along with these guards to the palace—"

"I, the Duchess of Rift Ridge, marched before the dynast like a common criminal! I could never show my face in court again!" Jera's pale skin flushed, her eyes blazed. "How can you even suggest such a thing!"

"I—I'm sorry, Your Grace," the monitor stammered. "I wasn't thinking. It's this crowd, you see, and the heat—"

"Then I suggest you do something about it," Jonathan stated loftily.

Alfred glanced at the cadavers, who stood stolidly in the center of the confusion swirling about them, faces set in expressions of fixed, albeit mindless, purpose.

"Sergeant," said the necromancer, turning to the cadaver in the lead of the small troop, "what is your assigned duty?"

"Guard prisoners. Take them to the palace," answered the cadaver, its hollow voice mingling with the other hollow voices of the dead milling about in the tunnel.

"What prisoners?" the monitor asked.

The cadaver paused, searching its past, latched on to a memory. "Prisoners of war, sir."

"What battle?" asked the monitor, a hint of exasperation in his voice.

"Battle." A trace of a smile seemed to touch the cadaver's blue lips. "Battle of the Fallen Colossus, sir."

"Ah," said Jera, bitingly.

The necromancer heaved a sigh. "I am extremely sorry, Your Graces. Would you like me to deal with this?"

"If you please. I could have done it myself, but there's so much less bother involved if you take care of the matter, you being a government official. You'll know how to submit the proper reports."

"And we didn't want to cause a scene," added Jonathan. "The dead can be so stubborn sometimes. Once they got it into their heads that we were their prisoners . . ." He shrugged. "Well, they might have proved difficult. Think of the scandal if Her Grace and I were seen arguing with cadavers!"

The monitor evidently thought of it, for he bowed, then began to wave his hands in the air, tracing the runes, and chanting. The cadavers' expressions wavered, became slightly confused, lost, helpless.

"Return to the palace," stated the monitor crisply. "Report to your superior that you lost your prisoner. I'll send someone with them, make certain that they don't annoy anyone else along the way. And now, Your Graces," said the monitor, touching his hand to the cowl of his robe, "if you will excuse me—"

"Certainly. Thank you. You've been most helpful." Jera raised her hand, traced a sigil of polite blessing.

The monitor returned it, hurriedly, then hastened off to deal with the traffic tie-up clogging the tunnel. Jera linked her arm into her husband's, who took hold of Alfred's elbow. They steered the Sartan down a tunnel heading in a direction at right angles to the one they'd been traveling.

Dazed by the noise, the crowd, the claustrophobic atmosphere of the tunnels, it took Alfred a moment to realize that he and his companions were free.

"What happened?" he asked, glancing behind, missing his footing, and stumbling over himself.

Jonathan balanced him. "A matter of timing, actually. Do you think you might speed up your pace a bit and keep an eye on where you're walking? We're not out of this yet and the sooner we reach the Rift Gate, the better."

"I'm sorry." Alfred felt his face burn. He paid close attention to where he was putting his feet and watched them travel in the most extraordinary places—down holes, onto other people's feet, turning corners never intended to be turned.

"Pons was in such haste to get you back to the dynast—here, allow me to help you up—he neglected to renew the dead's instructions. You have to do that periodically or they do what this lot did. They revert back to acting from memory, their own memories."

"But they *were* taking us to the palace—"

"Yes. They would have managed that task quite adequately. Clung to it tenaciously, in fact. One reason we didn't dare try to get rid of them ourselves. As it was, that other necromancer confused them enough to break the thin thread still attaching them to their orders. The smallest distraction can send them back to bygone days. That's one reason the monitors are posted around town. They take charge of any dead who're wandering about aimlessly. Look out for that cart! Are you all right? Just a bit farther, then we should be through the worst of the traffic."

Jera and Jonathan hustled Alfred along at a rapid rate, each glancing nervously about as they did so. They kept to the shadows when possible, avoiding the pools of light cast by the gas lamps.

"Will they come after us?"

"You may be sure of that!" the duke said emphatically. "Once the guards return to the palace, Pons will have fresh guards sent out with our descriptions. We must reach the gate before they do."

Alfred said nothing more—he couldn't say anything more, he didn't have breath left to say it. The passage through Death's Gate, followed by the emotional upheaval of the cycles' shocking events and the constant drain on his magic to help him survive, rendered the Sartan weak to the point of collapse. Blindly, wearily, he stumbled along where he was led.

He had only a vague impression of arriving at another gate, of emerging thankfully from the maze of tunnels, of Jera and Jonathan answering questions put to them by a dead guard, of hearing that someone was taken ill and wondering vaguely who, of a large fur-covered body of a pauka appear out of the mist, of falling, face first, into a carriage and hearing, as in a dream, the voice of Jera saying, ". . . my father's house . . ." and of the eternal, horrible darkness of this dreadful world closing over him.

CHAPTER ✦ 23

NECROPOLIS,

ABARRACH

✦

"AND, SO, PONS, YOU LOST HIM," SAID THE DYNAST, IDLY SIPPING AT A potent, fiery, red-hued liquor known as stalagma, the favored after-dinner drink of His Majesty.

"I am sorry, Sire, but I had no idea I would be responsible for transporting five prisoners. I thought there would be only one, the prince, and that I would take charge of him personally. I had to rely on the dead. There was no one else."

The Lord High Chancellor was not concerned. The dynast was fair-minded and would not hold his minister responsible for the inadequacies of the cadavers. The Sartan of Abarrach had learned long ago to understand the limits of the dead. The living tolerated the cadavers, responding to them with patience and fortitude, much as fond parents tolerate the inadequacies of their children.

"A glass, Pons?" asked the dynast, waving off the cadaver servant and offering to fill a small golden cup with his own hands. "Quite an excellent flavor."

"Thank you, Your Majesty," said Pons, who detested stalagma but who wouldn't have dreamed of offending the dynast by refusing to drink with him. "Will you see the prisoners now?"

"What is the hurry, Pons? It is nearly time for our rune-bone game. You know that."

The chancellor gulped down the bitter-tasting liquid as swiftly as possible, fought a moment to catch his breath, and mopped his sweating forehead with a handkerchief.

"The Lady Jera mentioned something, Sire, about the prophecy."

Kleitus paused in the act of lifting the glass to his lips. "Did she? When?"

"After the stranger had . . . er . . . done whatever he did to the captain of the guard."

"But you said he 'killed' it, Pons. The prophecy speaks of bringing life to the dead." The dynast drank off the liquor, tossing it to the back of his throat and swallowing it immediately, as did all experienced stalagma drinkers. "Not ending it."

"The duchess has a way of twisting words to suit her own convenience, Sire. Consider the rumors that she could spread concerning this stranger. Consider what the stranger himself might do to make the people believe in him."

"True, true." Kleitus frowned, at first worried. Then he shrugged. "We know where he is and with whom." The stalagma put him in a relaxed mood.

"We could send in troops . . ." suggested the chancellor.

"And have the earl's faction up in arms? It's possible they might join these rebels from Kairn Telest. No, Pons, we will continue to handle this matter subtly. It could give us the excuse we need to put that meddlesome earl *and* his duchess daughter out of the way for good. We trust you took the usual precautions, Pons?"

"Yes, Sire. The matter is already in hand."

"Then why worry over nothing? By the way, who takes over the ducal lands of Rift Ridge if young Jonathan should die untimely?"

"He has no children. The wife would inherit—"

The dynast made a fatigued gesture. Pons lowered his eyelids, indicative of understanding.

"In that case, his estate reverts to the crown, Your Majesty."

Kleitus nodded, motioned to a servant to pour him another glass. When the cadaver had done so and withdrawn, the dynast lifted his cup, prepared to enjoy the liquor. His gaze caught that of his chancellor and, with a sigh, he set the glass back down.

"What is it, Pons? That sour face of yours is ruining our enjoyment of this excellent vintage."

"I beg your pardon, Sire, but I wonder if you are taking this matter seriously enough." The chancellor drew nearer, speaking in an undertone, although they were quite alone, apart from the cadavers. "The other man I brought in with the prince is extraordinary in his own way! Perhaps more so than the one who escaped. I think you should see this prisoner immediately."

"You've been dropping vague hints about this man. Spit it out, Pons! What's so . . . extraordinary . . . about him?"

The chancellor paused, considering how to produce the greatest impact. "Your Majesty, I've seen him before."

"I am aware of your extensive social connections, Pons." Stalagma tended to make Kleitus sarcastic.

"Not in Necropolis, Sire. Nor anywhere around here. I saw him this morning . . . in the vision."

The dynast returned the glass, its contents left untasted, to the tray at his elbow.

"We will see him . . . and the prince."

Pons bowed. "Very good, Sire. Shall they be brought here or to the audience chamber?"

The dynast glanced around the room. Known as the gaming room, it was much smaller and more intimate than the grand audience hall and was well lighted by several ornate gas lamps. Numerous kairn-grass tables had been placed around the room. On top of each were four stacks of rectangular white bones adorned with red and blue runes. Tapestries lined the walls, portraying various famous battles that had been fought on Abarrach. The room was dry, cozy, and warm, heated by steam that swirled through wrought-iron, gold-trimmed pipes.

The entire palace was heated by steam, a modern addition. In ancient times, the palace—originally a fortress and one of the earliest structures built by the first-arriving Sartan—had not been dependent on mechanical means to provide comfortable living conditions. Traces of the old runes could be seen to this day in the ancient parts of the palace, sigla that had provided warmth, light, and fresh air to the people dwelling within. Most of these runes, their use forgotten through neglect, had been deliberately obliterated. The royal consort considered them an ugly eyesore.

"We will meet our guests here." Kleitus, another glass of stalagma in hand, took a seat at one of the gaming tables, and began idly setting up the rune-bones as if in preparation for a game.

Pons gestured to a servant, who gestured to a guard, who disappeared out a door and, after several moments, entered with a retinue of guards, marching the two prisoners into the royal presence. The prince entered with a proud, defiant air, anger smoldering like boiling lava beneath the cool surface of royal etiquette. One side of his face was bruised, he had a swollen lip, and his clothes were torn, his hair disheveled.

"Allow me to present, Sire, Prince Edmund of Kairn Telest," introduced Pons.

The prince inclined his head slightly. He did not bow. The dynast paused in setting up his game board, stared at the young man, eyebrows raised.

"On your knees to His Most Royal Majesty!" the scandalized chancellor hissed out of the corner of his mouth.

"He is not my king," said Prince Edmund, standing tall, head back. "As the ruler of Kairn Necros, I bid him greeting and do him honor." The prince inclined his head again, the gesture graceful and proud.

A smile played about the dynast's lips. He moved a bone into position.

"As I trust His Majesty does *me* honor," pursued Edmund, his face flushed, his brows contracting, "as prince of a land that has now admittedly fallen on evil times but was once beautiful, rich, and strong."

"Yes, yes," said the dynast, holding a rune-marked bone in his hand, rubbing it thoughtfully across his lips. "All honor to the Prince of Kairn Telest. And now, Chancellor"—the eyes, hidden in the shadow of the black cowl trimmed in purple and in gold, turned toward Haplo—"what is the name of this stranger to our royal presence?"

The prince sucked in an angry breath, but kept his temper, perhaps mindful of his people, who were, according to reports, starving in a cave. The other man, the one with the rune-marked skin, stood quietly, unabashed, unimpressed, one might say almost uninterested in what was going on around him except for the eyes that saw everything without betraying that they'd seen anything.

"He calls himself Haplo, Sire," said Pons, bowing low. A dangerous man, the chancellor might have added aloud. A man who lost control once, but who won't be goaded into losing it again. A man who kept to the shadows, not furtively, but instinctively, as if he'd learned long ago that to draw attention to himself was to make himself a target.

The dynast leaned back in his chair. He gazed at Haplo through eyes that were slits only. Kleitus appeared bored, lethargic. Pons shivered. His Majesty was at his most dangerous when he was in this mood.

"You do not bow before us. We suppose you're going to tell us that we're not your king either," he remarked.

Haplo shrugged, smiled. "No offense."

His Majesty covered twitching lips with a delicate hand, cleared his throat. "None taken . . . from either of you. In time, perhaps, we will come to an understanding."

He sat silent, brooding. Prince Edmund began to fidget with impatience. His Majesty glanced swiftly at him and raised his languid hand, gesturing at the table.

"Do you game, Your Highness?"

Edmund was taken aback. "Yes . . . Sire. But it has been a long time since I played. I have had little leisure for frivolous activities," he added bitterly.

The dynast waved such considerations aside. "We had thought to give up our game tonight, but we see no reason to do so now. Perhaps we can come to an understanding over the game board. Will you join us, sir? Forgive me, but are you a prince . . . or . . . or any sort of royalty that we should acknowledge?"

"No," said Haplo, and volunteered nothing else.

"No, you won't join us, or no, you are not a prince, or no, in general?" the dynast inquired.

"I'd say that pretty well describes the situation, Sire." Haplo's gaze was fixed on the gaming pieces, a fact that did not go unnoticed by His Majesty.

The dynast permitted himself an indulgent laugh. "Come, sit with us. The game is complex in its subtleties, but it is not difficult to learn. We will teach you. Pons, you will make up a fourth, of course."

"With pleasure, Sire," said the chancellor.

An inept rune-bone player at best, Pons was rarely called on to game with his dynast, who had little patience with the unskilled. But the true game tonight would be played on a far different level, one with which the Lord High Chancellor was vastly familiar.

Prince Edmund hesitated. Pons knew what the young man was thinking. Might such an activity reduce his dignity and dilute the seriousness of his cause? Or would it be politically expedient to give in to this royal whim? The chancellor could have assured the young man it didn't matter, his doom was sealed no matter what he chose to do.

The Lord High Chancellor felt sorry for this prince for a brief moment. Edmund was a young man with heavy burdens, who took his responsibilities seriously, who was obviously sincere in his desire to help his people. A pity that he couldn't see he was just another game piece, to be moved where it suited His Majesty, or removed . . . if it suited His Majesty.

The prince's well-bred courtesy won out. He walked over to the gaming table, sat down opposite the dynast, and began arranging the bones in the starting position, which required that they be lined up to resemble the walls of a fortress.

Haplo hesitated, as well, but his reluctance to move was perhaps nothing more than a reluctance to leave the shadow and venture into the strong light. He did so, at last, walking forward slowly to take his place at the table. He kept his hands beneath the table, lounged back in his chair. Pons seated himself opposite.

"You begin, sir," said the chancellor, acting on a cue from the dynast's upraised eyebrow, "by arranging the pieces thusly. Those marked with the blue runes are the base. Those with the red are stacked on top of the blue and those with both blue and red markings form the battlements."

The dynast had completed building his wall. The prince, frustrated and angry, was halfheartedly constructing his. Pons affected to be interested in putting his together, but his gaze crept to the man opposite. Haplo moved his right hand out from beneath the table, lifted a rune-bone, and slid it into place.

"Remarkable," said the dynast.

All movement at the gaming table ceased, all eyes were fixed on Haplo's hand.

There could be no doubt. The runes on the bones were far cruder in nature than the runes tattooed on the man's skin—a child's scrawl compared to the flowing script of a grown man—but they were the same.

The prince, after a moment's involuntary fascination, wrenched his glance away and continued to work on his wall. Kleitus reached out his hand to Haplo's, intending to seize it and study it closer.

"I wouldn't do that, Sire." Haplo said quietly, not moving his hand. He wasn't making an overt threat, but a quality in the voice caused the dynast to pause. "Perhaps your man there told you." Eyes flicked to Pons. "I don't like to be touched."

"He said that when you attacked the guard the marks on your

skin glowed. By the way, may we apologize for that tragic incident? It is one that we deeply regret. We had no intention of harming your pet. The dead tend to . . . overreact."

Pons, watching closely, saw Haplo's jaw muscle twitch, the lips tighten. Otherwise, the face remained impassive.

His Majesty was continuing, "You attacked a soldier, he said, without a weapon in your hands, and yet you seemed confident of your ability to fight one armed with a sword. But you didn't intend battling with bare hands, did you, sir? These marks"—the dynast did not touch, but pointed—"these sigla are magic. *Magic* was your intended weapon. I am certain you can understand that we are fascinated. Where did you come by these runes? How do they work?"

Haplo lifted another rune-bone, placed it beside the one he moved into position. Lifting another, he set it next to the first.

"We asked you a question," said the dynast.

"We heard you," replied Haplo, lips twisting in a smile.

The dynast flushed in anger at the mockery. Pons tensed. The prince glanced up from his building.

"Insolence!" Kleitus glowered. "You refuse to answer?"

"It's not a question of refusing, Sire. I've taken a vow, an oath. I could no more tell you how my magic works than"—Haplo's eyes flicked to the dynast, returned coolly to the game—"than you could tell me how your magic raises the dead."

The dynast sat back in his chair, turning a game piece over and over in his hand. Pons relaxed, emitting a long breath, unconscious, until now, that he'd been holding it in.

"Well, well," said Kleitus at last. "Chancellor, you are delaying the game. His Highness has almost completed his wall and even the novice, here, is ahead of you."

"I beg your pardon, Sire," said Pons humbly, knowing and understanding his role in this charade.

"This palace is old, isn't it?" said Haplo, studying the room.

Pons, affecting to be absorbed in building his wall, eyed the man from beneath lowered lids. The question had an idle, making-polite-conversation sound to it, but this wasn't the type of man who engaged in mindless chatter. What was he after? The chancellor, watching carefully, saw Haplo's gaze stray to several partially obliterated rune markings on the walls.

Kleitus took it on himself to respond. "The old part of the palace was built out of a natural formation, a cavern within a cavern, one might say. It stands on one of the highest points of elevation in Kairn Necros. The rooms on the upper levels once provided a quite magnificent view of the Fire Sea, or so we're led to believe by ancient report. That was, of course, before the sea withdrew." He paused to take a drink of liquor, glanced at his chancellor.

"The palace was originally a fortress," Pons obediently picked up the thread of the story, "and there is evidence that a vast number of people passed through here at one time, undoubtedly on their way to the more habitable upper regions."

The prince frowned. His hand jerked, he knocked several pieces off his partially completed wall.

"As you may have surmised," Pons continued, "this room is in one of the older parts of the palace. Although, of course, we've made considerable modern improvements. The royal family's living quarters are located back here; the air's purer, don't you agree? Official chambers and halls and ballrooms are to the front, near where you entered."

"Seems a confusing sort of place," Haplo pursued. "More like a bee's hive than a palace."

"Bee's hive?" asked the dynast, raising an eyebrow and stifling a yawn. "I'm not familiar with that term."

Haplo shrugged. "What I mean is, a fellow could get himself lost in here without too much trouble."

"One learns one's way around," said the dynast, amused. "However, if you would truly be interested in seeing a place in which it is easy to lose oneself, we could show you the catacombs."

"Or, as we know them, the dungeons," the chancellor inserted, with a snigger.

"Pay attention to your wall, Pons, or we shall be here all night."

"Yes, Sire."

Nothing more was said. The walls were completed. Pons noted that Haplo, who maintained that he had never played, constructed his wall with perfect accuracy, although many beginning players found the markings on the bones confusing. It was almost, the chancellor thought, as if the runes said something to him they said to no one else.

"Excuse me, my dear sir," said Pons fussily, leaning over to whisper to Haplo. "I believe you've made a mistake. That particular rune doesn't belong up on the battlements, where you've put it, but down below."

"Properly placed, it goes there," said Haplo in his quiet voice.

"He's right, Pons," said Kleitus.

"Is he really, Sire?" The chancellor was flustered, laughed at himself. "I—I must have it wrong, then. I've never been very good at this game. I confess that all the bones look alike. These markings mean nothing to me."

"They mean nothing to any of us, Chancellor," said the dynast severely. "At least they didn't, up until now." A glance at Haplo. "You have to memorize them, Pons. I've told you that before."

"Yes, Your Majesty. It's good of Your Majesty to have such patience with me."

"Your bid, Your Highness," said Kleitus to the prince.

Edmund stirred restlessly in his chair. "One red hexagon."

The dynast shook his head. "I'm afraid, Your Highness, that a red hexagon is an improper opening bid."

The prince sprang to his feet. "Your Majesty, I have been arrested, beaten, insulted. If I had been alone, without a responsibility for others, I would have rebelled against such treatment that is not due from one Sartan to another, let alone from one king to another! But I am a prince. I hold the lives of others in my keeping. And I cannot concentrate on a . . . a game"—he waved a hand contemptuously at the board—"when my people are suffering from cold and starvation!"

"Your people attacked an innocent village—"

"We did not attack, Sire!" Edmund was rapidly losing control. "We wanted to buy food, wine. We intended to pay for it, but the people attacked us before we had a chance to say a word! Strange, now that I think of it. It was as if they'd been led to believe we *would* attack them!"

The dynast cast a look at Haplo, to see if he had anything to add. Haplo toyed with a rune-bone, appeared bored.

"A perfectly natural precaution," said the dynast, returning his attention to the prince. "Our scouts sight a large force of armed barbarians, moving toward our city, coming from the outland. What would have been *your* assumption?"

"Barbarians!" Edmund went white to the lips. "Barbarians! We are no more barbarians than . . . than this fop of a chancellor is a barbarian! Our civilization is older than yours, one of the first established following the Sundering! Our beautiful city, open to the air, makes this one look like the stinking rat's warren that it is!"

"And yet I believe you've come to beg to be allowed to live inside this 'stinking rat's warren,' " said Kleitus, leaning back and looking languidly at the prince through slit eyelids.

The prince's livid face suffused with a red, feverish flush. "I have not come to beg! Work! We will work to earn our keep! All we ask is shelter from the killing rain and food to feed our children. Our dead and our living, too, if you want, will work in your fields, serve in your army. We will"—Edmund swallowed, as though forcing down the bitter stalagma—"we will acknowledge you as our liege lord . . ."

"How good of you," murmured the dynast.

Edmund heard the sarcasm. His hands closed over the back of the chair, the fingers punching holes through the strong kairn grass in the desperate need to control his raging anger. "I wasn't going to say this. You have driven me to it."

Haplo stirred at this juncture. It seemed he might have interrupted, but he apparently thought better of it, relapsed into his former state of impassive observer.

"You owe us this! You destroyed my people's homes! You leeched our water, you stole our heat and used it for your own. You made our beautiful lush land a barren and frozen desert! You killed our children, our elderly, our sick and infirm! I have maintained to my people that you brought this disaster on us through ignorance, that you knew nothing of our existence in Kairn Telest. We didn't come in retribution. We didn't come in revenge, although we could have. We came to ask our brethren to right the wrong they inadvertently committed. I will keep on telling them this, although I know, now, that it is a lie."

Edmund left his place behind his chair. His fingers bled, the sharp prongs of the splintered kairn grass had driven through the flesh. He didn't seem to notice. Moving around the table, he bent gracefully to one knee and spread his hands.

"Take my people in, Your Majesty, and I give you my word of honor that I will keep my knowledge of the truth from them. Take my people in and I will work with them, side by side. Take my people in, Sire, and I will bend my knees to you, as you require." Although in my heart, I despise you.

The last words were not spoken aloud. There was no need. They hissed in the air like the gas that lit the lamps.

"We were right, you see, Pons," said Kleitus. "A beggar."

The chancellor could not help but sigh. The prince, in his youth and beauty, graced by compassion for his people, had a majesty about him that lifted him in stature and in rank far above most kings, let alone beggars.

The dynast leaned forward, fingertips touching. "You'll find no succor in Necropolis, Edmund, prince of beggars."

The prince rose to his feet, suppressed anger leaving patches of chill white in the feverish crimson of his skin.

"Then there is nothing more to say. I will return to my people."

Haplo stood up. "Sorry to break up the game, but I'm with him," he said, jerking his thumb in the direction of the prince.

"Yes, you are," said the dynast in a soft and menacing tone that only Pons heard. "I suppose this means war, Your Highness?"

The prince didn't stop walking. He was halfway across the room, Haplo at his side. "I told you, Sire, my people do not want to fight. We will travel on, perhaps proceed farther down the shoreline. If we had ships—"

"Ships!" Kleitus sucked in a breath. "Now we come to it! The truth. That's what you've been after all along! Ships, to find Death's Gate! Fool! You will find nothing except death!"

The dynast gestured to one of the armed guards, who nodded in response. Lifting his spear, the cadaver aimed and threw.

Edmund sensed the threat, whirled around, raised his hand in an attempt to ward off the attack. Futile. He saw his death coming. The spear struck him full in the chest with such force that the point shattered the breastbone and emerged from the man's back, pinned him to the floor. The prince died the instant the blow was struck, died without a scream. The sharp iron tore apart the heart.

By the expression of sadness on the face, his last thoughts had been, perhaps, not of regret for his own young life, cut tragically short, but of how he had failed his people.

Kleitus gestured again, motioned toward Haplo. Another cadaver raised its spear.

"Stop him," the Patryn said, in a quick, tight voice, "or you'll never learn anything about Death's Gate!"

"Death's Gate!" Kleitus repeated softly, staring at Haplo. "Halt!"

The cadaver, arrested in the act of throwing the spear, let it slip from the dead hand. It fell, clattering, to the floor, the only sound to break the tense silence.

"What," demanded the dynast at last, "do you know of Death's Gate?"

"That you'll never get through it if you kill me," returned Haplo.

CHAPTER ♦ 24

NECROPOLIS,

ABARRACH

♦

IT HAD BEEN A GAMBLE, BRINGING UP THE SUBJECT OF DEATH'S GATE. The dynast might have blinked once, shrugged his shoulders, and ordered the cadaver to pick up the dropped spear and try again.

Haplo wasn't risking his life. His magic would protect him from the spear's deadly point, unlike the poor devil of a prince, who lay sprawled dead on the floor at the Patryn's feet. It was the revelation of his potent magical power that Haplo sought to avoid, one reason he'd faked unconsciousness when that cadaver had attacked him on the road.

Unfortunately, he hadn't counted on Alfred rushing to his rescue. Damn the man! The one time fainting would have been beneficial, the blasted Sartan weaves some inexplicably complex and powerful magical spell that stands everyone's hair on end. It was always better, Haplo had learned, to encourage your enemy to underestimate you rather than overestimate. You were far more likely to catch him napping.

But at least this gamble had apparently paid off. Kleitus hadn't blinked and shrugged. He knew about Death's Gate, would almost have *had* to know about it. Obviously intelligent, a powerful necromancer, such a man would certainly have looked for and found any ancient records those early Sartan had left.

His "opening bid" strategy flashed through Haplo's mind while the prince's splattered blood was still warm on the Patryn's rune-covered skin.

The dynast had recovered his composure, was affecting indifference. "Your corpse will provide me with whatever information I might require, including information about this so-called Death's Gate."

"It might," Haplo countered. "Or it might not. My magic is kin to yours, that's true, but different. Far different. Necromancy has never been practiced among my people and there could be a reason for it. Once the brain that controls these sigla"—he held up his arm—"is dead, the magic dies. Unlike you, my physical being is inextricably bound with the magic. Separate one from the other and you may have a cadaver who can't even remember its name, much less anything else."

"What makes you think we care what you remember?"

"*Ships, to find Death's Gate.* Those were the words you used, almost the last words this poor fool heard." Haplo gestured at Edmund's torn body. "Your world's dying. But you know it isn't the end. You know about the other worlds. And you're right. They exist. I've been there. And I can take you back with me."

The cadaver had picked up the spear and was holding it ready, aimed for Haplo's heart. The dynast made an abrupt gesture, and the cadaver lowered the weapon, brought it down butt end against the cavern floor, and resumed standing at attention.

"Don't harm him. Take him to the dungeon," ordered Kleitus. "Pons, take both of them to the dungeons. We must think this matter through."

"The prince's body, Sire. Shall we send it to oblivion?"

"Where are your brains, Pons?" the dynast demanded irritably. "Of course not! His people will declare war against us. The corpse will tell us everything we need to know to plan our defense. The Kairn Telest must be destroyed utterly, of course. *Then*, you may send the beggar to oblivion along with the rest of his clan. Keep his death hushed up the requisite number of waiting days until we can safely reanimate him. We don't want that rabble to strike before we're ready."

"And how long would you suggest, Sire?"

Kleitus gave the body a professional evaluation. "A man of his youth and vigor with a strong hold on life, a passage of three days will be necessary to make certain the phantasm is tractable. We will be performing the raising ritual ourselves, of course. It's liable to be a bit tricky. One of the dungeon necromancers can perform the preservation rites."

The dynast left the room, walking rapidly, the skirts of his robes flapping about his ankles in his haste.

Probably, thought Haplo with an inward grin, going straight to the library or wherever it is the ancient records are kept.

Cadavers hastened over at Pons's command. Two guards removed the spear from the body of the prince, lifted it between them and bore it away. Dead servants brought water and soap to cleanse the blood from floor and walls. Haplo stood patiently off to one side, observing the proceedings. The chancellor, he noticed, kept avoiding looking at him. Pons fussed about the room, exclaimed loudly over bloodstains on one of the wall tapestries, made a major production of dispatching servants in search of powdered kairn grass to sprinkle on it.

"Well, I suppose that's all that can be done." Pons heaved a sigh. "I don't know what I'm going to say to Her Majesty when she sees this!"

"You might suggest to her husband that there are less violent ways of killing a man," suggested Haplo.

The chancellor gave an unaffected start, glanced about fearfully at the Patryn. "Oh, it's you!" He sounded almost relieved. "I didn't realize—forgive me. We have so few living prisoners. I'd quite forgotten you weren't a cadaver. Here, I'll take you down myself. Guards!"

Pons gestured. Two cadavers hurried to his side and all of them, chancellor and Haplo in front, guards behind, left the game room.

"You appear to be a man of action," said the chancellor, glancing at Haplo. "You didn't hesitate to attack that armed soldier who killed your dog. The death of the prince offended you?"

Offended? One Sartan killing another in cold blood? Amused, maybe, not offended. Haplo told himself that was how he should feel. But he looked with distaste at the blood spattered on his clothing, rubbed it off with the back of his hand.

"The prince was only doing what he thought was right. He didn't deserve to be murdered."

"It was not murder," retorted Pons crisply. "Prince Edmund's life belonged to the dynast, as do the lives of all His Majesty's subjects. The dynast decided that the young man would prove more valuable to him dead than alive."

"He might have allowed the young man to give his opinion on the subject," Haplo observed dryly.

The Patryn was attempting to pay close attention to his whereabouts, but he'd become immediately lost in the maze of identical, interconnecting tunnels. He recognized they were descending only by the slope of the smooth cavern floor. Soon, the gaslights were left behind. Crude torches burned in sconces on the damp walls. Haplo could see, by the flaring light, faint traces of runes running along the walls at floor level. Ahead of him, he heard the echoing sound of footsteps, heavy and shuffling, as if bearing a burden. The prince's body, going to its not-so-final resting place.

The chancellor was frowning. "I find it very difficult to understand you, sir. Your words come to me out of a cloud of darkness, shot with lightning. I see violence in you, violence that makes me shudder, makes my blood run cold. I see vaunting ambition, the desire for power achieved by any means. You are no stranger to death. Yet I sense that you are deeply disturbed by what was, in reality, the execution of a rebel and a traitor."

"We don't kill our own," Haplo said softly.

"I beg your pardon?" Pons leaned nearer. "What was that?"

"I said, 'We don't kill our own,' " Haplo repeated shortly, succinctly. He snapped his mouth shut, troubled, angry at being troubled. And he didn't much like the way everyone around here seemed to be able to stare into the heart and soul of everyone else.

I'm going to welcome prison, he thought. Welcome the soothing, cooling darkness, welcome the silence. He needed the darkness, needed the quiet. He needed time to reflect and think, decide on a course of action. He needed time to sort out and quash these disturbing and confusing thoughts. Which reminded him. He needed a question answered.

"What's this I heard about a prophecy?"

"Prophecy?" Pons's eyes slid sideways to Haplo, slid rapidly away again. "When did you hear about a prophecy?"

"Right after your guard tried to kill me."

"Ah, but you'd only just regained consciousness. You had suffered a severe injury."

"My hearing wasn't injured. The duchess said something about a prophecy. I wondered what she meant."

"Prophecy." The chancellor tapped a finger thoughtfully on his chin. "Let me see if I can remember. I must admit, now I come to think of it, that I was rather baffled by her mentioning the subject. I can't imagine what she was thinking! There have been so many prophecies given to our people over the past centuries, you see. We use them to amuse the children."

Haplo'd seen the look on the chancellor's face when Jera mentioned the prophecy. Pons hadn't been amused.

Before the Patryn could pursue the subject, the chancellor began discussing, with seeming innocence, the runes on the game pieces, obviously trying to wheedle information. Now it was Haplo's turn to dodge Pons's questions. Eventually the chancellor dropped the subject, the two proceeded through the narrow corridors in silence.

The atmosphere of the catacombs was dank and heavy and chill. The smell of decay hung in the air so thickly that Haplo could have sworn he tasted it, like oil on the back of the throat. The only sounds he heard were the footsteps of the dead, leading them on.

"What's this?" came a strange voice suddenly.

The chancellor gasped, involuntarily reached out and grasped hold of Haplo's arm, the living clinging to the living. Haplo himself was disconcerted to feel his heart lurch in his chest and did not rebuke Pons for touching him, although he irritably shook the grasping hand free almost immediately.

A ghostly shape emerged from the shadows into the torchlight.

"Flame and ash, you startled me, preserver!" Pons scolded, mopping his forehead with the sleeve of his black robes, trimmed in green—the mark of his ranking in court. "Don't ever do that again!"

"I beg your pardon, My Lord, but we're not accustomed to seeing the living down here."

The figure bowed. Haplo saw—to his relief, although he didn't like to admit it—that the man was alive.

"You better get used to it," Pons said in acerbic tones, obviously attempting to compensate for his former weakness. "Here's a live prisoner for you and he's to be well treated, by orders of His Majesty."

"Live prisoners," said the preserver, with a cold glance at Haplo, "are a nuisance."

"I know, I know, but it can't be helped. This one—" Pons drew the preserver to one side, whispered earnestly into the man's ear.

The gaze of both men shifted to tattooed runes on the skin of Haplo's hands and arms. Their stares made his flesh crawl, but he forced himself to stand still beneath the scrutiny. He'd be damned if he'd give them the satisfaction of seeing that they made him uncomfortable.

The preserver didn't appear particularly mollified. "Freak or not, when all's said and done, he has to be fed and watered and watched, doesn't he? And I'm only one man down here during the sleep-half shift, with no help, although I've asked for it often enough."

"His Majesty is aware . . . deeply regrets . . . can't be done at this time . . ." Pons was murmuring.

The preserver snorted, waved a hand at Haplo, gave an order to one of the dead. "Put the live one in the cell next to the dead one who came in tonight. I can work on one and keep my eye on the other."

"I'm certain His Majesty will be wanting to speak to you on the morrow," said the chancellor, by way of bidding Haplo farewell.

I'm certain he will, Haplo answered, but not aloud. He pulled back from the cadaver's touch. "Make that thing keep its hands off me!"

"What did I tell you?" the preserver demanded of Pons. "Come with me, then."

Haplo and his escort marched past cells occupied by corpses, some of them lying on cold, stone beds, others up and moving aimlessly about. In the shadows, the phantasms could be seen hovering near their corpses, the faint pale glow they gave off softly illuminating the cell's darkness. Iron bars with locked doors prevented escape from the small, cavelike cells.

"You bolt the doors against the dead?" Haplo asked, almost laughing.

The preserver came to halt, fumbled with a key in the door of an empty cell. Glancing at the cell across from him, Haplo saw the prince's corpse, a gaping hole in its chest, being laid out on a stone bier by two cadavers.

"Of course, we keep them locked up! You don't suppose I want them wandering about underfoot? I have enough to do down here as it is. Hurry up. I haven't got all night. That newest arrival isn't getting any fresher. I suppose you'll be wanting something to eat and drink?" The preserver slammed shut the door, glared through the bars at his prisoner.

"Just water." Haplo didn't have much appetite.

The preserver brought a cup, shoved it through the bars, ladled water from a bucket into it. Haplo took a drink, spit it out. The water tasted decayed, like everything smelled. Using the remainder, he washed the prince's blood from his hands and arms and legs.

The preserver glowered, as if he considered this a waste of good water, but said nothing. He was obviously in haste to begin his work on the prince. Haplo lay down on the hard stone, cushioned by a few handfuls of scattered kairn grass.

A Sartan chant rose high-pitched and grating, echoing thinly through the cells. At the sound, it seemed another chant arose, almost unheard, a ghastly wailing groan of unutterable sorrow. The phantasms, Haplo told himself. But the sounds reminded him of the dog, of that last pain-filled yelp. He saw the eyes looking at him, confident that its master would be there to help, as Haplo had always been there. Faithful, believing in him, to the end.

Haplo grit his teeth, and blotted the sight from his mind. Digging his hand into his pocket, he drew out one of the rune-bones he'd managed to palm during the game. He couldn't see it, in the darkness, but he turned it over in his hand, fingers tracing the sigla carved into the surface.

CHAPTER 25

OLD PROVINCES,

ABARRACH

◆

"AND THEN, FATHER," SAID JERA, "THE PHANTASM BEGAN TO TAKE shape and form—"

"Become solid, Daughter?"

"No." Jera hesitated, thoughtful, frowning, trying to put her memories into words. "It remained ethereal, translucent. If I tried to touch it, my hand would feel nothing. But yet I could see . . . features, details. The insignia he wore on his breastplate, the shape of his nose, battle scars on his arms. Father, I could see the man's eyes! Yes, his eyes! He *looked* at me, looked at all of us. And it was as if he'd won a great victory. Then, he . . . disappeared."

Jera spread her hands. So provocative were her words and so eloquent her gesture that Alfred could almost see again the diaphanous figure dwindle and fade like morning mist beneath an ever-shining sun.

"You should have seen," added Jonathan with his warm, boyish laugh, "the expression on old Pons's face!"

"Mmmm, yes," muttered the earl.

Jera flushed delicately. "Husband dear, this matter is really quite serious."

"I know, darling, I know." Jonathan struggled to regain his self-composure. "But you have to admit, it *was* funny . . ."

A smile crept over Jera's lips. "More wine, Papa," she said, and hastily moved to fill her father's glass.

When she thought the earl wasn't watching, Jera shook her head in fond, mock reproof at her husband, who grinned back at her and winked.

The earl saw and wasn't amused. Alfred had the uncomfortable impression there wasn't much that went on around him that the earl didn't see. A dried-up, wizened husk of a man, the earl kept his beady black-eyed gaze constantly darting about the room, then suddenly sent the darts into Alfred.

"I'd like to see you do that spell of yours." The earl spoke as if Alfred had performed a rather ingenious card trick. The earl leaned forward in his chair, balancing himself on sharp-pointed elbows. "Do it again. I'll call one of the cadavers. Which one, Daughter, can we afford to spare—"

"I—I couldn't!" Alfred stammered, becoming more and more flustered as he sought to grope his way through the morass threatening to engulf him. "It was impulse. Act of the . . . the moment, you see. I looked up and . . . there was that sword c-coming down. The runes . . . just popped into my head . . . er . . . so to speak."

"And just popped back out again, eh?" The earl jabbed a sharp-boned finger into Alfred's ribs. Every part of the old man's body appeared to have been honed on a grindstone.

"So to speak," returned Alfred faintly.

The earl chuckled and poked him again. Alfred could almost envision truth being sucked out of him like blood whenever that knifelike finger or those knifelike eyes touched him. But what was the truth? Did he truly not know what he'd done? Or was one part of him hiding it from the other, as he'd grown so adept at doing over these many years of being forced to conceal his true identity?

Alfred passed a shaking hand through his thinning hair.

"Father, leave him be." Jera came to stand at Alfred's side, placed her hands on his shoulders. "More wine, Sir?"

"No, thank you, Your Grace." Alfred's glass stood untouched, untasted. "If you would excuse me, I'm very tired. I'd like to lay down . . ."

"Of course, Sir," said Jonathan. "We've been thoughtless, keeping you up well into the dynast's sleep time after what must have been a terrible cycle for you—"

More than you know, Alfred said to himself sadly, with a shudder. Far more than you know! He rose unsteadily to his feet.

"I'll show you to your room," Jera offered.

The faint sound of a bell chimed softly through the gas-lighted darkness. All four in the room hushed, three of them exchanged conscious glances.

"That will be news from the palace," said the earl, starting to rise on creaking limbs.

"I'll go," Jera said. "We daren't trust the dead." She left them, disappearing into the shadows.

"You'll want to hear this, I'm sure, Sir," said the earl, black eyes glittering. He waved a hand, inviting—or ordering—Alfred to be seated.

Alfred had no choice but to sink back down into the chair, although he was miserably conscious of the fact that he didn't want to hear whatever news came swiftly and secretly in what, for this world, were the waning hours of the cycle.

The men waited in silence, Jonathan's face was pale and troubled, the old earl looked crafty and enthused. Alfred stared bleakly, hopelessly at a blank wall.

The earl lived in Old Province, on what had once been a large and affluent estate. Ages ago, the land had been alive, worked by immense numbers of cadavers. The house had overlooked waving stands of kairn grass and tall, blue-flowered lanti trees. Now the house itself had become a cadaver. The lands round it were barren, lifeless seas of ash-mud created by the endless rain.

The earl's dwelling was not a cavern-formed structure, as were many in Necropolis, but had been built of blocks of stone, reminding Alfred strongly of the castles the Sartan had created during the height of their power in the High Realms of Arianus.

The castle was large, but most of the back rooms had been shut off and abandoned, their upkeep difficult to maintain because the only person who dwelt here was the earl and the cadavers of old servants. But the front part of the house was exceptionally well preserved, compared to other mournful and dilapidated dwellings they had passed during the carriage ride through the Old Provinces.

"It's the ancient runes, you see," the earl told Alfred, with a sharp glance. "Most people took them off. Couldn't read them and thought they made the place look old-fashioned. But I left them on, took care of them. And they've taken care of me. Kept my house standing when many another's sunk into dust."

Alfred could read the runes, could almost feel the strength of the magic upholding the walls over the centuries. But he said nothing, fearful of saying too much.

The lived-in portion of the castle consisted of downstairs utility rooms: a kitchen, servants' quarters, pantry, front and back entryways, and a laboratory where the earl conducted his experiments in attempting to bring life back to the soil of the Old Provinces. The two levels above were divided into comfortable family living quarters: bedchambers, guest rooms, drawing room, dining area.

A dynast clock[1] headed for its bedchamber, indicating the current time. Alfred thought longingly of bed, sleep, blessed oblivion, if only for a few hours before returning to this waking nightmare.

He must have actually dozed off, because when a door opened, he experienced the unpleasant tingling sensation of being awakened from a nap he had never meant to take. Blinking, he focused bleary eyes on Jera and a man wrapped in a black cloak, emerging from a doorway at the far end of the room.

"I thought you should hear this news from Tomas himself, in case you had any questions," said Jera.

Alfred knew, then, that the news was bad and he let his head sink into his hand. How much more could he take?

"The prince and the stranger with the rune-covered skin are both dead," said Tomas in a low voice. He stepped into the light, pulled the cowl from off his head. He was a young man, near Jonathan's age. His robes were dirty, fouled with mud as if he had ridden hard and fast. "The dynast executed both of them this very night in the palace gaming room."

"Were you present? Did you see it happen?" the earl demanded, sharp-hewn face jutting forward, seeming to slice the air in its eagerness.

"No, but I talked to a dead guard whose duty it was to take the bodies to the catacombs. It told me that the preserver was being set to work to maintain both men."

"The dead told you!" The old man sneered. "You can't trust the dead."

---

[1] A diminutive clay model of the dynast himself set within its own miniature duplicate of the palace. As originally designed, the dynast doll was attuned magically to the dynast and portrayed the current time by its position within its play palace. Thus when the doll went to bed, the hour was the dynast's sleeping hour. When the doll sat down to dinner, it was the dynast's dining hour. When the magic on Abarrach grew weaker, the dolls began to keep less-than-perfect time.

"I am well aware of that, Milord. I pretended that I didn't know the dynast had canceled his rune-bone game and blundered into the gaming room. The cadavers were cleaning up a great pool of blood— fresh blood. A blood-covered spear, its tip notched, lay nearby. There can be little doubt. The men are dead."

Jera shook her head, sighed. "Poor prince. Poor young man, so handsome, honorable. But one's ill fortune can be another's good luck, as they say."

"Yes," said the old man fiercely, eagerly. "*Our* luck!"

"All we need do is rescue the cadavers. The prince and your friend's." Jera turned briskly to Alfred. "It will be dangerous, of course, but—my dear sir," she said in sudden consternation, "are you all right? Jonathan, bring him a glass of stalagma."

Alfred sat staring at her, unable to move, unable to think in any rational manner. Words burst forth from him. He rose, clumsy and stumbling, to his feet. "Haplo, the prince—dead. Murdered. My own people. Killing wantonly. And you—you callous . . . Treating death as if it were nothing more than a mild inconvenience, a nuisance, like a cold in the head!"

"Here, drink this." Jonathan held out a glass of a foul-smelling liquor. "You should have eaten more at dinner—"

"Dinner!" Alfred cried hoarsely. He knocked the glass away, backed up until he bumped into a wall and could go no farther. "The lives of two people have been torn from them and you can talk only of eating more dinner! Of . . . of recovering their . . . their bodies!"

"Sir, I assure you. The corpses will be well treated." This from Tomas, the stranger. "I know the late-cycle preserver, personally. He is highly skilled in this art. You will note little change in your friend—"

"Little change!" Alfred ran his trembling hand over his bald head. "It is death that gives life its meaning. Death, the great equalizer. Man, woman, peasant, king, rich, poor: all of us fellow travelers to our journey's end. Life is sacred, precious, a thing to value, to cherish, not to be taken lightly or wantonly. You have lost all respect for death and thereby all respect for life. Stealing a man's life is no more a crime to you than . . . than stealing his money!"

"Crime!" countered Jera. "You talk of crime? *You* were the one who committed the crime! You destroyed the body, sent the phantasm into oblivion where it will chafe forever, bereft of any form or shape."

"It had form, it had shape!" Alfred cried. "You saw it! The man was finally free!" He paused, confounded by what he'd said.

"Free?" Jera stared at him in bewilderment. "Free to do what? Free to go where?"

Alfred flushed hotly, shivered with chills. The Sartan, demigods. Capable of forging worlds from one that was doomed. Capable of creation. But creation had been brought about by destruction. Our magic led the way to necromancy. This next step was inevitable. From controlling life, to controlling death.

Yet why is that so terrible? Why does every fiber of my being revolt against this practice?

He saw, once again, the mausoleum back on Arianus, the bodies of his friends lying in their tombs. He'd felt a sadness when he had visited them the last time before he'd left Arianus. His sorrow was not so much for them, he realized, as for himself. Left alone.

He recalled, as well, the deaths of his parents in the Labyrinth. . . .

No, Alfred remembered confusedly. That had been Haplo's parents. But he'd felt the tearing grief, the raging anger, the terrible fear. . . . Again, for himself. For Haplo, that is. Left alone. The mangled bodies who had fought and struggled had found peace at last. Death had taught Haplo to hate, hate the enemy who had locked his parents inside the prison that had killed them. But, although Haplo might not know it himself, death had taught him other lessons, as well.

And now Haplo was dead. And I'd almost begun to think there was a chance that he . . .

A whine broke in on Alfred's thoughts. The swipe of a tongue, cold and wet on his skin, made him jump.

A black, nondescript dog gazed up at him worriedly, cocked its head to one side. It raised a paw, placed it on Alfred's knee. Liquid brown eyes offered consolation for trouble felt, if not understood.

Alfred stared at the dog, then, recovering from his initial shock, he threw his arms around the animal's neck. He could almost have wept.

The dog had been prepared to offer sympathy, but such rough familiarity was apparently not to be tolerated. It wriggled out of Alfred's grasp, regarded the man in puzzlement.

Why all the fuss? it seemed to say. I'm only obeying orders.

Watch him. Haplo's final command.

"G-good boy," Alfred said, reaching out gingerly to pat the furry black head.

The dog submitted to the caress, indicating, with a dignified air, that head patting was acceptable and the relationship might advance to ear scratching, but a line had to be drawn somewhere and it hoped that Alfred understood.

Alfred did understand.

"Haplo's not dead! He's alive!" he cried.

Looking around, he saw everyone in the room staring at him.

"How did you do that?" Jera's face was livid, her lips white. "The beast's corpse was destroyed! We saw it!"

"Tell me, Daughter! What are you talking about?" her father demanded irascibly.

"That . . . that dog, Father! It was the one the guard threw into the mud pit!"

"Are you sure? Maybe it resembles—"

"Of course I'm sure, Father! Look at Alfred. He knows the dog! And the dog knows him!"

"Another trick. How did you manage this one?" the earl asked. "What marvelous magic is this? If you can restore cadavers that have been destroyed—"

"I told you, Father!" Jera gasped, hardly able to speak for awe. "The prophecy!"

Silence. Jonathan gazed at Alfred with the undisguised and fascinated wonder of a child. The earl, his daughter, and the stranger regarded the Sartan with shrewd, thoughtful eyes, perhaps plotting how best they could make use of him.

"No trick! Not me! I didn't do anything," Alfred protested. "It wasn't my magic that brought the dog back. It's Haplo's—"

"Your friend? But, I assure you, sir, he's dead," said Jonathan, with a glance at his wife that said plainly, *Poor man's gone mad.*

"No, no, he's not dead. *Your* friend, here, must be mistaken. You didn't actually see the body, did you?" Alfred asked.

"I didn't. But the blood, the spear—"

"I tell you," Alfred insisted, "that the dog would not be here if Haplo were dead. I can't explain how I know, because I am not even certain my theory about the animal is the correct one. But I do know this. It would take more than a spear to kill my . . . er . . . friend. His magic is powerful, very powerful."

"Well, well. There's no use arguing over it. Either he's alive or he isn't. All the more reason for us to get him, or what's left of him, out of the dynast's clutches," said the earl. He turned to Tomas. "And, now, sir, when will the resurrection on the prince be performed?"

"Three cycles hence, according to my source, Milord."

"That gives us time," Jera said, twining her fingers together, her expression thoughtful. "Time to plan. And time to get a message to his people. When Prince Edmund doesn't return, they will guess what has happened. They must be warned not to do anything until we're ready."

"Ready? Ready for what?" asked Alfred, perplexed.

"War," said Jera.

War. Sartan fighting Sartan. In all the centuries of Sartan history, there had never been such a tragedy. We sundered a world to save it from conquest by our enemy and we succeeded. We won a great victory.

And lost.

CHAPTER ♦ 26

NECROPOLIS,

ABARRACH

♦

ONE CYCLE FOLLOWING THE PRINCE'S DEATH, THE DYNAST CANCELED his audience hour, a thing he had never before been known to do. The Lord High Chancellor gave it out publicly that His Majesty was fatigued with pressures of state. Privately, Pons allowed it to be known to a privileged few, "in strictest confidence," that His Majesty had received disturbing reports concerning an enemy army camped across the Fire Sea.

As Kleitus had foreseen, the alarming news drizzled down among Necropolis's inhabitants like the incessant laze, creating an atmosphere of tension and panic quite conducive to his plans. He spent the cycle secreted in the palace library, quite alone, except for the dead who guarded him and they didn't matter anyway.

> Elihn, God in One, looked on Chaos with displeasure. He stretched forth his hand and this motion created the Wave Prime.[1] Order was established, taking the form of a world blessed with intelligent life. Elihn was pleased with his creation and granted all good things needed to sustain life thereon. Once he set the Wave in motion, Elihn left the world, knowing that the Wave would maintain the world and a Caretaker was no longer necessary. The three races created by the Wave, elves, humans, and dwarves, lived in harmony.

[1] Refer to *Magic in the Sundered Realms, Excerpt from a Sartan's Musings,* Vol. 1.

"Mensch," Kleitus declared in disdain and scanned rapidly over the next few paragraphs of text, which dealt with the creation of the first races, now known as the lesser races. The particular item of information he sought wouldn't be found in this section, although he remembered it as being near the beginning of the dissertation. It had been a long time since he'd read this particular manuscript, and at that time he'd paid scant attention to it. He'd been searching for a way out of this world, not a history of another world long dead and gone.

But, during the small hours of a sleepless sleep-half, a phrase had come to His Majesty's mind, a phrase he recalled reading from the pages of a text. The phrase brought him bolt upright in his bed. Its discovery was of such importance that it had prompted him to cancel the cyclical audience. A rummage through his memory brought the book to recollection. He had only to track it down and corner the words.

> In its effort to maintain balance and prevent degeneration back into Chaos, the Wave Prime constantly corrects itself. Thus the Wave rises and thus it dips. Thus there is light and thus darkness. Thus good and thus evil. Thus peace, thus war.
>
> At the world's beginning, during what were known falsely as the Dark Ages, people believed in magical laws and in spiritual laws, balanced by physical laws. But as time passed, a new religion swept the land. It was known as "science." Propagating physical laws, science ridiculed the spiritual and the magical laws, claiming that they were "illusions."
>
> The human race, because of their short-lived span of time, became particularly enamored of this new religion, which held out the false promise of immortality. They referred to this period of time as the Renaissance. The elven race maintained their belief in magic and were now consequently persecuted and driven from the world. The dwarven race, quite skilled with things mechanical, offered to work with the humans. But the humans wanted slaves, not partners, and so the dwarves left the world on their own, taking refuge beneath the ground. Eventually, humans forgot these other races, ceased to believe in magic. The Wave lost its shape, became erratic, one end bulged with strength and power, the other end was flat and weak.
>
> But the Wave would ever correct itself and it did, at horrific cost. At the end of the twentieth century, the humans unleashed a terrible war upon themselves. Their weapons were marvels of

scientific design and technology and brought death and destruction to untold millions. In that day, science destroyed itself.

The dynast frowned in displeasure. Certain parts of this work appeared to him to be wild surmise and speculation. He had never known any mensch—all those in Kairn Necros had died before he'd been born—but he found it extremely difficult to believe that any race would bring deliberate destruction on itself.

"I did find corroborating texts to back this up." He often spoke aloud to himself when in the library, to relieve the incessant, nerve-racking silence. "But the writers came out of the same early period of our history and probably shared the same faulty information. Thus they all might be considered suspect. I shall keep that in mind."

The survivors were plunged into what was known as the Age of Dust, during which they were forced to struggle to simply remain alive. It was during this struggle that there arose a mutant strain of humans who could, now that the incessant din of science was shattered, hear the flow of the Wave around them and feel it within them. They recognized and utilized the Wave's potential for magical power. They developed the runes, to direct and channel the magic. Wizards, male and female, banded together in order to bring hope to lives lost in darkness. They called themselves Sartan, meaning, in the rune language, "Those Who Bring Back Light."

"Yes, yes." The dynast sighed. He'd formerly had little use for history, for a past dead and gone, a corpse decayed beyond the point of resurrection.

Or, perhaps not.

The task proved enormous. We Sartan were few in number. In order to facilitate the rebirth of the world, we went forth and taught the most rudimentary use of magic to the lesser peoples, reserving the true nature and power of the Wave for ourselves, that we might maintain control and prevent the catastrophe that had occurred from reoccurring.

Fondly, we believed that we *were* the Wave. Too late, we realized that we ourselves were only a part of the Wave, that we had become a bulge in the Wave and that the Wave would take corrective action. Too late, we discovered that some of us had forsaken the altruistic goals of our work. These wizards sought power through the magic, they sought rulership of the world. Patryns, they called themselves, "Those Who Return to Darkness."

"Ah!" Kleitus took a breath and settled himself to read more carefully and concisely.

> The Patryns named themselves thus in mockery of us, their brethren, and because, in the beginning, they were forced to work in dark and secret places in order to remain hidden from us. They are a close-knit people, fiercely loyal to each other and to their one abiding goal, which is the absolute and complete domination of the world.

"Absolute and complete domination," the dynast repeated, rubbing his forehead with his hand.

> It proved impossible to penetrate such a closed society and learn their secrets. We Sartan tried, but those we sent among the Patryns disappeared; it can only be assumed that they were discovered and destroyed. Thus we know little about the Patryns or their magic.

Kleitus scowled in disappointment, but continued reading.

> It is theorized that the Patryns' use of rune-magic is grounded in the physical portion of the Wave, whereas our magic tends to be based in the spiritual. We sing the runes and dance them and draw them in the air, resorting to physically transcribing them when necessity dictates.
> The Patryns, on the other hand, rely heavily on the physical representation of the runes themselves, even going so far as to paint them on their own bodies in order to enhance their magic. I trace—

The dynast stopped, returned, and read the words over again. 'Paint them on their own bodies in order to enhance their magic.' He continued on, reading aloud. " 'I trace, as a curiosity, some of the rune structures that they have been known to use. Note the similarity to our runes, but note also that it is the barbaric manner in which the sigla are constructed that radically alters the magic, creating—as it were—an entirely new language of crude but forceful magical power.' "

Kleitus lifted several of the rune-bones from his game and placed them on the page, next to the drawings of that ancient Sartan author. The matches were almost perfect. "It's so blasted obvious. Why didn't I ever notice before?"

Shaking his head, vexed at himself, he resumed reading.

The Wave, for the moment, appears stable. But there are those among us who fear that the Patryns are growing stronger and that the Wave is beginning to bulge again. There are some who argue that we must go to war, stop the Patryns now. There are some, myself included, who caution that we must do nothing to upset the balance or the Wave will bulge in the other direction.

The treatise continued on, but the dynast closed the text. It contained nothing more about the Patryns, wandered into speculation about what might happen if the Wave bulged. The dynast already knew the answer. It had, and then had come the Sundering, and then life in this tomb of a world. So much he knew of the history of the Sartan.

But he had forgotten the Patryns, the ancient enemy, bringers of darkness, possessors of a "crude but forceful" magical power.

"Absolute and complete domination . . ." he repeated softly to himself. "What fools we've been. What complete and utter fools. But it isn't too late. They think they're clever. They think they can catch us unawares. But it won't work."

After several more moments' reflection, he beckoned to one of the cadavers. "Send for the Lord High Chancellor."

The dead servant left, returning almost instantaneously with Pons, whose value lay in the fact that he was always where he could be easily found when he was wanted and was conveniently absent when he wasn't.

"Your Majesty," said Pons, bowing low.

"Has Tomas returned?"

"Just this moment, I believe."

"Bring him to us."

"Here, Your Majesty?"

Kleitus paused, glanced around, nodded. "Yes, here."

The matter being an important one, Pons went on the errand himself. One of the cadavers might have been dispatched to fetch the young man, but there was always the possibility, with the dead servants, that the cadaver might bring back a basket of rez flowers, having completely forgotten its original instructions.

Pons returned to one of the public rooms, where large numbers of couriers and suitors were wont to be found. The dynast's appearance in the room would have struck them like a bolt of lightning from the colossus, shocking them into a frenzy of fawning and bowing and scraping. As it was, the appearance of the Lord High Chancellor sent a mild jolt through the throng. A few of the lower-ranking members of the nobility bowed humbly, the upper echelon ceased their rune-bone playing and conversations and turned their heads. Those who knew Pons well gave him greeting, much to the jealous envy of those who did not.

"What's up, Pons?" asked one languidly.

The Lord High Chancellor smiled. "His Majesty is in need—"

Numerous couriers rose instantly to their feet.

"—of a living messenger," Pons finished. He gazed about the room with apparent bored indifference.

"Errand boy, huh?" A baron yawned.

The upper echelon, knowing that this was a menial task, one that probably wouldn't even involve actually seeing the dynast, returned to their games and gossip.

"You, there." Pons gestured to a young man standing near the back of the room. "What is your name?"

"Tomas, My Lord."

"Tomas. You'll do. Come this way."

Tomas bowed in silent acquiescence and followed the Lord High Chancellor out of the antechamber into the private and guarded section of the palace. Neither spoke, beyond one brief exchange of significant glances on leaving the antechamber. The Lord High Chancellor preceded the young man, who walked several paces behind Pons as was proper, his hands folded in his sleeves, his black and untrimmed cowl drawn low over his head.

The Lord High Chancellor paused outside the library, made a sign to the young man to wait. Tomas did as he was bid, standing silently in the shadows. One of the dead guards thrust open the stone door. Pons looked inside. Kleitus had returned to his reading. On hearing the door open, he glanced up and—seeing his minister—nodded.

Pons beckoned to the young man, who slid out of the shadows

and in through the door. The Lord High Chancellor entered with him, shut the door softly behind him. The cadavers guarding His Majesty took up their positions.

The dynast returned to perusing the text spread out on the table before him.

The young man and Pons stood quietly, waiting.

"You have been to the earl's dwelling, Tomas?" Kleitus asked, without looking up.

"I have just now returned, Sire," said the young man, bowing.

"And you found them there—the duke and duchess and the stranger?"

"Yes, Your Majesty."

"And you did as you were told?"

"Yes, of course, Sire."

"With what result?"

"A—a rather peculiar result, Sire. If I may explain—" Tomas took a step forward.

Kleitus, eyes on his text, waved a negligent hand.

Tomas frowned, glanced at Pons, the young man asking if the dynast was paying attention.

The Lord High Chancellor answered with a peremptory raise of his eyebrows, meaning, "His Majesty is paying far more attention to you than you might wish."

Tomas, now appearing somewhat uncomfortable, launched into his report. "As Your Majesty is aware, the duke and duchess believe that I am one of their party, involved in this misguided rebellion." The young man paused to bow, to demonstrate his true feelings.

The dynast turned a page.

Tomas, receiving no acknowledgment, continued, discomfiture growing. "I told them of the prince's murder—"

"Murder?" Kleitus stirred, the hand turning the page paused.

Tomas cast Pons a pleading glance.

"Forgive him, Majesty," the Lord High Chancellor said softly, "but that is how the rebels would view the prince's lawful execution. Tomas must appear to join in their views, in order to convince them that he is one of them, and thus remain useful to Your Majesty."

The dynast resumed the turning of his page, smoothed it with his hand.

Tomas, with a small sigh of relief, continued, "I told them that the man with the rune-painted skin was dead, as well." The young man hesitated, uncertain how to continue.

"With what result?" Kleitus prompted, running a finger down the page.

"The man's friend, the one who killed the dead, denied the report."

The dynast looked up from his reading. "Denied it?"

"Yes, Your Majesty. He said he knew that his friend, whom they called 'Haplo,' was alive."

"He *knew* it, you say?" The dynast exchanged glances with the Lord High Chancellor.

"Yes, Sire. He seemed quite firmly convinced of the fact. It had something to do with a dog—"

His Majesty was about to say something, but the Lord High Chancellor raised a finger in a warding, albeit highly respectful, manner.

"Dog?" Pons asked. "What about a dog?"

"A dog entered the room while I was there. It went up to the stranger, whose name is Alfred. This Alfred appeared quite pleased to see the dog and he said that now he knew Haplo wasn't dead."

"What did this dog look like?"

Tomas thought back. "A largish animal. Black fur, with white eyebrows. It's very intelligent. Or seems so. It . . . listens. To conversations. Almost as if it understood—"

"The very animal, Sire." Pons turned to Kleitus. "The one that was thrown into the boiling mud pit. I saw it die! Its body sucked down beneath the ooze."

"Yes, that's exactly right!" Tomas appeared amazed. "That's what the duchess said, Your Majesty! She and the duke couldn't believe their eyes. The duchess Jera said something about the prophecy. But the stranger, Alfred, denied most vehemently that he'd had anything to do with it."

"What did he say about the dog, how it came to be alive?"

"He said he couldn't explain, but if the dog is alive, then Haplo must be alive."

"Exceedingly strange!" murmured Kleitus. "And did you find out, Tomas, how these two strangers managed to make their way to Kairn Necros?"

"A ship, Sire. According to the duke, who told me as I was leaving, they arrived in a ship which they left docked at Safe Harbor.

The ship is made of a strange substance and is, by the duke's account, covered with runes, much like the stranger Haplo's body."

"And what do the duke and duchess and the old earl plan to do now?"

"They are sending, this cycle, a message to the prince's people, telling them of their ruler's untimely death. In three cycles' time, when the resurrection is complete, the duke and duchess plan to rescue the prince's cadaver and return him to his people and urge them to declare war on Your Majesty. The earl's faction will join with the people of Kairn Telest."

"So, in three cycles, they plot to break into the palace dungeons and rescue the prince."

"That is true, Sire."

"And you offered them your willing assistance, Tomas?"

"As you commanded me, Sire. I am to meet with them this night, to go over the final details."

"Keep us apprised. You run a risk, you know that? If they discover you are a spy, they will kill you and send you into oblivion."

"I welcome the risk, Sire." Tomas placed his hand over his heart, bowed low. "I am completely devoted to Your Majesty."

"Continue your good work and your devotion will be rewarded." Kleitus lowered his eyelids, resumed his reading.

Tomas looked at Pons, who indicated that the interview was at an end. Bowing again, the young man left the library alone, escorted through the dynast's private chambers by one of the servant cadavers.

When Tomas was gone and the door shut behind him, Kleitus looked up from his book. It was obvious, from the staring, searching expression, that he hadn't seen the page lying open before him. He was looking far away, far beyond the cavern walls surrounding him.

The Lord High Chancellor watched the eyes grow dark and shadowed, saw lines deepen in the forehead. A tingle of apprehension knotted Pons's stomach. He glided nearer, treading softly, not daring to disturb. He knew he was wanted, because he had not been dismissed. Approaching the table, he sat down in a chair and waited in silence.

A long time passed. Kleitus stirred, sighed.

Pons, knowing his cue, asked softly, "Your Majesty understands all this: the arrival of the two strangers, the man with the runes on his skin, the dog that was dead and is now alive?"

"Yes, Pons, we believe we do."

The Lord High Chancellor waited, again, in silence.

"The Sundering," said the dynast. "The cataclysmic war that would once and for all bring peace to our universe. What if we told you that we didn't win that war as we have so fondly assumed all these centuries? What if we told you, Pons, that we lost?"

"Sire!"

"Defeat. That is why the help that was promised us never came. The Patryns have conquered the other worlds. Now they wait, poised, to take over this one. We are all that remains. The hope of the universe."

"The prophecy!" Pons whispered, and there was true awe in his tone. At last, he was beginning to believe.

Kleitus noticed his minister's conversion, noticed that faith came rather late, but smiled grimly and said nothing. It wasn't important.

"And now, chancellor, leave us," he added, coming out of his momentary reverie. "Cancel all our engagements for the next two cycles. Say that we have received disturbing news concerning the hostile enemy force across the Fire Sea and that we are making preparations to protect our city. We will see no one."

"Does that include Her Majesty, Sire?"

The marriage had been one of convenience, meant to do nothing more than maintain the dynastic rule. Kleitus XIV had produced Kleitus XV, along with several other sons and daughters. The dynasty was assured.

"You, alone, are excepted, Pons. But only in an emergency."

"Very good, Sire. And where will I find Your Majesty if I am in need of counsel?"

"Here, Pons," said Kleitus, glancing around the library. "Studying. There is much to be done, and only two cycles in which to do it."

CHAPTER • 27

OLD PROVINCES,

ABARRACH

♦

THE TIME PERIOD WAS KNOWN AS THE DYNAST'S WAKING HOUR AND, although the dynast himself was far away in the city of Necropolis, the household in Old Province was up and stirring. The dead had to be roused from their slumber time state of lethargy, the magic that kept them functional renewed, and their daily tasks urged on them. Jera, as necromancer in her father's house, moved among the cadavers, chanting the runes that brought the mockery of life to the servants and workers.

The dead do not sleep, as do the living. They are told at slumber time to sit down and not move about, for fear of disturbing the living members of the household. The cadavers obediently take themselves to whatever out-of-the-way spot can be found for them and wait, motionless and silent, through the sleeping hours.

"They do not sleep, but are they dreaming?" Alfred wondered, regarding them with wrenching pity.

It may have been his imagination, but he fancied that during this time when contact with the living was forgone, set aside until the morrow, the faces of the dead grew sad. The phantasm shapes hovering over their physical husks cried out in despair. Lying on his bed, Alfred tossed and turned, his rest broken by the restless sighs of whispered keening.

"What a quaint fancy," said Jera, over breakfast.

The duke and duchess and Alfred dined together. The earl had already broken his fast, she explained apologetically, and had gone downstairs to work in his laboratory. Alfred was able to obtain only a vague idea of what the old man was doing, something about experimenting with varieties of kairn grass to see if he could develop a hardy strain that could be grown in the cold and barren soil of the Old Provinces.

"The moaning sound must have been the wind you heard," Jera continued, pouring kairn-grass tea and dishing up rashers of torb.[1] (Alfred, who had been afraid to ask, was vastly relieved to note that a living female servant did the cooking.)

"Not unless the wind has a voice and words to speak," Alfred said, but he said it to his plate and no one else heard him.

"You know, I used to think the same thing when I was a child," said Jonathan. "Funny, I'd forgotten all about it until you brought it up. I had an old nanny who used to sit with me during sleep-time and, after she died, her corpse was reanimated and, naturally, she came back into the nursery to do what she'd always done in life. But I couldn't sleep with her in there, after she was dead. It seemed to me she was crying. Mother tried to explain it was just my imagination. I suppose it was, but at that time it was very real to me."

"What happened to her?" Alfred asked.

Jonathan appeared slightly shamefaced. "Mother eventually had to get rid of her. You know how children get something fixed in their minds. You can't argue logically with a child. They talked and talked to me but nothing would do but that nanny had to go."

"What a spoiled brat!" said Jera, smiling at her husband over her teacup.

"Yes, I rather think I was," said Jonathan, flushing in embarrassment. "I was the youngest, you know. By the way, dear, speaking of home—"

Jera set down her teacup, shook her head. "Out of the question. I know how worried you are about the harvest, but Rift Ridge is the first place the dynast's men will come searching for us."

"But won't this place be the second?" Jonathan inquired, pausing in his eating, his fork halfway to his mouth.

Jera ate her breakfast complacently. "I received a message from

---

[1] Most probably a descendant of the pig, which was brought by the Sartan to this world following the Sundering. A large portion of the diet of the Sartan on Abarrach consists of meat, vegetables being extremely scarce, and the torb is their primary source. Torb graze on kairn grass and are raised in the New Provinces and brought to market in Necropolis.

Tomas this morning. The dynast's men have set out for Rift Ridge. It will take them at least a half cycle's march to reach our castle. They'll waste time searching, and then another half cycle's journey back to report. If Kleitus even cares about us anymore, now that he has this war to fight, he'll order them to come here. They can't possibly arrive in Old Provinces before tomorrow. And we're leaving this cycle, once Tomas returns."

"Isn't she wonderful, Alfred?" said Jonathan, regarding his wife admiringly. "*I* would have never reasoned any of that out. I'd have run off wildly, without thinking, and landed right in the arms of the dynast's men."

"Yes, wonderful," mumbled Alfred.

This talk of troops searching for them and sneaking about in the slumber-time and hiding completely unnerved him. The smell and sight of the greasy torb on his plate made him nauseous. Jera and Jonathan were gazing lovingly into each other's eyes. Albert lifted a largish piece of torb off his plate and slipped it to the dog, who was lying at his feet. The treat was graciously accepted, with a wag of the tail.

After breakfast, the duke and duchess disappeared to make arrangements for the night's decampment. The earl remained in the laboratory. Alfred was left to his own dismal company (and that of the ever-present dog). He wandered the house, and eventually found the library.

The room was small and windowless, light came from glowing gas lamps on the walls. Shelves, built into the stone walls, housed numerous volumes. A few were quite old, their leather binding cracked and worn. He approached these in some trepidation, not certain what he feared finding; perhaps voices from the past, speaking to him of failure and defeat. He was vastly relieved to see that they were nothing more alarming than monographs written on agricultural topics: *The Cultivation of Kairn Grass, Diseases Common to the Pauka.*

"There's even," he said conversationally, glancing down, "a book on dogs."

The animal, hearing its name, pricked its ears and thumped its tail against the floor.

"Although I bet I wouldn't find mention of anything like you!" Alfred murmured.

The dog's mouth parted in a grin, the intelligent eyes seemed to be laughing in agreement.

Alfred continued his desultory search, hoping to come across something innocuous to occupy his mind, take it away from the turmoil and danger and horror surrounding him. A thick volume, its spine lavishly decorated in gold leaf, caught his eye. It was a handsome work, well bound and, although obviously well read, lovingly cared for. He drew it out, turned it over, to see the cover.

The Modern Art of Necromancy.

Shuddering from head to toe, Alfred attempted to place the book back on the shelf. His trembling hands, more clumsy than usual, failed. He dropped the volume and fled the room, fled even that portion of the house.

He roamed disconsolately through the earl's gloomy mansion. Unable to rest, unable to sit still, he gravitated from room to room, peering out the windows at the bleak landscape, his large feet displacing small articles of furniture or stumbling over the dog, his hands upending cups of kairn-grass tea.

What is it you fear? he asked himself, his thoughts constantly straying back to the library. Surely not that you will succumb to the temptation of practicing this black art! His gaze went to a servant cadaver, who had, in life, cleaned up spilled cups of kairn-grass tea and who was mechanically performing the same task after death.

Alfred turned to stare out a window at the black, ash-covered landscape beyond.

The dog, who had been trotting along behind him, obeying its master's last order, watched the man carefully. Deciding that, perhaps, at last, Alfred was going to stay put, the dog flopped down on the floor, curled its tail to its nose, sighed deeply, and closed its eyes.

I remember the first time I saw the dog. I remember Haplo, and the sight of his bandaged hands. I remember Hugh, the assassin, and the changeling Bane.

Bane.

Alfred's face grew haggard. He leaned his forehead against the window, as though his head were too heavy for him to support . . .

◆

. . . The hargast forest was on Pitrin's Exile, an island of coralite floating in the air world of Arianus. The forest was a terrifying place—to Alfred, at least. But then, most of the world outside the comforting peace of the mausoleum terrified the Sartan. The hargast tree is sometimes called the crystaltree. They are much prized in Arianus, where they are cultivated and tapped for the water they store in their brittle, crystalline trunks. But the forest wasn't a hargast farm, the trees weren't small and well tended.

In the wild, the hargast trees grow to hundreds of feet in height. The ground on which Alfred walked was littered with branches broken off in the wind currents that swept this end of the island. He stared at the branches, stared in disbelief at their razor-sharp edges. Loud cracks boomed like thunder, splintering crashes brought to mind fearful images of the giant limbs falling down on top of him. Alfred was feeling thankful he was walking on a road running along the forest's fringes when the assassin, Hugh the Hand, stopped and gestured.

"This way." He pointed into the forest.

"In there?" Alfred couldn't believe it. To walk in a hargast forest in a windstorm was madness, suicidal. But maybe that's what Hugh had in mind.

Alfred had long begun to suspect that Hugh the Hand couldn't go through with his "deal" to cold-bloodedly murder the child, Bane, who traveled with them. Alfred had been watching the assassin's inner struggle with himself. He could almost hear the curses Hugh was heaping on his own head, cursing himself for being a weak and sentimental fool. Hugh the Hand—the man who had killed many before this with never a qualm or a moment's regret.

But Bane was such a beautiful child, ingratiating, charming . . . with a soul blackened and warped by the whispered words of a wizard father the boy had never met or seen. Hugh had no way of knowing he, the spider, was being caught in a web far more devious and cunning than any he could ever hope to spin.

The three of them—Bane, Hugh, and Alfred—entered the hargast forest, forced to fight their way through a tangle of underbrush. At last they came to a cleared path. Bane was in high spirits, eager to see Hugh's famed flying ship. The boy darted ahead. The wind blew strong, the branches of the hargast trees clashed together, their crystalline tones harsh and ominous in Alfred's mind.

"Oh, sir, shouldn't we stop him?" the Sartan asked.

"He'll be all right," Hugh answered, and Alfred knew then that the assassin was sluffing off his responsibility, tossing the child's death into the lap of fate or chance or whatever deity, if any, this dark-souled man thought might bear the burden.

Whatever it was had accepted it.

Alfred heard the crack, like the booming of the perpetual storm of the Maelstrom. He saw the limb fall, saw Bane standing beneath it, staring up in rapt shock. The Sartan lunged forward, but he was too late. The limb fell on the child with a shattering crash.

He heard a scream, then, abruptly, silence.

Alfred dashed forward. The fallen branch was huge. It completely covered the path. The child's body was nowhere to be seen. He must be buried underneath the wreckage. Alfred gazed in hopeless despair at the broken branches, their edges sharp as spears.

Leave it. Don't meddle. You know what this child is! You know the evil that brought him forth. Let it die with him.

But he is a child! He's had no choice in his fate. Must he pay for the sin of the father? Shouldn't he have the chance to see for himself, to understand, to judge, to redeem himself, and perhaps redeem others?

Alfred glanced down the path. Hugh must have heard the branch fall, must have heard the scream. The assassin was taking his time, or perhaps offering up a prayer of thanksgiving. But he would be along soon.

The gigantic branch would take a team of men with cables and ropes to move—or one man with powerful magic. Standing over it, Alfred began to sing the runes. They wove and twined themselves about the tree branch, separated it into two halves, lifted each half up, deposited each half on either side of the path. Beneath the shattered limb lay Bane.

The child wasn't dead, but he was dying. He was covered with blood. Crystal shards had pierced the small body, there was no telling how many bones were crushed and broken.

Bring life to the dead. The Wave must correct itself. Bring life to one and another will die untimely.

The child was unconscious, in no pain, his life seeping away rapidly.

If I were a physician, I would try to help him live. Is what I am capable of doing wrong?

Alfred picked up a small shard of crystal. Hands, generally so clumsy, moved with delicacy and skill. The Sartan made a cut in his own flesh. Kneeling down beside the child, he traced in his own blood a sigil on the boy's mangled body. Then he sang the runes and, with his other hand, repeated them in the air.

The child's broken bones knit together. The torn flesh closed. The rapid, shallow breathing eased. The grayish skin grew pink, flushed with returning life.

Bane sat up and stared at Alfred with blue eyes sharper than the crystal branches of the hargast tree. . . .

♦

. . . Bane lived. And Hugh died. Died untimely. Alfred pressed his hand to his aching temples. But others were saved! How can I know? How can I know if I did right? All I know is that it was in my power to save that child and I did so. I couldn't let him die.

Then Alfred understood his fear. If he opened that book on necromancy, he would see on its pages the very rune he drew on Bane's flesh.

I have taken the first step down the dark and twisting path and who knows but that I shall not take a second and a third! Am I stronger than these, my brethren?

No, Alfred said to himself, and sank down, despairing, in a chair. No, I am the same.

CHAPTER 28

NECROPOLIS,

ABARRACH

♦

Haplo propped himself up on one elbow and gazed out the bars of his prison cell at the body of the prince, lying in the cell across from him. The preserver had done his job well. No grotesque stiffening of the limbs, face muscles relaxed; Edmund might have been peacefully sleeping, except for the gaping, bloody hole in the chest. The preserver had been ordered to leave the wound, visible evidence of the prince's terrible manner of death and one guaranteed to inflame his people to war when the cadaver was returned.

The Patryn rolled over on his back, made himself as comfortable as he could on the hard stone bed, and wondered how long it would be before the dynast came to pay him a visit.

"You're a cool one, aren't you?" The preserver, passing by the cell, on his way home after his cycle's duty, paused to stare at Haplo. "I've seen corpses more restless. That one, for example"—the preserver motioned gloomily at the prince—"will be a handful when it comes back to life. They keep forgetting they're locked up and crash into the bars. Then, when I make them understand, they pace: back and forth and back and forth. Then they forget again and hurl themselves against the bars. While you—lying there as if you hadn't a care in the world."

Haplo shrugged. "A waste of energy. Why wear myself out?"

The preserver shook his head and left, glad to return to his home and family after a long and arduous shift. If he had the suspicion that Haplo wasn't telling all he knew, the preserver was right. A prison is a prison only to a man who can't escape. And Haplo could have walked out of his cell any time he chose.

It suited his purpose to stay.

Kleitus was not long in coming. He was accompanied by Pons. It was the chancellor's duty to make certain that prisoner and ruler were not disturbed in their conversation. Pons slid his arm through the arm of the highly astonished wake-time preserver, who was making herself dizzy by repeated bowings and scrapings, and led her away. The only ones to overhear the dynast's conversation with his prisoner were the dead.

Kleitus stood outside Haplo's cell door, intently regarding the man inside. The dynast's face was shadowed by the hood of his purplish black robes. Haplo could not see the expression. But he sat quietly, gazing calmly back at the dynast.

Kleitus opened the cell door with a gesture of his hand and a spoken rune. Everyone else used a key. Haplo wondered if this magical show was intended to impress him. The Patryn, who could have dissolved the cell doors with a gesture and a rune, grinned.

The dynast glided inside, glanced around with distaste. There was nowhere for him to sit. Haplo slid to one side of the stone bed, patted it with his hand. Kleitus stiffened, as if to ask if the Patryn were joking. Haplo shrugged.

"No one sits while we stand," said Kleitus coldly.

Several appropriate remarks came to Haplo's tongue, but he swallowed them. No use antagonizing this man. The two of them were, after all, going to be traveling companions. Haplo slowly rose to his feet.

"Why did you come here?" Kleitus asked, lifting long-fingered, delicate hands and folding back the cowl so that his face was visible.

"Your soldiers brought me," Haplo replied.

The dynast smiled faintly, clasped his hands behind his back and began to walk about the cell. He made one complete turn—which didn't take long, the cell being extremely cramped—paused, and stared at Haplo.

"We meant, why did you come through Death's Gate to this world?"

The question took Haplo by surprise. He'd expected "Where is Death's Gate?" or perhaps "How did you get through it?" but not "why." The truth, or at least part of the truth, was necessary in answering. And they'd probably find it out anyway, because every word Haplo spoke seemed to create clouds of images in the brains of these Sartan.

"My Lord sent me, Your Majesty," Haplo replied.

Kleitus's eyes widened. Perhaps he'd caught a glimpse of the Lord of the Nexus from Haplo's mind. Just as well. He'd know the lord, then, when they met.

"What for? Why did your lord send you?"

"To look around, see how things were going."

"You've been to the other worlds?"

Haplo wasn't able to keep the images of Arianus and Pryan from flitting across his memory, and from his mind they were certain to enter Kleitus's.

"Yes, Sire."

"And what is it like on these other worlds?"

"Wars. Chaos. Turmoil. About what you could expect with the mensch in control."

"The mensch in control." Kleitus smiled again, this time politely, as if Haplo had made a bad joke. "Implying, of course, that we here on Abarrach, with our wars and turmoil, are no better than mensch." He tilted his head, stared down at Haplo from between half-closed eyelids. "Pons told us that you don't approve of the Sartan on Abarrach. What was it you said, 'We don't kill our own kind.' "

The dynast's gaze shifted, moved to the body of the prince lying on the stone in the cell opposite. He glanced back at Haplo, who didn't have time to rearrange the sardonic sneer on his lips.

Kleitus paled, frowned. "You, the ancient enemy, scion of a race of cruel and barbarous people, whose greed and ambition led to the destruction of our world, you dare pass judgment on us! Yes, you see we know about you. We've studied, found reference to you—to your people, rather—in the ancient texts."

Haplo said nothing, waited.

The dynast raised an eyebrow. "Tell us again, why have you come to our world?"

"I'll tell you again." The Patryn was growing impatient, decided to get to the point. "My Lord sent me. If you want to ask *him* why he sent me, you can do that yourself. I'll take you to him. I was going to propose just such a journey anyway."

"Indeed? You'd take me through Death's Gate with you?"

"Not only that, Your Majesty, I'll show you how to get through it, how to get back. I'll introduce you to My Lord, show you around my world—"

"And what do you want in return? We don't suppose, from what we've read of your people, that you will perform these services for us out of the goodness of your heart."

"In return," Haplo said quietly, "you will teach my people the art of necromancy."

"Ah." Kleitus's gaze went to the runes tattooed on the back of Haplo's hand. "The one magical skill you do not possess. Well, well. We will consider the idea. We could not, of course, leave when the peace of our city is threatened. You would have to wait until this matter between our people and those of the Kairn Telest is settled."

Haplo shrugged nonchalantly. "I'm in no hurry." *Kill off more of your people,* he suggested silently. *The fewer of you Sartan left alive to interfere with My Lord's plans the better.*

Kleitus's eyes narrowed and Haplo thought for a moment he had gone too far. He wasn't used to having his mind probed. *That fool Alfred had always been far too absorbed with his own worries to try to worm into Haplo's. I'll have to watch myself,* the Patryn counseled.

"In the interim," the dynast said slowly, "we hope you won't mind being our guest. We regret the accommodations aren't more comfortable. We would offer you a room in the palace, but that would occasion gossip and explanations. Far better if we keep you here, safe and quiet."

Kleitus started to leave, paused, turned back. "Oh, by the way, that friend of yours—"

"I don't have any friends," Haplo said shortly. He had started to sit down, but was now forced to remain standing.

"Indeed? I'm referring to the Sartan who saved your life. The one who destroyed the dead guard about to execute you—"

"That was self-preservation, Your Majesty. I'm the only way he gets back home."

"Then it wouldn't concern you to hear that this acquaintance of yours is in collusion with our enemies and has, therefore, placed his life in jeopardy?"

Haplo grinned, sat down on the stone seat. *If you're trying to use threats against Alfred to goad me into talking, Friend, you're sadly* mistaken. "It wouldn't concern me to hear that Alfred fell into the Fire Sea."

Kleitus slammed shut the cell door, using his hands this time, not the rune-magic. He began to walk away.

"Oh, by the way, Your Majesty—" Haplo called, scratching at the tattoos on his arm. Two could play at this game.

Kleitus ignored him, continued to walk away.

"I heard something mentioned about a prophecy . . ." Haplo paused, let his words hang in the chill, dank air of the catacombs.

The dynast stopped. He had drawn the cowl up over his head. The hood, turning toward Haplo, shadowed Kleitus's face. His voice, though he attempted to keep it cold and uncaring, had an edge of sharpened steel to it.

"Well, what about it?"

"Just curious to know what it was. I thought perhaps Your Majesty could tell me."

The dynast emitted a dry chuckle. "We could spend the remainder of our waking hours relating prophecies to you, Patryn, and half the slumbering hours into the bargain."

"There've been that many, have there?" Haplo marveled.

"That many. And most of them worth about what you might expect—the ravings of half-crazed old men or some dried-up old virgin in a trance. Why do you ask?" The voice probed.

So many, huh? Haplo thought. *The* prophecy, Jera said, and everyone knew—or seemed to know—exactly what she meant. I wonder why you don't want to tell me, you crafty dragon-spawn. Perhaps it hits a little too close to home, eh?

"I thought perhaps one of the prophecies might refer to My Lord," Haplo said, taking a risk.

He didn't know exactly what he hoped to accomplish with that shot, made completely in the dark. But if he'd intended it to draw blood, apparently he missed his mark. Kleitus didn't flinch or cringe. He made no comment, but turned as if completely bored with the conversation and walked off down the narrow hallway.

Haplo, listening closely, heard the dynast greet Pons in the same bored, casual tones. The echo of their voices gradually faded in the distance, and the Patryn was left alone with the dead for company.

At least the dead were a quiet group . . . with the exception of that incessant sighing or whining or whatever noise buzzed in his ears.

Haplo threw himself down on the stone bed to consider his conversation with the dynast, going over every word spoken and every word that hadn't been. The Patryn decided that he'd come out ahead in this first contest of wills. Kleitus wanted off this hunk of rock badly, that much was obvious. He wanted to visit other worlds, wanted to *rule* other worlds—that, too, was obvious.

"If there were such a thing as a soul, as the ancients believed, this man would sell his for the chance," Haplo remarked to the dead. "But, in lieu of his soul, he'll sell me the necromancy. With the dead fighting for him, My Lord will forge his own prophecy!"

He looked across at the still form lying in the cell opposite. "Don't worry, Your Highness," Haplo said quietly. "You'll have your revenge."

◆

"He's lying, of course, the cunning devil," the dynast told Pons, when the two Sartan were again alone in the library. "Trying to make us believe the mensch are in control of the worlds beyond! As if mensch could control anything!"

"But you saw—"

"We saw what he wanted us to see! This Haplo and his partner are spies, sent to discover our weaknesses, betray our strengths. It is this lord of his who rules. We saw the man." Kleitus fell silent, remembering. Slowly, he nodded his head. "A power to be reckoned with, Pons. An elder wizard of extraordinary skill and discipline and will."

"You could tell this by viewing him in a vision, Sire?"

"Don't be an idiot, Pons! We saw him through the eyes of his minion. This Haplo is dangerous, intelligent, skilled in his magical art, barbaric though it may be. He honors and reveres this man he calls 'his lord'! A man as strong as this Haplo would not give his body and mind to an inferior or even an equal. This lord will be a worthy foe."

"But if he has worlds at his command, Sire—"

"We have the dead, chancellor. And the art of raising the dead. He doesn't. His spy admitted it to us. He is trying to induce us to make a bargain."

"A bargain, Your Majesty?"

"He would lead us to Death's Gate and we would provide him with the knowledge of necromancy." Kleitus smiled, thin-lipped, devoid of mirth. "We allowed him to think we were considering it. And he brought up the prophecy, Pons."

The chancellor gaped. "He did?"

"Oh, he pretends he knows nothing about it. He even asked us to recite it to him! I am certain he knows the truth, Pons. And do you realize what that means?"

"I'm not sure, Sire." The chancellor was moving warily, not wanting to appear slow of thought. "He was unconscious when the Duchess Jera mentioned it—"

"Unconscious!" Kleitus snorted. "He was no more unconscious than we are! He is a powerful wizard, Pons. He could stroll out of that cell at this moment, if he chose. Fortunately, he believes himself to be in control of the situation.

"No, Pons, he was shamming that entire episode. We've been studying their magic, you see." Kleitus lifted a rune-bone, held it up to the light. "And we think we're beginning to understand how it works. If those fat, complacent ancestors of ours had taken the trouble to learn more about their enemy, we might have escaped disaster. But what do they do, in their smugness? They turn their paltry knowledge into a game! Bah!" The dynast, in a rare flash of anger, swept the rune-bone pieces from the table to the floor. Rising to his feet, he began to pace.

"The prophecy, Your Majesty?"

"Thank you, Pons. You remind us of what is truly important. And the fact that this Haplo knows of the prophecy is of monumental significance."

"Forgive me, Majesty, but I fail to see—"

"Pons!" Kleitus came to stand in front of his minister. "Think! One comes through Death's Gate who knows the prophecy. This means that the prophecy is known beyond."

Light shown on the benighted chancellor. "Your Majesty!"

"This Patryn lord fears us, Pons," Kleitus said softly, eyes gazing far away, to worlds he had seen only in his mind. "With our necromancy, we have become the most powerful Sartan who have ever lived. That is why he has sent his spies to learn our secrets, to disrupt our world. I see him, waiting for his spies to return. And he will wait in vain!"

"Spies plural. I assume that Your Majesty refers to the other man, the Sartan who destroyed the dead. May I respectfully remind you, Sire, that this man *is* a Sartan. He is one of us."

"Is he? Destroying our dead? No, if he is a Sartan, he is one of us turned to evil. It is likely that, over the centuries, the Patryns have corrupted our people. But not us. They will not corrupt us. We must have that Sartan. We must learn how he performed his magic."

"As I told you before, Sire, he did not use a rune structure that I recognized—"

"Your skills are limited, Pons. You are not a necromancer."

"True, Sire." The chancellor admitted this lack quite humbly. Pons knew of and was confident in his own particular area of expertise—how to make himself indispensable to his ruler.

"This Sartan's magic could prove to be a significant threat. We must know what he did to the corpse that ended its 'life.' "

"Undoubtedly, Sire, but if he is with the earl, capturing this Sartan may prove difficult—"

"Precisely why we will not attempt it. Nor will 'capture' be necessary. The duke and duchess are coming to rescue the prince, are they not?"

"According to Tomas, their plans are moving forward."

"Then, this Sartan we want will come with them."

"To rescue the prince? Why should he?"

"No, Pons. He will come to rescue his Patryn friend—who, by that time, will be dying."

CHAPTER 29

NECROPOLIS,

ABARRACH

•

THE NEXT CYCLE, THE CONSPIRATORS PLANNED THEIR MOVE TO THE CITY, to the house of Tomas. They would have no difficulty slipping into Necropolis under the cover of the slumber hours. Only one main gate led into the city and it was guarded by the dead. But, being a network of tunnels and caves, Necropolis had any number of other entrances and exits, too numerous for guards to be posted at each, particularly because there was usually no enemy to guard against.

"But now there is an enemy," said Jera. "Perhaps the dynast will order all the 'rat holes' stopped up."

But Tomas was confident that the dynast would not have issued such an order; the enemy was, after all, on the other side of the Fire Sea. Jera appeared dubious, but Jonathan reminded her that their friend Tomas stood high in the dynast's regard and was extremely knowledgeable concerning His Majesty's way of thinking. At length all agreed that they would sneak into the city through the rat holes. But what were they to do with the dog?

"We could leave him here," suggested Jera, eyeing the animal thoughtfully.

"I'm afraid the animal wouldn't stay," Alfred returned.

"He's got a point," Jonathan said in an undertone to his wife. "The dog wouldn't even stay dead!"

"Well, we can't let it be seen. Few in Necropolis are likely to pay any attention to us, but some zealous citizen would report a beast inside the city walls in a moment!"

Alfred could have told them they needn't have worried. The dog could be tossed into any number of boiling hot mud pits. It could be hauled off by any number of guards, locked into any number of cages, and, as long as Haplo lived, the dog would, sooner or later, turn up again. The Sartan didn't know quite how to put this into words, however. He let the discussion continue until it became obvious that their solution was to leave both him *and* the dog behind.

The old earl was in favor of this plan. "I've seen corpses dead fifty years who got around with less likelihood of falling apart!" he said to his daughter testily.

Moments before, Alfred had nearly broken his neck tumbling down a staircase.

"You'd be much safer here, Alfred," added Jera. "Not that smuggling the prince out of Necropolis will be all that dangerous, but still—"

"I'm coming," Alfred insisted stubbornly. To his surprise, he had an ardent supporter in Tomas.

"I agree with you, sir," the young man said heartily. "You should definitely be one of us." He drew Jera to one side, whispered something to her. The woman's shrewd eyes gazed at Alfred intently, much to his discomfiture.

"Yes, perhaps you're right."

She had a talk with her father. Alfred listened closely, picked out a few threads of conversation.

"Shouldn't leave him here . . . chance dynast's troops . . . remember what I told you I saw . . . the dead dying."

"Very well!" stated the old man disagreeably. "But you're not planning to take him into the palace, are you? He'd go bumbling into something and that'd be the end of us!"

"No, no," soothed Jera. "But what," she added with a sigh, "do we do about the dog?"

In the end, they decided to simply take their chances. As Tomas pointed out, they were entering the city during the slumber hours and the odds of meeting any living citizens who were likely to protest against a beast inside the city walls were slim.

They traveled the backroads of Old Provinces, and reached Necropolis during the deepest of the slumber hours. The main highway leading into the city was deserted. The city walls stood dark and silent. The gas lamps had been dimmed. The only light was a lambent glow shining redly from the distant Fire Sea. Dismounting from the carriage, they followed Tomas to what appeared to be a hole burrowing beneath the cavern wall. All the citizenry knew about the rat holes, as they were called, and used them because they were more convenient than entering by the main gate and trying to move through the congested tunnel streets.

"How does the dynast plan to defend these entrances against an invading army?" Jera whispered, ducking her head to walk beneath a glistening wet cavern ceiling.

"He must be wondering that himself," said Tomas, with a slight smile. "Perhaps that's why he's shut up in his room with his maps and military advisers."

"On the other hand, he may not be worried at all," pointed out Jonathan, assisting Alfred to his feet. "Necropolis has never fallen in battle."

"Wet pavement," murmured Alfred in apology, cringing at the earl's look of irritation. "Have there truly been that many wars fought among you?"

"Oh, yes," Jonathan answered, quite cheerfully. They might have been discussing rune-bone games. "I'll tell you about them later, if you're interested. Now, we should probably keep our voices low. Which way, Tomas? I get rather muddled down here."

Tomas indicated a direction, and the group entered a perfect maze of dark, intersecting tunnels that had Alfred completely lost and confused in a matter of moments. Glancing around, he saw the dog, trotting along behind.

The first streets, those nearest the wall, were empty. Narrow and dark, they wound among a confused jumble of shabby houses and small shops, built of blocks of black rock or carved out of lava formations.

The shops were shuttered for the sleep-half, the houses dark. Many of them appeared to be deserted, abandoned, left to fall to ruin. Doors hung crazily on hinges, rags and bits of bone littered the street. The odor of decay was unusually strong here. Curious, Alfred peeped through a broken window.

A cadaverous face loomed white in the darkness. A pair of empty, dark eye sockets stared sightlessly into the street. Alarmed, Alfred stumbled backward, nearly knocking Jonathan off his feet.

"Steady, there!" the duke remonstrated, catching his balance and helping Alfred reestablish his. "I admit it's a depressing sight. This part of the city used to be quite nice, or so the old records tell us. In the ancient time, this area housed the working class of Necropolis: soldiers, builders, storekeepers, and the lower echelon necromancers and preservers.

"I suppose," he added, lowering his voice after a warning glance from his wife, "that you could say they live here still, but they're mostly all dead."

So depressing were these empty streets with their tomblike houses that Alfred breathed a sigh of relief to actually emerge into a larger tunnel and see people moving about. Then he remembered the danger of the dog being observed. Despite Jera's whispered assurance that everything would be all right, Alfred crept nervously along, keeping near the wall, avoiding the pools of dim light cast by the sputtering lamps. The dog followed almost at his heels, as if the animal itself understood and was willing to cooperate.

The people in the streets passed them without a glance, not seeming to notice or care about them at all. Alfred realized, gradually, that these people were not living. The dead walked the streets of Necropolis during the slumber hours.

Most of the cadavers moved along purposefully, obviously intent on performing some task assigned to them by the living before the living took to their beds. But, here and there, they came on a cadaver roaming about aimlessly or performing some task it should have been performing during the waking time. Necromancers patrolled the streets of Necropolis, picking up any of these dead who had become confused, forgotten their tasks, or were making nuisances of themselves. Alfred's group took care to keep out of the way of these necromancers, slipping into the shadows of doorways until the black-robed wizards had passed.

Necropolis was built in a series of half circles that radiated out from the fortress. Originally, a small population of mensch and Sartan had dwelt inside the fortress, but as more and more people began to settle in the area permanently, the population soon overflowed the fortress and began building homes in the shadow of its sheltering walls.

In the days of Necropolis's prosperity, the then-current dynast, Kleitus III, took over the fortress as his castle. The nobility dwelt in magnificent homes located near the castle and the remainder of the population spread out around them, in order of rank and wealth.

Tomas's house was located about halfway between the poor houses on the city's outer walls and homes of the wealthy, near the castle walls. Depressed and weary from his journey, Alfred was extremely glad to escape the dark and drizzling atmosphere and enter rooms that were warm and well lighted.

Tomas apologized to the duke and duchess and the earl for the modesty of the dwelling, which was—as were many of the dwellings in the cavern—built straight up to conserve space.

"My father was a minor noble. He left me the right to stand around in the court with the other courtiers, hoping for a smile from His Majesty, and not much else," Tomas said, with a tinge of bitterness. "Now he stands around with the dead. I stand around with the living. Little difference between us."

The earl rubbed his hands. "Soon all that will change. Come the rebellion."

"Come the rebellion," said the others, in a sort of reverent litany.

Alfred sighed bleakly, sank into a chair, and wondered what he was going to do. The dog curled up at his feet. He felt numb, unable to think or react of his own volition. He wasn't a man of action, not like Haplo.

Events move *me*, Alfred reflected sadly, I don't move events. He supposed that he should be doing something to bring about an end to the practice of the long-forbidden art of necromancy, but what? He was one man, alone. And not a very strong man or a very wise one at that.

The only thought in his mind, his only wish, his only desire, was to flee this horrible world, run away, escape, forget it, and never be reminded of it again.

"Excuse me, sir," said the duke, coming up and touching Alfred deferentially on the knee.

Alfred jumped, and lifted a frightened face.

"Are you well?" Jonathan asked in concern.

Alfred nodded, waved a vague hand, mumbled something about a tiring walk.

"You mentioned being interested in the history of our wars. My wife and the earl and Tomas are planning our strategy for sneaking away the prince. They sent me off." Jonathan smiled, shrugged. "I simply don't have the head for plots. My task is to entertain you. But if you're too tired and you'd rather retire, Tomas will show you to your room—"

"No, no!" The last thing Alfred wanted was to be left alone with his thoughts. "Please, I'd be very interested in hearing about . . . wars." He had to force the word out past the lump in his throat.

"I can only tell you about the ones fought around here." The duke pulled up a chair, made himself comfortable. "Tea? Biscuits? Not hungry. Where shall I start? Necropolis was originally nothing more than a small town, mostly a place where people came to wait until they could move to other parts of Abarrach. But, after a while, the Sartan and the mensch—there were mensch back then—began to look around and decide that life was good here and that they didn't need to move. The city grew rapidly. People began to farm the fertile land. Crops flourished. Unfortunately, the mensch didn't."

Jonathan spoke in a carefree, cheerful manner that Alfred found quite shocking.

"You don't seem to care much about them," he observed, gently rebuking. "You were supposed to protect those weaker than your-selves."

"Oh, I think our ancestors were extremely upset, at first," said Jonathan defensively. "Devastated, in fact. But it really wasn't our fault. The help they were promised from other worlds never came. The magic needed to keep the mensch alive in this grim world was simply too great. Our ancestors couldn't provide it. There was noth-ing they could do. Eventually, they quit blaming themselves. Most of them, back then, came to believe that the era of the Dying of the Mensch was something inevitable, necessary."

Alfred said nothing, shook his head sadly.

"It was during this era, possibly in reaction to it," Jonathan continued, "that the art of necromancy was first studied."

"The *forbidden* art," Alfred corrected, but in such soft tones that the duke didn't hear him.

"Now that they no longer had to support the mensch, they discovered they could live quite well in this world. They invented iron ships to sail the Fire Sea. Colonies of Sartan spread throughout Abarrach, trade was established. The realm of Kairn Necros came into being. And as they progressed, so did the art of necromancy. Soon the living were living off the dead."

Yes, Alfred could see it all as Jonathan talked.

Life in Abarrach was good. Death was not bad, either. But then, just when everything (not counting the mensch, who by this time had been mostly forgotten anyway) seemed to be going so well, it all began to go terribly wrong.

"The Fire Sea and all the magma lakes and rivers and oceans were cooling and receding. Realms that had previously been trading neighbors became bitter enemies, hoarding their precious supplies of food, fighting over the life-giving colossus. That's when the first wars were fought.

"I guess it would be more correct to term them brawls or skirmishes, not really wars. Those," Jonathan said more seriously and solemnly, "would come later. Our ancestors apparently didn't know much about waging war at that time."

"Of course not!" Alfred said severely. "We abhor warfare. We are the peacemakers. We promote peace!"

"You have that luxury," said Jonathan quietly. "We did not."

Alfred was struck, startled by the young duke's words. Was peace a luxury available only to a "fat" world? He recalled Prince Edmund's people, ragged, freezing, starving; watching their children, their elderly die while inside this city was warmth, food. What would I do if I was in their position? Would I meekly die, watch my children die? Or would I fight? Alfred shifted in his chair, suddenly uncomfortable.

I know what I'd do, he thought bitterly. I'd faint!

"As time passed, our people became more adept at war." Jonathan sipped at a cup of kairn-grass tea. "The young men began to train as soldiers, armies were formed. At first, they tried to fight with magic as their weapon, but that took too much energy away from the magic needed to survive.

"And so we studied the art of ancient weaponry. Swords and spears are far cruder than magic, but they're effective. Brawls became battles and, inevitably, led to the great war of about a century ago—the War of Abandonment.

"A powerful wizardess named Bethel claimed that she had discovered the way out of this world. She announced that she was planning to leave and would take those who wanted to go with her. She drew a large following. If the people had left, it would have decimated the population that was rapidly dwindling anyway. To say nothing of the fact that everyone feared what might happen if the "Gate" as she called it was opened. Who knew what terrible force might rush in and seize control?

"The dynast of Kairn Necros, Kleitus VII, forbid Bethel and her followers to leave. She refused to obey and led her people across the Fire Sea to the Pillar of Zembar, preparatory to abandoning the

world. The battles between the two factions raged off and on for
years, until Bethel was betrayed and captured. She was being ferried
across the Fire Sea when she escaped her captors and flung herself
into the magma, to keep her corpse from being resurrected. Before
she jumped, she cried out what later became known as the prophecy
about the Gate."

Alfred pictured the woman standing on the bow, screaming
defiance. He pictured her hurling herself into the flaming ocean. He
lost the thread of Jonathan's tale, picked it up again only when the
young man suddenly lowered his voice.

"It was during that war that armies of the dead were first formed
and pitted against each other. In fact, it's said that some commanders
actually ordered the killing of their own living soldiers, to provide
themselves with troops of cadavers . . ."

Alfred's head jerked up. "What? What are you telling me? Murdered their own young men! Blessed Sartan! To what black depths
have we sunk?" He was livid, shaking. "No, don't come near me!"
He raised a warding hand, rose distractedly from his chair. "I must
get out of here! Leave this place!" It seemed, from his fevered attitude, that he meant to run out of the house that instant.

"Husband, what have you been saying to upset him like this?"
demanded Jera, coming into the room with Tomas. "My dear sir,
please sit down, calm yourself."

"I was only telling him that old story about the generals killing
their own men during the war—"

"Oh, Jonathan!" Jera shook her head. "Certainly, you can leave,
Alfred. Any time you want. You're not a prisoner here!"

Yes, I am! Alfred groaned inwardly. I'm a prisoner, a prisoner of
my own ineptness! I came through Death's Gate by sheer accident! I
would never have the courage or the knowledge to get back alone!

"Think about your friend," Tomas added soothingly, pouring out
a cup of kairn tea. "You don't want to leave your friend behind, do
you, Sir?"

"I'm sorry." Alfred collapsed back into his chair. "Forgive me.
I'm . . . tired, that's all. Very tired. I think I'll go to bed. Come on,
boy."

He laid a trembling hand on the dog's head. The animal looked
up at him, whimpered, slowly brushed its tail against the floor, but
didn't move.

The whimper had an odd note to it, a sound that Alfred had

never heard the dog make before. He took more notice, looked down at it intently. The dog tried to lift its head, let it sink back weakly on its paws. The tail wagging increased slightly, however, to indicate that it appreciated the man's concern.

"Is there something wrong?" asked Jera, staring down at the dog. "Do you think the animal's sick?"

"I'm not sure. I don't know much about dogs I'm afraid," Alfred mumbled, feeling dread shrivel him up inside.

He *did* know something about this dog, or at least suspected. And if what he suspected was true, then whatever was wrong with the dog was wrong with Haplo.

CHAPTER • 30

NECROPOLIS,

ABARRACH

•

THE DOG'S CONDITION GRADUALLY WORSENED. BY THE NEXT CYCLE, IT couldn't move at all, but lay on its side, flanks heaving, panting for breath. The animal refused all attempts to feed it or give it water.

Although everyone in the house was sorry for the dog's suffering, no one, except Alfred, was much concerned. Their thoughts were on the raid on the castle, the rescue of the prince's cadaver. Their plans were made, discussed and viewed from every conceivable angle for flaws. None could be found.

"It's going to be almost ridiculously easy," said Jera, at breakfast.

"I do beg your pardon," said Alfred in timid tones, "but I spent some time at court on . . . er . . . well, the world from which I come, and King Stephen's . . . that is . . . the king's dungeons were quite heavily guarded. How do you plan—"

"You're not involved." The earl snorted. "So don't concern yourself."

I may yet be involved, Alfred thought. His glance strayed to the sick dog. He said nothing aloud, however, preferring to bide his time until he had more facts.

"Don't be so cantankerous, Milord," said Jonathan, laughing. "We trust Alfred, don't we?"

Silence fell over the group, a faint blush suffused Jera's cheek. She glanced involuntarily at Tomas, who met her look, shook his head slightly, and lowered his gaze to his plate. The earl snorted again. Jonathan glanced from one to the other in perplexity.

"Oh, come now—" he began.

"More tea, sir?" Jera interrupted, lifting the stoneware kettle and holding it over Alfred's teacup.

"No, thank you, Your Grace."

No one else said anything. Jonathan started to speak again, but was stopped by a look from his wife. The only sounds were the labored breathing of the dog and the occasional rattle of cutlery or the clink of a pottery plate. All seemed vastly relieved when Tomas rose from the table.

"If you will excuse me, Your Grace." A bow to Jera. "It is time for my appearance at court. Although I am not of the least importance"—he added with a self-deprecating smile—"this cycle of all cycles I should do nothing to draw attention to myself. I must be seen at my regular place at my regular time."

Alfred lurked about on the fringes of the group until everyone had separated and gone about their morning tasks. Tomas was alone on the lower floor, heading out the door of his dwelling. Alfred emerged from a shadowy corner, plucked at the sleeve of the man's robe.

Tomas gave a start, stared around with livid face and wide eyes.

"Excuse me," said Alfred, taken aback. "I didn't mean to startle you."

Tomas frowned when he saw who had hold of him. "What do *you* want?" he demanded impatiently, shaking free of Alfred's grip. "I'm late as it is."

"Would it be possible—could you speak to your friend in the dungeons and find out the . . . the condition of my friend?"

"I told you before. He's alive, just as you said," Tomas snapped. "That's all I know."

"But you could find out . . . today," Alfred insisted, somewhat surprised at his own temerity. "I have the feeling he has fallen ill. Gravely ill."

"Because of the dog!"

"Please . . ."

"Oh, very well. I'll do what I can. But I don't promise anything. And now I must be leaving."

"Thank you, that's all I—"

But Tomas was gone, hastening out the door and joining the throng of living and dead crowding the streets of Necropolis.

Alfred sat down beside the dog, stroked its soft fur with a soothing hand. The animal was extremely ill.

Later that day, Tomas returned. It was near the dynast's dining hour, a time when the courtiers, those unfortunates who had not been asked to dinner, departed for their own pleasures.

"Well, what news?" Jera asked. "All is well?"

"All is well," Tomas answered gravely. "His Majesty will resurrect the prince during the lamp dimming hour."[1]

"And we have permission to visit the Queen Mother?"

"The queen was most pleased to grant permission herself."

Jera nodded at her father. "All is ready. I wonder, however, if we shouldn't—"

Tomas cast a significant glance at Alfred, and the duchess fell silent.

"Excuse me," Alfred murmured, rising stiffly to his feet. "I'll leave you alone—"

"No, wait." Tomas raised his hand. His expression grew more grave. "I have news for you, and this affects us all and affects our plans, I'm afraid. I spoke to my friend the sleep-shift preserver, before he left the castle this morning. I am sorry to relate that what you feared, Alfred, is true. Your friend is rumored to be dying."

◆

Poison.

Haplo knew it the moment the first cramps twisted his gut, knew it when the nausea swept over him. He knew it, but he wouldn't admit it to himself. It made no sense! Why?

Weak from vomiting, he lay on the stone bed, bent double by the clenching pain that stabbed at his vitals with knives of fire. He was parched, suffering from thirst. The waking-shift preserver brought him water. He had just strength enough to dash the cup from her hand. The cup smashed on the rock floor. The preserver withdrew hurriedly. The water seeped rapidly into the cracks in the floor. Haplo collapsed on the bed, watched it disappear, and wondered, Why?

He attempted to heal himself, but his efforts were feeble, half-hearted, and at length he gave up. He'd known from the outset healing wouldn't work. A cunning and subtle mind—a Sartan mind—had devised his murder. The poison was powerful, acting

---

[1] The hour following the dynast's gaming hour when His Majesty orders the light of the gas lamps to be dimmed. During the dynast's slumber hours, the gas lamps are turned off completely.

equally on his magic and his body. The complex, interconnecting circle of runes that was his life's essence was falling apart and he couldn't put it back together again. It was as if the edges of the runes were being burned away, they wouldn't link up. Why?

"Why?"

It took Haplo a dazed moment to realize that his question had been repeated out loud. He lifted his head—every movement was fraught with pain, every movement took extraordinary will and effort. His eyes dimming with death's shadow, he could barely make out the dynast, standing outside his cell.

"Why what?" Kleitus asked quietly.

"Why . . . murder me?" Haplo gasped. He gagged, wretched, doubled over, clutching his stomach. Sweat rolled down his face, he suppressed an agonized cry.

"Ah, you understand what is happening to you. Painful, is it? For that, we are sorry. But we needed a poison that was slow to do its work and we didn't have much time to devote to study. What we devised is crude, albeit efficient. Is it killing you?"

The dynast might have been a professor, inquiring of a student if his experiment in alchemy was proceeding satisfactorily.

"Yes, damn it! It's killing me!" Haplo snarled.

Anger filled him. Not anger at dying. He'd been near death before, the time the chaodyns attacked him, but then he'd been content to die. He'd fought well, defeated his enemies. He'd been victorious. Now he was dying ignominiously, dying at the hands of another, dying shamefully, without being able to defend himself.

Lunging off the stone bed, he hurled himself at the cell door, fell to the floor. He reached out a grasping hand and clutched at the hem of the dynast's robe before the startled man had time to withdraw.

"Why?" Haplo demanded, clinging to the purple-dyed black fabric. "I would have taken you . . . Death's Gate!"

"But I don't need you to take me," replied Kleitus calmly. "I know where Death's Gate is. I know how to get through it. I don't need you . . . for that." The dynast bent down, his hand moved to touch the rune-covered hand holding on to the black robes.

Haplo grit his teeth, but did not loosen his grasp. Delicate fingers traced over the runes on the Patryn's skin.

"Yes, now you begin to understand. It takes so much of our magical ability to bring life to the dead that it drains us. We hadn't realized how much until we met you. You tried to hide your power but we felt it. We could have thrown a spear at you, thrown a hundred spears at you, and none would have so much as scratched you. True? Yes, of course it's true. In fact, we could probably have dropped this castle on top of you and you would have emerged alive and well." The fingers continued to trace the tattooed runes, slowly, longingly, with desire.

Haplo stared, understanding, disbelieving.

"There is nothing more we can gain from our magic. But there is a great deal we can gain from yours! That is why," the dynast concluded briskly, rising to his feet, looking down at Haplo from what seemed to the dying man to be a tremendous height, "we couldn't afford to injure your body. The rune patterns must be left unblemished, unbroken, to be studied at our leisure. Undoubtedly your cadaver will be of assistance in explaining the meaning of the sigla to me.

" 'Barbaric' our ancestors called your magic. They were dolts. Add the power of your magic to ours and we will be invincible. Even, we surmise, against this so-called Lord of the Nexus."

Haplo rolled over on his back. His hand released its grip on the dynast's robe; he no longer had the strength left in his fingers to maintain it.

"And then there is your comrade, your ally—the one who can bring death to the dead."

"Not friend," Haplo whispered, barely aware of what he was saying or what was being said to him. "Enemy."

Kleitus smiled. "A man who risks his life to save yours? I think not. Tomas gathered, from certain things this man has said, that he abhors necromancy and that he would not come to restore your corpse, if you were dead. Most likely he would flee this world, and we would lose him. We inferred, however, that there must be some sort of empathic connection between the two of you. It turned out we were right. Tomas reports that your friend knows, somehow, that you are dying. Your friend believes that there is a chance you might be saved. There isn't, of course, but that won't matter to your friend. Or, at least it won't matter to him long."

The dynast drew aside the hem of his robe. "And now I must commence the resurrection of Prince Edmund."

Haplo heard the man's voice receding, heard the rustle of the robe's fabric along the floor and the voice became the rustle, or perhaps the rustle was the voice. "Don't worry. Your agony is almost over. We would imagine the pain eases, near the end.

"And so you see, Haplo, there is no need for you to ask why. The prophecy," came the rustling voice. "It is all for the prophecy."

Haplo lay on his back, on the floor, too weak to move. That bastard's right. The pain is beginning to fade . . . because my life is fading. I'm dying. I'm dying and there's not a damn thing I can do about it. I'm dying in fulfillment of a prophecy.

"What is . . . the prophecy?" Haplo cried out.

But his cry was, in reality, nothing more than a breath. No one answered. No one heard him. He couldn't even hear himself.

CHAPTER 31

NECROPOLIS,

ABARRACH

♦

THE CONSPIRATORS PLEADED, ARGUED, AND BEGGED, AND FINALLY PER-
suaded the old earl to allow Alfred to accompany them on their
mission to the palace. Tomas spoke eloquently on Alfred's behalf, a
fact that considerably astonished the Sartan. Prior to this, Alfred had
received the distinct impression that Tomas didn't trust him. Alfred
wondered, rather uneasily, at the cause for this change.

But he was determined to go to the castle, determined to go to
Haplo's aid, despite the nagging, inner voice that kept insisting it
would be better, easier, simpler to let the Patryn die.

You know what villainy he plots, what villainy he's done. He
started a world war on Arianus.

Haplo was the spark, perhaps, Alfred argued with himself, but
the powder was poured and ready to ignite long before he arrived.
Besides, he countered, I need Haplo in order to escape this terrible
world!

You don't need Haplo! the inner voice scoffed. You could go back
through Death's Gate on your own. Your magic is strong enough. It
took you to the Nexus. And if he is dying, what will you do? Save his
life? Save his life as you saved Bane? The boy was dying, and he was
brought back by you! Necromancer!

Alfred's conscience squirmed in indecision. Again I'm confronted with that awful choice. And what if I save Haplo, only to save
him for evil? The Patryn is capable of committing dreadful crimes, I
know that. I've seen it in his mind. It would be easy, so very easy, to
stay here, to turn my back, to let the Patryn die. If the situation were

reversed, Haplo would not lift one rune-covered hand to save me. And yet . . . and yet . . . What about mercy? Compassion?

A whimpering sound drew the Sartan back from his confused musings, his attention drawn to the dog, lying at his feet. The animal could not lift its head, it could only feebly wag the tail that thumped weakly against the floor. Alfred had barely left the dog's side all cycle; the animal appeared to rest easier when he was nearby and it could see him. Several times, he'd feared the animal had died, and had been forced to put his hand on its flanks to feel for a heartbeat. But the life's pulse was present, fluttering beneath his gentle fingers.

The dog's eyes gazed at him with an expression of confidence that seemed to say, *I don't know why I'm suffering like this, but I know you're going to make everything all right.*

Alfred reached down, stroked the animal's head. The patient eyes closed, the dog was comforted by the touch.

Let's just say, he told that bothersome inner voice, that I'm not saving Haplo, I'm saving Haplo's dog. Or, rather, I will try to save him, he added, worried and unhappy.

"What was that?" Jera asked. "Alfred, did you say something?"

"I . . . I was just wondering if they knew what was wrong with my friend?"

"It is the preserver's considered opinion," answered Tomas, "that your friend's magic is incapable of sustaining him in this world. Just as the mensch's magic was incapable of sustaining them."

"I understand," Alfred murmured, but he didn't understand and, what's more, he didn't believe it. Alfred hadn't been in the Labyrinth (in Haplo's body) long, but he was positive that a person who had survived that fearsome place would not drop over dead in Abarrach. Someone was lying to Tomas . . . or Tomas was lying to them. A nervous tremor convulsed one of Alfred's legs. He clasped his hand over the twitching muscle and tried to keep his voice from quavering.

"In that case, I must insist on going with you. I'm certain I can help him."

"And whether he can help his friend or he can't," Jera said to her father, who was glowering at Alfred, "we'll need *his* help ourselves. Jonathan and I will be guiding the prince. Tomas can't handle by himself a sick man or a—forgive me, sir, but we must be realistic about this—a dead one. We don't want to leave Haplo behind, no matter what his condition, for the dynast."

"If I were twenty years younger—"

"But you're not, Father," Jera admonished.

"I can get around better than he can!" the earl thundered, pointing a bony finger at Alfred.

"But you can't do anything to help Haplo."

"All our plans will remain the same, My Lord," added Tomas. "We just include one more in our numbers, that's all."

"Perfectly simple and safe, the way my wife and Tomas have worked it out," Jonathan stated, regarding the duchess with pride. "When we have the prince, we'll meet you at the gate, just as we've planned."

"Everything will be fine, Father." Jera leaned over, kissed the old man's wrinkled cheek. "This slumber time will mark the beginning of the end for the Kleitus dynasty!"

The beginning of the end. Her words passed through Alfred like the ripple of the Wave, tingling his nerves, leaving him feeling wrung out and flattened when the sensation had passed.

◆

"You can't appear at court in those clothes," Jera told Alfred, eyeing his faded velvet knee breeches and shabby velvet jacket. "You would call far too much attention to yourself. We'll have to find robes that fit you."

"Begging your pardon, my dear," said Jonathan, after Alfred's transformation had been effected, "but I don't think you've improved matters much."

Alfred's stoop-shouldered walk gave a false impression of his height, making him seem shorter than he actually was. Jera had first thought of clothing him in a gray robe of Tomas's, but the young man was short for a Sartan and the robe's hem hit Alfred about mid-calf. The effect was ludicrous. The duchess searched for the longest garment she could find and eventually outfitted the Sartan in one of Tomas's cast-off court robes.

Alfred felt extremely uncomfortable in the black robes of a necromancer and made a feeble protest but no one paid the least attention to him. The robes hit him at a point slightly above his large, rawboned ankles. He was able to wear his own shoes, at least; no other pair could be found that came close to fitting over his feet.

"They're bound to take him for a refugee," said Jera, with a sigh. "Just keep your hood over your head," she instructed Alfred, "and don't say a word to anyone. Let us do the talking."

The robe was worn loosely belted around the waist. Tomas added an embroidered purse to be carried at the belt. Jera would have added an iron dagger—to be hidden in the purse—but Alfred adamantly refused.

"No, I won't carry a weapon," he said, recoiling from the dagger as he might have recoiled from one of the deadly jungle snakes of Arianus.

"It's only a precaution," said Jonathan. "No one thinks for a moment we'll actually have to use these weapons. See, I have mine." He displayed a dagger made of silver, inlaid with precious jewels. "It was my father's."

"I won't," Alfred said stubbornly. "I took a vow—"

"He took a vow! He took a vow!" the earl mimicked in disgust. "Don't force it on him, Jera. It's just as well. He'd probably cut off his own hand."

Alfred did not carry a weapon.

He had supposed that they would sneak into the palace in the dead of the dynast's slumber hours. He was considerably astonished when Tomas announced shortly after dinner that it was time they departed.

The farewells were brief and matter-of-fact, as between those who know they will meet again shortly. Everyone was excited, on edge, and didn't appear in the least fearful or cognizant of danger. The possible exception was Tomas.

Having caught him in what he was certain was a lie about Haplo, Alfred watched Tomas carefully and fancied that the easygoing smile was forced, the carefree laugh was just a split second too late to be natural, the eyes had a tendency to dart away whenever anyone looked at him directly. Alfred considered mentioning his suspicions to Jera, but rejected the idea.

I'm a stranger, an outsider. They've known him far longer than they've known me. She wouldn't listen to me and I might make matters worse instead of better. They don't trust me, as it is. They might decide to leave me behind!

Alfred took a last look at the dog before he left.

"The beast is dying," stated the earl bluntly.

"Yes, I know." Alfred stroked the soft fur, petted the heaving flanks.

"What am I supposed to do with it, then?" the old man demanded. "I can't haul a corpse with me to the gate."

"Just leave it," said Alfred, rising to his feet with a sigh. "If all goes well, the dog will come to meet us. If not, it won't matter."

◆

Despite the fact that the dynast was not appearing in public, the court was thronged with people. Alfred had thought the tunnel streets crowded and claustrophobic until he entered the castle. Most of the living inhabitants of Necropolis could be found there at night, dancing, sharing the latest gossip, playing at rune-bone, eating the dynast's food.

Entering the crowded antechamber, doing his best not to trip over Jonathan's heels or tread on the hem of Jera's robe, Alfred was almost suffocated by the heat, the perfume of the rez flower, the raucous noise of laughter and music. The fragrance of the rez was delightful, sweet and spicy. But it couldn't quite mask another odor prevalent in the ballroom, an underlying odor, pervasive, cloying, sickening in the heat—the odor of death.

The living ate and drank, joked and flirted. The dead moved among the living, waiting on them, serving them. Trailing behind the cadavers, the phantasm shadows almost disappeared in the glitter of bright lights.

Everyone they met greeted the duke and duchess with enthusiasm.

"Did you hear the news, my darlings? There's to be a war! Isn't it too shocking!" cried a woman in mauve robes, rolling her eyes with intense enjoyment.

Jera, Jonathan, and Tomas laughed and danced and exchanged gossip and skilfully oiled their way through the throng in the antechamber, dragging, pushing, and prodding a stumbling and distressed Alfred along with them. From the antechamber, they passed into the ballroom, which was even more crowded, if such a thing were possible.

A surge in the throng suddenly separated Alfred from his group. He took a hesitating step toward where he'd last seen Jera's shining hair, and found himself in the midst of a crowd of young people amusing themselves by watching a corpse dance.

The cadaver was that of an older man of grave and stately mien. From the dilapidated appearance of both the cadaver and the clothing it wore, the corpse had been around a long, long time. Urged on by the giggling young people, the cadaver was performing a dance that it had probably performed in its own youth.

The young people hooted and jeered and began to dance around the corpse in mockery of the old-fashioned steps. The cadaver paid no attention to them, but continued to dance on its decaying legs, moving solemnly with a pathetic grace to the tune of music only it could hear.

"I've found him. Fire and ash! He's going to faint!" gasped Tomas, grabbing hold of Alfred and propping him up as the Sartan started to keel over.

"I've got him," said Jonathan, catching hold of Alfred's limp, dangling arm.

"What's the matter with him?" Jera demanded. "Alfred? Are you all right?"

"The . . . heat!" Alfred panted, hoping they would mistake the tears on his face for sweat. "The noise . . . I'm . . . most frightfully sorry . . ."

"We've been seen around the ballroom long enough to allay suspicion. Jonathan, go find the chamberlain and ask if the Queen Mother is receiving yet."

Jonathan wormed his way through the crowd. Tomas and Jera between them guided Alfred to a somewhat quieter corner, where they dislodged a portly and grumbling necromancer from his chair and plunked the shaken Alfred down into it. The Sartan closed his eyes and shivered and hoped he could avoid being sick.

Jonathan returned shortly with the news that the Queen Mother was receiving and that they had permission to wait on her and pay their respects.

Between the three of them, they hauled Alfred to his feet and propelled him through the throng, out of the ballroom, and into a long, empty hallway that, after the heat and noise of the ballroom, was a cool and quiet haven of rest.

"Your Graces." The chamberlain stood before them. "If you will follow me."

The chamberlain led them down the hallway, advancing several steps before them, his staff of office striking the rock floor with a ringing sound at about every five paces. Alfred followed, extraordinarily confused, wondering why they were taking time out of a desperate attempt to free an imprisoned prince's corpse to pay a royal visit. He might have asked Jonathan, who was beside him, but the slightest sound seemed to reverberate through the hallway, and he was fearful of the chamberlain overhearing.

Alfred's confusion grew. He had assumed they were going to the royal family's quarters. But they left the sumptuous, beautifully decorated halls far behind. The corridor they walked was narrow, winding, and began to dip downward. The gas lamps were infrequently spaced and soon ended altogether; the darkness was deep and heavy, tainted strongly with the smells of decay and must.

The chamberlain spoke a rune and a light gleamed on the top of his staff, but it merely guided the way. The light did little to aid their steps. Fortunately, the rock floor was smooth and unobstructed and they traversed it without undue difficulty, not counting Alfred, who fell over a minuscule crack in the floor and landed flat on his face.

"I'm quite all right. Please, don't bother," he protested. Nose pressed against the floor, he happened to get a very close look at the base of the rock walls.

Rune markings. Alfred blinked, stared, his thoughts going back to the mausoleum, to the underground tunnel built by his people far beneath the Geg's realm of Drevlin on Arianus, to the rune markings that ran along the tunnel floors and, when activated by the proper magic, became small, lighted guides through the darkness. In Arianus, the tunnels had been kept in good repair, the rune markings were easy to see for those with eyes to see them. On Abarrach, the sigla were faded, some obscured by dirt, in a few places completely obliterated. They had not been used in a long time. Perhaps their use had been completely forgotten.

"My dear sir, are you injured?" The chamberlain was coming back to check on him.

"Get up!" Tomas hissed. "What's the matter with you?"

"Uh, nothing. I'm fine." Alfred clambered to his feet. "Th-thank you."

The tunnel wound around, was met by other tunnels, was intersected by other tunnels, flowed through and over and under and into other tunnels. Each tunnel looked exactly like every other tunnel. Alfred was completely confused and disoriented, and he marveled at the chamberlain, who moved through the maze without hesitation.

Finding the way would have been easy, if the chamberlain had been reading the guide-runes on the floor, but he never so much as glanced in their direction. Alfred couldn't see them in the dark and he dared not call attention to himself by activating their magic, and so he stumbled on ahead blindly, knowing only that they were moving downward, ever downward, and thinking that this was a very odd place for the Queen Mother to keep her parlor.

CHAPTER 32

THE CATACOMBS,

ABARRACH

♦

THE SLOPING FLOOR GREW MORE LEVEL, GAS LAMPS REAPPEARED, gleaming yellow in the darkness. Alfred heard Jera's breathing quicken slightly in excitement. He felt Jonathan's body tense. Tomas, passing beneath a gas lamp, appeared almost as livid as one of the corpses. Alfred judged by these signs that they were nearing their goal. His heart fluttered, his hands shook, and he banished the comforting thought of fainting firmly from his mind.

The chamberlain brought them to a halt with an imperious gesture of his staff. "Please wait here. You will be announced." He moved off, calling, "Preserver! Visitors for the Queen Mother."

"Where are we?" Alfred took advantage of the moment to whisper to Jonathan.

"In the catacombs!" Jonathan answered, eyes glittering with fun and excitement.

"What?" Alfred was amazed. "The catacombs? Where Haplo and the prince—"

"Yes, yes!" Jera murmured.

"We told you it would be simple," Jonathan added.

Tomas, Alfred noticed, said nothing, but stood off to one side, keeping in the shadows, out of the light of the gas lamps.

"Of course, we'll have to go through with this farce of visiting the Queen Mother," Jera whispered, peering impatiently into the catacombs for some sign of the chamberlain. "I wonder where he's gone off to?"

"The Queen Mother. Down here." Alfred was completely baffled. "Did she commit some crime?"

"Oh, dear no!" Jonathan was shocked. "She was a very great lady when she was alive. It was her corpse that proved rather difficult."

"Her corpse," Alfred repeated weakly, leaning against the damp stone wall.

"Constantly interfering," said Jera in a low voice. "She simply could not understand that she was no longer wanted at royal functions. Her cadaver kept barging in at the most inopportune moments. Finally, there was nothing the dynast could do but lock the corpse away down here, where she can't cause trouble. It's quite fashionable to visit her, however. And it *does* please the dynast. He was a good son, if not much else."

"Hush!" Tomas said sharply. "The chamberlain's returning."

"This way, if you will be so good," called the man in sonorous tones.

The narrow hall and dank walls echoed back the sounds of rustling robes and shuffling feet. A man clad in untrimmed black robes bowed, stood deferentially to one side. Was it Alfred's imagination or did Tomas and this black-robed apparition exchange telling glances? Alfred began to shiver with cold and apprehension.

They came to an intersection that formed the shape of a cross; narrow hallways branched off in four directions. Alfred darted a swift glance down the hall to his right. Darkly shadowed cells ranged along either side of the hall. The Sartan tried to catch a glimpse of the prince, or possibly Haplo. He saw nothing, and he didn't dare take time for a closer inspection. He had the uncanny feeling that the preserver's eyes were fixed on him.

The chamberlain turned to the left and the group trooped behind him. Rounding a corner, they stepped into a blaze of light that nearly blinded them after the dim light of the hallways. Sumptuously adorned and appointed, the cavern might have been lifted intact from the royal chambers, except for the iron cell bars, which marred the effect. Behind the bars, surrounded by every possible luxury, a well-preserved cadaver sat in a high-backed chair drinking air from an empty teacup. The corpse was clad in robes of silver thread, and gold and jewels glittered on waxen fingers. Her silver hair was beautifully coiffed and cared for.

A young woman clad in plain black robes sat in a chair near her, making desultory conversation. Alfred realized, with a shock, that the young woman was alive; the living actually serving the dead.

"The Queen Mother's private necromancer," said Jera.

The young woman brightened when she saw them, her expression grew eager. She rose quickly and respectfully from her seat. The cadaver of the Queen Mother glanced their way, made a stately invitational motion with its wrinkled hand.

"I will wait to accompany you out of the catacombs, Your Graces," said the chamberlain. "Please do not remain long. Her Most Gracious Majesty is easily tired."

"We could not think of taking you from your duties," Jera protested smoothly. "Don't let us inconvenience you. We know the way."

At first the chamberlain would not hear of such a thing but Her Grace was persuasive and His Grace was careless with a bag of golden coins that happened to fall into the chamberlain's hands by accident. The chamberlain left them, returning down the hallway, his staff thumping against the floor. Alfred watched him depart, thought he saw the chamberlain nod once at the black-robed preserver. Alfred broke out into a cold sweat. Every fiber in his body was urging him to either run or faint or perhaps do both simultaneously.

The young woman had moved to open the cell door.

"No, my dear, that won't be necessary," Jera said softly.

The conspirators stood together, listening, waiting for the sound of the chamberlain's staff to disappear in the distance. When it could no longer be heard, the preserver beckoned.

"This way!" he called, motioning them toward him.

They moved swiftly. Alfred, glancing back, saw the bitter disappointment in the young woman's face, saw her sink back down into her chair, heard her resume—in a dull, lifeless voice—her conversation with the corpse.

The preserver led them down the hall opposite to the one in which the Queen Mother was housed. It was far darker than the hall they'd just left, far darker than any hall they'd walked yet. Alfred, hurrying along next to Tomas, saw numerous gas lamps on the wall, but for some reason most of them were unlit. Either they'd blown out . . . or they'd been turned off.

Only one lamp in the hallway remained lighted. It beamed out from somewhere ahead, making the surrounding darkness that much darker by contrast. Drawing near, Alfred saw that the light shone on a corpse sitting on a stone slab. The eyes stared straight ahead, its arms dangled listlessly between its knees.

"That's the prince's cell!" said Tomas, his voice tight and hard. "The one with the light in it. Your friend is in the cell across from the cadaver."

Jera, in her eagerness, darted ahead. Jonathan kept close pace behind his wife. Alfred was forced to concentrate on keeping both his feet headed in the same general direction. He found himself at the rear and he suddenly realized that the preserver, who had been in the lead, had unaccountably dropped back behind him. Tomas, too, was no longer around.

From out of the darkness came the clank and rattle of armor. Alfred saw the danger, saw it clearly in his mind, if not with his eyes. He drew a breath to shout a warning, forgot to watch where he was going. The toe of one foot caught on the heel of his other foot. He pitched forward, came down hard on the rock surface, the force of his impact slamming the breath from his body. His cry became nothing more than a whoosh of air, followed by a twanging sound behind him. An arrow flew over his head, pierced the air where he'd been standing.

Peering ahead, fighting desperately to breathe, Alfred saw Jonathan and Jera, two shapes silhouetted against the light—perfect targets.

"Jonathan!" Jera screamed. The two shapes converged confusingly. A flight of arrows sped at them.

Unconsciousness sought to claim Alfred, to draw him into its comfortable oblivion. He battled it back and managed to gasp out the runes, his subconscious bringing words to lips that had no idea what they were speaking.

A heavy weight crashed on top of Alfred, who wondered dazedly if he'd brought the cavern roof down on them. But he realized, from the smell and the feel of chill flesh and cold armor plate against his skin, that he'd succeeded in performing the magic he'd performed once before. He had killed the dead.

"Jera!" Jonathan's voice, panic-stricken, disbelieving, rose to a shriek. "Jera!"

The soldier's corpse had fallen across Alfred's legs. The Sartan pulled himself out from beneath it. A phantasm floated around him, taking on the living form and shape of the body it had left, before it wafted away into the darkness. Alfred was vaguely aware of footsteps—living footsteps—running swiftly back down the hallway and of the preserver kneeling beside the soldier-corpse, speaking to it imperatively, commanding it to rise.

Alfred had no clear idea in his mind of what to do, where to go. He made it to his feet and peered around in terrified confusion. Grief-choked, ragged sobs drew him forward, into the darkness.

Jonathan knelt on the floor. He held Jera in his arms.

The two had almost reached the prince's cell. The light of the gas lamp above it streamed over them, shone off the shaft of an arrow, buried deep, lodged in Jera's right breast. Her eyes were fixed on her husband's face and, just as Alfred reached them, her lips parted in a sigh that took the last breath from her body.

"She jumped in front of me," Jonathan cried dazedly. "The arrow was meant for me and . . . she jumped in front of me. Jera!" He shook the corpse, as if he were trying to waken a deep sleeper. Her lifeless hand slid to the floor. Her head lolled to one side. The beautiful hair fell over her face, covering it like a shroud.

"Jera!" Jonathan clasped her to his breast.

Alfred could still hear the voice of the preserver, attempting to raise the dead guard.

"But he'll soon realize that's futile and summon other guards. Maybe that's where Tomas, the traitor, went." Alfred was talking to himself, knew he was talking to himself, but he couldn't seem to help it. "We have to get away, but where do we go? And where's Haplo?"

A soft groaning came to him as if in response to the sound of the name, cutting beneath Jonathan's cries and the preserver's chants. Alfred looked around hurriedly, saw Haplo lying on the floor near his cell door.

Swift-spoken runes and a graceful weaving of the hands, all done without conscious thought on Alfred's part, reduced the iron bars of the cell to small piles of rust lined up in a neat row.

Alfred touched the Haplo's neck. He could not find the heartbeat, the life's pulse had sunk low, and he feared he was too late. Reaching out a gentle, trembling hand, he turned the man's head to the light. He saw the eyelids flutter. He could feel a soft stirring of warm breath on the skin of the hand that he held near the Patryn's cracked and parched lips. He was alive, but just barely.

"Haplo!" Alfred leaned near, whispering urgently. "Haplo! Can you hear me!" Watching anxiously, he saw the man's head nod with a feeble motion. Relief flooded through him. "Haplo! Tell me what happened to you? Is it sickness? A wound? Tell me! I"—Alfred drew a deep breath, but there had really never been any doubt over his decision—"I can heal you—"

"No!" The crusted lips could barely move, but Haplo managed to form the word, managed to summon enough breath to speak it aloud. "I won't . . . owe my life . . . Sartan." He ceased talking, shut his eyes. A spasm convulsed his body and he cried out in agony.

Alfred hadn't foreseen this, couldn't think how to handle it. "You wouldn't owe your life to me! I owe you!" He was babbling, but it was the only thing he could think to do under the circumstance. "You saved my life from the dragon. On Arian—"

Haplo sucked in a breath. He opened his eyes, reached out and gripped Alfred's robes. "Shut up and . . . listen. You can do . . . one thing for me . . . Sartan. Promise! Swear!"

"I—I swear," Alfred said, not knowing what else to say. The Patryn was very near death.

Haplo was forced to pause, summon his waning strength. He ran his swollen tongue over lips coated with a strange, black substance. "Don't let them . . . resurrect me. Burn . . . my body. Destroy it. Understand." The eyes opened, gazed intently into Alfred's. "Understand?"

Slowly, Alfred shook his head. "I can't let you die."

"Damn you!" Haplo gasped, his weak hand losing its grasp.

Alfred traced the runes in the air, began his chant. His only question now, the only dread left in his heart was: would his magic work on a Patryn?

Behind him, he heard, like an echo of his own words, the soft phrase, "I won't let you die!" And he heard the chanting of runes. Alfred, concentrating on his work, paid no attention.

"Damn you!" Haplo cursed him.

CHAPTER 33

THE CATACOMBS,

ABARRACH

◆

FOLLOWING ALFRED'S FIRST ENCOUNTER WITH HAPLO ON ARIANUS, the Sartan took pains to study the Patryns, the ancient enemy. The early Sartan were meticulous record keepers, and Alfred delved into the mass of histories and treatises kept in the record vaults in the mausoleum beneath Drevlin. He searched particularly for information on the Patryns themselves and their concepts of magic. He found little, the Patryns having been wary of revealing their secrets to their enemies. But one text struck him particularly, and it came now to his mind.

It had been written, not by a Sartan, but by an elven wizardess, who had formed a romantic liaison (brief and volatile) with a Patryn.

The concept of the circle is the key to the understanding of Patryn magic. The circle rules not only the runes they tattoo upon their bodies and how those runes are structured, but it also extends into every facet of their lives—the relationship between the mind and body, relationships between two people, relationships with the community. The rupture of the circle, whether it be injury to the body, the destruction of a relationship, or rupture in the community, is to be avoided at all costs.

The Sartan and others who have encountered the Patryns and are familiar with their harsh, cruel, and dictatorial personalities are continually amazed at the strong loyalty these people feel for their own kind. (And only their own kind!) To those who understand the concept of the circle, however, such loyalty is not surprising. The circle preserves the strength of their community by cutting the community off from those the Patryns consider beneath them. [*There followed irrelevant material concerning the wizardess and her failed love affair.*]

Any illness or injury that strikes down a Patryn is seen to have broken the circle established between body and mind. In healing practices among the Patryns, the most important factor is to reestablish the circle. This may be done by the wounded or sick person himself or it may be done by another Patryn. A Sartan who understood the concept might possibly be able to perform the same function, but it is highly doubtful 1: if the Patryn would permit it and 2: if even a Sartan would be inclined to exhibit such mercy and compassion for an enemy who would turn around and slaughter him without compunction.

The mensch wizardess had not had much use for either Patryns or Sartan. Alfred, on originally reading the text, was somewhat indignant at the woman's tone, feeling sure his people were being unfairly maligned. Now, he wasn't so certain.

Mercy and compassion . . . to an enemy who would show you none himself. He had read the words lightly, glibly, without thinking about them. Now he didn't have time to think about the question, but it occurred to him that somewhere in that sentence was the answer.

The circle of Haplo's being was broken, shattered. Poison, Alfred guessed, noting the black substance on the lips, the swollen tongue, the evidence around him that the man had suffered terrible sickness.

"I must mend the circle, then I can mend the man."

Alfred took hold of Haplo's rune-tattooed hands—the Patryn's left hand held in the Sartan's right, the Sartan's right hand holding the Patryn's left. The circle was formed. Alfred closed his eyes, shutting out every sound around him, banishing the knowledge that more guards were coming, that they were still in deadly peril. Softly, he began to sing the runes.

Warmth surged through him, blood pulsed strongly in his body, life welled up inside him. The runes carried the life from his heart and head to his left arm and his left hand and he sensed it passing through his hand to Haplo's hand. The chill skin of the dying man grew warm to the touch. He heard, or thought he heard, the man's breathing grow stronger.

Patryns have the ability to block Sartan spells, to obviate their power. Alfred was truly afraid, at first, that Haplo might do just that.

But he was either too weak to tear apart the weaving of the runes Alfred spun around him, or the urge to survive was too strong.

Haplo was growing better, but, suddenly, Alfred himself was gripped with pain. The poison entered his system, flowing from the Patryn to the Sartan, stabbing at his insides with knives of flame. Alfred gasped and moaned and doubled over, nausea twisting bowels and stomach, seeming likely to tear him apart.

An enemy who would turn around and slaughter him without compunction.

A horrifying suspicion came over Alfred. Haplo was killing him! The Patryn cared nothing about his own life, he would die and use this opportunity to take his enemy with him.

The suspicion vanished in an instant. Haplo's hands, growing warmer and stronger, clasped the Sartan's more tightly, giving what life and strength he had to give back to Alfred. The circle between the two was truly forged, truly complete.

And Alfred knew, with a feeling of overwhelming sadness, that Haplo would never forgive him.

"Stop! No! What are you doing?" Someone was yelling in panic.

Alfred came back to his surroundings, to their peril, with a jolt. Haplo sat upright and, although he was pale and shivering, he was breathing normally, his eyes were clear, their gaze fixed on Alfred with grim enmity.

Haplo broke the circle, jerking his hands from Alfred's grip.

"Are . . . are you all right?" Alfred asked, peering at Haplo anxiously.

"Leave me alone!" Haplo snarled. He attempted to stand, fell back.

Alfred stretched forth a solicitous hand. Haplo shoved him away roughly.

"I said leave me alone!"

Gritting his teeth, he leaned against the stone bed and pulled himself up off the floor. He was about to attempt to stand, when he glanced out the cell, over Alfred's shoulder. The Patryn's eyes narrowed, his body tensed.

Becoming aware of the panicked shouting behind him, Alfred swung around hastily. The preserver was yelling, but he was yelling at the duke, not at Alfred.

"You're insane! You can't do such a thing! It is against all the laws! Stop it, you fool!"

Jonathan was singing the runes, working the magic on the body of his dead wife.

"You don't know what you are doing!"

The preserver lunged at Jonathan, attempted to drag him away from the corpse. Alfred heard the preserver add something about a "lazar," but the Sartan didn't understand the incoherent shout.

Jonathan flung the preserver off him with a strength born of grief, despair, and madness. The man slammed into a wall, struck his head, and crumpled to the floor. The duke paid no attention to him, paid no attention to the sounds of pounding footsteps, far away, but drawing closer. Holding the still-warm body of his wife to his breast, Jonathan continued to sing the runes, tears running down his face.

"The guards are coming," said Haplo, his voice sharp-edged, cutting. "You've probably saved my life just to get me killed again. I don't suppose you gave any thought as to how we get out of here?"

Alfred looked involuntarily back down the way they'd come, realized the sound of the pounding boots emanated from precisely the same direction. "I . . . I—" he stammered.

Haplo snorted in derision, glanced grimly at the duke. "He's too far gone to be of any help to us." The Patryn stood up, somewhat shakily, nearly falling back on the stone bed. A furious look warned Alfred to keep his distance. Haplo regained his balance, staggered out of the cell, peered down the hallway that continued on into impenetrable darkness.

"Does it lead out of here? Or does it dead-end? If it comes to a dead end, then so do we. Or we could wander around in a maze forever. Still, it's our—Well, hullo, boy! Where did you come from?"

The dog, seeming to materialize out of the darkness, leapt on its master with a joyous bark. Haplo bent down to fondle it. The dog wriggled and danced and nipped at his master's ankles in a frenzy of affection.

The footsteps were nearer, but they had slowed and now Alfred could hear voices, indistinct but audible. From the fragments of conversation, it appeared that they were wary about entering the catacombs, facing the dread magic of the mysterious stranger.

Haplo patted the dog's flanks, looked inquiringly at Alfred.

"I know what you're going to ask me!" Alfred cried distractedly. The Sartan rose hastily, avoiding the Patryn's gaze, and crossed the hall to where the preserver lay in a heap on the floor. He knelt beside the body of the comatose man. "And, no! I can't remember the spell that I used to kill the dead. I'm trying but it's impossible. It's like my fainting. It's something I can't control!"

"Then what the hell are you doing wasting time?" Haplo demanded angrily. "We've got to get out of here! If we knew the way—"

"The runes!" Alfred remembered, stared at the wall of the catacomb, shining in the light. He pointed a shaking hand. "The runes!"

"Yeah? So?"

"They'll lead us out! I—Wait!"

Alfred's fingers traced the carvings on the wall, ran over the whorls and notches and intricate designs. Touching one, he spoke the rune. The sigil beneath his fingers began to glow with a soft, radiant blue light. A rune carved beside the one he touched caught the magical fire and began to glow. Soon, one after the other, a line of runes appeared out of the darkness, running down the length of the hallway and vanishing beyond their line of vision.

"Those'll lead us out of here?"

"Yes," said Alfred confidently. "That is . . ." He hesitated, wavering, recalling what he'd seen in the halls in levels above. His shoulders sagged. "If the sigla haven't been destroyed or defaced . . ."

Haplo grunted. "Well, at least it's a start." The voices were louder. "C'mon. It sounds like they're massing the whole damn army! You go on ahead. I'll get the prince. Knowing Baltazar, I have a feeling we may run into trouble trying to reach the ship without His Highness along."

The preserver was knocked unconscious, but he was alive. Alfred could leave him with a clear conscience. The Sartan hurried over to the duke's side, bent down, not certain what he could do or say to persuade the grief-stricken man to flee for a life that he must now care little about.

Alfred started to speak, stopped, sucked in a breath.

Jonathan's magic had worked. Jera's eyes were open, staring about her. She looked up at her husband with the warm and shining eyes of the living. He reached out to her but at that moment, her visage wavered, dissolved, and she was staring at him with the cold, vacant gaze of the dead.

"Jonathan!" her living voice moaned in pain. "What have you done?"

And there came a chill echo, as if from the grave, moaning, "What have you done?"

Horror filled Alfred, numbed him. He shrank back, bumped into Haplo, and clutched at him thankfully.

"I thought I told you to go on ahead!" the Patryn snapped. He had one hand on the prince's arm, the cadaver moving along quite docilely. "Leave the duke, if he won't come. He's no use to us. What the devil's the matter with you now? I swear—"

Haplo's eyes shifted, his voice trailed off. The Patryn's jaw sagged.

Jonathan was on his feet, helping his wife to stand. The arrow was lodged in her breast, the front of her robes were stained with her life's blood. That much of her image remained fixed and solid in their minds. But her face . . .

"Once, on Drevlin, I saw a woman who had drowned," Alfred said softly, voice tinged with awe. "She was lying beneath the water and her eyes were open, the water stirred her hair. She looked alive! But I knew all the time that . . . she wasn't."

No, she wasn't. He remembered the ceremony he'd witnessed in the cave, remembered the phantasms, standing behind the corpses, separate and apart from the body, divided.

"Jonathan?" the voice cried again and again. "What have you done?"

And the dreadful echo, "What have you done?"

Jera's phantasm had not had time to free itself from the body. The woman was trapped between two worlds, the world of the dead and the world of the spirit. She had become a lazar.[1]

---

[1] From the proper name, Lazarus. Originally, in ancient times, the word was used to refer to a person with a loathsome disease, such as leprosy, considered to be living death. In more modern times, following the Sundering, Sartan practicing the forbidden art of necromancy used the word to refer to those who were brought back from the dead too quickly.

CHAPTER ◆ 34

THE CATACOMBS,

ABARRACH

◆

THE PRESERVER GROANED AND STIRRED, REGAINING CONSCIOUSNESS. The footsteps were on the move again, the arguing voices silenced. Apparently they had their orders and were coming after them.

The animated corpse of Prince Edmund gazed about with the dazed air of a rudely awakened sleeper; its phantasm, hovering at the prince's shoulder, whispered incoherently, sounding like the hissing of a chill wind. The duchess's cadaver was a frightful apparition. Her image constantly shifted, dissolving one moment into that of a writhing phantasm, only to coalesce again into a pale and bloody corpse. Her husband could do nothing except stare at her; the enormity of his terrible crime had stunned him senseless. Alfred was deathly white, whiter than the corpse, and looked as if he were going to keel over any moment. The dog barked frantically.

"It would be easier," Haplo said to himself bitterly, "just to lay down and die . . . except that I don't dare leave my body behind.

"Get moving!" he ordered, poking Alfred none too gently in the ribs. "I've got the prince. Go on!"

"What about—" Alfred's gaze was fixed on the duke and the terrible form that had been the duchess.

"Forget them! We've got to get out of here. The soldiers and most likely the dynast himself are coming." Haplo shoved a reluctant Alfred down the hall. "Kleitus will deal with the duke and duchess."

"They will send me to oblivion!" the lazar shrieked.

". . . oblivion . . ." came the echo.

Fear jolted both the lazar's body and spirit into movement. Haplo glanced behind him in the eerie, blue, rune-lit darkness, and had the awful impression that two women were running after him.

Jera's flight impelled Jonathan to movement. The duke followed after his wife. His hands reached out to her, but he couldn't seem to bring himself to touch her. His hands dropped limp at his sides.

Alfred chanted. The runes on the walls shone brightly, lighting their way deeper into the catacombs. The light rarely failed. If one line of sigla on one side of the wall grew dim or darkened, the sigla on the other side was almost certain to be visible.

The runes led them far below the catacombs. The floor sloped downward at a steep angle that made it difficult to traverse. The cell block soon came to an end, as did the modern improvements such as gas lamps on the walls.

"This part . . . is ancient!" gasped Alfred, panting from the exertion of running, staggering, and stumbling. "The runes . . . are undisturbed."

"But just where the hell are they leading us?" Haplo demanded. "They're not going to drop us in a hole, are they? Or run us smack into a blank wall?"

"I—I don't think so."

"You don't *think* so!" Haplo sneered.

"At least, the runes aren't leading our enemy to us," Alfred ventured. He pointed back at the path they had taken. It had been swallowed up by darkness, the runes had gone out.

Haplo listened carefully. He couldn't hear the footsteps or the voices. Perhaps the fool Alfred had finally managed to do something right. Perhaps the dynast had given up the pursuit.

"Either that, or he has sense enough not to come down here," Haplo muttered. He felt sick and wobbly on his legs. It took an effort just to draw each breath. The runes swam in his blurred vision.

"If I could rest . . . a moment. Have time to think—" Alfred suggested timidly.

Haplo didn't want to stop. He couldn't imagine that Kleitus would just let them slip through his fingers. But the Patryn knew, though he'd never admit it, that he couldn't walk another step.

"Go ahead." He sank down thankfully onto the floor. The dog curled up at his side, crowding close, resting its head on Haplo's leg.

"Watch them, boy," he commanded, turning the dog's head in a slow sweep to include everyone in the narrow tunnel. The prince's cadaver had come to a halt and stood staring at nothing. Jera's body

and spirit flitted restlessly from one side of the hall to another.
Jonathan collapsed onto the tunnel floor, buried his face in his arms.
He hadn't spoken a word since they'd fled.

The Patryn closed his eyes, wondered wearily if he had strength
enough to complete the healing process. Or was healing possible,
considering the powerful poison that had been used on him. . . .

The dog lifted its head, barked once sharply. Haplo opened his
eyes.

"Don't go anywhere, Your Highness."

The prince's cadaver turned around. It had been heading down
the hallway. Purpose had apparently replaced dazed confusion.

"You are not my people. I must return to my people."

"We'll get you there. But you've got to be patient."

The answer appeared to satisfy Edmund's cadaver, which again
stood stock-still. His phantasm, however, wavered and whispered.
The lazar stopped its restless pacing, turned its head as if a voice had
spoken to it.

"Is that what you desire? The experience will not be a pleasant
one! Look at me!" it cried in a ghastly voice.

". . . at me . . ." came the echo.

The phantasm appeared resolute.

The lazar lifted its arms, its bloody hands wove strange runes
around the prince's cadaver. Edmund's face, once peaceful in death,
twisted in pain. The phantasm disappeared, life gleamed in the
corpse's eyes. The lips moved, mouthing words, but only one among
them heard what he said.

The lazar turned to Haplo. "His Highness wonders why you are
helping him."

Haplo attempted to look at the lazar, to meet the eyes, but found
he couldn't. The sight of the blood, the arrow, the shifting face was
too horrible for him to bear. He cursed himself for his weakness,
kept his gaze on the prince.

"How can *it* wonder anything? It's dead."

"The body is dead," the lazar answered. "The spirit is alive. The
prince's phantasm is aware of what is transpiring around it. It could
not speak, could not act. That is why this living death in which we
are trapped is so terrible!"

". . . terrible . . ." came the echo.

"But now," continued the lazar, the awful visage cold with pride,
"I have given him, as far as I am able, the power of speech, of

communicating. I have given him the ability to act, spirit and body as one."

"But . . . we can't hear him," Alfred said in a weak voice.

"No, his spirit and body were too long divided. They have joined together, but the joining is painful, as you can see. It will not last long. Not like mine. My torment is eternal!"

". . . eternal . . ."

Jonathan groaned, writhed in agony nearly as acute as his wife's. Alfred blinked, incredulous, and opened his mouth. Haplo gave him a vicious nudge, warning him to silence.

"His Grace repeats the question: Why are you helping him?"

"Your Highness," said Haplo, speaking to the prince slowly, carefully considering his words, "in helping you, I'm helping myself. My ship . . . remember my ship?"

The cadaver may have nodded.

"My ship," Haplo continued, "is on the other side of the Fire Sea, docked at Safe Harbor. Your people now control Safe Harbor. I'll get you across the Fire Sea, if you'll keep your people from attacking me and grant me passage out of the docks."

The cadaver stood without moving, only the dead eyes flickered in answer.

The lazar listened, then said, with a slight sneer, "His Highness understands and accedes to the arrangement."

So much, thought Haplo, for my plan to abandon the duchess and her traumatized husband. She—or whatever it is she's turned into—could prove extraordinarily useful. He leaned over, caught hold of Alfred's robes.

"Have you come up with something? Do you know where these runes are taking us?"

"I . . . I believe so." Alfred's voice lowered, his gaze shifted to Jera. "But do you realize—she can communicate with the dead!"

"Yes, I realize it! And so will Kleitus, if he gets hold of her." Haplo rubbed his arms, his skin prickled and burned. "I don't like this. Someone's coming. Someone's following us. And whoever or whatever it is, I'm in no condition to fight. It's up to you to save us, Sartan."

"And now I understand," the lazar was saying softly, speaking either to the prince or to the other half of its tortured being. "I hear your words of bitter sorrow. I share your regret, your despair, your frustration!"

The lazar wrung its hands, its voice rising. "You want so desperately to make them listen, and they can't hear! The pain is worse than this arrow in my heart!" Grasping the arrow's shaft, the lazar jerked it free, hurled it to the floor. "That pain ended swiftly. This pain will last forever! Never ending! Oh, my husband, you should have let me die!"

". . . should have let me die . . ." came the mournful echo that faded into the silence of the tunnel.

"I know how she feels," Haplo said grimly. "Pay attention to *me*, Sartan! There'll be enough time later for your tears . . . if we're lucky. The runes, damn it!"

Alfred wrenched his gaze from Jera. "Yes, the runes." He swallowed. "The sigla are leading us in a definite direction, keeping in one path. If you've noticed, we've passed by several other tunnels, branching off from this one, and they haven't taken us down those. When I spoke the runes, it was in my mind that I wanted out and so I think that the runes are leading me where I asked to go. But—" Alfred hesitated, appeared uncomfortable.

"But?"

"But that exit might very well be the front entrance to the palace," Alfred concluded miserably.

Haplo sighed, fought back a strong desire to curl up in a ball and be sick. "We've got no choice except to keep going." The burning of the runes on his skin was strong. He rose slowly and painfully to his feet, whistled to the dog.

"Haplo." Alfred stood up, laid a tentative hand on the Patryn's arm. "What did you mean, you know how she feels? Do you mean I should have let you die?"

Haplo jerked away from the man's touch. "If it's thanks you want for saving my life, Sartan, you won't get them. By bringing me back, you may have imperiled my people, your people, and all those fool mensch out there you seem to care so much about! Yes, you should have let me die, Sartan! You should have let me die, then you should have done what I asked and destroyed my body!"

Alfred stared, confused, frightened. "Imperiled . . . I don't understand."

Haplo lifted a tattooed arm, thrust it into Alfred's face, pointed at the runes on his skin. "Why do you think Kleitus used poison, instead of a spear or an arrow to murder me. Why use poison? Instead of a weapon that *would damage the skin*?"

Alfred went livid. "Blessed Sartan!"

Haplo laughed, briefly. "Yeah! Blessed Sartan! You're a blessed bunch, all right! Now go on. Get us out of here."

Alfred started down the hallway. The sigla on the walls flamed into soft blue light at his approach. The prince's cadaver waited for the lazar, held out its hand with regal dignity, despite the gaping hole in its chest.

The lazar looked from the dead prince to her husband.

Jonathan's head was bowed, his hands clutched at his long hair, tearing it in his bitter regret.

The lazar regarded him without pity, its face smooth, cold, frozen in its death mask. The phantasm, trapped within, gave the lazar its life, a terrible life that stared out of the dead eyes with sudden, dreadful menace.

"It is the living who have done this to us," she hissed.

". . . done this to us . . ." whispered the echo.

The duke lifted a ravaged face, his eyes widened. The lazar took a step toward him. Cringing, he shrank away from what had once been his wife.

The lazar regarded him in silence. The two halves of her being shifted, separated, the spirit attempting futilely to free itself from the body's prison. Turning, without a word, the lazar joined the dead prince, its feet trampling heedlessly over the blood stained arrow it had hurled to the floor.

Wild-eyed, Jonathan plucked an object from beneath his robes. Steel flashed in the already fading light of the runes.

"Dog!" Haplo shouted. "Stop him!"

The dog leapt, teeth slashing. Jonathan cried out in pain and astonishment. The knife he held clattered to the tunnel floor. He made a grab for it, but the dog was swifter. Standing over it, the animal bared its teeth, growling. Jonathan fell back, nursing a bleeding wrist.

Haplo put his hand on the duke's arm, steered him down the tunnel after Alfred. A whistle brought the dog trotting along behind.

"Why did you stop me!" Jonathan asked in a dull voice. His feet dragged. He walked blindly. "I want to die!"

Haplo grunted. "All I need is another corpse! Get moving!"

CHAPTER ♦ 35

THE CATACOMBS,

ABARRACH

♦

THE CATACOMB TUNNEL CONTINUED TO DESCEND AT A MODERATE slope, the runes lighting a smooth path that appeared to be delving straight into the depths of the world. Haplo had doubts about anything that Alfred undertook, but the Patryn was forced to concede that the tunnel, although ancient, was dry, wide, and had been kept in good repair. He hoped he was right in deducing, therefore, that it had been designed to accommodate a considerable amount of traffic.

Why? he reasoned, if not to take a large number of people to a specific place. And wouldn't that place more than likely be out?

It made sense. Still, he reminded himself gloomily, there was no telling with the Sartan.

But, wherever the path was leading them, they were forced to follow. There was no turning back. Haplo paused often to listen, and now he was certain he heard footsteps, the clank of armor, the rattle of sword and spear. He glanced over at his charges. The dead were in better condition than the living. The lazar and the prince's cadaver walked down the tunnel with calm, purposeful steps. Behind them, Jonathan stumbled aimlessly, paying little attention to his surroundings, his gaze fixed with a puzzled horror on the tortured figure of his beloved wife.

Haplo wasn't moving all that well himself. The poison was still in his system. Only a healing sleep would cure him completely. The runes on his flesh glowed in a sickly manner. His magic fought to place one foot in front of the other. The runes on his skin might flicker and die out completely if the sigla had to fight anything more challenging. Silent, watchful, the dog padded along, keeping at the duke's heels.

The Patryn edged his way through the narrow tunnel, past the living and the dead, to catch up with Alfred. The Sartan sang the runes softly beneath his breath, watched the sigla flame to life and light their path.

"We're being followed," Haplo announced in a low voice.

The Sartan was concentrating on the runes, had no idea Haplo was near. Alfred jumped, tripped, and nearly fell. He saved himself by clinging to the smooth, dry wall and glanced nervously behind him.

Haplo shook his head. "I don't think they're close, although I can't be certain. These damn tunnels distort the sound. They can't be sure which way we went. My guess is that they're having to stop and investigate every intersection, send patrols down every bran- ching path to make certain they don't lose us." He gestured at the glowing blue marks on the wall. "These sigla wouldn't be likely to light up again, show them the way, would they?"

"They might," Alfred paused, considering. He looked unhappy. "If the dynast knew the proper spells . . ."

Haplo stopped walking, began swearing fluently. "That damn arrow!"

"What arrow?" Alfred cringed back against the wall, expecting barbed shafts to come flying past him.

"The arrow Her Grace yanked out of her body!" Haplo pointed in the direction they'd just come. "Once they find that, they'll know they're on the right track!"

He took a step in that direction, hardly knowing what he was doing.

"You can't be thinking of returning!" Alfred cried, panicked. "You'd never find the way back!"

Is that what I'm thinking? Haplo wondered to himself silently, nerves tingling with the idea. I use retrieving the arrow as an excuse, double back on our own trail. The soldiers will keep going forward. All I'd have to do is hide until they're gone, then be on my merry way and leave these Sartan to their well-deserved fate.

It was tempting, very tempting. But that left the problem of returning to his ship, a ship that was now moored in hostile enemy territory.

Haplo resumed walking beside Alfred.

"I'd find a way back," he said bitterly. "What you mean is that *you'd* never find the way back—the way back through Death's Gate. That was the reason you saved my life, wasn't it, Sartan?"

"Of course," returned Alfred softly, sadly. "Why else?"

"Yeah. Why else?"

Alfred was apparently deeply absorbed in his chanting. Haplo couldn't hear the words, but he saw the Sartan's lips move, the runes continue to light. The slope in the floor had decreased markedly. It ran level, which might indicate they were getting somewhere. The Patryn didn't know if this was good or bad.

"It wouldn't be on account of the prophecy, would it?" he asked abruptly, keeping his gaze fixed intently on Alfred.

The Sartan's entire body jerked as if dancing on a puppeteer's string—head, hands flew up, eyes opened wide. "No!" he protested. "No, I assure you! I don't know anything about this . . . this prophecy."

Haplo studied the man. Alfred was not above lying, if driven to it, but he was a terrible liar, offering up his prevarications with a wistful, pleading expression, as if begging you to believe him. He was looking at Haplo now and his look was frightened, miserable. . . .

"I don't believe you!"

"Yes, you do," answered Alfred meekly.

Haplo fumed, angry, disappointed. "Then you're an idiot! You should have asked them. After all, the prophecy was mentioned in connection with you."

"The one reason that I never want to know of it!"

"*That* makes a hell of a lot of sense!"

"A prophecy implies that we are destined to do something. It dictates to us, we have no choice in the matter. It robs us of our freedom of will. Too often, prophecies end up being self-fulfilling. Once the thought is in our minds, we act, either consciously or unconsciously, to bring it to pass. That can be the only explanation . . . unless you believe in a higher power."

"Higher power!" Haplo scoffed. "Where? The mensch? I don't plan to believe in this 'prophecy.' These Sartan believe in it, and that's what interests me. As you say"—Haplo winked—"that prophecy could be 'self-fulfilling.' "

"You don't know what it is either, do you?" Alfred guessed.

"No, but I intend to find out. Don't worry, though. I don't plan to tell you. Say, Your Grace—" He turned toward Jonathan.

"Haplo!" Alfred sucked in his breath, caught hold of the Patryn's arm.

"Don't try to stop me!" Haplo tore himself free. "I'm warning you—"

"The runes! Look at the runes!"

Alfred pointed a trembling finger at the wall. Haplo glared at the Sartan, thinking it was a ruse to keep him from talking to the duke. But Alfred appeared truly upset. The Patryn reluctantly and warily shifted his gaze.

The sigla, lighting one by one, had been running consistently along the base of the wall ever since they left the dungeon. At this point, however, they left the base of the wall, traveled upward to form an arch of glowing blue light. Haplo squinted his eyes against the brilliance, peered ahead. He could see nothing beyond but darkness.

"It's a door. We've come to a door," said Alfred nervously.

"I can see that! Where does it lead?"

"I—I don't know. The runes don't say. But . . . I don't think we should go any farther."

"What do you suggest we do instead? Wait here to pay our respects to the dynast?"

Alfred licked his lips. Sweat beaded on his balding head. "N-no. It's just . . . I mean I wouldn't—"

Haplo walked straight for the arch. At his approach, the runes changed color, blue turned to flaring red. The sigla smoldered, burst into flame. He put his hand in front of his face, tried to advance. Fire roared and crackled, smoke blinded him. The superheated air seared his lungs. The runes on his arms glowed blue in response, but their power could not protect him from the burning flames that scorched his flesh. Haplo fell back, gasping for air. He'd be immolated if he went through that doorway.

The Patryn glared at Alfred, irrationally blaming him. At Haplo's retreat, the sigla's fire faded to a red-yellow glow.

"Those are runes of warding. You can't enter," said Alfred, wide eyes reflecting the rune light. "None of us can enter! There's another hallway over here." He indicated a tunnel running at right angles to the one in which they stood.

They left the flaring archway, whose runes dimmed to darkness behind them, and entered the hallway. Alfred began to chant, the blue runes lit up along the base of the wall, leading them onward. But after taking about forty steps, they discovered that the corridor bent around to the right, leading them back in the direction from which they'd come. Haplo wasn't surprised to see another archway light up before them.

"Oh, dear," murmured Alfred, distressed. "But this can't be the same one!"

"It isn't," said Haplo, voice grim.

"Look, the hall continues on around—"

"—and my guess is that it will only take us to another arch. You can go look, but—"

"The dead are coming." The lazar spoke suddenly, chill lips curved in a strange and eerie smile. "I can hear them."

". . . hear them . . ." murmured the phantasm.

"I can hear them, too," Haplo said, "the clash of cold steel." He eyed Alfred. The Sartan shrank back against the wall. By his expression, it seemed he wished very much he could crawl into the rock. "Runes of warding, you said. That means they would 'ward' people away, *not* prevent them from entering."

Alfred flicked a despairing glance at the sigla. "No one who came across these runes would *want* to enter."

Haplo checked a bitter, frustrated comment, turned to Jonathan. "Do you have any idea what could be in there?"

The duke raised glazed eyes, glanced around without interest. He had little or no idea where he was and obviously cared less. Haplo swore softly, turned back to Alfred. "Can you break the runes?"

Sweat trickled down the Sartan's face. He gulped, swallowed. "Yes." His voice was tremulous, barely audible. "But you don't understand. These runes are the strongest that could possibly be laid down. Something terrible lies beyond that door! I will not open it!"

Haplo eyed Alfred intently, measuring what it would take to force the Sartan to act. Alfred was very pale, but resolute, stooped shoulders braced, eyes meeting Haplo's with unflinching, unexpected resolve.

"So be it," Haplo muttered and, turning, started walking toward the arch. The sigla flared red, he could feel the heat on his face and arms. Gritting his teeth, he continued to walk forward. The dog gave a frantic bark.

"Stay!" Haplo commanded, and kept on walking.

"Wait!" Alfred cried in a tone no less frantic than the dog's. "What are you doing? Your magic can't protect you!"

The heat was intense. Breathing was difficult. The doorway was ablaze, an arc of fire.

"You're right, Sartan," Haplo said, coughing, moving steadily forward. "But . . . it will be over quickly. And"—he glanced backward—"my body won't be of much use to anyone afterward . . ."

"No! Don't! I'll . . . I'll open them!" Alfred cried, shuddering. "I'll . . . open them," he repeated. Pushing himself up from the wall, he shuffled forward.

Haplo came to a stop, stepped to one side, watched with a quiet, satisfied smile. "You weakling," he said in disdain as Alfred moved slowly past.

CHAPTER ✦ 36

THE CHAMBER OF

THE DAMNED, ABARRACH

✦

STANDING BEFORE THE ARCHWAY, A PREPOSTEROUS, UNGAINLY FIGURE in his too-short black robe, Alfred began to perform a solemn dance.

The feet that could not take ten steps without falling over themselves were suddenly executing intricate steps with extraordinary grace and delicacy. His face was grave and solemn, wholly absorbed in the music. He accompanied himself with a grave and solemn song. Hands wove the runes in the air, his feet replicated the pattern on the floor. Haplo watched until he discovered some wayward part of himself feeling touched and entranced by the beauty.

"How long is this going to take?" he demanded, his voice harsh and discordant, breaking in on the song.

Alfred paid no attention to him, but the dancing and the singing ended soon after Haplo spoke. The red light of the warding runes glimmered, faded, glimmered, and died. Alfred shook himself, drew a deep breath, as if he were emerging from deep water. He looked up at the dying light of the runes and sighed.

"We can go in now," he said, wiping sweat from his forehead.

They passed through the arch without incident, although Haplo was forced to fight down a sudden overwhelming reluctance to enter, and he experienced an unpleasant tingling sensation on his skin.

If I were in the Labyrinth, I'd heed these warnings. He was the last to walk beneath the arch, the dog trotting along at his heels. The runes lit again almost immediately, their red glow illuminating the tunnel.

"That should stop whoever's following us, or at least slow them down. Most of the Sartan may have forgotten the old magic but I wouldn't put it past Kleitus—" Haplo paused, frowning. The red-glowing sigla gleamed on both sides of the arch. "What does that mean, Sartan?"

"The runes are different," said Alfred softly, fearfully. "The sigla on the opposite side were designed to keep people out. These"— he turned, staring into the darkness—"are meant to keep something in."

Haplo leaned wearily back against the tunnel wall. Patryns are not noted for their imagination or creativity, but it took little of either for Haplo to conjure up visions of various terrible monsters that might be lurking in the depths of this world.

And I haven't got the strength left to fight an angry house cat.

He felt eyes on him and glanced up swiftly. The lazar was watching him. The eyes in the dead face were fixed and staring, without expression. But the eyes of the phantasm, that sometimes looked out of the dead eyes, like a sentient shadow, were regarding him steadfastly.

Their look was fey, dire. A slight smile touched the lazar's blue-gray lips. "Why struggle? Nothing can save you. In the end, you will come to us."

Fear twisted inside Haplo, turned his guts to water, clenched his bowels; not the adrenaline-pumped fear of battle that gave a man strength he didn't possess, stamina and endurance he didn't have. This fear was the child's fear of the darkness, the terror of the unknown, the debilitating fear of a thing he didn't understand and, therefore, couldn't control.

The dog, sensing the menace, growled, hackles raised and stepped between its master and the lazar. The corpse's malevolent eyes lowered, their dreadful spell broke. Alfred had moved on down the hallway, murmuring the runes to himself. Blue sigla on the walls were once again leading them forward. Prince Edmund's cadaver stalked after him. Its phantasm had again separated from the body, trailed along behind the cadaver like a ragged silk scarf.

Shaken and unnerved, Haplo remained leaning against the wall until the rune's light had almost faded, attempting to recover himself. A voice, speaking out of the dimness, set every nerve jumping and twitching.

"Do you suppose all the dead hate us that much?" It was Jonathan's voice, torn, anguished.

Haplo hadn't been paying attention, hadn't known the duke was near. Such a lapse would have cost the Patryn his life in the Labyrinth! Cursing himself, the tunnel, the poison, and Alfred, Haplo cursed Jonathan for good measure. Grabbing the duke by the elbow, he propelled him roughly along down the hallway.

♦

The tunnel was wide and airy, the ceiling and walls dry. A thick coating of dust lay undisturbed on the rock floor. No sign of footprints or claw marks or the sinuous trails left by serpents and dragons. No attempt had been made to obliterate the sigla, the guide-runes shone brilliantly, lighting their way to whatever lay ahead of them.

Haplo listened, smelled, felt and tasted the air. He kept close watch on the runes on his skin, was alert to every fiber of his body that might warn him of danger.

Nothing.

If it hadn't seemed too preposterous, he could have sworn he actually felt a sense of peace, of well-being that relaxed taut muscles, soothed frayed nerves. The feeling was inexplicable, made no sense, and simply increased his irritation.

No danger ahead, but he distinctly sensed pursuit behind.

The tunnel led them straight forward, no twists or turns, no other tunnels branched off this one. They passed beneath several archways, but none were marked with the warding runes as had been the first. Then, without warning, the blue guide-runes came to an abrupt halt, as if they'd run into a blank wall.

Which, Haplo discovered, catching up to Alfred, was exactly the case.

A wall of black rock, solid and unyielding, loomed before them. It bore faint markings on its smooth surface.

Runes, Sartan runes, observed Haplo, studying them closely by the reflected light of the blue sigla. But there was something wrong with them, even to his untrained eye.

"How strange!" Alfred murmured, gazing at the wall.

"What?" demanded Haplo, jumpy and on edge. "Dog, watch," he commanded. A hand motion sent the animal back to stand guard over the path down which they'd come. "What's strange? Is this a dead end?"

"Oh, no. There's a door here . . ."

"Can you open it?"

"Why, yes. A child could open it, in fact."

"Then let's find a child to do it!" Haplo seethed with impatience.

Alfred gazed at the wall with academic interest. "The rune structure is not complicated, rather like locks one places on one's bedroom door in one's own home, but . . ."

"But what?" Haplo suppressed a strong desire to wring the Sartan's scrawny neck. "Quit rambling!"

"There are two sets of runes here." Alfred lifted a finger, traced it over the wall. "Surely, you can see that?"

Yes, Haplo could see it and realized that's what he'd noticed when he'd first approached.

"Two sets of runes." Alfred was talking to himself. "One set apparently added later . . . much later, I would guess . . . inscribed on top of the first." Lines wrinkled the high, domed forehead; thin, gray brows came together in thoughtful consternation.

The dog barked once, loudly, warning.

"Can you open the damn door?" Haplo repeated, teeth and hands clenched, keeping a tight grip on himself.

Alfred nodded, in an abstract manner.

"Then do it," Haplo spoke quietly to keep from shouting.

Alfred turned to face him, the Sartan's expression unhappy. "I'm not sure I should."

"You're not sure you *should*?" Haplo stared at him, disbelieving. "Why? Is there something so formidable written on that door? More runes of warding?"

"No," admitted Alfred, swallowing nervously. "Runes of . . . sanctity. This place is sacred, holy. Can't you feel it?"

"No!" Haplo lied, fuming. "All I can feel is Kleitus, breathing down my neck! Open the damn door!"

"Holy . . . sanctified. You're right," Jonathan whispered in awe. He had regained some color in his face, looked about in reluctant astonishment. "I wonder what this place was? Why no one ever knew it was down here?"

"The sigla are ancient, dating back almost to the Sundering. The runes of warding would have kept everyone away and, over the centuries, I imagine people forgot it was here."

Those runes of warding had been put up to stop whatever was

beyond that door from going farther. Haplo shoved the unwelcome thought out of his mind.

The dog barked again. Turning tail, it dashed back to its master and stood at his feet, body tense, panting.

"Kleitus is coming. Open the door," Haplo said again. "Or stand here and die."

Alfred glanced fearfully behind, looked fearfully ahead. Sighing, he ran his hands over the wall, tracing rune patterns, chanting them beneath his breath. The stone began to dissolve beneath his fingers and, faster than the eye could capture, an opening in the wall appeared, outlined by the blue guide-runes.

"Get back!" Haplo ordered. He flattened himself against the wall, peered into the darkness beyond, prepared to meet slavering jaws, slashing fangs, or worse.

Nothing, except more dust. The dog sniffed, sneezed.

Haplo straightened, lunged through the door and into the darkness. He almost hoped something *would* leap out at him, something solid and real that he could see and fight.

His foot encountered an obstacle on the floor. He shoved against it gently. It gave way with a clatter.

"I need light!" Haplo snapped, looking back at Alfred and Jonathan, who stood huddled in the doorway.

Alfred hastened forward, stooping his tall body to duck beneath the arch. His hands fluttered, he recited the runes in a singsong tone that set Haplo's teeth on edge. Light, soft and white, began to beam out of a sigla-etched globe that hung suspended from the center of a high, domed ceiling.

Beneath the globe stood an oblong table carved of pure, white wood—a table that had not come from this world. Seven sealed doorways in the walls undoubtedly led to seven other tunnels, similar to the one down which they'd passed, all of them leading to the same place—this room. And all of them, undoubtedly, marked with the deadly runes of warding.

Chairs that must have once stood around the table lay scattered over the floor, upended, overturned. And amid the wreckage . . .

"Merciful Sartan!" Alfred gasped, clasping his hands together.

Haplo looked down. The object his foot had disturbed was a skull.

CHAPTER ✦ 37

THE CHAMBER OF

THE DAMNED, ABARRACH

✦

The skull lay where he had nudged it, sending it rolling onto a pile of dry bones. More bones, and more skulls—almost too numerous to count—filled the chamber. The floor was carpeted with bones. Well preserved in the sealed atmosphere, undisturbed through the centuries, the dead lay where they had fallen, limbs twisted grotesquely.

"How did they die? What killed them?" Alfred glanced this way and that, expecting to see the killer emerge at any moment.

"You can relax," said Haplo. "Nothing killed them. They killed each other. And some of them weren't even armed. Look at these two, for example."

A bony hand held the hilt of a sword, its bright metal had not rusted in the dry, hot atmosphere. The notched blade lay beside a head that had been severed from its shoulders.

"One weapon, two bodies."

"But then, who killed the killer?" Alfred asked.

"Good question," Haplo admitted.

He knelt down to examine one of the bodies more closely. The skeletal hands were wrapped around the hilt of a dagger. The dagger's blade was lodged firmly in the skeleton's own rib cage.

"It seems the killer killed himself," said Haplo.

Alfred drew back in horror. Haplo looked quickly about, saw evidence that more than one had fallen by his or her own hand.

"Mass murder." He stood up. "Mass suicide."

Alfred stared, aghast. "That's impossible! We Sartan revere life! We would never—"

"Just as you never practiced necromancy?" Haplo interrupted curtly.

Alfred closed his eyes, his shoulders sagged, he buried his face in his hands. Jonathan stepped gingerly inside, stared dazedly around the room. Prince Edmund's cadaver stood stolidly against one wall, evincing no interest. These were not his people. The lazar glided among the skeletal remains, its dead-living eyes quick and darting.

Haplo kept one of his own eyes on Jera. He walked over to Alfred, slumped dispiritedly against the wall.

"Get a grip on yourself, Sartan. Can you shut that door?"

Alfred lifted an anguished face. "What?"

"Shut the door! Can you shut the door?"

"It won't stop Kleitus. He came through the warding runes."

"It'll slow him down. What the hell's the matter?"

"Are you sure you want me to? Do we want to be . . . locked in here?"

Haplo gestured impatiently at the six other doors in the chamber.

"Oh, yes, well, I see," Alfred mumbled. "I *suppose* it will be all right . . ."

"Suppose all you want. Just shut the damn door!" Haplo turned, surveying the exits. "Now, there must be some way to figure out where these lead. They must be marked—"

A grating sound interrupted him; the door starting to slide shut.

Why, thank you, Haplo was about to comment sarcastically, when he caught a glimpse of Alfred's face.

"I didn't do it!" the Sartan protested, staring wide-eyed at the stone door that was grinding its way inexorably across the opening.

Suddenly, irrationally, Haplo didn't want to be trapped in this place. He leapt forward, interposed his body between the door and the wall.

The massive stone door bore down on him.

He pushed against it with all his might. Alfred grabbed wildly at the door with his hands, fingers scrabbling at the stone.

"Use magic!" Haplo commanded.

Desperately, Alfred shouted a rune. The door continued to shut. The dog barked at it frantically. Haplo made an attempt to stop it using his own magic, hands trying to trace runes on the door that was near to squeezing the life from him.

"It won't work!" Alfred cried, ending his attempt to stop the door. "Nothing will work. The magic's too powerful!"

Haplo was forced to agree. Near being crushed between the door and the wall, he lunged sideways, pulled himself free. The door shut with a dull boom that sent dust into the air, rattled the bones of the skeletons.

So the door shut. It's what I wanted. Why did I panic like that? Haplo demanded of himself angrily. It's this place, a feeling about this place. What drove these people to kill each other? To kill themselves? And why those warding runes, preventing anyone from coming, anyone from leaving? . . .

A soft blue-white light began to illuminate the chamber. Haplo looked up swiftly, saw runes appear, running in a circle around the upper portion of the chamber walls.

Alfred drew in a deep breath.

"What is it? What do they say?" Haplo braced himself.

"This place is . . . sanctified!" Alfred breathed in awe, staring up at the runes whose glow grew brighter, bathing them in radiant light. "I think I'm beginning to understand. 'Any who bring violence in here . . . will find it visited on themselves!' That's what they say."

Haplo breathed a sigh of relief. He'd begun to have visions of people trapped inside a sealed room, dying of suffocation, going mad, ending it swiftly.

"That explains it. These Sartan began fighting among themselves, the magic reacted to put a stop to it, and that was that."

He shoved Alfred toward one of the doorways. It didn't matter where it led. Haplo wanted only to get out of here. He almost flung the Sartan into the door. "Open it!"

"But why is this chamber sacred? What is it sacred to? And why, if it is sacred, should it be so strongly guarded?" Alfred, instead of studying the runes on the door, was peering vaguely about the room.

Haplo flexed his hands, clenched them tightly. "It's going to be sacred to your own corpse, Sartan, if you don't open that door!"

Alfred set to work with infuriating slowness, hands groping over the stone. He peered at it intently, murmured runes beneath his breath. Haplo stood near, to make certain the Sartan wasn't distracted.

"This is our perfect chance for escape. Even if Kleitus does manage to make it this far, he won't have any idea which way we've gone—"

"There are no phantasms here," came the lazar's voice.

". . . no phantasms here . . ." whispered its echo.

Haplo glanced around, saw the lazar flitting from one corpse to another. The prince's cadaver had left the doorway and moved over near the white wood table in the center of the chamber.

Is it my imagination, wondered Haplo, or is the prince's phantasm gaining shape and form?

The Patryn blinked, rubbed his eyes. It was this damn light! Nothing looked like it was supposed to look.

"I'm sorry," said Alfred meekly. "It won't open."

"What do you mean, it won't open?" Haplo demanded.

"It must be something to do with those runes," the Sartan said, gesturing vaguely up at the ceiling. "While their magic is activated, no other magic can work. Of course! That's the reason," he continued in a pleased tone, as if he'd just solved some complex mathematical equation. "They didn't want to be interrupted in whatever it was they were doing."

"But they were interrupted!" Haplo pointed out, kicking at one of the skulls with his foot. "Unless they went mad and turned on themselves."

Which seemed like a very real possibility. I have to get out of here! Haplo couldn't breathe. Some strange force in the room was expanding, squeezing the air out. The light was intensely bright, painful, hurt his eyes.

I have to get out of here, before I go blind, before I suffocate! Clammy sweat dampened his palms, chilled his body. I have to get out of here!

Haplo shoved Alfred aside, hurled himself at the sealed door. He began to trace runes on the rock, Patryn runes. He was frantic, his hands shaking so that he could barely form the sigla he had known how to shape since childhood. The sigla burned red, dimmed, went out. He'd made a mistake. A stupid mistake. Swearing, he grit his teeth and began again. He had a vague sense of Alfred attempting to stop him. Haplo brushed him away, as he would have brushed away a stinging fly. The white, blue light was growing stronger, more brilliant, beating down on him like the sun.

"Stop him!" The lazar's shrill voice. "He's leaving us!"

". . . leaving us . . ." came the echo.

Haplo began to laugh. He wasn't going anywhere and he knew it. His laughter had a hysterical edge. He heard it, didn't care. Die. We're all going to die . . .

"The prince!" Alfred's voice and the dog's warning bark came at the same time, were almost indistinguishable, as if the Sartan had given the dog words.

Body and mind numb from sickness, fatigue, and what could only be described as panic, Haplo saw that at least one member of their group had discovered a way out.

The prince's cadaver slumped over the table, the dreadful magic that had kept it alive was gone. Edmund's phantasm was walking away from the husk that had been its prison, the spirit's form tall and regal as the prince had been in life, its face transfigured by an expression of rapt wonder. The arms of the cadaver lay flaccid on the marble. The arms of the phantasm reached out. It took a step forward, moving through the solid wooden table as if *it* were a phantasm. Another step and another. The phantasm was leaving its body behind.

"Stop him!" The lazar's shifting features, blending those of the living and the dead, faced Haplo. "Without him, you will never recover your ship! Even now, his people are attempting to break down the runes you have placed on it. Baltazar plans to sail across the Fire Sea and attack Necropolis."

"How the hell can you know that?" Haplo shouted. He heard himself shouting, but couldn't stop. He was losing control.

"The voices of the dead cry out to me!" the lazar answered. "From every part of this world, I hear them. Stop the prince or your voice will join them!"

". . . your voice will join them . . ." hissed the echo.

None of this made sense anymore. It was all an insane dream. Haplo shot Alfred an accusing glance.

"I didn't cast the spell! Not . . . not this time!" Alfred protested, wringing his hands. "But it's true. He is leaving!"

The prince's phantasm, arms outstretched, glided through the wood table, approaching the center. The spirit grew clearer in the vision of those watching, the lifeless cadaver began to slide to the floor. Where was he going? What was drawing him away?

What would bring him back?

"Your Highness," Jonathan called out, voice cracking with frantic urgency. "Your people! You can't leave them. They need you!"

"Your people!" The lazar added its persuasion. "Your people are in danger. Baltazar rules now, in your stead, and he is leading them to war, a war they cannot hope to win."

"Can he hear us?" Haplo demanded.

The phantasm heard. It hesitated in its movement, gazed at those standing around it, the expression of wonder blurring, marred by doubt, sorrow.

"It seems a pity to call him back," Alfred murmured.

Haplo could have made a sarcastic comment, but he lacked the energy. He was irritated with himself for having been thinking the very same thing.

"Return to your people." The lazar was luring the phantasm back to its corpse, crooning to it gently, as a mother lures a child from the perils of the cliff's edge. "It is your duty, Your Highness. You are responsible. You have always been responsible. You cannot be selfish and leave them when they need you most!"

The phantasm dwindled, faded until it was nothing more than the gibbering ghost it had been before. And then, it vanished, disappeared altogether.

Haplo shut his eyes, hard, thinking again that the eerie blue light was playing tricks on them. Blinking, he glanced around to see if anyone else had noticed.

Alfred stared vacantly at the white wooden table. Jonathan was assisting the reanimated corpse to stand.

Would anyone notice if a man, walking down a street in broad daylight, cast no shadow?

"My people," the corpse said. "I must return to my people."

The words were the same, the intonation was different. The difference was subtle, a change in the pitch, the modulation. He wasn't reciting them by rote, he was thinking about them. And Haplo realized that Edmund's corpse had become a "he," no longer an "it." The sightless eyes were sightless no longer. They were fixed on the lazar and in the eyes was the shadow of doubt. Haplo knew then where Edmund's phantasm had gone. It had, once again, joined with the corpse.

Glancing at the lazar, he saw that it had seen the same phenomenon and that it was not pleased.

Haplo didn't know why, he didn't care. Strange things had happened—were happening—in this room. The longer he stayed, the less he liked it and he hadn't liked it much from the beginning. There had to be some way to shut off those damn blue lights . . .

"The table," said Alfred suddenly. "The key is the table." He approached it, stepping carefully over the bodies that littered the floor. Haplo went with him, keeping up with him, step for step. "And look at this! The bodies around the table are facing outward, as if they had fallen defending it."

"And they're the ones who weren't armed," Haplo added. "The sacred runes, a table these people died to protect. If they had been mensch, I'd say this table was an altar." His eyes met Alfred's, the same question was in both.

The Sartan considered themselves to be gods. What could they possibly have worshiped?

He and Alfred drew close to the table now. Jonathan was examining it closely, brow furrowed. He reached out a hand.

"Don't touch it!" Alfred exclaimed.

The duke snatched his hand back. "What? Why not?"

"The sigla on it. Can't you read them?"

"Not very well." Jonathan flushed. "The runes are old."

"Very old," Alfred agreed solemnly. "The magic has to do with communication."

"Communication?" Haplo was disappointed, disgusted. "Is that all?"

Alfred began slowly unraveling the tangled skein. "This table is ancient. It did not come from this world. They brought it with them from the old world, the sundered world. They brought it with them and they established it here, beneath the first structure they ever built. For what purpose? What would be one of the first things these ancient Sartan would attempt to do?"

"Communicate!" Haplo said, studying the table with more interest.

"Communicate. Not with each other on this world, they could do that by means of their magic. They would try to establish contact with the other worlds."

"Contact that failed."

"Did it?" Alfred studied the table. He held his hands above the sigil-inscribed wood, fingers spread, palms facing down. "Suppose that, in attempting to contact the other worlds, they made contact with . . . something, someone else?"

The force that opposes us is ancient and powerful. It cannot be fought, cannot be placated. Tears do not move it, nor do all

the weapons we have at our command. Too late, we have come
to admit its existence. We bow before it . . .

Haplo recalled the words, couldn't think, for the moment, where
he'd heard them. On another world. Arianus? Pryan? An image of a
Sartan speaking them came to mind, but Haplo had never spoken to
another Sartan, except Alfred, before coming to this place. It didn't
make any sense.

"Does it say how we get the hell out of here?" Haplo demanded.

Alfred, hearing the jagged edge to the Patryn's voice, looked
grave. "One of us must attempt the communication himself."

"Just who are you going to communicate with?"

"I don't know."

"All right. Anything to end this. No, wait, Sartan. I'm in on this,
too," Haplo said grimly. "Whatever you hear, I'm going to hear."

"And you, Jonathan?" Alfred turned to the duke. "You are the
representative of this world."

"Yes. Perhaps I can learn how to help . . ." Jonathan's glance
strayed to his wife, the words died on his lips. "Yes," he said again in
a low voice.

"I will guard the door," offered the lazar, moving to stand beside
the sealed rock.

"That's not really necessary." Alfred found it difficult to look
directly at the dead woman. He tried, but his gaze kept shifting,
sliding away from her. "No one can enter this hallowed chamber."

"They entered the last time," the lazar said.

". . . the last time . . ." whispered her phantasm.

"So they did!" Alfred licked dry lips, swallowed.

"We can't worry about that now," Haplo said shortly. "What do
we do?"

"Put your . . . uh, put your hands on the table. You can see the
indentations where the hands are to be placed. Like this, palm
down, thumbs touching, fingers spread. Haplo, make certain none
of the sigla on your skin come in contact with the wood. Make your
mind a blank—"

"Think like a Sartan, huh? I can manage that." Haplo did as
instructed. Gingerly, he placed his hands on the table. Muscles
twitched involuntarily, expecting a jolt, pain, he didn't know what.
He touched wood, solid beneath his hands, cool, reassuring.

"I warn you, I don't know what's going to happen," Alfred reiterated, nervously placing his hands on the table.

Jonathan, opposite them, did the same.

Alfred began to chant the runes. The duke, after a moment's hesitation, joined in, speaking the language of the arcane clumsily and uncertainly. Haplo sat still, kept silent. The dog curled up on the floor near its master.

Soon, the three men heard nothing except Alfred's chanting. And, soon, they couldn't hear that.

◆

The lazar stood near the door, watching in silence, watched Alfred slump forward, watched Haplo's head rest on the table, watched Jonathan cradle his cheek on the cool, white wood. The dog's eyes blinked sleepily, closed.

The lazar raised its chill voice. "Come to me. Follow my call. Fear no runes of warding. They are for the living. They have no power over the dead. Come to me. Come to this chamber. They will open the door for you, as they opened it long ago, and invite their own doom inside. It is the living who have done this to us."

". . . done this to us . . ." came the echo.

"When the living are no more," the lazar intoned, "the dead will be free."

". . . free . . ."

CHAPTER 38

THE CHAMBER OF

THE DAMNED, ABARRACH

◆

... A SENSE OF REGRET AND SADNESS FILLED ALFRED. AND ALTHOUGH painful to him, the sorrow and unhappiness were better—far better—than the lack of feeling he'd experienced prior to joining this brotherhood. Then he had been empty, a husk, a shell containing nothing. The dead—those dreadful creations of those who were beginning to dabble in necromancy—had more life than he. Alfred sighed deeply, lifted his head. A glance around the table revealed similar feelings softening the faces of the men and women gathered together in this sacred chamber.

The sadness, the regret wasn't bitter. Bitterness comes to those who have brought tragedy on themselves, through their own misdeeds, and Alfred foresaw a time for his people when bitter sorrow must encompass them all, unless the madness could be halted.

He sighed again. Just moments before, he had been radiant with joy, peace had spread like a balm over the boiling magma sea of his doubts and fears. But that heady sense of exaltation could not last in this world. He must return to face its problems and perils and thus the sadness, the regret.

A hand reached out, clasped his. The hand's grip was firm, the hand's skin smooth and unwrinkled, a contrast to Alfred's aged, parchment-paper skin, his weakened grasp.

"Hope, brother," said the young man quietly. "We must have hope."

Alfred turned to look at the man seated beside him. The young face was handsome, strong, resolute—fine steel from a forging fire.

No doubts marred its shining surface, its blade was honed to a sharp, cutting edge. The young man looked familiar to Alfred. He could almost put a name to him, but not quite.

"I try," answered Alfred, blinking back the tears that suddenly misted his eyes. "Perhaps it's because I've seen so much during my long life. I've known hope before, only to watch it wither and die, as did the mensch, left in our care. Our people are rushing headlong into evil—madmen rushing to the edge of the cliff, intent on hurling themselves into the abyss below. How can we stop them? Our numbers are too few—"

"We will stand before them," said the young man. "Reveal to them the truth . . ."

And be carried over the edge of the cliff with them, thought Alfred. He kept the words to himself; let the young man live while he could in the bright dream.

"How," he said instead, sadly, "do you suppose it all went wrong?"

The young man had the answer, the young always have the answers. "Throughout history, man has feared the forces in the world he could not control. He was alone in an immense universe that appeared uncaring. Thus in the ancient days, when the lightning flashed and thundered, he cried to the gods to save him.

"In the more recent past, man began to understand the universe and its laws. Through technology and science, he developed the means to control the universe. Unfortunately, like the rabbi who created the golem, man discovered he could not control his own creation. Instead of coming to control the universe, he came near to destroying it.

"After the holocaust, man had nothing to believe in; all his gods had abandoned him. He turned to himself, to the forces within himself. And he found the magic. Over time, the magic brought us more power than we'd ever attained in our many thousand years of striving. We didn't need the gods anymore. We *were* the gods."

"Yes, so we believed," agreed Alfred, pondering. "And being a god was a heavy responsibility, burdensome—or so we told ourselves: ruling over and controlling the lives of those weaker than ourselves, depriving them of their freedom to determine their paths through life, forcing them to walk the one path *we* deemed good. . . ."

"Yet how we enjoyed it!" said the young man.

Alfred sighed. "How we enjoyed it. How we enjoy it still and hunger after it! That's why it is going to be difficult, so very difficult—"

"Brethren." A woman, seated at the head of the table, broke in. "They are coming."

No tongue spoke a word, only the eyes communicated. Heads turned, each person looked searchingly at those beside him, receiving strength and reassurance. Alfred saw resolution and fierce joy light the eyes of the young man.

"Let them come!" he said suddenly. "We are not misers, bent on hoarding the gold we have discovered! Let them come and we will share it with them, gladly!"

The other young people who were gathered around the table caught fire from the young man's torch. Burning with inspiration, they cried out in agreement. Their elders smiled indulgently, sorrowfully. Many lowered their eyelids, not wanting their own bitter knowledge and unfortunate wisdom to snuff out the life of the bright flame.

Besides, thought Alfred, perhaps we are wrong. Perhaps the young are right. After all, why should this be revealed to us if we are not to carry it forth . . .

Sounds could be heard outside the sealed chamber, sounds indicative of many people. And it was not the sound of footsteps marching in response to order and discipline. It was the shuffling, stomping, confused sound of indiscipline, of chaos and riot, of the mob. The Sartan seated around the table again exchanged glances, doubtful, questioning.

No one can enter this chamber unless we open it. We can stay sealed up in here forever, reveling in our knowledge, keeping it only for ourselves.

"Our brother is right," said the eldest Sartan among them. A venerable woman whose body was frail and fragile as that of a bird's, her indomitable spirit and powerful magic had led them to the marvelous discovery. "We have been the miser, hiding our wealth beneath the mattress, living in poverty by day, taking our gold out in the darkness of the night to gaze at it with covetous eyes and then returning it to its hiding place. Like the miser, who does no good with his gold, we will soon shrivel and dry up inside. It is not only our responsibility to share our wealth, it is our joy. Remove the runes of protection."

It is the right thing to do, I know, thought Alfred, lowering his head. But I am not strong. I am afraid.

A hand closed over his, a hand that was warm and strong and tried to share the confidence of the self that guided it.

"They will listen to us," said the young man softly, exultantly. "They must!"

The bright and beautiful white-blue light faded, dimmed, and died. The sounds beyond the sealed doors were suddenly louder and far more ominous, sounds of shouts and jeers, anger and hatred. Alfred's heart quailed. His hand, held fast in the young man's, trembled.

We are right. What we do is right, he kept reminding himself. But, oh, it is hard!

The stone doors ground open. The mob burst into the room, those in back shoving those in front of them to reach their goal. The people in front, however, came to a halt, nonplussed by the calm demeanor and grave, solemn countenances of those gathered around the table. A mob feeds off fear. Faced by reason and calm, the mob finds some of its energy begin to drain away.

The enraged shouts dwindled to mutterings, broken occasionally by the yell of someone in the back, demanding to know what was happening. Those who had crowded into the room, intent on violence, looked foolish and sought among themselves for a leader, someone to rekindle the comforting flame of rage.

A man stepped forward. Alfred's heart, which had been lifted by a sudden flutter of hope, sank in despair, wings broken. The man was clad in black, one of those practicing the newly discovered and previously forbidden art of necromancy. He was powerful, charismatic, and it was rumored that he was seeking to set himself up as king.

He opened his mouth, but before he could speak, the old woman, gazing on him as she might have gazed on an obstreperous child who has just interrupted its elders, asked mildly, "Why have you and your followers disturbed us in our work, Kleitus?"

"Because your work is the work of heretics and we have come to put an end to it," the necromancer answered.

"Our work here was established by the council—"

"—who deeply regret their actions!" Kleitus sneered.

Those standing behind him voiced their approbation. He knew himself to be in control, now. Or perhaps, Alfred realized with a sudden flash of terrifying insight, Kleitus had been in control all along. His was the spark that had ignited the fire. Now he had only to blow on the coals to create a raging inferno.

"The council set you the task of contacting the other worlds, to explain to them our desperate peril and beg them to send the aid promised to us before the Sundering. And what was the result? For months you did nothing. Then, suddenly, you come forward prattling nonsense that only a child would believe—"

"If it is nonsense," cut in the old woman, her voice smooth and calm, a contrast to the rising, strident tones of her accuser, "then why disturb us? Let us continue on—"

"Because it is dangerous nonsense!" Kleitus shouted. He lapsed into silence, seeking to gain control over himself. An intelligent man, he knew that wild hacking and slashing was as self-destructive in verbal parry as it was in actual swordplay. His voice, when he spoke, had regained its discipline. "Because, unfortunately, there are some of our people who have the guileless minds of children. And others, like this one." Kleitus's gaze rested on the young man. The necromancer's eyes darkened in anger. "Young people who have been lured into your trap by the bright bauble you dangled in front of them!"

The young man said nothing, the hand holding Alfred's tightened its firm grip, the handsome face became more serene. What was this young man to Kleitus? He couldn't be his son, Kleitus wasn't old enough to have fathered one this age. Younger brother, perhaps, who had looked to the older brother in worship before finding out the truth? Apprentice to a once-idolized teacher? It occurred to Alfred that he didn't know the young man's name. Names had never been important to those gathered around the table. Something told Alfred, deep inside, that he would never know it. And that, somehow, it would not matter.

Alfred felt stronger. He was able to return the pressure of the young man's grip. The young man looked at him, and smiled.

Unfortunately, this smile was oil thrown on Kleitus's smoldering blaze. "You stand accused of corrupting the minds of our youth! There"—he pointed a stabbing finger at the young man—"is our proof!"

The crowd surged forward, its anger rumbled like the belching of the Fire Sea, breaking out of the cracks in the ground.

The old woman thrust aside the hands of those of her brethren who respectfully sought to assist her and rose to her feet under her own power. "Take us before the council, then!" she returned in a voice that quelled the fiery tide. "We will answer any charges brought against us!"

"The council is a bunch of doddering fools, who, in their misguided efforts to preserve peace, have put up with your rantings far too long. The council has turned over leadership to me!"

The mob cheered. Kleitus, emboldened, moved the accusing finger from the young man to the old woman.

"Your heretical lies will do no more harm to the innocent!"

The mob's cheering grew louder, more sinister. They surged forward again. Blades flashed, blades of sword and knife.

"Those who wield steel in this sacred chamber will find the point turned to their own breasts!" the old woman warned.

It was Kleitus who raised a hand, brought the mob to a halt, brought their clamor to a grumbling quiet. He didn't act to stop the threat out of fear or mercy; he was demonstrating his control, letting it be known that he could release his wolf pack any time he chose.

"We mean you no harm," he said smoothly. "Agree to go forth publicly and tell the people that you have been lying to them. Tell them . . ." Kleitus paused, spinning his web. "Tell them that you did, in fact, contact the other worlds. That you hoped to preserve their riches for yourselves. Actually, now that I think of it, such a scheme is probably not far from the truth."

"Liar!" cried the young man, jumping to his feet. "You know what we have done! I told you! I told you everything! I only wanted to share with you—" Hands outspread, he turned to those gathered around the table. "Forgive me. I have brought this on us."

"It would have come," said the old woman softly. "It would have come. We are too early . . . or too late. Resume your place at the table."

Sorrowing, the young man slumped back into his chair. It was Alfred's turn to offer comfort, what comfort there could be. He rested his hand on the young man's arm.

Brace yourself, he told him silently. Brace yourself for what must come. Too early . . . too late. Please, not too late! Hope is all we have left.

Kleitus was saying something: ". . . appear in public, denounce yourselves as charlatans. Suitable punishment will be determined. And now stand aside from that table!" he commanded, his voice cold and grinding as the stone door. Several of his followers came forward, iron hammers and chisels in their hands.

"What do you intend to do, Kleitus?"

He shifted the pointing finger again, this time to the white wood. "It will be destroyed, lest it lead others to evil!"

"To the truth, don't you mean?" the old woman said quietly. "Isn't that what you fear?"

"Stand aside! Or you will meet the same fate!"

The young man raised his head, stared, stricken, at Kleitus. Only now, he was beginning to understand what terrible purpose the necromancer had in mind. Alfred felt profoundly sorry for the young man. The old woman remained standing. As a body, the men and women gathered around the table rose to stand with her.

"You are wasting your time and possibly your lives, Kleitus. You may silence our voices, but others will come after us. The table will not be destroyed!"

"You plan on defending it?" Again, Kleitus sneered.

"Not with our bodies. With our prayers. Brethren, do no violence. Harm no one. These are our people. Raise no magical defenses. None will be needed. I warn you again, Kleitus!" The old woman's voice rose strong and proud. "This chamber is sacred, blessed. Those who bring violence will—"

A bow snapped, an arrow sped over the table, thudded into the woman's breast.

"—be forgiven," she whispered, and slumped down, red blood staining the white wood.

A flash of movement. Alfred turned. A man raised his bow, arrow aimed straight at Alfred. The man's face was twisted with fear and the anger fear breeds. Alfred couldn't move. He couldn't have cast a magical defense if he'd wanted to. The man drew back the bowstring, prepared to let fly. Alfred stood waiting for death. Not courageously, he realized sadly, but rather foolishly.

A strong hand, coming from behind Alfred, shoved him to one side, and he was falling. . . .

CHAPTER • 39

THE CHAMBER OF

THE DAMNED, ABARRACH

•

"DAMN IT, SARTAN! WHAT THE HELL DO YOU THINK YOU'RE DOING?"

A hand caught hold of him, shook him roughly.

Alfred raised his head, gazed confusedly about. He was lying on the floor, and expected to see the bloodstained hems of white robes, the trampling feet of the mob. Instead, he saw a dog, standing over him, and Haplo. He could hear voices, shouts, and the tramping of feet. The mob. The mob was coming. But, no, the mob had come—

"Must . . . guard the table . . ." Alfred struggled to stand.

"There's no time for any more of your tricks!" Haplo fumed. "Do you hear that? The soldiers are coming!"

"Yes, the mob . . . attacking . . ."

Haplo grabbed him, shook him as if to shake up his scattered wits. "Give your magic up as a bad try and concentrate on how you're going to get us out of here!"

"I don't understand . . . please! Tell me what's going on! I . . . I truly don't understand!"

The Patryn kept his watchful gaze on the door, dropped his hands from Alfred's robes in exasperation. "Why should that surprise me? All right, Sartan. Apparently during the 'performance' you put on for our benefit—"

"I didn't—"

"Shut up and listen! Our duchess managed somehow to douse the sacred lights and activate the runes that open that door. And you're going to do the same to the runes on that door"—Haplo pointed to another door located at a forty-five-degree angle from the first—"when I give the word. Do you think you can walk now?"

"Yes," Alfred said, somewhat hesitantly. He swayed unsteadily on his feet, clung to the table for support. He was confused, felt as if he were in two different places at the same time, and he had a strong reluctance to leave the last place, despite the danger. The overwhelming sense of peace and . . . and of having found something long sought . . . now gone again . . .

"I don't know why I asked." Haplo glared at him. "You couldn't walk all that well in the first place. Keep low, damn it! You're of no use to me with an arrow stuck in your craw! And if you faint, I'll leave you here!"

"I'm not going to faint," Alfred said, with dignity. "And my own magic is now strong enough to protect me from . . . from attack," he added, faltering.

Brethren, do no violence. Harm no one. These are our people. Raise no magical defenses.

I did her bidding. I had no magical defenses. Haplo knew that. He knew it because he was there with me! He was beside me! He saw what I saw. . . . What did we see?

A deep voice could be heard outside the door. It sounded distant, but the clamoring of the dead soldiers hushed.

"Kleitus," said Haplo grimly. "We'll have to run for it!" He propelled the Sartan forward, guiding him over and around the tangle of bones on the floor, dragging him to his feet when he stumbled.

"Jonathan!" Alfred attempted to twist around to see the duke.

"I have care of him," came a voice.

Prince Edmund's cadaver was following behind them, leading a bewildered, seemingly stupefied young duke.

"Your spell worked on him." Haplo sneered. "Blasted fool has no idea where he is!"

"It wasn't *my* spell!" Alfred protested. "I didn't do—"

"Shut up and keep moving. Save your breath to activate the runes on the door."

"What do we do about Jera?—"

The lazar stood near the open door. The cadaver's eyes stared straight ahead, the spirit twined about the body, sometimes looking at them from its own vantage point, sometimes peering out of the dead eyes. The dead lips formed words, and Alfred could hear them, realized that he'd been hearing them ever since he'd awakened from the vision.

"The living hold us in bondage. We are slaves to the living. When the living are no more, we will be free."

". . . we will be free . . ." whispered the echo.

"Blessed Sartan!" Alfred shuddered.

"Yeah," Haplo said briefly. "She's out to recruit more for her side. Maybe Kleitus cast a spell of some sort on her—"

"No," said Prince Edmund. "It is no spell. She has seen, as I have seen. But she does not understand."

You've seen it! And I've seen it, too! Only I haven't seen it! Alfred looked back longingly at the table. Outside the chamber, he could hear shouted commands, the shuffling of feet. He had only to activate the runes to open the door. The sacred light had disappeared, the door would work. But the words stuck in his throat, the magic twisted around in his head. If I stay, if I spend a little more time, I will remember. . . .

"Do it, Sartan!" Haplo hissed through clenched teeth. "If Kleitus takes me alive, we . . . our people, our worlds are finished!"

Two forces, pulling him apart. The people's hope, the people's doom, both in this chamber! If I leave, I will lose one forever. If I don't leave . . .

"Look what we have found, Pons." Kleitus's black-robed bulk filled the entryway, the smaller figure of his minister scuttled in beside him. "You see before you the Chamber of the Damned. It would be interesting to know how these wretches found it and also how they managed to break the warding runes. Unfortunately, we can't allow them to live long enough to tell us."

"The Chamber of the Damned!" Pons's words were faint, he seemed barely able to speak. The minister stared around the room, stared at the corpses littering the floor, stared at the white wood table. "It *is* real! Not legend!"

"Of course it's real. And so is its curse. Guards." Kleitus's motion brought forward dead soldiers, as many as could crowd through the door. "Slay them."

Brethren, do no violence. Harm no one. These are our people. Raise no magical defenses.

Alfred fumbled for the runes to open the door, the old woman's voice rang in his ears, obliterating the construction. He was dimly aware of Haplo standing beside him, the exhausted Patryn braced to fight, if not for his life, then to make certain that his body proved useless.

But the soldiers weren't fighting.

"Did you hear my command?" Kleitus demanded angrily. "Kill them!"

The dead guards stood with weapons raised, arrows notched, swords drawn, but they did not attack. Their phantasms, barely visible, stirred as if shaken by a hot wind. Alfred could almost feel their agitated whisperings breathe against his cheek.

"They will not obey you," said the lazar. "This chamber is sacred. Violence will turn on the one who uses it."

". . . the one who uses it . . ." spoke the echo.

Kleitus turned. His eyes narrowed, black brows came together at the sight of the woman's horrifying visage. Pons gasped, and shrank away from her, attempted to hide himself among the troops of the dead.

"How do you know what the dead think?" the dynast demanded, studying the lazar intently.

The runes! Alfred said to himself frantically, and began to trace them in his mind. Yes, yes. The sigla on the door caught fire, began to glow a soft blue.

"I can communicate with them. I understand their thoughts, their needs, their desires."

"Bah! The dead think nothing! Need nothing! Desire nothing!"

"You are wrong," the lazar said in the hollow voice that brought out a sheen of sweat on Pons's face. "The dead want one thing: their freedom. We will have our freedom when our tyrants are dead!"

". . . tyrants are dead . . ."

"You see this, Pons," said Kleitus with a ghastly smile, affecting to speak in nonchalant tones, although he was working hard to control the tremor in his voice. "She has become a lazar. This is what happens when the dead are raised too soon. Now you understand the wisdom of our ancestors, who teach that the body must be left at rest until the phantasm has completely abandoned it. We will have to experiment with her cadaver. The books suggest that, in this instance, the body should be 'killed' again. Although we're not quite certain . . ." The dynast paused, then shrugged. "But we will have time to study it further. Guards, take her."

The slight, terrible smile played on the chill blue lips. The lazar began to chant. The wispy phantasms hovering about their cadavers suddenly vanished. Dead eyes came to life. Dead arms reached out. Dead hands lifted weapons but not against the lazar. The dead eyes turned on Kleitus and the Lord High Chancellor, dead eyes turned on the living.

Pons clasped hold of the dynast's black robes. "Your Majesty! It is this accursed chamber! Leave it! Seal it up! Leave them all trapped inside! Please, Majesty!"

The lights of Alfred's runes flared brilliantly. The door started to grind open. At last! He'd done something right!

"Haplo—"

A flash of movement. Alfred turned.

Kleitus had grabbed a bow from a guard.

A man raised it, arrow aimed straight at Alfred. The man's face was twisted with fear and the anger fear breeds. Alfred couldn't move. He couldn't have cast a magical defense if he'd wanted to. . . .

"Do no violence!"

The man drew back the bowstring, prepared to let fly. Alfred stood waiting for death. Not courageously, he realized sadly, but rather foolishly.

A strong hand, coming from behind Alfred, shoved him to one side, and he was falling. . . .

Red light filled the room, blinding, stabbing the eyes, searing the brain with fire. Alfred was on the floor, groping about on his hands and knees, aware of legs stumbling into him and over him and the warm body of the dog crowding beside him. A hand grasped hold of the collar of his robes, jerked him to his feet. A harsh voice shouted in his ear, "Now, we're even, Sartan!" The same hand shoved him toward the door that, by the grinding sound, was sliding closed again.

"Run, damn you!"

Alfred staggered forward. He was running through flame, smoke. Everything around him had caught fire, was burning: Prince Edmund, Jonathan, Haplo, the dog, the rock walls, the stone floor, the door. Burning, burning . . .

Haplo jumped through the opening, pulled Alfred after him. The Sartan could feel the heavy stone weight of the door press against him, sliding shut. But, even at this moment, his heart wrenched. He was leaving behind something wonderful, something of immense value, something . . .

". . . only when the living are dead!" cried out the lazar's voice.

Alfred peered through the fiery light. Steel flashed red in the duchess's dead hand. The knife plunged hilt-deep into Kleitus's chest.

His bellow of anger degenerated into a scream of pain.

The lazar wrenched the bloody knife free, stabbed again.

Kleitus howled in agony, clutched at her, trying to wrest the blade from her hand. She stabbed him again, and the dead guards joined her in the attack. The dynast fell, disappeared beneath flailing hands and stabbing swords and slashing spears.

Alfred's arm was nearly yanked out of the socket. He tumbled headfirst into Haplo's grasp. Alfred heard a pleading scream cut off in an agonized gurgle—the Lord High Chancellor.

The door ground shut. But everyone standing in the dark tunnel could hear the lazar, either through the walls or in their hearts.

"Now, dynast, I will show you true power. The world of Abarrach will belong to us, to the dead."

And her echo, ". . . to the dead . . ."

The lazar's voice raised, chanting the runes of resurrection.

CHAPTER • 40

THE CATACOMBS,

ABARRACH

•

ALFRED'S EYES GRADUALLY ADJUSTED TO THE DARKNESS INSIDE THE TUNnel. The darkness wasn't absolute, as he'd first feared when he emerged from the bright light of the chamber, but was red tinged, dimly lit by reflected light shining down a slick-walled corridor. From the light and from the heat, a magma pool was not far distant. Alfred turned to ask Haplo if he should activate the guide-runes, saw the Patryn slump to the floor.

Concerned, he hastened to Haplo's side.

The dog stood over its master, teeth bared, a warning growl in its throat.

Alfred tried to reason with the animal. "I want to see if he's injured. I can help—" He took another step, his hand outstretched.

The dog's growl deepened, the eyes narrowed, ears flattened. *We've shared some good times*, the dog appeared to be advising Alfred. *And I think you're a fine fellow and I'd be sorry to see you come to harm. But that hand comes any closer and you'll find my teeth in it.*

Alfred withdrew the hand hastily, retreated a step.

The dog watched him warily.

Peering over the dog's shoulder at Haplo, Alfred studied the man and decided that, after all, he wasn't injured. He had fallen sound asleep—either the height of bravery or the height of folly, Alfred couldn't decide which.

Perhaps, however, it was really only common sense. He seemed to recall something to the effect that Patryns had the ability to heal themselves in their sleep. Now that he thought of it, Alfred himself was bone weary. He could have kept moving, the sheer horror of what he'd witnessed in that chamber would have propelled him on until he dropped. As it was, it was probably better that he rest, conserve his strength for whatever lay ahead. He glanced nervously and fearfully, at the sealed door.

"Do . . . do you suppose we're safe here?" he asked aloud, not quite certain to whom he was addressing the question.

"Safer here than anywhere else in this doomed city," answered Prince Edmund.

The cadaver seemed more alive than the living. The phantasm had once more departed from the body, but the two appeared to act in conjunction. This time, however, it was as if the corpse were the shadow.

"What's wrong with him?" Alfred's pitying gaze encompassed Jonathan. The duke, lost in a rapt vision, had been led like a child from the chamber by the prince, the cadaver's cold hand grasping the duke's that was not much warmer. "Is he . . . insane?"

"He saw what you saw. Unlike you, he continues to see."

Witness to that tragic, ancient slaughter, Jonathan was apparently oblivious to the current terror surrounding him. At the cadaver's gentle urging, he sat down on the stone floor. His eyes stared back into the past. Occasionally he cried out or made motions with his hands as though endeavoring to help someone he could not see.

Prince Edmund's phantasm was clearly visible in the darkness, a reverse shadow, a shining white-blue outline of a corpse shrouded in darkness. "We will be safe," he repeated. "The dead have more urgent business to do than chase after us."

Alfred shuddered at the grim, solemn tone. "Business? What do you mean?"

The phantasm turned glittering eyes back toward the door. "You heard her. 'We will have our freedom only when the tyrants are dead.' She means the living. All the living."

"They're going to kill—" Alfred was appalled. His mind recoiled from the supposition. He shook his head. "No, it's impossible!" But he recalled the lazar's words, recalled the expression on the face that was sometimes dead, sometimes horribly alive.

"We should warn the people," he mumbled, although the thought of forcing his weak and weary body to continue on was enough to make him weep. He hadn't realized how exhausted he was.

"Too late," said the phantasm. "The slaughter has begun and will continue, now that Kleitus has joined the ranks of the lazar. As Jera told him, he will discover true power—power that can be his eternally. The living are his only threat, and he will take care to see to it that such a threat does not long survive."

"But what can the living do against him?" Alfred demanded, shuddering at the horrible memory. "He's . . . he's dead!"

"Yet you cast a spell that caused the dead to die," said Prince Edmund. "And if you could do it, then so could another. Kleitus cannot take the chance. And even if it were not so, the lazar would kill out of hatred. Kleitus and Jera both understand now what the living have done to the dead."

"But not you," said Alfred, staring at the phantasm, puzzled. "You said you understand. And yet I sense in you only deep regret, not hatred."

"You were there. You saw."

"I saw, but I don't understand! Will you explain it to me?"

The phantasm's eyes were suddenly hooded, invisible lids closing. "My words are for the dead, not the living. Only those who seek shall find."

"But I'm seeking!" Alfred protested. "I truly want to know, to understand!"

"If you did, you would," said the prince.

Jonathan gave a fearful cry, clutched his chest and pitched forward, writhing in pain. Alfred hastened to the man's side.

"What happened to him?" he gasped, looking over his shoulder. "Are we being attacked?"

"It is not a weapon of our time that has hit him," said the phantasm, "but a weapon of the past. He is still in the vision of what has been. You had better wake him, if you can."

Alfred turned Jonathan over, saw the pinched, blue lips, the bulging eyes, felt the clammy skin, the thudding heartbeat. The duke was so completely wrapped in the spell that he might very well die of shock. Yet to waken him might be worse. Alfred glanced at the slumbering Haplo, saw the wan face peaceful, lines of sickness and suffering smoothed out.

Sleep. Or, as the ancients had termed it, "little death."

Alfred held the duke in his arms, soothed the young man, murmured comforting words and interspersed them with a singsong chant. Jonathan's stiffened limbs relaxed, the pain-twisted features eased. He drew a deep, shivering breath. His eyes closed. Alfred held Jonathan a moment longer, to make certain he was truly asleep, then eased him down onto the stone floor.

"Poor man," said Alfred softly. "He will have to live with the knowledge that he brought this terrible evil on his people."

Prince Edmund shook his head. "What he did, he did for love. Evil has come out of it, but—if he is strong—good will prevail."

Such a sentiment might read well in a child's bedtime story, but in this fire-lighted tunnel, with unspeakable horrors raging in the city above . . .

Alfred slumped back against the wall, sank down to the floor.

"What about your people?" he asked, suddenly remembering the Kairn Telest. "Aren't they in danger? Shouldn't you be doing something to warn them, help them?"

The prince's expression altered, grew sad. Or perhaps Alfred only sensed the sadness, and his mind willed the cadaver's expression to change accordingly.

"I grieve for my people and their suffering. But they are the living and no longer my responsibility. I have left them and gone beyond. My words are for the dead."

"But what will you do?" Alfred asked helplessly. "What can you do for them?"

"I don't know yet," said the phantasm. "But I will be told. Your living body needs sleep. I will keep watch while you rest. Fear nothing. No one will find us. For the time being, you are safe."

Alfred had little choice except to trust the prince and give way to weariness. Magic, even Sartan magic, had its physical limitations, as had been proven on this terrible world. He could draw on it only so long before his strength needed replenishing. He made himself as comfortable as possible on the hard rock floor.

The dog, who had been keeping a wary eye on Alfred, was satisfied that it, too, could relax. Curling up beside its master, the animal rested its head on Haplo's chest, but kept its eyes open.

◆

Haplo awoke from a long sleep that had healed his body, but had not brought peace or ease to his mind. He was unaccountably restless, vague anger gnawed at him. Lying on the floor in the darkness, he stroked the dog's head, and attempted to figure out what was the matter with him.

He had something of extreme importance to do or say or tell

someone. Something urgent, something of value and . . . he couldn't remember what it was.

"Arrant nonsense," he told the dog. "Impossible. If it were that important, I'd remember it." But, try as he might, he couldn't, and the lost knowledge burned within him, another kind of poison.

Added to his disquiet were hunger and a raging thirst. He'd had nothing to eat or drink since the supper that had nearly been his last. He sat up, glanced about, searching for water—perhaps a tiny rivulet streaming through a crack in the wall, a drop falling from the ceiling. He could use a drop to create more with his rune-magic, but he couldn't conjure water out of solid rock.

No water. Nothing. Everything was going wrong, had gone wrong ever since he'd arrived on this blasted world. At least he knew where to lay the blame.

Alfred lay hunched up on his side, his mouth wide open, snoring softly.

I should have let the bastard die back there. Especially after he cast that spell on me, made me see those people around that table, made me say—Haplo shook free of the unpleasant memory. But at least now we're even. I saved his life in return for him saving mine. I don't owe him a damn thing.

Haplo stood up suddenly, startling the dog, who jumped to its feet and stared at him with an air of faint reproach.

"You are setting off on your own." Prince Edmund's cadaver stood motionless at the end of the corridor, near the sealed door, near where Jonathan lay in spellbound sleep on the floor.

"I travel faster that way." Haplo stretched his arms, rubbed a stiff neck. He didn't like looking at the phantasm. The sight made him think again of whatever it was he'd forgotten.

"You're going to leave without the guiding runes." The phantasm wasn't attempting to persuade him, apparently. It didn't seem to care, was merely pointing out the obvious. It was probably lonely, liked hearing itself talk.

"I figure we're at the bottom of the catacombs," said Haplo. "I'll find a corridor that leads back up, follow it until I get to the top. I can't end up much worse than I've ended up following him!"

He gestured at Alfred, who had rolled over on his stomach, his backside hunched up in a most undignified position.

"Besides," Haplo grunted, "I've been in worse places. I was born in one. C'mon, dog."

The dog yawned and stretched, front paws extended, rocked forward, back legs extended, then shook itself all over.

"Do you know what is going on up there?" The phantasm's gleaming-eyed gaze lifted.

"I can guess," Haplo muttered, not liking to discuss it.

"You will never reach your ship alive. You will become like Kleitus and Jera—souls trapped in dead bodies, hating the mockery of life that binds them to this realm, fearing the death that would free them."

"That's my risk," retorted Haplo, but the palms of his hands grew clammy. Sweat broke out on his body, chilling him, although the air in the tunnel was warm and oppressive.

All right, I'm afraid! We respect fear, we're not ashamed of it—so the elders taught us in the Labyrinth. The rabbit feels no shame fleeing the fox, the fox feels no shame fleeing the lion. Listen to your fear, confront it, understand it, deal with it.

Haplo walked over, faced the phantasm of the prince. He could see through it, see the wall in back of it, and he knew from the cool, intent stare of the eyes that, in much the same way, it could see through him.

"Tell me the prophecy."

"My words," said the prince, "are for the dead."

Haplo turned abruptly, moving swiftly, and fell over the dog, who had been trotting along behind. He stepped on the animal's fore paw. The dog yelped in pain, sprang backward, cringing, wondering what it had done wrong.

Alfred woke with a start. "What—? Where—?" he gabbled.

Haplo cursed fluently, held out his hand to the dog. "I'm sorry, boy. Come here. I didn't mean it."

The animal accepted the apology, came forward graciously to be scratched behind the ears, indicated that there were no hard feelings.

Seeing only Haplo, Alfred gulped in relief, mopped his brow. "Are you feeling better?" he asked anxiously.

The question annoyed Haplo almost beyond endurance. A Sartan, concerned for my health! He gave a brief, bitter laugh and turned away, continued his search for water.

Alfred sighed, shook his bald head. He was obviously in misery, his stiff body twisted like an old gnarled tree. He watched Haplo a moment, guessed what he must be doing.

"Water, that's a good idea. My throat is raw. I can barely talk—"

"Then don't!" Haplo made a fourth fruitless circuit of the tunnel, the dog trotting along at his heels. "Nothing here. There's bound to be water near the surface. We better get started." He walked over to the duke, nudged him with his foot. "Wake up, Your Grace."

"Oh, dear! I forgot." Alfred flushed. "He's under a spell. He was dying. Well, he wasn't, but he thought he was and the power of suggestion . . ."

"Yeah. I know all about the power of suggestion! You and your spells! Wake him up and let's get out of here. And no more guide-runes, either, Sartan!" Haplo held up a warning finger. "The Labyrinth only knows where they'd lead us next! This time, you follow me. And be quick about it or I'll leave without you."

But he didn't. He waited. He waited for Alfred to wake the duke, waited for the wretched Jonathan to come to his senses.

Haplo waited, fretting with impatience, tormented by his thirst, but he waited.

When he asked himself why he had changed his mind about going off alone, he answered himself that traveling in numbers made sense.

CHAPTER 41

THE CATACOMBS,

ABARRACH

♦

THE TUNNEL CLIMBED STEADILY UPWARD, LED THEM OUT AND AWAY FROM the Chamber of the Damned to the shores of a vast pool of magma. Its fire lit the cavern's eternal night with a red glow. There was no way around it, they could only go over it. A narrow rock bridge spanned the molten lava, a thin black line snaking over an inferno. They moved across it in single file.

The sigla tattooed on Haplo's skin glowed blue, their magic protected him from the heat and the fumes. Alfred chanted beneath his breath; either his magic was aiding his breathing or his walking. Haplo wasn't certain, but he guessed the walking, amazed that the clumsy-footed Sartan made it over the treacherous span.

Jonathan followed after, his head bowed, ignoring the others' talk, absorbed in his own thoughts. He had changed since yesterday, however. His step was no longer aimless and stumbling, but firm and resolute. He took an interest in their surroundings and in his own well-being, walking the span with care and caution.

"He's young, after all," said Alfred softly, watching anxiously as the duke, accompanied by the cadaver, arrived at the end of the bridge. "His instinct for self-preservation has won out over the desire to end his despair by ending his life."

"Look at his face," said Haplo, wishing for the hundredth time that Alfred would keep out of his brain and stop saying what he, Haplo, was thinking.

Jonathan had lifted his head to stare at the prince's phantasm hovering near him. The young face, lit by the magma's fiery glow, was prematurely aged; grief and horror had tightened the once-smiling mouth, shadowed the light of the eyes. But the sullen uncaring desperation and despair were gone, replaced by a thoughtful, introspective study. His gaze was fixed most often on the prince.

The tunnel continued to carry them upward, the floor slanting upward at a steep angle as if it couldn't wait to leave behind the horror of what lay below. But what horror lay ahead? Haplo didn't know and at this point didn't care.

"What did you do to him with that spell of yours?" He kept talking to distract himself, keep his mind off his thirst. A gesture sent the dog back to watch over the duke and the cadaver.

"It was only a simple sleep spell—" Alfred stumbled, fell headlong over his own feet.

Haplo walked grimly on, ignoring sounds of scrabbling and panting behind.

"It's grown rather dark," Alfred said timidly, catching up with Haplo. "We could use the guide-runes for light—"

"Forget it! I've had enough Sartan magic to last a lifetime. And I wasn't referring to your sleep spell. I meant that spell you cast over him in that chamber back there."

"You're mistaken. I didn't cast any spell. I saw what you saw and what he saw. At least, I think I did . . ." Alfred glanced at Haplo sideways, an open invitation to talk about what they'd seen.

The Patryn snorted and continued on in silence.

The tunnel widened, grew lighter. Other tunnels branched off from it, heading in several different directions. The air was cooler, more moist, easier to breathe. Gas lamps hissed, formed pools of yellow light that alternated with pools of darkness. Haplo had no doubt they were nearing the city.

What would they find once they reached the top? Guards posted, waiting for them? All exits blocked?

Water. That was all Haplo cared about at this moment. At least, there would be water. He'd fight an army of the dead for one swallow.

Behind him, the prince and Jonathan spoke together in low tones. The dog trotted along at their feet, a quiet, unobtrusive spy on their conversation.

"Whatever happens, it will all be my fault," Jonathan was saying. His tone was sad, regretful. He was accepting blame, not whining in self-pity. "I've always been heedless, reckless! I forgot all I'd been taught. No, that's not quite true. I *chose* to forget it. I knew what I was doing was wrong when I worked the magic on Jera. . . . But I couldn't bear to let her go!"

He paused a moment, added, "We Sartan became obsessed with life. We lost our respect for death. Even a semblance of life, a horrible mockery of life, was better for us than death. Such an attitude came from thinking of ourselves as gods. What is it, after all, that separates man from the gods? Ultimate rule over life and death. We were able to control life with our magic. We worked until we were able to control death—or thought we had."

He's speaking about himself and his people in the past tense, Haplo realized. He might have been eavesdropping on a conversation between two cadavers, instead of one.

"You are beginning to understand," said the prince.

"I want to understand more," Jonathan spoke humbly.

"You know where to look for the answers."

Back in that damn chamber, no doubt. Or just have good, old Alfred sing his blasted runes at you again. What is it I'm supposed to remember? I saw it all so clearly. . . . Saw *what* clearly? . . . I understood . . . understood *what*? If only I could recall. . . .

The hell with it! I know everything I need to know. My lord is all-powerful, all-wise, all-knowing. My Lord will one day rule this world and all others. My duty is to My Lord and to his cause. These doubts, these confusing vagaries are a trick of the Sartan's.

"Haplo . . ." Alfred's voice.

"What now?"

Turning around, Haplo saw that the Sartan had again come to grief. Alfred lay sprawled on the stone floor, his face twisted with pain. He raised his hand, held it palm out.

"If you think I'm helping you, forget it. You can lie there and rot for all I care."

The dog hurried up to Alfred, began to lick the man's cheek. Haplo turned away in disgust.

"No, it's not that! I think—that is . . . I've found water. I—I'm lying in a puddle."

◆

Alfred had, unfortunately, soaked up quite a bit of the water on his clothes, but once they had a small amount of the precious liquid, they could magically replicate more. Haplo searched until he discovered the source, a steady drip of water draining through a crack in the ceiling.

"We must be near the upper level. Best stay alert. Don't drink too much," he cautioned. "It'll cramp the stomach. Slowly, in small sips." He found it difficult to follow his own advice. The liquid was muddy and tasted faintly of sulfur and iron, even after magic had purified it. But it quenched thirst, kept the body going.

"Some gods *we* are," said Haplo to himself, sucking on a piece of cloth he'd dipped in the puddle. He caught Alfred's swift glance and scowled, turned away in irritation. Why had such a thought crossed his mind? The Sartan had put it there, no doubt . . .

The dog lifted its head, ears pricked. It growled low and softly.

"Someone's coming!" Haplo whispered, twisting, catlike, to his feet.

A figure in black robes emerged from the shadows at the end of the corridor. It moved slowly, haltingly, as if injured or greatly fatigued, and made frequent stops to look back over its shoulder.

"Tomas!" cried Jonathan suddenly, although how he could tell one black-robed necromancer from another was beyond Haplo's ability to fathom. "Traitor!" Before anyone could stop him, the young duke sprinted forward, robes flapping behind him.

Tomas whirled around to face them, his panicked shriek echoed through the corridors. He tried to run. An injured leg or ankle gave out, and he fell to the stone floor. Crawling on hands and knees, he attempted to drag himself away. Jonathan caught up with him easily, placed a hand on the man's shoulder.

Screaming fearfully, Tomas lurched over on his back, raised his hands over his face. "No, please! Don't! Please! No!" he babbled, over and over, writhing in a paroxysm of terror, his body twitching and rolling on the floor.

The duke stared at the man. "Tomas! I'm not going to hurt you! Tomas!" Jonathan attempted to catch hold of the wretched man, soothe him. But the sight of hands approaching him only increased his panic.

"Shut him up!" ordered Haplo furiously. "He'll have every guard in the palace down on us!"

"I can't!" Jonathan looked helpless. "He's . . . he's gone mad!"

Alfred knelt beside Tomas, began weaving his hands over him, chanting the runes.

"Don't put him to sleep, Sartan! We need information."

Alfred shot Haplo a stern, reproachful glance.

"You want to carry him through the corridors with us?" Haplo demanded. "Or just leave him here, unconscious?"

Abashed, Alfred nodded. The motion of his hands formed an invisible blanket over the man. Tomas's cries ceased, he began to breathe easier. But he continued to stare at them with wide eyes, his limbs shivered and shook. Haplo crouched on the floor near the man. The dog, coming up alongside, sniffed and pawed at Tomas's robes with intense interest. Haplo reached out and touched the robe's fabric. It was wet and sodden. He held up his hand to the light, his fingers were stained crimson.

Alfred shoved the man's robe aside, looked at the leg beneath. It was bruised, but otherwise uninjured. The blood wasn't his own. Alfred went extremely pale.

"You know this man?" Haplo asked Jonathan.

"Yes, I know him."

"Talk to him. Find out what's going on up there."

"Tomas. It's me, Jonathan. Don't you recognize me?" The duke had forgotten his anger in pity. He reached out his hand, gingerly.

Tomas's eyes followed the hand, his gaze suddenly shifted to Jonathan's face. "You're alive!" he gasped. He grasped Jonathan's hand convulsively, held it fast. "You're alive!" he whispered over and over, and burst into dry, heaving sobs.

"Tomas, what happened to you? Are you hurt? There's blood—"

"Blood!" The man gasped, shuddered. "It's in the air. I can taste it! Breathe it! It stands in pools, burns like the magma. It drips, drips. I can hear it. All cycle. Drip, drip."

"Tomas . . ." Jonathan urged.

The man paid no attention. He clutched the duke's hands, stared out into the shadows. "She came . . . for her father. His blood seeped down through the floor . . . drip, drip."

Jonathan's face went livid. He let loose Tomas's grasping hands, sat back on his heels.

Haplo decided it was time to intervene. Roughly crowding the duke aside, he caught hold of Tomas and shook him. "What's going on in the city? What's going on up there?"

"Only one alive. Only one—" He began to choke, his eyes bulged from his head, his tongue protruded from his mouth.

"Sartan! Do something, damn it! He's having some sort of fit! I have to know—"

Alfred moved to minister to him. Too late. Tomas's eyes rolled back in the head, his body stiffened, then went limp.

Haplo felt for a pulse, shook his head.

"Is he—? Is he . . . dead?" Jonathan's voice was barely audible. "How?"

"His own fear killed him," Alfred replied. "Whatever he saw up there."

" 'Only one alive,' " Haplo repeated the words slowly.

"I hear the voices of the dead," said the phantasm. Prince Edmund's cadaver stood near Jonathan, the phantasm's gleaming eyes gazed dispassionately at the corpse. "They are many and they are filled with anger. Be at ease, poor spirit," the prince added, speaking to a thing unseen. "Your wait will not be long. Time grows short. The prophecy is about to be fulfilled."

The prophecy! Haplo'd forgotten all about it. He rose to his feet. "Tell me about this—"

The dog growled, lowered its head.

"Damn! Get out of the light!" Haplo ordered, melting back into the darkness. "Keep quiet!"

Shadowed forms appeared, hooded faces hidden.

"The man ran this way," said one. "I am positive. I can sense warmth. There is life down here!"

". . . life down here . . ." came the faint, sibilant whisper.

"Lazar . . ." Alfred said, gave a gentle sigh, and slid down the wall.

"He's fainted!" whispered Jonathan.

Just when the bastard might have proved useful! Haplo swore beneath his breath. He glanced down the hallway, back the way they'd come. We passed other corridors. Alone, I could make a run for it. I'd stand a good chance of escaping, particularly because the lazar would be otherwise occupied with the duke and Alfred. That's how you escape wolfen. Toss them a freshly killed carcass. The beasts stop to feast, you make tracks.

He looked at Alfred, lying on the floor, looked at Jonathan, bending over him. The strong survived. The weak did not.

"Dog! Here, boy!" Haplo called softly. "C'mon!"

The dog stood over Alfred.

The lazar had stopped to stare searchingly down another corridor. Now was the time.

"Dog!" Haplo ordered.

The animal wagged its tail, began to whimper.

"Dog! Now!" Haplo insisted, snapping his fingers.

The dog took a few steps toward Haplo, then circled back to Alfred. The lazar were on the move again. Jonathan glanced up at Haplo.

"Go on. You've done enough. I can't ask you give up your life for us. I'm sure your friend would want it this way."

He's not my friend! Haplo started to shout. He's my enemy! You're my enemy! You Sartan murdered my parents, you imprisoned my people. Countless thousands have suffered and died because of you. Damn right I won't give up my life for you! You're getting no more than you deserve.

"Dog!" Haplo yelled furiously, grabbing for the animal.

The dog glided out of his reach, turned, and dashed straight at the lazar.

CHAPTER ◆ 42

THE CATACOMBS,

ABARRACH

◆

IT WAS DIFFICULT TO COUNT THE NUMBER OF LAZAR. SEEN IN SHADOW, their bodies and spirits merged and separated constantly, confusing to the eye, appalling to the brain. They were clad in black robes, necromancers—those who had the power to turn other newly dead into those who were neither dead nor alive.

Haplo had one consolation. They wouldn't be interested in his skin. They'd just butcher him outright. He supposed he should be grateful.

The lazar came to a halt. Strong hands reached out to capture the pesky dog, throttle it, twist its neck.

Haplo traced a sigil in the air. It caught fire, streaked from his hands, flashing like lightning, and struck the dog. Blue and red flame engulfed the animal. It grew in size and continued to grow with each bounding leap. Its massive head brushed against the ceiling, huge paws shook the ground. Its eyes were fire, its breath hot smoke.

The dog leapt on the lazar, crushed their bodies beneath its gigantic paws. The animal's teeth sank into dead flesh. It didn't rip out the throat, it tore off the head.

"This will stop them, but not for long," Haplo shouted above the dog's hoarse growling. "Get Alfred on his feet and start moving!"

Jonathan tore his horrified gaze from the carnage at the end of the hallway. Grabbing hold of a groggy Alfred, who was just starting to come to his senses, the duke and the prince's cadaver managed to lift the Sartan to his feet.

Haplo took a moment to consider his strategy. Going back was out. Their hope lay in reaching the city, in joining forces with the rest of the living. And to reach the city, they had to get past the lazar.

He started down the corridor at a run, not looking behind him. If the others followed, fine. If they didn't, it was all the same to him.

The dog stood in the center of a grisly battlefield of dismembered corpses and torn, black robes. The stone floor was slippery with blood and gore.

Haplo kept close to the wall, watching his footing. Behind him, he heard the young duke's breath rattle in his throat, his footsteps falter.

"Haplo!" he cried in a fear-choked voice.

One of the mangled corpses started to move. An arm crawled toward a trunk, a leg slithered over to join it. The lazar's phantasm, shimmering in the darkness, was exerting its magical power, bringing its severed body back together.

"Run!" Haplo shouted.

"I—I can't!" Jonathan gasped. The man was frozen stiff with terror.

Alfred swayed on his feet, looked around dazedly. Prince Edmund's cadaver stood stock-still, unmoved by the threat.

Haplo gave a low, piercing whistle. The flames around the dog flickered and died, the animal shrank back to its normal size. It jumped lightly over the reassembling corpses, ran over, and nipped Alfred on a bare, bony ankle.

The pain brought the Sartan to his senses. He saw their danger, understood Jonathan's predicament. Grasping hold of the duke by the shoulders, Alfred dragged him past the lazar. The dog raced around them, darting forward to bark threateningly at the various twitching pieces of the corpses. Prince Edmund's cadaver marched gravely, solemnly behind. One of the dead hands clutched at him. He shook it off, heedless, uncaring.

"I'm all right," Jonathan said through stiff lips. "You can let go of me now."

Alfred glanced at him anxiously.

"Really," the duke assured him. He started to turn his head, drawn by a terrible fascination. "It . . . it was just the shock of seeing . . ."

"Don't look back!" Haplo grabbed Jonathan, forced him around.

"You don't want to see what's going on. Do you know where we are?"

The catacombs had come to an end. They stood at the entrance to brightly lighted, sumptuously decorated corridors.

"The palace," said Jonathan.

"Can you lead us out, back into the city?"

The Patryn feared at first that Jonathan had been through too much, that he was going to fail him. But the duke drew on reserves of strength he undoubtedly never knew he had. Color tinged the pallid cheeks.

"Yes," said Jonathan, voice faint but steady. "I can. Follow me." He walked ahead, Alfred keeping by his side, the prince coming along behind.

Haplo cast a last glance back at the lazar. I should try to get hold of a weapon of some sort, he thought. A sword wouldn't kill them, but it would put them out of action long enough to escape—

A cold nose pressed into his hand.

"Don't hang around here with me," snapped Haplo, pushing the animal away. He started walking. "You like the Sartan so much, you go be *his* dog. I don't want you."

The animal grinned. Tail wagging, it trotted along close to Haplo's side.

◆

The only one alive.

Haplo had seen many dreadful sights in his lifetime. The Labyrinth killed without mercy or compassion. But what he saw that day in the palace of Necropolis would haunt him the remainder of his life.

Jonathan knew his way around the palace, led them swiftly through the twisting corridors and confused maze of rooms. They moved warily, cautiously at first, keeping to the shadows, hiding in doorways, fearing at every corner to meet more of the lazar, searching for new victims.

The living hold us in bondage. We are slaves to the living. When the living are no more, we will be free.

The echo of Jera's voice lingered in the halls, but there was no sign of her or any other being, either living or half-living.

The dead, however, were everywhere.

Corpses littered the corridors, lying where they'd fallen, none of them resurrected, none of them treated with any ceremony at all. A woman cut down by an arrow held a murdered baby clasped in her arms. A man taken unaware, stabbed from behind, stared sightlessly at them, an almost comical expression of astonishment on the dead face.

Haplo yanked the sword from the body, appropriating it for his own use.

"You will not need that weapon," said the prince. "The lazar no longer pursue us. Kleitus has called them. They have more urgent business."

"Thanks for the advice, but I feel better with it, all the same."

Swiftly, working as he walked, keeping his group moving, the Patryn traced in blood several sigla on the blade. Looking up, he met Alfred's horrified stare.

"Crude, I admit," Haplo told him. "But I don't have time for anything fancy."

Alfred opened his mouth to protest.

"This spell might," the Patryn added coolly, "sever the magical life that binds those lazar, holds their bodies together. Unless you think you can remember that spell you cast on them?"

Alfred shut his mouth, averted his eyes. The Sartan looked ill, haggard. His skin was gray, his hands trembled, his shoulders were bent beneath a crushing weight. He was suffering acutely, and Haplo should have been exultant, should have reveled in his enemy's torment.

He couldn't, and the feeling angered him. He drew a sigil in the blood of his ancient enemy and felt only gut-wrenching pain. *Like it or not, Alfred and I spring from the same source. Branches far removed from each other, one at the top of the tree, one at the bottom; one reaching toward the light, the other keeping to the shadow. But we each grow from the same trunk. The blade of the ax is biting into the trunk, intent on bringing down the whole tree. In the Sartan's doom, Haplo could read his own.*

Do I take this knowledge of necromancy back to My Lord? Or do I conceal its discovery? That would mean lying to My Lord. Lying to the man who saved my life.

What am I thinking? Of course, I'll take the knowledge back to My Lord. I'll take Jonathan. What's the matter with me? I'm growing weak! Sentimental! All the fault of that damn Alfred. He goes back with me, too. My Lord will deal with him.

And I'll watch and enjoy every minute . . .

♦

Only one left alive.

They came to the antechamber, near the throne room. The courtiers who'd waited on Kleitus, currying his favor, hoping for even a
glance from the dynastic eye, lay dead on the floor. None had been
armed, none had been able to fight for their lives, although it appeared that a few had sought desperately to escape. They'd been
stabbed from behind.

"They got what they wanted," said Jonathan, gazing at the
bodies dispassionately. "Kleitus paid attention to them at last, every
one."

Haplo glanced at the young man. Alfred was enduring vicari-
ously every agony the dead had experienced. Jonathan, by contrast,
might have been one of the corpses. He and the dead Prince Edmund
bore an uncanny resemblance to each other. Calm, solemn, untouched by the tragedy.

"And where is Kleitus?" Haplo wondered aloud. "And why did
he leave these dead behind? Why not turn them into lazar?"

"You will note that there are no necromancers among this
group," Alfred answered in a low, shaken voice. "Kleitus must maintain control. He will return, in a few days' time, and raise these dead,
as has been done in the past."

"Except," added Jonathan, "that now Kleitus can communicate
with the dead directly. Through the intervention of the lazar, the
dead have gained intelligence."

Armies of dead advancing with purpose and resolve, bent on
slaughtering those they envied and hated—the living.

"That is why we have found no one in the palace," said the
prince. "Kleitus and Jera and their army have moved on. They are
preparing to cross the Fire Sea, preparing to attack and destroy the
last remaining people left alive on this world."

"Your people," said Haplo.

"They are my people no longer," said the prince. "Now my
people are these." The white, glistening phantasm stood among the
corpses, its cold light casting a pale glow over the chill faces. The
whisperings of the unhappy spirits filled the air as if they were
answering him.

Or pleading with him.

"We have to warn Baltazar. And what about your ship?" asked

Alfred suddenly, turning to Haplo. "Will it be safe? Will we be able to leave?"

Haplo started to snap that, of course, his ship was safe, protected. But the words died on his lips. How could he be sure? He didn't know what powers these lazar possessed. If they destroyed his ship, he'd be trapped here until he could find a new one. Trapped, battling against armies of dead, battling against those who could never be stopped, never be defeated. Haplo's breathing shortened. The Sartan's panic was catching.

"What's he doing now? Where is Kleitus at this moment? Do you know?"

"Yes," the prince answered. "I hear the voices of the dead. He is mobilizing his forces, gathering his army together, preparing to send them forth. The ships swing at anchor, waiting. It will take some time for him to board all his troops." Haplo could have sworn the phantasm smiled. "The dead cannot be herded about like sheep now. They are intelligent, and intelligence brings independence of thought and action, and that leads, inevitably, to confusion."

"So we have time," Haplo said. "But we have to cross the Fire Sea."

"I know of a way," said the prince, "if you have the courage to use it."

It wasn't a question of courage anymore.

Alfred spoke Haplo's thought. "We have no choice."

CHAPTER 43

NECROPOLIS,

ABARRACH

♦

NECROPOLIS HAD FULFILLED THE DREAD PORTENT OF ITS NAME. MANGLED bodies lay huddled in doorways, struck down before they could reach refuge. Nor would they have escaped, even then. Doors had been split asunder, beaten down by the dead, in their efforts to wrest life from the living. They had been successful. The water that ran in the gutters was stained dark with blood.

The phantasm of Prince Edmund led them through the winding tunnels of the City of the Dead. They avoided the main gate, which might be guarded, escaped the city through one of the rat holes. Once outside the walls, they could hear, in the distance, a dull rumbling sound that echoed off the high cavern ceiling and shook the ground on which they stood. The armies of dead, preparing for war.

Numerous pauka, still harnessed to their carts, roamed the outskirts of Necropolis. The animals were bewildered, frightened at the smell of blood. Owners and riders were dead, bodies left to lie where they'd fallen or resurrected and borne away to assist in the slaughter. Haplo and Jonathan commandeered a carriage, dragged the bodies of a man, a woman, and two children out of it. Alfred climbed inside, scarcely knowing what he was doing, acting completely under guidance, usually Jonathan's, but sometimes—roughly—Haplo's.

The carriage rattled off. The pauka appeared relieved to have someone in control of its life once more. Jonathan drove, Haplo sat beside him, keeping watch. The cadaver of Prince Edmund sat upright in the passenger seat next to Alfred. The prince's phantasm acted as guide. They headed eastward for several miles, traveling in the direction of Rift Ridge. Reaching an intersection, the carriage turned southward toward the Fire Sea. The dog ran alongside, occasionally barking at the pauka, much to that animal's discomfiture.

Jonathan drove as fast as he dared. The carriage rocked and bounced over the rock-strewn highway, fields of kairn grass whipped past them in a dizzying blur of greenish brown. Alfred clung to the side of the lurching carriage, expecting every moment to be pitched out of it or overturned in it. He rode in fear of his life, a thing he couldn't understand, for his life had very little meaning left to it.

What base animal instinct in us drives us? Alfred wondered to himself bitterly. Forces us to continue living, when it would be far easier to sit down and die.

The carriage rolled around a corner on two wheels. The Sartan was thrown violently against the chill form of the cadaver. The carriage righted itself. Alfred righted himself, Prince Edmund's corpse assisting him with its accustomed dignity.

Why do I cling to life? What is there left for me, after all? Even if I escape this world, I can never escape the knowledge of what I've seen, the knowledge of what my people have become. Why should I race to warn Baltazar? If he survives, he'll continue to look for Death's Gate. He'll figure out how to enter and carry the contagion of necromancy into the realms beyond. Haplo himself has threatened to bring the art to the knowledge of his lord.

Yet, Alfred pondered, the Patryn spoke of that when we first came. He hasn't mentioned it since. I wonder how he feels about it now. Sometimes I imagine I've seen the same horror that I've felt in my soul reflected in his eyes. And in the Chamber of the Damned, he was the young man seated next to me! He saw what I saw—

"He fights against it, as do you," said the prince, breaking in on Alfred's thoughts.

Startled, Alfred tried to speak, to protest, but the words were jounced out of his mouth. He nearly bit off his tongue. Prince Edmund understood, however.

"Only one out of the three of you opened his heart to the truth. Jonathan doesn't understand completely, yet, but he is near, much closer than you."

"I want . . . to know . . . the truth!" Alfred managed to get out, shooting the words from between clenched teeth to keep from biting his tongue again.

"Do you?" asked the phantasm, and it seemed to Alfred that he saw it coolly smile. "Haven't you spent your life denying it?"

His fainting spells: used consciously at first to keep from revealing his magical powers, had now become uncontrollable. His clumsiness: a body at odds with its spirit. His inability—or was it refusal—to call to mind a spell that would give him too much power, unwanted power, power that others might try to usurp. Constantly putting himself in the role of observer, refusing to act for good or for evil.

"But what else could I have done?" Alfred asked defensively. "If the mensch once found out I had the power of a god, they would force me to use that power to intervene in their lives."

"Force you? Or tempt you?"

"You're right," Alfred admitted. "I know I'm weak. The temptation would have been too strong, was too strong. I gave in to it— saving the child Bane's life when his death would have averted the tragedies that followed."

"Why did you save the child? Why"—the prince's ghostly gaze shifted to Haplo—"did you save the man? Your enemy? An enemy who has vowed to kill you? Search your heart for the answer, the true answer."

Alfred sighed. "You'll be disappointed. I wish I could say I acted because of some noble ideal—chivalrous honor, self-sacrificing courage. But I didn't. In Bane's case, it was pity. Pity for an unloved child who would die without ever knowing a moment's happiness. And Haplo? I walked in his skin, for a few brief moments. I understand him." Alfred's gaze went to the dog. "I think I understand him better than he understands himself."

"Pity, mercy, compassion."

"That's all, I'm afraid," said Alfred.

"That is everything," said the phantasm.

◆

The road on which they traveled was empty, deserted. It had been trampled by many feet, part of the army of the dead had passed this way, flowing out of the city onto the many highways leading to the Fire Sea. Helmets, shields, bits and pieces of armor, bones and, here and there, a fallen, shattered skeleton lay scattered in the army's wake. Farm carts or carriages were discovered abandoned, their passengers either murdered or they had fled the rumor of the dead army's coming.

Alfred had first believed Tomas to have been correct. They had not seen one living being since they emerged from the catacombs. He feared that everyone in or around Necropolis must have fallen victim to the dead's fury. But on their journey, he thought more than once that he caught a glimpse of furtive movement in the tall kairn grass, thought he saw a head lift, eyes—living eyes—peer fearfully out at them. But the carriage whirled past too swiftly for him to confirm what he'd seen or mention it to the others.

But it was a tiny crack of hope, splitting the darkness like light shining from beneath a closed door. His spirits raised, whether because of the newfound hope or the phantasm's comforting words, he couldn't tell. His brain was too jounced and jostled for coherent thought. He clung to the side of the carriage, hanging on to it in grim resolve. Life did have meaning and purpose. He wasn't certain what that was, yet. But he had decided at least to keep searching.

The carriage neared the Fire Sea, neared danger. Topping a rise, Alfred gazed down on the docks far below, gazed down on an army of dead, swirling and milling about the ships in chaos. He was reminded of a colony of coral grubs invaded by a hungry dragon hatchling. At first each grub sought only to escape the crunching jaws. After the initial confusion and panic, however, the threat united the insects and they turned, as one, to repel the invader. The mother dragon had rescued her young just in time.

Confusion and panic might reign on the docks at this moment, but a single goal would soon unite them.

The carriage dashed down the hill, veering in an easterly direction that would take them clear of the docks. Jonathan drove the maddened pauka at a breakneck pace. The army and ships vanished from Alfred's sight.

The wild ride finally came to a halt. The carriage brought up on a rock shore of the Fire Sea. The pauka collapsed in the traces, sinking to the ground, breathing heavily.

Before them, the vast ocean of flaming magma gleamed orange-red, its fiery light reflecting off the glistening black stalactites spiraling downward from the cavern's roof. Huge stalagmites, dark against the red background of the sea, formed a jagged-toothed shoreline. The magma washed and pushed against them sluggishly. A meandering stream of water, that had escaped from the city above, plunged, hissing, into the sea, sending rolling clouds of steam into the hot, sulfurous air.

The living and the dead stood on the beach and stared out across the sea. Barely visible, in the distance, Alfred thought he could make out the opposite shore.

"I thought you said we'd find a boat here," said Haplo, eyeing the prince grimly, suspiciously.

"I said you would find the way to cross here," corrected Prince Edmund. "I said nothing about a boat." The white, gleaming arm of the phantasm raised, an ethereal finger pointed.

At first Alfred thought Edmund meant them to use their magic to cross the sea of flame.

"I can't," the Sartan said meekly. "I'm too weak. It's costing me nearly all my energy, just to stay alive."

He had never before felt the weight of his own mortality, never before realized that his powers had physical limits. He was beginning to understand the Sartan of Abarrach, beginning to understand them as he had begun to understand Haplo. He was walking in their skins.

The phantasm said nothing; again Alfred thought he saw a smile flicker on the translucent lips. It continued to point.

"A bridge," said Haplo. "There's a bridge."

"Blessed . . ." Alfred had been about to say, Blessed Sartan. The words died on his lips. That was one oath he'd never use again, at least not without serious thought.

Now that Haplo had pointed it out, Alfred could see the bridge (he supposed one could dignify it by that appellation). In reality it was nothing more than a long row of large, oddly shaped boulders that happened to be arranged in a straight line extending from one shoreline to the other. It looked almost as if a gigantic column of rock had crashed into the sea, its skeletal remains forming the bridge.

"The fallen colossus," said Jonathan, in understanding. "Except it was located in the middle of the ocean."

"It used to be in the middle of the ocean," said the prince. "The sea is shrinking, and now one may reach it and use it to cross."

"If we have the courage," Haplo murmured. He fondled the dog, scratching it on the head. "Not that it makes any difference." His eyes flicked to Alfred. "As you said, Sartan, we have no choice."

Alfred tried to reply, but his throat burned, the moisture in his mouth had gone dry. He could only stare at the broken bridge, at the huge gaps yawning between segments of the shattered column, at the magma sea, flowing beneath.

One slip, one false step . . .

And what has my life been, Alfred wondered dismally, but an endless series of slips and false steps?

◆

They scrambled down among the boulders on the shoreline. The way was treacherous—hands and feet lost their grip on wet rock, mists floated before their eyes, obscuring their vision. Alfred chanted runes until he lost his voice and came near losing his breath. He was forced to concentrate on each footstep, each handhold. By the time they reached the base of the broken colossus, he was exhausted, and the difficult part lay ahead of them.

They halted at the base to rest, survey the way before them. Jonathan's pallid face glistened with sweat, his hair straggled down around his temples. His eyes were sunken, dark shadows surrounded them. He wiped his hand across his mouth, licked his tongue across parched lips—they'd been attacked before they could carry off water—and gazed across at the opposite shore as if he fixed one end of his will on that dark horizon, planned to use it as a rope to pull himself along.

Haplo walked out on the first segment of broken colossus, examined the stone beneath his feet. The first segment, the base, was the longest and would be the easiest to cross. He squatted down on his haunches, stared curiously at the rock, ran his hand over it. Alfred sat gasping for breath on the shore, envying the Patryn his strength, his youth.

Haplo motioned. "Sartan," he said peremptorily.

"My name . . . is Alfred."

Haplo glanced up, scowled, frowned. "I don't have time for games. Make yourself useful, if that's possible. Come take a look at this."

They all ventured out onto the colossus. It was wide—three large farm carts might have been driven abreast across it and left room on either side for a carriage or two. Alfred crept across it as gingerly as if it had been the branch of a small hargast tree spanning a rushing stream. Nearing Haplo, the Sartan's foot slipped, sending him sprawling on his hands and knees. He closed his eyes, fingers dug into the rock.

"You're safe," said Haplo in disgust. "Hell, you'd have to work at throwing yourself off this thing! Open your eyes, damn it. Look, look there."

Alfred opened his eyes, gazed fearfully around. He was a long way from the edge, but he was acutely conscious of the magma sea flowing beneath him, and that made the edge seem much closer. He wrenched his gaze from the orange-red viscous flow and stared down beneath his hands.

Sigla . . . inscribed on the rock. Alfred forgot his danger. His hands traced lovingly the ancient runes carved on the stone.

"Can these help us in any way? Is their magic good for anything anymore?" Haplo asked in a tone that implied the magic had never been good for much in the first place.

Alfred shook his head. "No," he said, voice husky. "The magic of the colossus cannot help us. Their magic was meant to give life, to carry life from this realm below to those realms above."

The prince's cadaver raised its head, dead eyes looked above to a land it could see perhaps more clearly than the land on which it now walked. The expression on the face of the phantasm grew grim and sad.

"The magic is broken now." Alfred drew a deep breath, looked back at the shoreline, at the broken, jagged edges of the column's base. "The colossus didn't fall by accident. It couldn't have, its magic would have prevented such an occurrence. The colossus was knocked down, deliberately. Perhaps by those who feared it was sucking life out of Necropolis and carrying it to realms above. What-ever the reason, its magic is gone, can never be renewed."

Like this world, the world of the dead.

"Look!" cried Jonathan. His face, his eyes reflected the heat of the fire.

They could barely see, in the distance, the first ships setting out from the shoreline.

The dead had begun the crossing.

CHAPTER ◆ 44

FIRE SEA,

ABARRACH

◆

THEY HURRIED FORWARD, TRAVELING AS FAST AS THEY DARED ACROSS the rune-inscribed column. They had an advantage over the ships, in that the shrinking Fire Sea flowed at its narrowest point there. They were much closer to the shore than Kleitus and his army. The sight of the ships gave them impetus, renewed strength. The sigla may have lost their magic, but the runes carved into the stone provided traction, sure footing on a slippery surface.

And then they came to the end of the broken segment.

A huge, V-shaped gap separated one part of the colossus from another. The magma sea churned in between, roiling among the sharp, jagged edges.

"We can't cross that!" said Alfred, staring at the gap in dismay.

"Not up here we can't." Haplo measured it with his eye. "But we might down below. Even *you* could make that jump, Sartan."

"But I'll slip! Fall in! I—I . . . I'll try." Alfred gulped, lowering his eyes before Haplo's narrow-eyed, angry glare.

"No choice. No choice. No choice," Alfred chanted, instead of the runes. What magical resources he had left, he had to conserve. And, somehow, the litany seemed to help.

"You're a fool," Haplo said, overhearing him. The Patryn stood at the bottom of the vee, legs akimbo, balanced easily, catlike, on uneven strata of rock. He gripped Alfred's thin arm, steadied the shaking man. "Jump for it."

Alfred stared fearfully across what looked to him to be an

immense stretch of flowing lava. "No!" He shrank back. "I can't! I'll never make it! I—"

"Jump!" Haplo roared.

Alfred bent his knees, and suddenly he was flying through the air, propelled by a strong boost from behind. Arms flailing, as if he might flap his way across, he landed heavily on the edge of a lip of rock about twenty feet above the lava sea. He was slipping. His hands scrabbled for purchase. Pebbles slid beneath his fingers. He was falling, sliding into the magma beneath him.

"Hold on!" Jonathan shouted frantically.

Alfred made a wild grab at a jutting piece of rock. His fingers curled around it, and he managed to stop his fall. His hands were wet with sweat, he started to lose his grip, but his foot found a toehold, and he stopped himself. Arms and legs aching with the strain, he hauled himself up over the lip and hunched there, shivering in reaction, not daring to let himself believe he was safe.

He didn't have time to relax. Before he knew what was happening, Jonathan leapt across the gap, assisted from behind by Haplo's tireless arms. The young duke landed easily and gracefully. Alfred caught hold of him, balanced him.

"There isn't room for both of us. Go on up." Alfred told him. "I'll wait here."

Jonathan started to protest.

Alfred pointed. The top edge of the column protruded outward, forming another shelf, this one overhead. It would take strong arms to hoist oneself over that ledge.

Jonathan saw, understood, and began climbing up to the top. Alfred watched him anxiously, for a moment, and was intensely startled to find that the cadaver of Prince Edmund was standing on the shelf beside him. How the corpse managed to cross was beyond Alfred's ability to explain. He could suppose only that the phantasm had assisted its body.

The gleaming white shape was the cadaver's glistening shadow, barely distinguishable from the mists curling around them. The phantasm seemed so independent. Why does it bother to drag the shell along with it?

"Stand clear, Sartan!" Haplo shouted. "Go on up with the others!"

"I'll wait! Help you!"

"I don't want your"—the next words were unclear, lost in the churning sound of the magma—"help!"

Alfred pretended he didn't hear any of it, waited stolidly, back braced against the rock.

Haplo fumed on the shore, but there wasn't time to argue. He checked the sword that he had thrust into his belt, made sure it was secure. Leg muscles bunched. He launched himself outward, hurtled through the air above the magma, and landed like a fly against a wall on the smooth-sided rock beneath Alfred. He began to slip. The dog, across the way, barked loudly.

Alfred reached down, caught hold of the Patryn's rune-covered wrists, and pulled. Pain shot up his back, muscles gave way, feet scraped over the surface of the ledge on which he stood. He was losing his hold. He must let go or risk sliding over the edge.

Alfred refused to give up. He searched inside himself, found physical resources he never knew he possessed. He held on tightly and, with a last, desperate burst of energy, lunged backward. His feet slid out from beneath him, but not before he had pulled Haplo up onto the ledge.

The Patryn grabbed hold of rocks and Alfred and hung on until he caught his breath, then dragged himself the rest of the way over. Without warning, the dog sailed across in a graceful bound. Landing beside them, nearly crowding both off the ledge, the animal gazed at each of them with bright eyes, obviously enjoying itself immensely.

"More ships are crossing!" Jonathan reported from up above. "We've got to hurry!"

Alfred's body ached, muscles burned. A pain in his side was like someone jabbing him with a knife. He was cut and bruised and wondered if he'd have the strength to walk, let alone climb over that shelf. And how many segments of this colossus remained left to cross? How many gaps, perhaps wider than this? He shut his eyes, then, drawing a breath that brought his burning lungs no relief, he wearily prepared to go on.

"I suppose I should thank you—" Haplo began in his usual sneering tone.

"Forget it! I don't want your thanks!" Alfred yelled at him. It felt good to yell. Felt good to be angry and let his anger loose. "And don't feel like you have to pay me back for saving your damn life, because you don't! I did what I had to do. That's all!"

Haplo stared at Alfred in blank astonishment. Then the Patryn's lips started to twitch. He tried to control himself, but he, too, was tired. He began to laugh. He laughed until he was forced to lean against the rock wall to support himself, laughed until tears crept from beneath his eyelids. Dabbing at blood seeping from a cut forehead, Haplo grinned, shook his head.

"That's the first time I ever heard you swear, Sar—" He paused. "Alfred," he amended.

♦

They had made it safely across one gap but it was only the first of many. The steam-driven dragonships of the dead churned through the magma sea, black against fiery red. Alfred trudged over the broken column, tried not to look at the ships, tried not to look at or think about jumping over the next crevice. One foot after the other, over and over and over and—

"We'll never reach the shore in—"

"Hush! Freeze! Stop!" Haplo hissed, cutting Jonathan off in midsentence.

Alfred jerked around, the alarm in the Patryn's tense call tore through the lethargy of aching body and despairing mind. The runes on Haplo's skin glowed, the normally blue color tinged purple in the red glare of the magma. The dog stood near its master, growling, ruff bristling, legs stiff. Frantically Alfred glanced behind, expecting to see hordes of dead following them across the colossus.

Nothing. Nothing was chasing them. Nothing blocked their path ahead. But something was wrong. The sea was moving, gathering itself together, rising up around them. A tidal wave? Of magma? He stared harder at the sea, attempting to convince himself it was an optical illusion.

Eyes! Eyes watching him. Eyes in the sea. Eyes *of* the sea. A fiery red head poked up from the depths of the magma, slid toward them. The unblinking eyes kept them under constant surveillance. The eyes were enormous. Alfred could have walked into the black slit of the pupils without ducking his head.

"A fire dragon," Jonathan gasped.

"So this is how it ends," said Haplo softly.

Alfred was too tired to care. His first thought, in fact, was one of relief. I won't have to jump over another damn crack.

Smooth and sharp as a spear point, the dragon's head thrust

upward. Its neck was long, narrow, and graceful, topped by a spiky mane that resembled stalagmites. Scales glowed bright red when the body lifted from the sea. Contact with air cooled them instantly, turning them black, with a lingering red glow, like coals in a banked fire. Only the eyes remained vivid, flame red.

"I don't have the strength to fight it," said Haplo.

Alfred shook his head. He lacked the strength to talk.

"We may not need to," Jonathan said. "They attack only when they feel threatened."

"But they have little love for us," added the prince, "as I have good reason to know."

"Whether it attacks us or not, the delay could prove fatal," Haplo pointed out.

"I have an idea." Jonathan walked slowly and deliberately across the colossus toward the approaching dragon. "Don't make any threatening moves or gestures."

The beast glanced at him, but the red eyes were far more intent on the phantasm of the prince.

"What are you?"

The dragon spoke to the prince, ignored Jonathan, ignored everyone else standing on the broken column. Haplo put his hand on the dog's head, keeping it quiet. The animal trembled, but obeyed its master.

"I have never seen anything like you."

The dragon's words were perfectly intelligible, clearly understood, but they weren't spoken aloud. The sound seemed to run through the body, like blood.

"I am what was always meant to be," said the phantasm.

"Indeed." The slit eyes flicked over the group. "And a Patryn, too. Stranded on a rock. What next? The fulfillment of the prophecy?"

"We are in desperate need, Lady," said Jonathan, with a low bow. "Many of the people in the city of Necropolis now lie dead—"

"Many of *my* people now lie dead!" The dragon made a hissing sound, its black tongue flickered. "What is this to me?"

"Do you see those ships, crossing the Fire Sea?" Jonathan pointed. The dragon did not turn her head, she was obviously aware of what was passing in her ocean. "They carry lazar and armies of the dead—"

"Lazar!" The slit eyes of the dragon narrowed. "Bad enough the dead walk. Who brought lazar into Abarrach?"

"I did, Lady," said Jonathan. His hands clasped together, holding tight, keeping his pain within.

"You will get no help from me!" The dragon's eyes flared in anger. "Let the evil you have brought into this world take you down with it!"

"He is innocent of that charge, Lady. He acted out of love," stated the phantasm. "His wife died, sacrificed her life for his. He could not bear to let her go."

"Folly, then. But criminal folly. I will have nothing further—"

"I want to make amends, Lady," Jonathan said. "I have been given the wisdom to do so. Now, I am trying to find the courage. . . ." Words failed him. He swallowed, drew a deep breath. Hands clasped tighter. "My companions and I must reach the opposite shore, ahead of the lazar and the dead they command."

"You want me to carry you," said the dragon.

"No . . ." Alfred shook in his shoes.

"Shut up!" Haplo laid a silencing hand on the Sartan's arm.

"If you would so honor us, Lady." Jonathan bowed again.

"How can I be certain you will do what you say? Perhaps you will only make matters worse."

"He is the one of whom the prophecy speaks," said the prince.

Haplo's hand, on Alfred's arm, twitched. Alfred saw the man's lips twist, the brows knot in frustration. The Patryn kept silent, however. His major concern now was to reach his ship in safety.

"And you are with him in this?" the dragon queried.

"I am." Prince Edmund's cadaver stood straight and tall, the phantasm was its shining shadow.

"The Patryn, as well?"

"Yes, Lady." Haplo's words were brief, bitten off at the end. What else could he say, with those fire red eyes intent on him?

"I will take you. Be quick."

The dragon glided nearer the broken colossus, spike-maned neck and head towering over the puny figures who stood beneath. A sinuous, twisting body rose out of the sea, flat backed, spikes extending the full length of the spine. The tip end of a spiny tail could be seen slashing through the lava far, far behind it.

Jonathan descended swiftly, grabbing hold of one of the spikes and using it to steady his landing. The cadaver followed, its gleaming phantasm guided the corpse's steps. Alfred came after, touching the mane gingerly, expecting it to be hot. The scales were quite cool, however, hard and shining as black glass.

The Sartan had ridden dragonback on Arianus and, although this dragon was considerably different from those in the air world, he wasn't nearly as frightened as he'd expected to be. Only Haplo and the dog remained standing on the column, the Patryn eyeing the dragon warily, his gaze shifting to the column ahead of him, as if measuring what his best decision might be. The dog whimpered and cringed and ducked behind its master, doing its best to avoid the dragon's eye.

Alfred knew enough about the Labyrinth to understand the Patryn's fear, his dilemma. Dragons in the Labyrinth are intelligent, malevolent, deadly; never to be trusted, always to be avoided. But the steam-powered ships of the dead were nearing the middle of the ocean. Haplo made his decision, jumped onto the dragon's back.

"Here, dog!" he called.

The animal ran back and forth on the column, made a tentative try at a jump, gave it up at the last moment, ran up and down the column again, whining.

"Hurry!" the dragon warned.

"Dog!" Haplo commanded, snapping his fingers.

The animal gathered itself together and made a desperate jump right into Haplo's arms, nearly bowling him over.

The dragon whipped around with a speed that caught Alfred unaware. He had let go of the mane and now almost slid off the back. Grabbing hold of a spike that stood taller than he did, he clung to it with both hands.

The fire dragon swam through the magma as easily as the dragons of Arianus flew through the air, using slithering motions and the push of its strong tail to propel the wingless, gigantic body forward. The hot wind of their passing blew Alfred's wispy hair back from his head, fluttered his robes behind him. The dog howled in terror the entire way.

The dragon moved at an angle to cut off the ships, then raced ahead of them. At home in her element, her speed was formidable. The iron ships could not match it. But they were now more than halfway across. The dragon was forced to cut close, swinging across the bow of the lead ship. The dead saw them. A hail of arrows rained down around them, but the dragon was sailing too rapidly for the archers to find a good target.

"My people," said the cadaver in its hollow voice.

The army of the dead of Kairn Telest was drawn up on the docks, prepared to meet the army of the dead of Necropolis and drive them back before they could establish a foothold.

Baltazar's strategy was sound, but he didn't know of the lazar, had no word of what had happened in Necropolis. He was prepared for war—a war between cities. He had no idea that now it was a war between the dead and the living. He had no suspicion that he and his people were among the last living beings on Abarrach and that, soon, they might be fighting for their lives against their own dead.

"We're going to make it," said Haplo, "but not by much." His gaze flicked to Alfred. "If you're coming back with me through Death's Gate, run straight for the ship. The duke and I will join you."

"Duke?" Alfred was puzzled. "But he won't come. Not voluntarily." And then he understood. "You don't mean to give him a choice, do you?"

"I'm taking the necromancer back to the Nexus. If you're coming along, head for the ship. You should thank me, Alfred," Haplo added with a grim smile. "I'm saving his life. How long do you think he could survive here?"

They were within sight of those waiting on shore. The cadaver of Prince Edmund, prompted by its phantasm, raised its arms. A cheer greeted him; swarms of the dead soldiers began running along the wharf to assist them, protect them from attack as they disembarked.

The dragon surged in among the docks, her momentum sent waves of lava crashing onto the shoreline. The ships of the dead arrived so close behind that Alfred could see the dreadful writhing image of the lazar Kleitus standing on the prow of the lead vessel. At his side—Jera.

CHAPTER 45

SAFE HARBOR,

ABARRACH

♦

HAPLO'S SHIP SWUNG AT ANCHOR, UNHARMED, SAFE, INTACT. WITHIN moments, they could be aboard, the Patryn's runes keeping them safe from assault. Alfred was in a quandary. What Haplo said was undoubtedly true. The duke would not survive long on Abarrach. None of those still living on Abarrach could survive the fury of the dead, driven to vengeance and destruction by the lazar.

At least I would be able to save one person, one Sartan. Mercy, compassion, pity. . . . Surely I could devise some means of keeping a necromancer out of the hands of the so-called Lord of the Nexus! But what if I failed? What terrible tragedies would follow if a necromancer entered the other worlds? Wouldn't it be better for him to die here?

The troops of Kairn Telest raced along the docks, intent on saving their prince. Archers covered their advance, flights of arrows vaulted through the air to land, clattering, against the sides of the iron dragonships. The dead plucked the arrows from their chill flesh and tossed them into the magma, where they vanished with snake-like hisses. Kleitus tore out an arrow that had lodged in his breast and brandished it aloft.

"We are not your enemy!" he shouted, his voice ringing over the magma sea, silencing the army of the dead of Kairn Telest on the docks below. "They, the living"—he pointed to the black-robed figure of Baltazar—"are the true enemy! They have enslaved you, robbed you of your dignity!"

"Only when the living are dead, will the dead be free!" Jera cried.

". . . dead be free . . ." echoed her tormented spirit.

The army of Kairn Telest hesitated, wavered. The air was filled with the moaning wails of its phantasms.

"Now's our chance!" said Haplo. "Jump for it!"

He leapt from the dragon's back to the stone dock. Alfred followed, landed in a confused jumble of hands and knees that took him some moments to sort out. When he was erect and more or less walking, he saw Haplo grip the duke firmly by the arm.

"Come along, Your Grace. You're going with me."

"Where? What do you mean?" Jonathan pulled back.

"Through Death's Gate, Your Grace. Back to my world." Haplo gestured toward his ship.

The duke glanced at it, saw safety. He hesitated, wavering, much as the dead around him. The dragon swam a short distance from shore, stopped, its slit eyes watching, waiting.

Jonathan shook his head. "No," he said softly.

Haplo's grip tightened. "Damn it, I'm saving your life! If you stay here, you'll die!"

"Don't you understand?" Jonathan said, looking at the Patryn with a strange, detached calm. "That is what I am meant to do."

"Don't be a fool!" Haplo lost control. "I know you think you communicated with some sort of higher power, but it was a trick! *His* trick!" He jabbed a finger at Alfred. "What you and I saw was a lie! *We* are the highest power in the universe! My Lord is the highest power. Come back with me and you will understand—"

A higher power! The revelation was devastating. Alfred staggered where he stood, his legs sinking beneath him. Now he understood, understood what had happened to him in the chamber! He remembered the feeling of peace and contentment that had filled him, understood the reason why he felt such sorrow when he'd awakened from that vision to discover the feeling was gone. But it had taken the Patryn to show him!

Deep within, I knew the truth, but I couldn't admit it to myself, Alfred realized. Why? Why did I refuse to listen to my heart?

Because, if there is a higher power, then we Sartan have made a dreadful, an appalling, an unforgivable mistake!

The idea was too awful to comprehend. His brain was barely capable of handling the flood of emotions that rolled over him, waves of concepts and new ideas slammed into him one after the other. The solid ground on which he stood was suddenly washed out from beneath him, casting him adrift on a perilous sea with no ship, no compass, no anchor.

A shaft whistled past Alfred, jolted him to conscious awareness of their surroundings, of their danger. The dead of Kairn Telest were raising their weapons, turning those weapons on their own.

A thrown spear had struck Haplo on the arm. Blood flowed from the wound that wasn't serious; but it was a mark of the Patryn's weakening magic that the point had penetrated the sigla tattooed on his skin.

"Can't you stop them?" Alfred cried at Prince Edmund, trusting him to do something, prevent what must be the massacre of the last living beings on Abarrach. "They're your people!"

The cadaver stood silent, more silent than death in this world. The phantasm's gleaming eyes were fixed on Jonathan.

"Leave us, Patryn," said the duke. "You have no part in what happens on Abarrach. We brought this on ourselves. We must do what we can to make amends. Return to your world and share with your people the knowledge you have gained in this one."

"Pah!" Haplo spit on the ground. "C'mon, dog!" The Patryn ran toward his ship. The dog, after one backward glance at Alfred, dashed after its master.

Kleitus's ship docked. The ramps were lowered, the dead swarmed out to join their brethren on land. The duke would soon be surrounded by an army. On board ship, Kleitus and Jera stood together. The duchess's hand was outstretched, she was shrieking at the dead to slay her husband.

Jonathan stood unmoved by the chaos. He stared up at his wife, his face pale with grief and sorrow. A brief, bitter struggle shadowed the eyes.

He knows what he must do, thought Alfred, but he is afraid. Is there any way for me to help? Frustrated, the Sartan wrung his hands. How can I help? I don't understand what's happening.

Another flight of arrows flew past Alfred like hordes of wasps. One stuck in his robes, another landed point first on the toe of his shoe. An arrow thudded into Haplo's thigh. He clutched at his leg, tried to keep running. Blood welled from between his fingers. His leg gave out, he collapsed onto the dock.

The dead cheered, several broke from their ranks and ran toward him. The dog whirled to face them, teeth bared, hackles raised. Haplo stood up, tried to limp on, but he knew he couldn't move fast enough to outpace the dead. He drew the sword, turned, and prepared to fight.

The arrows that showered down around Jonathan might have been drops of rain. He paid no attention to them, and they didn't touch him. He was calm, resolute. He raised his hand for quiet and such was the commanding presence of the young man with the grief-ravaged face that the dead fell silent, the lazar hushed their calls for revenge. Even the faint plaintive moaning of the phantasms sunk into stillness.

Jonathan raised his voice. "In ancient days, when we Sartan first came to this world we had created, we worked to build lives for ourselves and the mensch and the creatures that were a sacred trust to us. In the beginning, all went well with one exception: we did not hear from our brethren in the other worlds.

"Their silence was, at first, disquieting. Then it became alarming, for our world was failing us. Or, perhaps it is more correct to say that we were failing our world. Instead of studying how to conserve our resources, we wantonly exploited them, always believing that, in time, we would be connected with those other worlds. They would provide us with what we lacked.

"The mensch were the first to succumb to the poisons of this world that was growing chill and barren around us. The creatures were next. And then our own population began to dwindle. At that critical juncture, our people took two steps—one forward into light, one backward into darkness.

"One group of Sartan sought to fight death, to end dying. They turned to necromancy. Instead of conquering death, however, they became enslaved by it. At the same time, another group of Sartan pooled their magical talents and resources in an effort to establish contact with the other three worlds. They built a chamber, devoted to this purpose, and brought into it a table that was one of the last surviving relics of another place and time. They established contact . . ."

Jonathan's voice softened. "But not with our brethren in other worlds. They established contact with a higher order. They spoke to One who had been long, long forgotten."

"Heresy!" cried Kleitus and "Heresy!" came the sibilant echo rising from the dead.

"Yes, heresy." Jonathan shouted above the clamor. "That was the charge leveled at those Sartan long years ago. After all, we are the gods, are we not? We sundered worlds! Created new ones! We had defeated death itself! Look around you."

The duke spread his arms, turned to the left, to the right, gestured forward and behind. "Who has won?"

The dead were silent. Alfred, glancing up at Kleitus, standing on the prow of the dragonship, saw by the twisted, sneering smile on the lazar's crawling visage that the dynast was playing out the rope, allowing his victim to wrap the noose around his own neck. The lazar would cinch it tight and watch with pleasure as his victim's body twitched and writhed.

Jonathan was making matters worse, not better, but Alfred had no idea how to stop him . . . or even if he should. Never before had the Sartan felt so completely, utterly helpless.

A cold touch on the back of his leg nearly sent Alfred leaping into the sea. He thought it was one of the hands of the cadavers, and he shuddered, waited for death, until he heard a soft, pathetic whine.

Alfred opened his eyes, sighed in relief. The dog stood at his side. Certain it had the Sartan's full attention, the animal darted sideways several steps, then darted back, and looked at Alfred expectantly.

The dog wanted him to go to its master, of course. Haplo stood on the pier, propped up against a bale of kairn grass. The Patryn's shoulders sagged. His face was deathly pale. Only his indomitable will and strong sense of survival kept him conscious.

Mercy, compassion, pity . . .

Alfred drew a deep breath. Expecting to be halted, challenged, cut down by arrow, spear, or sword, he gripped his courage in both hands and began to edge his way through the dead toward Haplo.

Jonathan continued his speech, a speech now pitiable in Alfred's estimation. He knew how it must end and so, he realized suddenly, did the young duke.

"Our ancestors feared these people who now came forward, crying out against the necromancers, warning that we must change or we would end up destroying not only ourselves, but the fragile balance that exists in the universe. The answer of our ancestors was to murder the 'heretics,' seal their bodies up in the chamber

that became known as 'Damned' and surround it with runes of
warding."

The dead eyes of the cadavers followed Alfred's movements, but
they made no attempt to stop him. He reached Haplo's side, knelt
down near the wounded man. "What . . . what can I do?" he asked
in a low voice.

"Nothing," Haplo answered, teeth clenched against his pain,
"unless you can shut that fool up."

"At least, while he's talking, we have time—"

"For what?" Haplo demanded bitterly. "Write a last letter home,
maybe?"

"They didn't do anything to me."

"Why should they bother? They know we're not going anywhere."

"But your ship—"

"Make one move toward it, and that move will be your last."
Haplo drew a shuddering breath, bit off a groan. "Look on board
the dragonship. The lady isn't paying attention to her husband's
speech."

Alfred looked up, saw Jera looking directly at him.

"She knows about the ship, about Death's Gate. Remember?"
Haplo pushed himself into a more upright position, gasping at the
agony the move caused him. The dog, standing over him, whimpered in sympathy. "My guess is . . . they want to take it for themselves, try to enter . . ."

"Enter worlds of the living! Enter to kill! That's . . . that's awful!
We've got to do something!"

"I'm open to suggestion," Haplo said dryly.

He had managed—at what terrible cost in pain Alfred couldn't
begin to imagine—to hack off much of the shaft of the arrow in his
thigh. But the arrow's head remained lodged in his flesh, his pant leg
was soaked with blood. His shirt had stuck to the wound on his
arm, forming a crude bandage. The deep slash would break open
and begin to bleed the moment he moved.

"We might have one chance," he said softly, his gaze intent on
the young duke. "You can see, of course, where this tale of his is
leading?"

Alfred didn't answer.

"When they move in for the kill, we make a run for the ship.
Once we're on board, the runes will protect us. I hope."

Alfred looked back at Jonathan, standing, alone.

"You mean . . . abandon him?"

Haplo's bloody hand snaked out, grabbed Alfred's collar, dragged the Sartan's face to within an inch of his.

"Listen to me, damn you! You know what will happen if these lazar come through Death's Gate! How many innocents will die? How many on Arianus? How many on Pryan? Balance that against one man's life on this world. You made him believe in this 'higher power.' You're the one who sent him to his death! You want to be responsible for bringing death itself through Death's Gate?"

Alfred's tongue felt swollen. He couldn't talk, could only stare at Haplo in wordless confusion.

Jonathan's voice, firm, strong, powerful, caught their attention. He drew even Jera's dead eyes.

"Your warding runes couldn't keep out those who went searching for the truth! I saw. I heard. I touched. I don't understand yet. But I have faith. And I will prove to you what I have discovered."

Jonathan took a step forward, raised his arms in appeal. "Beloved wife, I wronged you deeply. I would make amends. Slay me where I stand. I will die by your hands. Then raise me up. I will join your ranks, the ranks of the eternally damned."

The lazar that had once been Jera left Kleitus's side. It walked down the ramp that stretched from the ship to the pier. Her phantasm, trapped in its dead shell, surged as far ahead as it could, ephemeral hands outstretched in eager anticipation.

Tears slid down Jonathan's cheeks. "So you came to me as my bride, Jera . . ."

He waited for her. The dead gathered around them, waited. The corpse of Prince Edmund and its shadowy phantasm, floating free beside it, waited. Out in the magma sea, the dragon drifted on the burning lava, waited. The lazar of Kleitus, standing on board ship, laughed, and waited.

The cadaver's hands reached out as if to clasp her husband to her breast. The cruel fingers, strong in death, closed instead around Jonathan's throat.

"Now!" cried Haplo.

CHAPTER 46

SAFE HARBOR,

ABARRACH

◆

HAPLO REACHED OUT A HAND TO ALFRED TO SUPPORT HIM. ALFRED cast a stricken glance back over his shoulder. He couldn't see Jonathan, for the wall of dead surrounding the young man. He saw fists flail, saw a sword flash, heard a muffled groan. When the sword was raised again, it was dark with blood.

Blackness crept toward Alfred, comforting, soothing oblivion, a place where he could hide and not be responsible for anything that happened, including his own death.

"Alfred, don't pass out! Damn it, Sartan, for once in your miserable life, accept the responsibility!"

Responsible. Yes, we're responsible. I'm responsible for this . . . for all this. I've been like the dead myself, walking the land in a shell of a body, my soul buried in a tomb. . . .

"There's nothing you can do for Jonathan," Haplo's voice grated, "except die with him. Help me reach the ship!"

The blackness receded, but seemed to take all feeling and rational thought with it. Numb, Alfred did as he was told, obeying Haplo like a puppet or a child. The Sartan put his arm around the Patryn's shoulder and back. He aided Haplo's limping footsteps, Haplo aided Alfred's limping spirit.

"Stop them!" Kleitus howled in fury. "I need that ship! Let me through to stop them!"

But a thousand dead, milling around the dock, eager to kill, stood between Kleitus and his prize. Some of the cadavers heard the dynast's cry; most heard only the screams of their victim, joining them in death.

"Don't look back!" Haplo commanded with what breath he had remaining. "Keep running!"

Alfred's arm ached with the strain of supporting Haplo, the fire of the magma sea glowing around him seemed to burn in his lungs. He tried calling on his magic, but he was too frightened, too exhausted, too weak. Sigla swam in his mind, burst in dazzling flashes before his eyes. A forgotten language, they meant nothing to him.

Haplo sagged against his supporter, his footsteps slipped, although they never faltered their pace. Alfred glanced at him, saw the Patryn's face ashen gray, jaw clenched tight, sweat glistened on his skin. They were near their goal, the ship loomed above them. But shuffling footsteps sounded close behind.

The footsteps goaded Alfred on. He was close, very close—

A blur of black robes rose up in front of them like a wall of night.

"Damn it all . . ." Haplo sighed, sounding weary to the point of not caring.

In their fear of the dead, they'd forgotten the living. Baltazar stood before them. Pale, composed, black eyes red with the reflected light of the magma, he blocked their way to the ship. He raised grasping hands and Alfred shuddered in terror. But the hands clasped together, pleading.

"Take us with you!" Baltazar begged. "Take me, take my people! As many as we can crowd on board!"

Haplo regarded Baltazar intently, but for the moment the Patryn couldn't answer, he lacked the breath to speak. Alfred guessed that the necromancer had already tried to board; the Patryn's protective sigla had prevented him. The footsteps behind them grew louder. The dog barked a warning.

"I'll teach you the necromancy!" Baltazar said softly, urgently. "Think of the power in the worlds beyond! Armies of the dead to fight for you! Legions of the dead to serve you!"

Haplo flicked a glance at Alfred. The Sartan lowered his gaze. He was tired, defeated. He'd done all he could and it hadn't been enough. Hope—inexplicable and not clearly understood—had been born within him in the chamber. It had died with Jonathan.

"No," said Haplo.

Baltazar's black eyes widened in astonishment, stared in disbelief, then narrowed in fury. The dark brows came together, the pleading hands clenched to fists. "That ship is our only means of escape! Your living body will not tell me how to break the runes, but your corpse will!" He took a step toward Haplo.

The Patryn gave Alfred a push that sent the Sartan staggering into a bale of kairn grass.

"Not if my corpse is in there, it won't." Haplo pointed at the magma sea. Balancing precariously on his good leg, his sword in a bloodstained hand, he stood on the edge of the obsidian wharf, only a step or two from flesh-searing death.

Baltazar halted. Alfred was dimly aware of Kleitus's shouts growing louder, of more footsteps rushing toward them. The dog had ceased to bark, the animal stood at Haplo's side. Alfred picked himself up, not certain what he could do, trying desperately to summon his magic.

A chill voice sounded close by his ear.

"Let them go, Baltazar."

The necromancer cast the prince a sorrowful glance, shook his head. "You are dead, Edmund. You no longer have power over the living." Baltazar took a step nearer Haplo.

Haplo took a step nearer death.

"Let them go," repeated Prince Edmund sternly.

"Your Majesty dooms his own people!" Baltazar cried. Foam flecked the necromancer's lips. "I can save them! I—"

The cadaver raised its waxen hand, a bolt of lightning crackled, flashed out, and struck the ground at the necromancer's feet. Baltazar fell back, staring at the prince in fear and astonishment.

Prince Edmund gave Alfred a gentle shove. "Go to your friend. Help him on board the ship. You had better hurry. The lazar are coming to take you."

Dazed, stupefied, Alfred did as he was told and reached Haplo just as the Patryn's strength began to fail him. They hastened toward the ship, the Sartan assisting the flagging steps of his ancient enemy.

Alfred slammed up suddenly against an invisible barrier. He had the startling impression of sigla flashing blue and red around him. A word from Haplo, barely audible, caused the barrier to disappear. Alfred continued on, Haplo leaning on him heavily. He grimaced in pain with every movement.

Baltazar saw the defenses lowered, took a defiant step toward them.

"Do so, and I will kill you, my friend," said Prince Edmund, not in anger, but in sorrow. "What is one dead more or less in this world of ours?"

Alfred caught his breath in a choked sob.

"Just get us on board, damn you!" Haplo spoke through clenched teeth. "You'll have to do it. I can't . . . I've lost . . . too much blood . . ."

The ship floated above the magma sea, a wide gulf of burning red stretching between them and escape from Abarrach. No gangplank, no ropes. . . . Behind them, Kleitus had made his way off his ship. He was marshaling the dead, leading them to the assault, urging them to seize the coveted winged ship, urging them to sail into Death's Gate.

Alfred blinked back his tears and he could see the sigla again, he could read them, understand. He wove the runes together in a bright and shining net that wrapped around him, around Haplo, around Haplo's dog. The net raised them in the air, an invisible fisherman hauling in his catch, and lifted them on board the *Dragon Wing*.

The runes of his enemy closed protectively behind the Sartan.

◆

Alfred stood on the bridge, stared out the porthole. The dead, led by the lazar, swarmed around the dragonship, beating unsuccessfully against the runes. Baltazar was nowhere to be seen. He was either dead, murdered by the lazar, or he'd managed to flee in time.

The people of Kairn Telest were abandoning Safe Harbor, escaping back to the Salfag Caverns or beyond. Alfred could see them, a long, thin, ragged line, straggling across the plain. The dead, momentarily distracted by their desire to seize the ship, were letting them go. It didn't matter. Where could the living hide that the dead would not find them? It didn't matter. Nothing mattered . . .

Kleitus shouted a command. The other lazar ceased their fruitless struggle, gathered around their leader. The crowd of dead parted, and Alfred caught a glimpse of Jonathan lying still and unmoving on the pier. Jera bent over him, clasped the body in her dead arms. Her lazar began the chant that would restore him to terrible, tormented life.

Alfred turned away.

"What are the lazar doing?" Haplo crouched on the deck, his hands on the steering stone. The sigla tattooed on his hands glowed blue, but only a faint blue, barely discernible. He swallowed, removed his hands, flexed them, and shut his eyes.

"I don't know," Alfred answered dispiritedly. "Does it matter?"

"Hell, yes, it matters! They may be able to unravel my magic. We're not out of this yet, Sartan, so quit blubbering and tell me what's going on."

Alfred gulped, looked back out the porthole. "The lazar are . . . are plotting something. At least that's what it looks like. They're gathered around Kleitus. All of them except . . . Jera. She's . . ." His voice died.

"That's what they're doing," said Haplo softly. "They're going to try to break down the runes."

"Jonathan was so certain." Alfred stared out the window. "He had faith—"

"—in nothing but your trickery, Sartan."

"I know you won't believe me, Haplo, but what happened to you in the chamber happened to me, as well. Just as it happened to Jonathan. I don't understand it." Alfred shook his head, added in a low voice, "I'm not certain I *want* to understand it. If we're not gods . . . if there is some higher power . . ."

The ship moved beneath his feet, nearly throwing him off balance. He looked back at Haplo. The Patryn had his hands on the steering stone. The sigla glowed a bright, intense blue. Sails shivered, ropes tightened. The dragonship spread its wings, prepared to fly. On the pier, the dead began to clamor and clashed their weapons together. The lazar lifted their horrible visages, moved as a group toward the ship.

Apart from them, at the far end of the dock, Jonathan rose to his feet. He was a lazar, he had become one of the dead who was not dead, one of the living who was not living. He began walking toward the ship.

"Stay! Stop!" Alfred cried, pressing his face against the glass. "Can't we wait a minute longer?"

Haplo shrugged. "You can go back if you want to, Sartan. You've served your purpose. I don't need you any longer. Go on, get out!"

The ship began to move. Haplo's magical energies flowed through it, the blue light beamed brightly, welled up from between his fingers, surrounding him in a brilliant halo.

"If you're going, go!" he shouted.

I should, Alfred told himself. Jonathan had faith enough. He was willing to die for what he believed. I should be prepared to do the same.

The Sartan left the porthole, started toward the ladder that led up from the bridge. Outside the ship, he could hear the chill voices of the dead, shouting in fury, enraged at seeing their prey escape. He could hear Kleitus and the other lazar raise their voices in a chant. From the strain suddenly apparent on Haplo's face, they were attempting to break down the *Dragon Wing's* fragile, protective rune structure.

The dragonship jolted to a halt. It was caught, held fast like a fly in a web of the lazar's magic. Haplo closed his eyes, focused his mental powers, his concentration visible in the rigidity of the hands pressed against the steering stone. His fingers—red against the light welling up from beneath—seemed to be made of flame.

The dragonship lurched, sank a few feet.

"Perhaps the choice will be taken from me," Alfred murmured, almost relieved. He turned back to the porthole.

Haplo gasped, grit his teeth, and held on. The ship rose slightly.

A spell came, unbidden, to Alfred's mind. He could enhance the Patryn's failing energy. He could help break free of the web before the spider stung them.

The choice, far from being taken away, was being laid squarely on him.

The lazar that was Jonathan stood apart from the other lazar, the eyes of the soul not quite torn from the body gazed up at the ship, gazed through the runes, through the wood, through the glass, through flesh and bone into Alfred's heart.

"I'm sorry," Alfred said to the eyes. "I don't have the faith. I don't understand."

The Sartan turned away from the window. Walking over to Haplo, Alfred placed his hands on the Patryn's shoulders and began to chant.

The circle was joined. The dragonship gave a great shudder, broke free of the magical toils, lifted its wings and soared upward, leaving behind the fiery sea, leaving behind the dead and the living on the stone world of Abarrach.

♦

The ship floated before Death's Gate.

Haplo lay on a pallet on the deck, near the steering stone. He had collapsed moments after they'd freed themselves. Hovering on the brink of unconsciousness, he'd fought to keep himself awake, fought to guide their ship to safety. Alfred had watched over him anxiously, until Haplo ordered him irritably to go away and leave him alone.

"All I need is sleep. When we reach the Nexus, I'll be fine. You

better find yourself a place to lie down, Sartan, or you'll end up
breaking your neck when we go through Death's Gate. And this
time, when we go through, keep your mind out of mine!"

Alfred stood by the porthole, staring out, his mind walking back
on Abarrach, regret gnawing at him. "I didn't mean to pry into your
past life. I don't have much control—"

"Shut up and sit down."

Alfred sighed and sat—or rather tumbled—into a corner. He
huddled there dejectedly, his bony knees level with his chin.

The dog curled up beside Haplo, put its head on his chest. The
Patryn settled himself comfortably, stroked the dog's ears with his
hand. The animal closed its eyes, and its tail wagged contentedly.

"Sartan. You awake?"

Alfred kept silent.

"Alfred." Grudgingly.

"Yes, I'm awake."

"You know what'll happen to you in the Nexus." Haplo didn't
look at him when he spoke, he kept his gaze on the dog. "You know
what My Lord will do to you."

"Yes," Alfred answered.

Haplo hesitated a moment, either deciding on his next words or
deciding whether or not to say them. When he made his decision, his
voice was hard and sharp, cutting through some barrier within
himself.

"Then, if I were you, I wouldn't be around when I woke up."
Haplo closed his eyes.

Alfred stared in amazement, then smiled gently. "I understand.
Thank you, Haplo."

The Patryn didn't respond. His labored breathing grew even and
easy. Lines of pain relaxed from his face. The dog, sighing, wriggled
closer.

Death's Gate opened, drew them slowly inside.

Alfred leaned back against the bulkheads. Consciousness was
slipping away from him. He thought he heard, though it may have
been a dream, Haplo's sleepy voice.

"I never did find out about the prophecy. I don't suppose it
matters. No one will be left alive down there to fulfill it. Who
believes in that crap anyway? Like you said, Sartan. If you believe in
a prophecy, you have to believe in a higher power."

Who believes? Alfred wondered.

CHAPTER ♦ 47

SAFE HARBOR,

ABARRACH

♦

THE LAZAR, ANGERED AT LOSING THE DRAGONSHIP, TURNED THEIR WRATH on the living who yet remained on Abarrach. Kleitus led the armies of the dead in an attack on the small band of refugees from Kairn Telest.

The living were led by Baltazar, who barely escaped with his life from the docks. Protected by Prince Edmund, the necromancer hastened back to his people, hiding in the Salfag Caverns. He brought them the terrible news that their own armies of dead had turned against them.

The people of Kairn Telest fled the coming of the dead, running out into the open plains of the land that was itself, dying. They fled without hope, however, for among their number were many sick and many children, who could not stand the forced pace. The cycles of their suffering and hardship were mercifully brief. The dead were hard on their heels and soon the last living beings on Abarrach were brought to bay. They had no choice but to turn and fight.

During this time, I walked among the lazar, pretending to be one with them, for I knew that my hour had not yet come. Prince Edmund remained by my side. Although I knew his grief for his people was acute, he, too, waited for his hour.

The people of Kairn Telest chose for their field of battle a level plain not far from the Pillar of Zembar. They gave some thought to trying to protect the children, the sick and infirm, the elderly. In the end, they decided that it mattered little. Against the dead, there could be only one outcome. Men and women, old and young gathered what weapons they could and prepared to fight. They formed their ranks into a single line—families together, friend beside friend. The fortunate ones would be those who died first and swiftest.

The dead ranged themselves in ranks in the field across from the living. Their army was huge, outnumbering the people of Kairn Telest almost a thousand to one. Kleitus and the lazar walked before them, the dynast exhorting the cadavers to bring the dead necromancers among the Kairn Telest to him for resurrection.

I knew what was in Kleitus's mind, for I had attended his council meetings with the rest of his lazar. Once the Kairn Telest were destroyed, he planned to enter Death's Gate and from there pass on to other worlds. His ultimate goal—to rule over a universe of dead.

The trumpets of the cadavers sounded, blowing thin, iron notes that echoed through the kairn. The army of dead prepared to advance. The living of Kairn Telest closed ranks, silently awaiting their fate.

Prince Edmund and I stood together on the front lines of battle. His phantasm turned to face me and I saw then that he had been given the knowledge for which he'd been waiting.

"Bid me farewell, brother."

"Fare you well, my brother, on your long journey," I said. "May you know peace at last."

"I could wish the same for you," he said.

"When my work is done," I told him.

We walked together, side by side, and took our places among the foremost ranks of the dead. Kleitus watched us warily, suspiciously. He would have confronted us but the dead began to cheer, thinking that Edmund had himself come out to lead the battle against his own people.

Kleitus could do little against us. My strength and my power had grown during those last days, shining down on me like the sun I had never seen except in the visions of the Sartan from another world, the one who called himself Alfred. I knew its source. I knew the sacrifice I would have to make to use the power, and I was prepared.

Prince Edmund raised his hand, calling for silence. The dead obeyed, the cadavers ceased their hollow cries, the phantasms hushed their endless moaning.

"This cycle," Prince Edmund shouted, "death comes to Abarrach!"

The dead raised their voices in a mighty shout. The writhing visage of Kleitus darkened.

"You mistake my meaning. Death will not come to the living," Edmund's voice rang out, "but to us, to the dead. Let go of your fear, as I let go of mine. Trust in this one." He knelt down before me, looked up at me. "For he is the one of whom the prophecy spoke."

"Are you ready?" I asked.

"I am," he said firmly.

I began reciting the chant, the words I had first heard spoken by the Sartan, Alfred. Blessed be the One who sent him to us.

Prince Edmund's body stiffened, jerked, as if it felt again the spear plunge into its chest. The face contorted with both the physical pain and the mental, the knowledge of failure, the brief and bitter struggle life makes leaving the body, the world.

My heart was filled with pity, but I continued the chant. The body slumped down to the ground at my feet.

Kleitus, realizing what was happening, tried to stop me. He and the other lazar raged around me, but they were nothing more to me than the hot wind blowing from the sea of fire.

The dead spoke no word, only watched.

The living murmured and clasped hands, wondering if we offered hope or a deepening of their despair.

The corpse lay still and silent, the dreadful magical strings that animated it were severed. The phantasm of Edmund, his spirit, grew stronger and more clearly defined. For a brief instant he appeared to me and to his people as he had been in life—young, handsome, proud, compassionate.

His last look went to his people, to the living and the dead, and then he vanished, as the morning mists burn away in sunshine.

A battle was fought that day, but not between the living and the dead. It was fought between myself and the dead and Kleitus and the other lazar. When it was ended, the lazar had been beaten, their dread power reduced. They fled, plotting to increase their strength and continue the fight. Some of the dead joined them, fearful of giving up what they know, fearful of the unknown. But many more of the dead came to me afterward and begged me to release them.

Following the battle, the living of Kairn Telest made their way across the Fire Sea and entered the tragic city of Necropolis, joined there those few who had managed to survive the slaughter. Baltazar is their leader. The first law he passed was to prohibit the practice of necromancy. His first decree was that the bodies of the victims of the dead's vengeance be committed with reverence to the Fire Sea.

The lazar have disappeared, but their threat hangs like the dreary clouds of laze over the living of Necropolis. The city's gates are shut, the rat holes have been bricked up, the walls are heavily guarded. Baltazar is of the opinion that the lazar are searching for the means to enter Death's Gate and may perhaps have done so.

I think it quite likely that Kleitus does seek a way through Death's Gate, but I do not believe he has found the means to enter. He remains in this world, all the lazar remain in this world. I hear their voices, sometimes, during the sleepless hours of the long nights. I hear their cries of hatred and agony and torment. It is their hatred that binds them to this world, their hatred of me in particular, for they know that, in me, the prophecy has been fulfilled.

The torment we lazar endure is indescribable. The soul longs for freedom, yet cannot detach itself from the body. The body longs to give up its heavy burden, but is terrified to part from the soul. We cannot sleep, we cannot find rest. No food can give us sustenance, no drink can ease our terrible thirst. The body aches with fatigue, the restless spirit forces that body to constantly roam the world.

I walk the streets of Necropolis, streets that were once crowded but are now pitifully empty. I walk the deserted halls of the palace and listen to the echoes of my own footfalls. I walk the fields of Old Province, desolate and abandoned. I walk the fields of New Province and watch the living toil in place of the dead. I walk the shores of the shrinking Fire Sea. When the pain of my existence becomes too much to bear, I return again to the Chamber of the Blessed to find strength.

My suffering is my penance, my sacrifice. My beloved Jera walks with the lazar, out there, somewhere. Her hatred for me is sharp, keen, but only because her hatred must wage constant battle against her deeper love. When the time for waiting is ended, when my work is accomplished, I will take my beloved in my arms again and together we will find the peace now denied us. I keep that dream in my heart, the only dream allowed these sleepless eyes. It is my comfort, my hope. My love and the knowledge of my duty sustain me in my waiting. The time of the prophecy is not now, but soon.

"He will bring life to the dead, hope to the living, and for him the Gate will open."[1]

[1]*A Collection of the Writings of Jonathan the Lazar,* compiled by Baltazar, ruler of Necropolis, Abarrach.

EPILOGUE

My Lord,

You may remove Abarrach completely from your calculations. I found evidence to indicate that the Sartan and the mensch did once inhabit that hunk of worthless, molten rock. The climate undoubtedly proved too harsh for even their powerful magic to sustain them. They apparently tried to contact the other worlds, but their attempts ended in failure. Their cities have now become their tombs.

Abarrach is a dead world.

My Lord will, I'm certain, understand why I do not make my report to him in person. An emergency has arisen that calls me away. On my return from Abarrach, I learned that the Sartan I discovered living on Arianus, the one who calls himself Alfred, has entered Death's Gate. Evidence indicates that he has gone to Chelestra, the fourth world the Sartan created, the world of water. I am following him there.

I remain your loyal and devoted son.[1]

HAPLO

Haplo, my loyal and devoted son, YOU ARE A LIAR.[2]

[1] Haplo's report on the world of Abarrach, from the files of the Lord of the Nexus.

[2] Scrawled on the margin of the report.

APPENDIX

NECROMANCY

as described in the Journal of Alfred

◆

FROM VOL. 3, (NOTE ON INSIDE COVER)
To the Untroubled Mensch and being written in your own language for your understanding: These are my Rune Journal Notes which I kept secretly and sporadically during the time of my travels through the Death Gates. I confess that I have never been very good about my journal entries— especially during those first years of travel. On reflection, my journal must seem rather disjointed to you. The text includes everything from meal selections in Pryan to long discourses on obscure magical principles. It's punctuated by observations and insights as my whim suited me at the time, usually served up without preamble or connection to previous texts.

I write knowing that you may not comprehend everything. My narrative is without clear sequence. Further complicating your understanding are the differences between Sartan and Mensch language structures. Sartan language is bound as one with its rune structure. As such, it is a non-sequential language, holding its concepts simultaneously rather than one after the other. While such structures work well for magic and other concepts, it has difficulty conveying a procession of events through time. Such sequences of events are better understood, organized and conveyed in the common language of the mensch.

I have kept my journal in both Sartan runic and several mensch languages, choosing whichever, in my judgement, seemed like the most appropriate conveyance for my thoughts and observations . . .

FROM VOL 2: PAGE 132—
ALFRED BELOW THE CITY OF NECROPOLIS

. . . I was riveted by the runes in that sacred chamber of the catacombs. Their structure filled my mind in the instant although, with a shudder, I forced myself to look away. Now their form troubles my sleep. In order to banish their shadows, I am translating them here. As I hide them from my sight by closing the cover on this book, perhaps I can also hide their memory from my consciousness.

I have chosen to translate the rune structure seen there into a rough equivalent in the common mensch language so as to better understand the sequence of events surrounding it rather than its conceptual whole. I will include as much of the original runestructure and linkages as I can. It is nevertheless impossible to truly translate a simultaneous language into a sequential one.

The runes begin apparently mid-thought concerning communication with other Sundered Realms—the subject of group research as the text later makes clear.

Translation: Subroot rune from the Altar[1]

Cycle 275[2] Origins of Necromancy
Kinilan[3] observed that the current problem was similar to that facing the ancient necromancers. This suggested that the solutions to those ancient problems might give some clue to resolving our own mission[4] . . . We began an exploration of the ancient texts to deter-

---

[1] Noticed and read eighty-three runes above the farthest hand placement impressions along the Sulistic LArc from the right hand. This is obviously a subroot of a larger structure and shows it is a minor part of the whole.

[2] Cycles refer to the periods by which time is measured in Abarrach. I have reorganized the narrative along the sequence of these cycles to gain a better perspective of the progress made.

[3] A Sartan magical researcher. By his position in the rune structure it is likely that he is the person who is building the rune. In mensch language structures he would be considered the voice or narrator of the text.

[4] Branches back to higher order subroot runes ignored. Tenor of the text is high spirited and hopeful.

mine if their own thinking may lead to a solution to our current problem of communication between the worlds.

INITIAL FAILURES: THE AUTOMATONIC AGE

Early attempts at reanimating our dead were unsatisfactory though its success was becoming necessary for our survival. The reanimated dead were no better than mindless automatons, capable of nothing more than doing tasks directly designated for them by the necromancer controlling them.[5] Such undead were unacceptable as a work force since they did little to free the necromancer from the actual work itself. The necromancer would be required to direct every movement of the animated corpse—a task that was tedious at best and a waist of magical energies at worst. The necromantic research continued to show promise, however, and found its solution in an aging mage of House Advocate.

THE DELSART SOLUTION

Delsart Sparanga, a Sartan researcher of considerable years, discovered the Delsart Near State or Delsart Similitude.[6]

> "... discovered a second state of existence that was resonating with the physical state. In rune magic this state is known as the Delsart Near State, referring to both the necromancer who discovered its existence and the concept that this second existence of all objects is a near state to that of its physical presence. This second state was alluded to in the ancient texts as a spiritual state usually associated with a deity or religious belief system. For this and simplification of language, the Delsart Near State is commonly referred to as the spiritual state as well.
>
> "The spiritual state of all things is a much finer reflection of

---

[5] Reference branches back to the original rune structures for necromancy which would only animate the dead. Buffer runes prevent the power of those runes from entering into the equation of the full rune structure.

[6] Branch runes lead to a large treatise on the Delsart State. The portion quoted here concerns those runes which were most closely tied by entry point to the reference runes just left. I did not gather—nor did I wish to know—more concerning the subject.

the physical state. All things that exist in the physical are also expressed in this spiritual state. Delsart taught that no thing exists in what he terms the coarse physical state except that it also have existence in the spiritual state.

"Through Delsart's research, it was discovered that this second state changes radically upon the death of a living being. While the corpse retains a form of spiritual existence, its new second state is radically different from that of the living being it once was. It was this difference, he surmised, that caused the reanimated dead to be without any self motivation.

"Delsart failed in his lifetime to discover the nature of this second state nor could his runes have control over it. Delsart's contribution, however, was a set of runes that could recall the original spiritual state and bind it again to the coarse physical state. It was this discovery that ushered in the current age of Necromancy.

Early Failures of the Delsart Solution. Necromancy was not without its early problems, despite the common teachings of our day.[7] Our research group has studied rune texts from that period. Early notes on those initial experiments speak of terrible problems in implementing Delsart's spiritual connection. The rituals and important waiting periods were not initially known. As a result, early efforts bound the spirit state to the dead subject too quickly and thus too closely to its original state. This caused many Lazar created in that early time. The Lazar were subsequently destroyed. It is secret knowledge,[8] known only among runes hidden deep in these walls, that the Rebellion and subsequent battles of the Pillar of Zembar were caused in part by the creation of several Lazar at that time, who subsequently threatened much of the kingdom.

Delsart Rune Refinements. Even as the Battles of the Pillar of Zembar raged, corrections and ceremonies were made in necromantic rune structures to properly revive the dead for service to their living masters and the state. The important waiting period between the

[7] Mild warning runes direct that this text is considered privileged information.

[8] This rune branch was prefaced with a number of warding runes to warn the reader. The scribe was apparently worried that the reader was about to see something that they should not know about.

time of death and that of reanimation was discovered. This period allowed sufficient disparity to grow between the physical state and the spiritual state to prevent their exercise of free will after reanimation. The dead could now act on simple directions rather than as puppets under the necromancer's constant vigil. A new age of necromancy had come.

Cycle 279: Search for Delsart Equivalents
     If all things in the world—living and otherwise—had such a spiritual resonance to their physical state, could this resonance be tapped as a source of communication between worlds? The sheer mass of creation seemed to prohibit our magical contact with the other worlds of the Sundering. Perhaps contact could be established through this spiritual state more easily than through the physical.
     By order of the Council, our group convened here in the sanctuary around the Table of Elders to contemplate this very thing.[9] The Table of Elders[10] was made of stone brought through Death Gate at the time of the Sundering. Being comprised of material from another world and therefore, according to Delsart, having a spiritual echo also from that foreign world, this tone might provide the medium through which we may communicate with the world from which it came—if not with all the other worlds of the Sundering.[11]
     Being well beyond the time of Delsart, however, it was not sufficient for us to know that the Spirit State was a fact that worked—we needed to know *why* it worked. Our next step, then, would be to contemplate a line of research begun over four centuries ago and, having then born fruit, was discarded.[12] From the ancient texts we unraveled Delsart's thoughts and methods in search of a more complete understanding of his work than even he had possessed.

[9] This was the subroot rune point of entry into the text.

[10] Meaning the stone table from which this rune was read.

[11] The phrasing of this paragraph shows a basic lack of understanding by the researchers concerning the nature of their world. Their own realm was once a part of the greater realm that was once sundered by our great a terrible magic. The stone touched on all other worlds but touched on their own as well. This shows a loss or corruption of knowledge even during the time of their research.

[12] Tenor of the text turns smug at this point. The rune scribe thought the original research should not have been abandoned.

Cycle 290: Coarse and Fine Existence

Our research is beginning to bear new fruit. Peartree[13] explored the facet of Delsart's work which dealt with the physical as a coarse state compared to the spiritual state. By examining the measurable differences between the two states, Peartree came to startling insights.

MATERIAL AS COARSE EXISTENCE STRUCTURE

Our ability to measure the coarse state ended at the Runestate Boundary[14]. This is elemental and foundational as far as the concepts of Sartan magic are concerned. All physical objects seem bound by the limits of this barrier in their coarse physical state. Their complete existence, however, crosses over this boundary into realms where magic and runes can no longer be defined.

SPIRITUAL AS FINER EXISTENCE STRUCTURE

Beyond this Runestate Boundary we had formerly believed was chaos. Yet it is in the very realm of this chaos that the spirit state seems to be defined. Peartree's measurements of the effects of the spirit state (this state being unmeasurable by definition) indicate order, pattern and structure beyond the chaotic boundary. That order should exist in that chaos beyond the reach of the most powerful runes is a discovery that many find heretical.[15]

Cycle 330: Refined Rune Structure Application

Orstan[16] has devised a rune structure that, through cancelling oscillation of rune structures may provide us the medium of communication through the Table of Elders. The waves form a null-carrier

---

[13] Obviously the name of a researcher by its rune position. It does not refer to a fruit bearing plant.

[14] The Runestate Boundary is an advanced magic concept concerning that point of detail beyond which magic will not function and all certainty is lost. This chaotic boundary between order and the unknown may be the same as the Barrier of Uncertainty referred to in Sartan writings.

[15] Caution and fear enter into the runes here.

[16] A fellow researcher?

wave of magic and thought beyond the Runestate Boundary. By modulating the frequency of the null-state wave[17] we hope to break through the Deathgate and make contact with the world from which the table was cut.

Cycle 332: Revelation[18]

What have we done to ourselves and our ancestors? Anguish and rage. Despair and shame. Orstan's structures worked beyond expectation. We do not speak with the Sundered Realms. We hear words beyond our worlds. We hear voices long dust and those yet to be heard. We are children playing with razor edged swords.[19]

---

[17] What an interesting approach!

[18] The runes take on a strange texture here. The scribe writes with both awe and horror but I'm not sure whether he's referring to their own actions as researchers or the collective action of their people.

[19] I translate no more. Here the runes branch into speculation on that which I might consider to be either lunatic rantings or prophesy. The runes also become heavily bound here in the runes which establish the communication with whatever or whoever they have reached.

Death Masque

The cadaver was that of an older man of grave and stately mien. From the dilapidated appearance of both the cadaver and the clothing it wore, the corpse had been around a long, long time. Urged on by the giggling young people, the cadaver was performing a dance that it had probably performed in its own youth.

The young people hooted and jeered and began to dance around the corpse in mockery of the old-fashioned steps. The cadaver paid no attention to them, but continued to dance on its decaying legs, moving solemnly with a pathetic grace to the tune of music only it could hear.

by Janet Pack

For Dave and Traci

N O T E :

In the somber Realm of Stone now known as the world of Abarrach, merriment is rare. Songs are no longer sung and seldom accompany dance.

10-96

WEI   Weis, Margaret.

Fire sea.

7-2-96

$20.00

DATE			